Naughty
or Nice?

Naughty or Nice?

—FOUR NOVELLAS BY—

Patricia Ryan

Sherrilyn Kenyon

Carly Phillips

Kathryn Smith

St. Martin's Paperbacks

NAUGHTY OR NICE

"Santa, Baby" Copyright © 2001 by Patricia Ryan.
"Love Bytes" Copyright © 2001 by Sherrilyn Kenyon.
"Naughty Under the Mistletoe" Copyright © 2001 by Karen Drogin.
"A Christmas Charade" Copyright © 2001 by Kathryn Smith.

For information address St. Martin's Press, 175 Fifth Avenue, New York, NY 10010.

ISBN: 0-312-98102-3
EAN: 80312-98102-0

Printed in the United States of America

St. Martin's Paperbacks edition / November 2001

St. Martin's Paperbacks are published by St. Martin's Press, 175 Fifth Avenue, New York, NY 10010.

10 9 8 7

CONTENTS

Santa, Baby

—

PATRICIA RYAN

*For Morgan, who was perusing the personal ads
over brunch one Sunday morning and said,
"Hey, Mom—check this out."*

CHAPTER ONE

—

"I want you to steal my husband's girlfriend from him."

Jack O'Leary, lazing back in his squeaky old leather swivel chair, his blue-jeaned legs braced on the battered Steelcase desk that took up about a third of what passed for his office, stilled. He looked up from the snow globe he'd been absently toying with while Celeste Worth growled on about the lying, cheating bastard she couldn't afford to divorce because of the pre-nup from hell.

It was a variation on a theme that was all too familiar to Jack, two-thirds of whose private investigations involved the extramarital hijinks of his clients' husbands. He'd sat through more than his share of hysterics, rage, and—oh, man, the worst—quiet weeping by any number of Wronged Wives.

Madame Celeste had actually been a good deal more composed than most when he'd first broken the news to her. It had been three or four weeks ago, right before Thanksgiving, that he'd called her into the office to show her the results of his brief but productive inquiry into the illicit frolics of one Preston Wrigley Worth III. She'd skimmed the report with refreshing stoicism, glanced coolly at the eight-by-ten glossies, written him a check and left. He'd been relieved to have gotten off so easily . . . until half an hour ago, when she'd shown up without an appointment, bulled her way past Grady in the outer office, planted herself on the other side of the desk, and launched into an anti-Preston diatribe that was notable only for its unoriginality.

Until she came to the part about Jack stealing Preston's girlfriend from him.

"Come again?" Reaching out, Jack set the snow globe down on his desk. Within it, a swarm of little white flakes drifted and swirled around a three-dimensional representation of Santa crawling into a rooftop chimney, a bulging sack thrown over his shoulder.

"You heard me." Celeste flipped open a monogrammed cigarette case, slid a black Balkan Sobranie between her collagen-plumped, frosted coral lips, and regarded him with an air of listless expectation.

Taking his time, Jack lowered his feet to the floor and rummaged in his middle desk drawer for the book of matches he'd snagged from that topless joint on Seventh Avenue last weekend. He'd gone there to check out the owner, whose wife had suspected him of dallying with the dancers. He'd lingered long after confirming those suspicions because—and this was the pathetic part, and the reason he'd ended up tying one on that night, which he almost never did anymore—it was the first time he'd seen a woman naked, or just about, since . . .

Damn, had it really been a year? Sure enough; it was last December that Jessica had given him the heave-ho.

No, wait a minute. There'd been that blind date his cousin Davy had hooked him up with, but that was last summer, a good what—four or five months ago? And all it had amounted to was a forgettable one-night stand. Ditto that motor-mouthed little waitress and that bar pickup he'd regretted as soon as she'd started undressing and he'd gotten a load of the piercings.

So that made three naked women in the twelve months since Jess had walked away from the Brooklyn walk-up they'd shared and the plans they'd made amid vague protestations that "something is missing." Five days later, she was on a plane to Jamaica with Roger Babcock, her married boss. It had taken Jack about ten minutes of quick 'n' dirty detective work to ascertain the sorry truth, which was that Jess had been nailing ol' Roger on the side for over five months. Sorry and almost comically ironic, considering Jack's line of work.

He took the diamond engagement ring he'd meant to give her on Christmas Eve back to Tiffany's, then ripped down all the pine swags and wreaths she'd tacked up around the apartment and stuffed them down the incinerator.

Ho ho ho.

Celeste studied him through contacts the color of green Life Savers as he leaned forward to light her cigarette. He managed not to stare back despite his morbid fascination with the results of an over-zealous facelift, which made her look like one of those Eyeliner Barbies from the 1950s as reflected in a fun house mirror.

Spewing a plume of smoke toward the ceiling, Madame extracted from her faux leopard-print handbag a carefully scissored little newspaper clipping, which she handed across the desk to him. "I placed this ad in the personals section of the *Village Voice* two weeks ago."

Jack snapped on his desk lamp and held the clipping under its smoke-hazed corona of light:

WANTED: SEDUCTIVE, SELF-ASSURED MALE to take my husband's girlfriend from him. She is an attractive blonde in her early thirties who enjoys travel, fine dining, and the theater. Generous reward. Photo required.

He looked up. "You've got to be kidding."

Celeste took another drag on the cigarette, her hard green gaze fixed on him as she exhaled. "I'm not actually much of a kidder, Jack."

"How do you know she likes this stuff?" Jack asked. "Travel? The theater?"

Celeste shrugged negligently. "Doesn't everybody?"

Jack shook his head in disbelief as he re-read the ad. "You get any takers?"

"Scores of them. Every vile, larcenous knuckle-dragger in New York answered that ad. At least half of them appeared to be petty criminals and ex-cons. The few letters that were actually legible scared the hell out of me. And, my God, the photos!" She shuddered delicately. "Apes, trolls . . . You'd be astounded, the men who regard them-selves as seductive. A woman like that . . ." Celeste aimed a coral-lacquered fingernail at the top print on the stack of black-and-white surveillance photos in the open file on Jack's desk. "No way would she let one of those troglo-dytes within a hundred feet of her."

Celeste had a point, Jack thought as he contemplated the photograph, which was one of the last batch he'd taken for this job. It was a nighttime shot of Preston Worth and his lady friend waiting beneath the awning over the entrance to the Four Seasons restaurant while a uniformed doorman ventured out in the stinging rain—or had it already turned to sleet by that point?—to hail a cab. Preston, a silver-haired, tennis-muscled blue blood, frowned in a preoccu-pied way as he burrowed in the pockets of his cashmere topcoat for tip money. The girlfriend, a lissome, ash-blond knockout by the name of Katherine Peale, who had evi-dently neglected to watch the Weather Channel that evening, hunched her shoulders as she buttoned up the jacket of her gunmetal silk dinner suit. Even with the rain and the dark and Jack's distance from the subjects—he was shooting with a telephoto lens from the recessed doorway of a palm reader's shop a dozen doors down on the other side of East Fifty-second Street—he could see that the woman was wracked with shivers.

Preston, you schmuck, he'd muttered to himself as he aimed and focused. *What's the matter with you? Give her your freakin' coat.*

"The first time Preston cheated on me was during our honeymoon, and he's kept it up ever since." Celeste tapped the ash from her cigarette into the potted poinsettia on the corner of Jack's desk. "Literally and figuratively. He was raised to take what he wanted when he wanted it. And from the moment he hit puberty, what he wanted was sex, and plenty of it. You wouldn't know it to look at him, but the man is utterly ravenous. He's probably been with a thousand women during the course of our marriage, and age does *not* seem to have slowed him down."

"If that's the case," Jack said, "why do you care so much about this Katherine Peale?"

"Because she's different. He's buying her expensive gifts, taking her out three, four nights a week—*courting* her from all appearances. He never does that. Oh, there might be a bouquet of roses or a dinner out, but once he's lured them into the sack, they're history. This new woman, though—God knows how long he's been seeing her. I didn't suspect a thing till I found those receipts."

Ah, yes, the telltale receipts. Three of them, tucked into her husband's wallet, documenting cash purchases made in mid-November: 3.25-carat emerald-cut diamond stud earrings from Harry Winston; a "bronze, easel-style Tiffany picture frame, dark patina, green slag glass, twelve by fourteen inches, signed," from Moody and Ives Antiques; and a "gossamer camisole and thong," both black and size small, from La Petite Coquette. *Yes, I'm sure they're not for me,* Celeste had told Jack during their initial meeting the next morning, adding, with an almost imperceptible little squirm, *He knows how I feel about thongs.*

"They didn't strike me as a couple that had been together that long," Jack said as he tossed the newspaper clipping on top of the photograph. "They were still laughing at each other's jokes that weren't funny, you know?"

"All I know is, if that woman is angling to be the next Mrs. Preston Worth, it's got to be stopped. There's far too much at stake."

"Yeah, I can see that." Jack glanced at the shopping bags Celeste had hauled in with her and dumped in the corner—Prada, Saks Fifth Avenue, Gucci, Chanel . . .

She noticed the direction of his gaze. " 'Tis the season, Jack. I'll bet even you buy Christmas presents."

"You'd lose that bet."

"Surely you're not *that* much of a hard-ass."

"Let's just say I've lost my taste for tinsel."

Celeste raised a dubious eyebrow as she took in the

snow globe and poinsettia on his desk, the glittery gold garland festooning the walls, the electric candle in the window, the wreath on the door, the fleece stockings taped to the file cabinet . . . "Looks like *somebody*'s been decking the halls."

"That's Grady's handiwork." Jack's nephew and assistant, although scarily efficient thanks in part to a ten-cup-a-day latte habit, had a few odd quirks, one of which was his insistence on decorating their dinky little midtown Manhattan office suite for the holidays. All the holidays. Every last one. Columbus Day; who decorated for Columbus Day? And Father's Day? With his penchant for frosty blond man-eaters devoid of maternal aspirations, Jack somehow doubted he'd be playing that particular role any time soon. As for twenty-something Grady, his childhood conviction that girls were icky and boys were cool had only gained strength with the passage of time; no patter of little feet in his future, either.

"How's ten grand sound?" Smoke trickled from Celeste's nostrils.

Jack cocked his head. "Sorry?"

"To do the dirty deed." Rolling her eyes at Jack's evident bemusement, Celeste said, "To get this woman away from my husband."

"For God's sake. No."

"Twenty."

"What?" He thought about it for a second. "No. Celeste—"

"Fifty, then." She stubbed her cigarette out in the poinsettia.

"Fifty thousand dollars?" Jack sat up straight in his chair.

"But that's as high as I can go. Here." Celeste withdrew a bulging six-by-nine kraft envelope from her handbag. "This is only a down payment, of course. Five thousand now, in cash, and a check for the other forty-five when she breaks things off with Preston. That's all I can get my hands on without him finding out. Take it or leave it."

"I'm not playing hardball, Celeste, I just . . ." Jack scrubbed a hand over the beard stubble he hadn't bothered to shave off this morning, since he hadn't expected to meet with any clients today. Fifty thousand dollars. Almost exactly the amount he still needed to come up with to launch the high-tech security consultancy that had been his dream ever since he realized what private eyes actually do for a living. Saving that kind of scratch the old-fashioned way would take years.

"You want to count it?" Prying open the envelope's clasp with the tips of her nails, Celeste upended it onto his desk. Five packets of bills slid out—twenties bound by a paper ribbon marked "$1000." Paper money had a certain sweet, softly rumpled smell even when the bills were fairly new, as these were. It was a smell that made it hard to think straight.

His gaze riveted on the money, Jack said, "It's just about the sleaziest job I've ever been asked to do. Deceiving this woman into thinking I'm interested in her, only to get her away from—"

"Spare me your qualms, Jack. And spare yourself, too. She's a conniving, opportunistic home-wrecker angling for a rich husband. *My* rich husband."

Home-wrecker. It wasn't a word that got bandied about all that much anymore. Jack had heard it often enough as a kid, though. His most indelible memory, from when he was nine, was of their upstairs neighbor, Mrs. Kaminsky, screaming it out the window at his mother as she heaved her suitcases into the trunk of Mr. Kaminsky's black Thunderbird. There was a wet snow falling; her high heels were buried in slush. It was the last time Jack ever saw her.

Celeste plucked another cigarette from her case; this time she lit it herself, with a slim gold lighter. "She's not the kind of woman you should be feeling sorry for, Jack."

"I don't," he said, with real feeling.

Jack wondered if Roger Babcock's wife, who evidently knew about Jess, thought of *her* as a "home-wrecker." Technically, she wouldn't qualify unless Roger threw the wife over for her. It could happen. Jess was the type of woman men got stupid over.

Jack's mother had been that type. So, evidently, was this Katherine Peale. It was like there was some secret sorority of femmes fatale who didn't care what kind of havoc they wreaked in the lives of those around them, as long as they Got Their Man.

"So, will you do it?" Celeste asked on an exhalation of smoke.

Jack glanced from the packets of bills to the photograph of Katherine Peale standing next to Preston under that awning. Her hair was caught up in that artfully half-assed way some women affect, with wisps sprouting every which way, a breezy contrast to the snugly tailored silk suit with its rhinestone buttons. She had stiletto-heeled Rockette legs and, despite her slenderness, nicely rounded hips. Tame the hair and she could have been Grace Kelly's *To Catch a Thief* stand-in.

Spots of light winked on her earlobes.

Jack squinted to get them into focus. Diamond earrings.

He wondered if she was wearing the camisole and thong, too.

"Not such distasteful work when you think about it, eh, Jack?" Celeste watched him, smiling, as she drew on her cigarette. "Mostly indoors. No heavy lifting."

"What makes you so sure she'll have anything to do with me?"

"Because you're what women mean—*exactly* what they mean—when they say 'tall, dark, and handsome.' Although a shave and a decent set of clothes wouldn't hurt. Spend some of this"—she shoved the pile of money toward him— "at the Armani shop over on Madison and you'll fulfill the job requirements quite nicely, I think."

"Job requirements?"

" 'Seductive and self-assured.' You read the ad."

" 'Seductive' as in . . . you don't expect me to . . ."

"Consider it a job perk."

"Sex for hire? There's a name for that, Celeste."

"Why, Jack," she purred through a cloud of smoke. "I never knew you harbored such delicate sensibilities. How tedious." Stabbing her cigarette out, she said, "Suit yourself. Take her to the malt shop and woo her with ice-cream sodas. Preston and I leave for Aspen tomorrow to spend Christmas and New Year's with friends. We go every year for three weeks. That should be plenty of time to get the job done. In any event, it's all the time you've got." Snatching a pen out of the cracked coffee mug on his desk, she scrawled something on the inside cover of the file folder—a phone number. "Call me in Aspen when you've run her to ground. If Preston answers, hang up and try again later."

"I haven't said I'll do it."

She smiled all too knowingly as she plunked the pen back in the mug. "You haven't said you won't."

CHAPTER TWO

—

She was even prettier up close. Smaller, younger-looking. Fragile, almost.

Or seemingly so.

Jack forced himself to reflect, as he tailed Katherine Peale from department to department at FAO Schwarz—taking pains to conceal himself among the throngs of holiday shoppers packing the celebrated toy emporium this Saturday morning—that women like her were never quite what they appeared to be.

Indeed, today she appeared as artlessly unaffected as a college girl. Jack almost hadn't recognized her when she'd walked out of her apartment building this morning dressed in a cinched trench coat and khakis, her hair pulled haphazardly back in a ponytail. Grady, swilling lattes in the front passenger seat of Jack's gray Saturn half a block away on East Thirty-seventh, had nudged him and pointed. *That's not her, is it?*

I'm not sure.

Nah, can't be, Grady said decisively. *What kind of femme fatale wears penny loafers?*

But it *was* her, as they realized when she walked past. They'd waited thirty seconds, then got out of the car and pursued her on foot across to Fifth Avenue and up to Fifty-eighth Street and FAO Schwarz. Jack had followed her inside, instructing Grady to wait for him in the plaza out front.

The subject toured pretty much the entire store, finally settling down in the second-floor "Bookmonster" department, where she perused titles with an expression of focused intensity while Jack watched from behind one of the two giant monster legs that disappeared up into the ceiling. She was drawn to young adult novels, of which she gathered an armload.

When she entered the robot-shaped elevator to go back downstairs, Jack made a beeline for the escalator at the rear of the store, but she had already dissolved into the crowd by the time he got to the first floor. That swaying flaxen ponytail made her easy to spot, though, and before long he caught sight of her again, in the stuffed-animal department, taking in the life-size giraffe with an oddly contemplative expression. She had big blue-gray eyes with that slightly heavy-lidded, sensually languid look that Jack associated more with a Mediterranean than a Nordic brand of beauty. With the arm that wasn't holding the books, she cradled a stuffed furry brown koala bear against her chest as if it were a baby.

Jack fished around for something clever to say as he approached her, but he must have been out of circulation too long, because the only opening gambits that came to him—all playing off the giraffe—sounded like the punch lines of bad *Playboy* cartoons: *Pretty impressive, but do you think size really matters?* Or: *They say he's an animal in the bedroom.* Or: *Why don't you just slap my face now and get it over with?*

"Cool, huh?" was what he finally opted for. *Cool, huh? What are you, nineteen?*

She lowered the koala, her hand automatically resting on her shoulder bag—the urban woman's first instinct when accosted by a stranger. She glanced at him, gave him a too-polite half-smile, said, "Yep," and turned away.

"Christmas shopping?" Jack cringed inwardly at his own inanity. *Get it together, man. Fifty grand is riding on this. Do you want to spend your whole life spying on cheating husbands?*

"That's right." She assessed him swiftly, taking in his empty hands along with the upscale threads in which Grady had costumed him for his role—Lower East Side knockoffs of sportswear by some designer Jack had never heard of, which had saved him, Grady estimated, somewhere in the neighborhood of a thousand bucks over the real thing. Contrary to Celeste's advice, he'd chosen not to dip into her five grand quite yet; he made it a practice not to touch a client's down payment until the job was in the can.

"I'm just getting started," Jack said. "On my Christmas shopping."

She nodded, looked away.

"For my nieces and nephews," he continued, a veritable glutton for punishment. "I've got, like, a thousand of them." *A thousand. A thousand nieces and nephews. Just shut up, why don't you? Shut up and walk away. This is humiliating.*

"Well, this is the place for it," she said as she turned to leave.

"Look, I'm no good at this," he said quickly as he darted in front of her. "I don't know what to say to women in situations like this. You know, when you see a woman and you think maybe . . ."

She was staring at him.

"Can I buy you a cup of coffee?" he asked.

"Um . . ." She looked away again, and he knew she was composing a tactful rejection.

"There's a place right around the corner—Moe's. Just a cup of coffee. Ten minutes. Just so I can, like, prove that I really can hold a conversation and I'm not some—"

"I'm sorry." She took a step back, the polite smile back in place. "I really can't."

"Because you don't know me? Okay. Name. Johnathan Rory Patrick O'Leary, but my friends call me Jack. I don't smoke, take drugs, or drink to excess. I box at Gleason's Gym in Brooklyn four or five nights a week. I own my own business and I'm healthy and well adjusted. References and test results on request. I'm a nice guy—really. Not some . . . you know. I mean—"

"I know what you mean, and I'm sure you're a nice guy, but I'm, like . . ." She tucked the koala more firmly against her. "I'm involved, and . . ."

"Ah."

"He wouldn't, you know . . ."

"Like it if you went out to coffee with some guy you just met at FAO Schwarz."

She smiled. "References and test results notwithstanding. So I'm afraid . . ."

"How come he's not here with you?" Jack was feeling a little more confident now that she was actually engaged in conversation with him, even if it was just to make excuses for not being able to have coffee with him. "If you were *my* girlfriend, I wouldn't let you out of my sight."

She gave him an *Oh, brother* look, but not before he caught a subtle little wavering in her eyes that spoke volumes. She was flattered. Maybe even a little interested—or would be, if it weren't for Preston.

"He left town yesterday," she said. *With his wife,* Jack mentally added, although naturally she would choose to omit that particular detail. "But trust me, he would not be amused if I had coffee with you, and yes, he would find out because I tell him everything, so I'm sorry, but I can't."

"But—"

"Sorry. Really. Enjoy your shopping." She turned and strode off purposefully in the direction of the cash registers.

Jack knew better than to pursue her. The line between "earnest nice guy" and "total pain in the ass" could be excruciatingly thin.

Instead, he exited the store through its imposing Fifth Avenue entrance with those mile-high windows, slid on his RayBans and scanned the crowd—thankfully sparse—for Grady, whose defensive-lineman build and orange-dyed buzz cut made him hard to miss. Maybe he'd ducked inside; it was chilly, despite the dazzling sunshine.

Jack finally spied him over at the edge of the plaza, chatting with a guy roasting chestnuts on a cart; their sweetly scorched aroma greeted Jack as he approached. "Front and center, Grady. Time to earn your pay."

His nephew shot him a beseeching look. "Can it wait?" The chestnut vendor, giving Jack a lazily curious once-over, was slim, goateed, and earringed, just Grady's type.

"Sorry, pal. She'll be coming out any second now." Grabbing Grady by the sleeve of his bomber jacket, Jack propelled him across the plaza. "Here's what I need you to do."

The mugger struck the moment Katherine Peale left the store with her two shopping bags, materializing as a hulking blur at the edge of her field of vision.

She dropped the bags and grabbed her purse just as the brute reached for it, cried "No!" as he yanked at it.

She impulsively yanked back.

Seizing the purse with both hands, her assailant tore it out of her grip, throwing her off balance in the process.

"No!" she screamed as her legs skidded out from under her. She broke her fall with her hands, crying out in pain as she landed.

The mugger, fleeing with her purse, heard her and glanced back over his shoulder. To her surprise, he turned and gaped when he saw that he'd knocked her down. He hesitated, almost as if he couldn't decide whether to run off with her purse or double back and help her up.

"Are you all right?" Someone—a man—crouched over her. The few other onlookers stood and watched as if it were street theater. Customers exiting the store just circled around them.

"My purse." Kat flinched when she tried to rise; her palms felt like they were on fire.

"Stay put." The good Samaritan leaped up. Even from behind, he looked familiar—dark hair, that tobacco-brown suede jacket, those shoulders. And she recognized that scratchy-deep voice; it was the guy who'd asked her to coffee just now. Jack . . . O'something. "What do you think you're doing?" he bellowed as he stalked toward the orange-haired behemoth of a mugger.

Uh-oh. Kat struggled to sit up. This was real life, not a boxing ring at Gleason's Gym. "Jack, don't."

The mugger was not only a little taller than Jack—no

pygmy himself at six feet or more—but he carried half
again as much bulk, with a tree-trunk neck and bone-
cracking hands. Yet he backed away a step as Jack approached, the handbag clutched to his chest—a ludicrous
image, given his brawn and the fact that he'd just snatched
it away from her. "I . . ."

"Give me that." Wresting the purse out of the mugger's
hand, Jack gave him a shove—a hard one that sent him
stumbling backward. "What's the *matter* with you?"

"I'm sorry, man." Meeting Kat's gaze, he said, "I didn't
mean to hurt you. Sorry." He shrugged helplessly, then
turned and sprinted away.

The onlookers whooped and applauded as Jack returned
with her purse.

"Wow," Kat said. "That was . . ." Strange. Cool, but . . .
"He just . . . buckled when you confronted him. How'd you
know he'd react that way and not"—she shrugged—"slug
you, or whip out a knife, or something?"

"Dumb luck, I guess." He knelt beside her and slid off
his sunglasses, giving her a close-up of those knee-
weakening hazel eyes that had so taxed her composure as
he'd held forth with goofy sincerity about boxing and references and being well adjusted. Right now they were dark
with compassion. "That never should have happened. That
was . . ." He looked away, swearing under his breath.

"Hey, that's life in the big city," she said, striving to
keep from shaking now that it was all over.

"Yeah, well . . ." He shook his head. "I'm sorry it happened."

"It's not your fault."

He looked at her. She thought he was going to say something, but then he just sort of sighed. "It's broken." He
showed her where the purse's shoulder strap had gotten
ripped out.

"They can fix that at the shoe repair place. At least you
got it back for me. Thank you, Jack. I can't tell you how
grateful I am. You really went above and beyond."

He grimaced. "Yeah, I'm a real swell guy." Rising, he

reached for her hands. "Here, let me . . . oh, my God. You're hurt."

She groaned when she got a good look at her palms, which were scraped raw—especially the balls of her hands, one of which was bleeding.

"Are you okay otherwise?" he asked, gingerly patting her arms through her coat sleeves. "Should I take you to the emergency room? Or maybe you've got a doctor . . ."

"I'm fine. I mean, except for my hands. I just need to get them cleaned up."

"Here." Gripping her by the upper arms, he lifted her easily to her feet. "I know a place nearby where we can get you fixed up. That coffee shop I mentioned before— Moe's."

"No, really," she said. "I'll be fine. I'll take care of it at home."

"How are you gonna get home?" Lifting her shopping bags, he said, "You can't even carry these with your hands like that. Come on, let me help you out here. It's the least I can do."

"Why? You don't even know me."

"So, introduce yourself."

She hesitated, a reluctant smile tugging at her mouth. What the heck . . . "Name. Margaret Peale, but people call me by my middle name, which is Katherine, except for close friends and family, who call me Kat. Let's see. I don't box, but I do kickbox—three times a week, san shou style, at this place on West Twenty-fourth. No smoking or drugs for me, either, although I do like a glass of wine with dinner—red only, merlot or pinot noir, even if it's fish or poultry. Or sometimes a beer, especially if it's a nice pale ale. As for employment . . . I'd guess you'd have to say I'm self-employed."

"Doing what?"

"It's . . . hard to describe in a nutshell."

Jack regarded her thoughtfully. "All right . . . Kat, is it?"

"Well, to my close—"

"You've talked me into it, Kat. I'll take you to Moe's."

Two minutes later, he ushered her into an unprepossessing little breakfast and lunch place around the corner, where the white-aproned owner greeted him with garrulous enthusiasm. Moe—yes, there actually was a Moe, and he was it—guided Kat and Jack through the kitchen and into a small, dimly lit storage room with a utility sink in the corner. Tsk-tsking over Kat's abraded palms, Moe fetched the first-aid kit Jack asked for, then left them to attend to business.

"Nice guy," Kat said as Jack eased her coat off and hung it on a nearby coat rack, along with her purse. His eyes widened slightly when he got a good look at her sweater, and his mouth twitched, but he was too diplomatic to laugh out loud.

"Moe is my cousin." Shucking off his suede jacket, Jack pushed up the sleeves of his own sweater—a handsome heathered wool pullover, the antithesis of hers—and set about washing his hands in the utility sink with a bar of Ivory soap.

She smiled. "One of your thousands of cousins?"

He shook his head, smiling, as he opened up the first-aid kit on a stack of cardboard cartons and proceeded to paw through its contents. "That's nieces and nephews you're thinking about. I've only got about three, four hundred cousins. Five, tops."

"That's all?"

"Us O'Learys don't know when to stop." He set out a tube of antibiotic ointment, a roll of adhesive tape, and two paper-wrapped gauze pads. "We have to rent out convention centers when we throw a wedding—which is, like, every other weekend."

At the mention of weddings, Kat found her gaze homing in on the ring finger of his left hand, which was bare.

He noticed and held the hand up, fingers wriggling. "Always the usher, never the groom."

"Never?"

He pushed her sleeves up, then opened her hands to inspect the damage. "I'm not sure, but I just might be the only straight thirty-seven-year-old male in New York City who's never once made that long walk down the aisle. *National Geographic*'s thinking about doing a special on me."

Kat chuckled, wishing it didn't sound quite so nervous.

He frowned as he studied her hands. "You're trembling."

She swallowed. "Adrenaline." *And you. Being here with you in this small, dark room with my hands in yours. Being afraid to look directly at you, for fear you'll see something in my eyes that you shouldn't see.* "It'll pass."

He rubbed his thumbs over the delicate skin of her inner wrists, as if to soothe her. Only it made her heart race even worse. "Have you ever had your purse snatched before?"

"No, and I've lived in Manhattan my entire life. I must emit kickboxing vibes or something."

Jack turned on the tap and adjusted the temperature, warning, "This is gonna sting, I'm afraid."

She sucked in her breath, but somehow kept from yanking her hands away as he guided them under the warm stream.

"You're a good patient." He soaped up her wounds with gentle, dextrous fingers. "Why'd you hold on so hard to that purse? I mean, not that it was your fault, any of it. He didn't have to . . . he shouldn't have been so . . ." Jack's jaw clenched.

"I guess I should have just given it up," she said. "But that purse is special to me. It was my Grandmother Augusta's. She had a weakness for Italian handbags, and that was her favorite one, from Adela Borse in Florence. It was the one she carried to St. Bart's every Sunday when I was growing up, except for Easter, when she always let me borrow it."

"Is she . . . ?"

"She died in her sleep two years ago."

"I'm sorry." Jack blotted her hands carefully with paper towels, then opened up a gauze pad and smeared it with antibiotic ointment. "Sounds like you two were close."

"Very. My favorite belongings are the things she gave

me, especially the things she made herself. She knitted me this sweater when I was a teenager."

Jack regarded the sweater with an expression that could only be described as politely jaundiced as he taped the gauze pad over the abrasion on her right hand. "Nice."

"You think it's ludicrous."

"Not ludicrous." He grinned. "Unusual, maybe."

She smiled, too. "Unusually ludicrous." Not only had Grandma Augusta knitted every conceivable Christmas symbol right into the sweater—Santa, tree, stockings, candles, wise men, wreaths, reindeer, angels, candy canes, you name it—but she had further embellished it with generous applications of sequins, buttons, ribbons, pom-poms, beads, and googly eyes. There was nothing remotely tasteful about Grandma's Christmas sweater.

"If you feel that way about it," Jack asked as he prepared the second gauze pad, "how come you wear it?"

" 'Cause it makes me happy to wear it. Sure, it's busy and silly and more than a little tacky. But so is Christmas, and everybody loves Christmas."

Jack looked as if he were going to say something, but thought better of it. Something stiffened in his expression as he applied the bandage to her left hand. For the first time she noticed a rigid, almost surly thrust to his jaw. It wasn't unattractive—actually, quite the opposite, when contrasted with his warmly expressive eyes—but she wondered about the subtle mood shift.

"You don't like Christmas," she said.

He shrugged with an indifference that looked forced. "I don't like it or dislike it. It's just another day. Or it would be, if the stores would stop hyping it for months beforehand. By the time it comes around, aren't you just a little sick of it?"

"No," she said with quiet sincerity. "Never. I mean, yeah, the 'buy, buy, buy' thing can be a bit much. But underneath it all, Christmas is a time of heartfelt giving and rebirth. It's a season of miracles."

"Hey, if that's the way you feel, that's cool," Jack said

as he repacked the first-aid kit and tidied up. "Different strokes, and all that."

"Isn't there *anything* you like about Christmas?"

"You mean, besides fruitcake?"

"No, seriously."

"Seriously. I can't get enough of the stuff. You know who makes an awesome fruitcake this time of year? Moe."

"Moe?" She pointed through the doorway to the kitchen, where Jack's cousin Moe was banging around and yelling at the help. "That Moe?"

"Come on—let's get a booth and I'll buy you a slice." Grabbing their outerwear, Jack led her with a hand on her back through the doorway. "I'm telling you, it'll rock your world."

CHAPTER THREE

"Oh, my God," Kat moaned, her head thrown back, her expression rapturous. "Oh, my *God*."

If she didn't have a fork in her bandaged hand, and a plate of half-eaten fruitcake in front of her, Jack might have taken her for a woman transported by a very different, and more carnal, sort of pleasure. He pictured her writhing against a mountain of satin pillows instead of opposite him in a corner window booth at Moe's. The Christmas sweater would have to go. She'd be naked. Or maybe wearing that sheer black camisole and thong that Jack was beginning to wish he'd never heard about.

"This is incredible," she said dreamily, her head resting against the back of the red vinyl bench, her eyes half-closed, cheeks flushed, sunlight igniting her hair, gilding her skin. "Definitely the best I've ever had."

Jack's own plate was empty but for a sprinkling of crumbs. He'd inhaled his fruitcake while Kat had lingered over hers, savoring every bite as if it were the most transcendent sensual experience imaginable. He lifted his coffee cup just to have something to do with his hands, but he couldn't for the life of him stop staring at her.

"This redefines fruitcake," she said as she forked up another mouthful. Her voice was warm, velvety, but with a hint of texture to it, like age-softened corduroy. "All these nuts. It's like pecan pie meets cherry pie, with a hint of something . . . almost smoky."

"That would be the bourbon."

"Yeah?" She grinned as she swallowed. "You trying to get me drunk, Jack?"

He grinned back. "Would it do me any good?"

She lowered her gaze as she pried a pecan out of the fruitcake with her fingertips. " 'Fraid not. I'm still, like . . ."

"Spoken for."

She nodded, touched the pecan to the tip of her tongue.

Coffee sloshed out of Jack's cup as he set it back down. "Tell me about him."

"Preston?"

"Is that his name?" Jack sopped up the spilled coffee with a paper napkin. "Sounds like some guy in a cartoon, some pompous old rich guy."

She hacked off another bite. "I guess he's rich, by most people's standards. He's from this prominent old Connecticut family. But he's not just living off inherited wealth. He works. He's a partner in a law firm down on Wall Street—Gardner and Worth."

Where he was a rainmaker, Jack knew, luring deep-pocket clients because of his social connections, but billing almost no hours in actual legal work. His most direct contribution to the firm's revenue, according to Celeste: playing tennis with their clients for the legal fee, double or nothing. His father had bought him a spot at Harvard Law with the expectation that he'd enter politics, but as it turned out, he'd had neither the disposition nor the interest.

"As for being old," she said around a bite of fruitcake, "he *is* older than I am. By about twenty years or so."

It would be closer to thirty. Preston Worth was almost twice Kat's age. Jack assumed she knew that but was trying to make the May-December thing sound more like a May-October thing.

"I've never dated a guy that much older than me," she said. "I almost refused to go out with him for that reason. I thought it would be . . ." She made an *ick* face. "But he's . . ." She chewed thoughtfully. "The maturity is actually refreshing. Guys my age can be so . . . unsure of themselves. Preston doesn't have that problem."

Jack was ambushed by the mental image of Preston lowering Katherine Peale into that mound of satin pillows, pressing his lips to her throat, slipping his hand inside that filmy thong . . .

He was brought up to take what he wanted when he wanted it . . . The man is utterly ravenous.

"Mm, that was great," she sighed, eyeing her empty plate wistfully. "I just wish there was more."

Jack signaled the waitress. "One more slice, please."

"Jack, no!" Kat protested laughingly. "I'll explode."

"We'll share it. I'd like some more."

She hesitated when the waitress set the plate of fruitcake down between them and topped off their coffee cups.

"Come on." He lifted his fork, gestured to her to lift hers. "I've got nothing communicable. Dig in."

She did. He couldn't get over the way her eyes grew unfocused with every bite she chewed, the way she closed them as she swallowed, a satisfied little smile curving her lips.

They were excellent lips, lush and pink. Naturally pink, because she didn't appear to be wearing lipstick—or makeup of any kind, that he could tell. Her skin had a sunny translucence that couldn't possibly have come out of a bottle.

She didn't seem to be wearing perfume, either, but he was less sure about that. Maybe there *was* something you could buy that smelled the way she smelled, very sweet and clean, but with a hint of . . . sky? Grass? Earth?

She smelled like rain, that was it. A soft, drenching spring rain.

No wonder Preston Worth was wooing her with diamonds and dinners at the Four Seasons. Married or not, it would take a strong man to resist the dewy allure of a Katherine Peale. Preston hadn't had the backbone for it.

As for Jack . . .

He sat up straighter, pressed his back against the bench. If he was feeling a little low on spinal fortitude at the moment, well . . . he'd just have to fake it.

"So, what do you do, Jack?" Kat asked, leaning forward

on her elbows as she twirled the fork slowly. "You said you own your own business?"

"It's a security firm," he said, having decided it would be the height of dumb to let on that he was a PI. "High-tech alarm systems and the like for businesses, mostly. Also state-of-the-art locks, closed-circuit video surveillance . . ."

"Sounds fascinating."

"It is," he said earnestly. "There are new breakthroughs every day, what with advances in computer technology and all. It's a great field to be in." Which was precisely why he was here, so he could afford to be a player in that field. It was why he was feeding her this line of bull, why he'd staged that mugging outside FAO Schwarz, so that he could play the hero by retrieving her purse, whereupon she'd feel obligated to put up with his attentions just long enough for him to get his foot firmly planted in the door.

Damn, he wished Grady hadn't gotten carried away and yanked so hard on that purse. Jack knew he hadn't meant to knock Kat down, and he'd be feeling bad about it for days. Still, Jack had every intention of chewing him out good the next time he saw him.

Because you want to chew out yourself. In a way, he was glad the purse-snatching had gone awry, thereby ratcheting up his guilt quotient a few abject degrees. If this wasn't quite the sleaziest job he'd ever been offered, it was certainly the sleaziest he'd ever accepted. Guilt was the trade-off. That was the way these things worked.

"Were you a computer major in college?" she asked.

"No. No, I, uh, never went to college. Never even graduated from high school."

"Really?"

Jack mentally kicked himself. He needed to get over with this woman. He should be telling her what she wanted to hear—*sure, I graduated cum laude from MIT*—not just blurting out the unvarnished and all-too-unimpressive story of his life.

Although maybe there was a certain wisdom to offering up the truth whenever possible and only doing an end run around it when absolutely necessary. The truth was easier to remember, after all, and would come off as more credible than a series of increasingly muddled fabrications.

Not that he was averse to lying outright to this woman when necessary. Hadn't she already committed a whopper of omission by withholding from her description of Preston the little fact that he was married? Jack didn't—strike that, *shouldn't*—feel a moment's guilt about misleading her.

"Why didn't you finish high school?" She kept her gaze trained on him as she questioned him about himself, her expression one of utter absorption. There was something undeniably gratifying—seductive, even—about having a beautiful woman draw him out this way, as if riveted by the banal details of his life. Was it a ploy, part of her temptress's bag of tricks? Maybe she was actually as interested in him as she appeared to be.

Yeah, and maybe Jack should start thinking with his brain instead of with unreliable old Mr. Stupid, and then maybe he could execute this job with the necessary detachment, score his fifty grand, and be done with it.

"Finishing high school would have meant staying in my house, and . . ." He lifted his coffee cup, took a sip. "That wasn't an option at the time."

"Didn't get along with your parents?"

"My mother was long gone. And to say I didn't get along with my father would be a laughable understatement. I enlisted in the army and did a couple of tours as an MP. Came home, got my GED, and went to work for an executive protection agency."

"You were a bodyguard?"

He nodded. "Yeah, foreign businessmen mostly, some political types."

"How did you go from that to owning your own security firm?"

He shrugged, not sure how to fudge the intermediary step of Jack O'Leary, Private Investigations. "I got lucky," he lied. "Fell into some cash and was able to pursue my dream a few years earlier than I otherwise might have been."

"That's great."

Yeah, it would have been. Then he wouldn't be sitting here snowing her this way. Jack was tempted to inquire about *her* work, ask her what she'd meant by being self-employed . . . only he was all too sure he knew.

Margaret Katherine Peale hadn't held down an actual job for two years, a fact that Jack had unearthed through his cousin Moira, who worked for the Social Security Administration in their Queens program center. Although it was strictly verboten for SSA employees to tap into the agency's database for personal reasons, Jack had found his cousin more than willing to sniff out a subject's employment history from time to time in exchange for a nice, crisp fifty-dollar bill.

Armed with a name and a date-of-birth range of 1967 to 1970, Moira had snagged Kat's social security number, plugged that into an earnings database, and discovered that she'd worked for the New York City public school system from 1990 to 1999. Since then, she had been either unemployed or employed off the books somewhere. Had she truly been self-employed, Moira assured Jack, she would be paying Social Security tax and the system would have a record of her.

Despite her official lack of income, Kat was hardly living in poverty. She dressed well and seemed to have plenty of cash to throw around. Not to mention the upscale building she lived in, a nineteenth-century limestone townhouse down the street from the Morgan Library in the tony Murray Hill section of Manhattan. One-bedroom apartments in buildings like that rented for around two grand a month. Could a woman who hadn't pulled down a paycheck in two years afford a place like that?

Maybe, if she was young and gorgeous and not squeamish about sleeping with married men. Especially if— strike that, *only* if—they could provide her with costly gifts and a snazzy apartment and, he assumed, a generous allowance.

How many other sugar daddies had there been before Preston? She probably hooked up with just one at a time; men who could afford mistresses of her caliber would expect fidelity, wouldn't they? Which was why she'd burned Jack off at first, or tried to.

It struck him suddenly that getting Kat away from Preston would be about a hundred times harder than he had anticipated. Why should she even agree to see him again? What was in it for her? And if he actually pulled it off and got her to trade in Preston for him, what then? Turn around and dump her once he had that fifty grand in his pocket?

Somehow he couldn't picture it. But what was the alternative? A *relationship*? With someone he'd been paid to essentially scam?

Maybe he should just pack it in now—pay the check, wish Katherine Peale a happy life, and walk away with his dignity intact. Not to mention his self-respect. Screw the money. It wasn't worth it.

"So, do you think you'd be interested?" she asked.

"Hm?" He'd zoned out while she was talking. *Real smooth, O'Leary.*

"In checking out my apartment."

He stared at her. "Um . . ."

"To see if you can boost the security. It's got first-floor exposure, is the problem. As a woman living alone, it makes me a little nervous."

"Oh." *Say no. Get out while you can.* "Yeah. Sure. I don't see why not." *Sure you do.* "Uh, but really the best thing you could do is to put bars on the windows. You don't need me for that."

"Bars . . . that's not really an option, I'm afraid."

"Why not?"

"You'd have to see the place to understand." She glanced at him, then frowned and looked away. Savvy New York women weren't in the habit of inviting virtual strangers into their apartments, regardless of how "nice" they claimed to be. Brightening, she said, "I know. You could come over next Friday night. I'm having a few people over for a little Christmas party—a couple of old friends, some women I work with . . ."

Work with? Did the demimonde of New York have a union?

"You'll like them." She started rummaging around in her purse—a laborious undertaking, given her bandages. "They'll like you, too. I've got a couple of girlfriends, they're really my best friends—Pia and Chantal. They'll probably get into a shrieking catfight over you the second you walk in the door."

"I hate it when that happens."

"Here." She retrieved a business card and handed it to him: cream vellum engraved in a graceful script. It gave her home address on East Thirty-seventh, with "Apartment One" spelled out on its own line. There was no company name or indication of profession. "This is where I live. Say, eight o'clock? Oh, I should warn you, it'll be dressy. I invited this big-time Internet tycoon, and I mean to wow him."

Could she already be scouting out a successor to Preston? "Um . . ."

"Say you'll come." Her hopeful smile undid him.

He rubbed a hand over his jaw. *Oh, hell . . .* "Can I bring anything?"

"Just yourself. Unless you, uh, want to bring a date. That'd be . . . I mean, you should feel free to . . ." She glanced away briefly, but not before he saw it again, that little waver in her expression, the fleeting hint that maybe, just maybe, if there were no Preston in the picture, she might not be inviting him to bring a date. "You *should* bring someone." She smiled and shrugged. "You'd avoid the catfight, if nothing else."

"No, that's okay." He met her gaze, returned her smile. "What's life without a little risk?"

CHAPTER FOUR

—

"Don't tell me—you're Jack," greeted the woman who opened the door to Apartment One at half past eight the following Friday evening, where Jack found Kat's party already in full swing. "I'm Chantal," she said over the tapestry of conversation and lively piano music. Chantal was a willowy, sepia-skinned beauty with extravagant dreadlocks and earrings that rattled when they brushed her shoulders.

"Uh, hi," Jack muttered as Chantal led him through the foyer and into a palatial, high-ceilinged room filled with richly upholstered antiques and Oriental rugs, the focal point of which was a Christmas tree that must have been fourteen feet tall. Flames leapt in a monumental fireplace surmounted by a proportionately outsized wreath, around which several guests stood laughing and sipping champagne. The back wall was mostly one giant leaded-glass window overlooking a moonlit private garden, in which fairy lights twinkled through a dusting of snow that looked as if it had been special-ordered for the occasion.

This was a duplex, Jack realized when he noticed the curved staircase heaped with poinsettias, and an immense one, given what he glimpsed through open doorways—a huge formal dining room, a more intimately scaled room next to it with leather furniture and sage-green walls, and a library with a baby grand in the corner, at which a tuxedoed pianist was launching into a spirited rendition of "I Saw Mommy Kissing Santa Claus."

"Pia!" Chantal was waving someone over, a young woman with spiky black hair and rhinestone-studded cat-eye glasses who had a mug of eggnog in her hand. "Look who's here," Chantal exclaimed, yelling to be heard over some guests who had gathered around the piano for a sing-along. "It's Kat's knight in shining armor. Jack O'something."

"O'Leary," Jack clarified, hand outstretched.

"Well, don't be!" Pia said loudly as she took his hand. "We won't bite."

"Uh, no, what I—"

"We love you!" Tugging him close, Pia kissed him on the cheek. "You're our hero!"

"Kat told us how you faced down that purse snatcher," Chantal shouted as she took the bottle of wine Jack had brought and helped him off with his snow-dusted topcoat, handing both to a white-jacketed young man hovering nearby. "Way to go!"

"Is she around?" Jack scanned the room, grateful to Grady for having talked him into buying a new suit for this gig.

"She's over there, strutting her stuff for Daddy War-bucks." Pia pointed toward the Christmas tree. Sure enough, there was Kat, half-hidden by its branches as she leaned toward her tall, entirely bald companion to say something. Whatever it was made Daddy Warbucks chuckle appreciatively.

"That's Harry Livermore," Chantal said into Jack's ear. "Kat's newest project—one of those dot-com zillionaires who *didn't* crash and burn. What can I get you to drink, hon?"

"Anything, as long as it's a double." Jack couldn't wrest his gaze away from Kat, incandescent in a gleaming black sheath adorned with a jeweled brooch the size of his hand that was shaped like a sprig of holly; he assumed the emeralds and rubies were real. The dress skimmed her curves and was short enough to show off those nonstop legs to excellent advantage. Her carelessly upswept hairdo revealed a good-size pair of diamonds sparkling on her ears.

Shouldn't there be some unwritten rule, Jack wondered,

against wearing diamonds given to you by one man while you were "strutting your stuff" for his prospective replacement?

Or maybe this Harry Livermore wouldn't be so much a replacement as a supplement. Was it possible Kat wasn't constrained by fidelity after all, that she permitted herself to be kept by more than one man at a time? More to the point, would the men permit it? It seemed to Jack that he'd heard of courtesans in Paris and Venice who were shared by several wealthy protectors. Did the same sorts of arrangements exist today?

It could happen. And where was it more likely to happen than in Manhattan, the world capital of jaded sophistication?

Was Kat the type to juggle three or four deep-pocket benefactors that way? Not that she couldn't pull it off if she wanted—just look at her—but did she have the stomach for it?

No way, he thought, picturing her in that goofy Christmas sweater, talking about going to church every Sunday with her grandma. But then he looked around at all this opulence, watched her smiling at Harry Livermore, laughing at his jokes, and he wasn't so sure.

"Here you are." Chantal handed him a hefty crystal glass filled with whiskey on the rocks. "I hope you like scotch."

Jack had detested the stuff ever since he'd gotten sick on it at fourteen, thereby reaping a particularly memorable ass-kicking from the old man, but he tossed it back anyway, in one burning tilt.

When he lowered the glass he found Kat watching him from across the room. She smiled a little tentatively, mouthed *Glad you could make it.* He nodded, his gaze fixed on her, his hand tightening around the glass.

Her smile faded, and he realized too late that he hadn't returned it. They stared at each other for a few long seconds, and then Harry Livermore said something to Kat and she turned toward him and Jack raised the glass to his mouth again.

It was empty, of course. He'd already drained it.

Chantal and Pia exchanged a look.

"Come on, Jack—let's go to the den, where it's quieter." Chantal took one of his arms, Pia the other, and together they guided him to the small, sage-colored room. The light was dimmer here—most of it came from candles—and the crowd thinner, and you didn't have to yell to be heard. There was another, smaller fireplace in this room, its mantel draped in evergreen swags. Jack breathed in a pleasantly sharp fusion of woodsmoke and pine.

"How about a refill?" Chantal plucked the glass out of his hand as she gestured him into a milk-chocolate leather sofa.

"Better not," he said, but she was already fetching him another one from the built-in carved-oak wet bar in the corner, manned by a middle-aged woman in a tuxedo shirt, cummerbund, and earrings shaped like Christmas lights.

If he sat all the way back and tilted his head, he could still see Kat, he discovered, only now she was facing away from him. Her dress, modestly cut in front, scooped down to her waist in back, displaying a sweep of bare, creamy flesh that he hadn't anticipated.

"It's Vera Wang."

"Huh?" He turned to find Chantal lowering herself into the squishy couch next to him; Pia had already settled in on the other side.

"Her dress." Chantal handed him a fresh scotch and took a sip of the eggnog she'd snagged for herself. "It's a Vera Wang. Doesn't she look faboo?"

"Kat could wear a feed sack and she'd look faboo," Pia said.

Jack raised his glass. That distinctive scotch aroma, which always reminded him of burned rubber tires, merged with the unctuous nutmeg-and-cream eggnog smell to make him feel woozier than he should have after just the one drink.

A waiter came around with a tray of skewered shrimp wrapped in prosciutto. Pia and Chantal helped themselves;

Jack waved it away. "So, how do you ladies know Kat?" he asked.

"We're on staff at her old junior high," Pia said. "I teach vocal music. Chantal teaches English."

"You two are teachers?"

Jack's tone must have betrayed his incredulity, because Chantal deadpanned, "We left our schoolmarm costumes at work."

"No, I mean . . . I didn't mean . . ." Jack chuckled uneasily. "You gotta understand, I was educated by hatchet-faced, ruler-swinging nuns. If it had been you two instead, I might have stuck around to graduate."

"Kat was a school counselor," Pia said, "before she left to do her thing."

"My ears are burning. You guys talking about me?"

Jack looked up to find Kat standing over him. He braced himself one-handed to rise, but it was the kind of couch that swallowed you up and didn't want to let you go.

"Don't get up." She waved him back down and perched on the edge of the marble-topped coffee table. "I just stopped by to say hi. I *am* glad you came." She reached out and lightly touched his knee, her fingers warm through the wool of his trousers, her smile shyly luminous. It was as if a mild electric current were shivering through him, scrambling his brainwaves and rendering him incapable of speech.

"How's it going with Harry Livermore?" Chantal asked Kat. "Got him eating out of your hand yet?"

Kat gave her friend a *look*. "Harry happens to be a swell guy, and we're hitting it off just fine, thank you. But Kirsten wandered off before I could sweet-talk her, and she's the key."

"Kirsten?" Jack inquired as he raised his glass to his mouth.

"Harry's wife," Kat said. "I've got to try and get the three of us together and show her what I can do."

Jack's scotch went down the wrong hole. "The three of you?" he choked out.

Chantal slapped him on the back. "They say he never makes a move without her."

"Uh . . ."

"Kirsten's been a sucker for glitz ever since their ship came in," Kat said in a low voice, glancing around. "That's why I pulled out all the stops this year. My Christmas parties usually aren't quite this *Dynasty*-esque."

Pia barked with laughter. "Most years, Kat cons us into decorating her tree for her, then we get maybe a bowl of popcorn and a six-pack while she makes us watch *It's a Wonderful Life* for, like, the umpteenth time."

Chantal chuckled. "That's Kat's idea of heaven—washing popcorn down with ice-cold beer and weeping like a baby at the end of that movie, like it's the first time she's seen it."

"Which only goes to show," Kat said with mock loftiness, "what a genius Frank Capra was, to get to me every time like that. And it's not like I'm alone. *It's a Wonderful Life* is ranked—"

"Eleventh," Chantal and Pia recited in eye-rolling unison, "on the American Film Institute's list of the one hundred greatest movies ever made."

"Because it's a masterpiece," Kat said, "which I'm sure even Jack the Grinch will agree with."

"Uh . . ." Jack winced exaggeratedly. "Truth be told, I'm not that crazy about it."

Kat's jaw actually dropped. Pia snickered as Chantal shook her head, murmuring, "Boy, you done blown it now," into her eggnog.

"I mean, I don't hate it," he hurriedly amended. "I've only seen, like, bits and pieces on TV now and then. It just struck me as being a little . . ."

"Sappy?" Kat asked.

"Let's just say I watch movies for amusement, not to have big, gooey life lessons wrapped up in tinsel and shoved down my throat." *Nice going, Scrooge,* Jack chided himself even as Chantal gored him in the ribs with her elbow. "Nothing personal," he added. "I'm sure it's basically a good movie. It's just not really . . . my scene."

Not really my scene? Who do you think you are, Maynard G. Krebs?

Kat said, "You should try watching the whole thing sometime. I've got a videotape I could lend you, because unfortunately I don't think either of my so-called best friends, or should I say *former* best friends"—she made a face at Pia and Chantal, who stuck their tongues out at her—"is going to be willing to watch it with me this year."

"You don't have it on DVD yet?" Pia asked.

"You know how low-tech I am," Kat said. "I'm going to be the last kid on the block with a DVD player."

Ask Preston for one when he comes back from Aspen, Jack thought uncharitably as he took another odious swallow of scotch. *Or Harry Livermore. Or . . .* How many more were there? he wondered.

Chantal said, "I saw an ad for the DVD version. It's got a couple of those making-of-the-movie type documentaries on it, and the original theatrical trailer."

"Really?" Kat sat forward, her eyes girlishly wide.

"Argh! Chantal!" Pia reached across Jack to playfully slap her friend. "Now look what you've done. She's gonna upgrade to DVD, lure us here on some pretext, and make us watch it again. I thought we'd get a reprieve this year."

"You can rest easy," Kat said. "I won't be upgrading any time soon. You know how much I've got on my plate lately. And it took me two days just to figure out how to hook up the VCR after I bought it, so the idea of taking the time to replace it with . . ." She trailed off, tilting her head to see something through the doorway. "There she is."

"Who?" Jack asked.

"Kirsten Livermore. She's talking to Harry in the living room. Time for me to kiss a little booty." Kat stood and smoothed her skirt, whispering, "Wish me luck," as she turned and disappeared through the doorway.

"Okay . . ." Leaning forward, Jack thunked his glass down on the coffee table. "You two are gonna have to brief me on the whole Harry Livermore thing, 'cause my imagination is pretty much making an ass out of me here."

Chantal's perplexed stare turned into a grin of disbelief. "Omigod, you thought she had designs on him! Or *them*."

"As *if*." Pia joined her in an uproarious burst of laughter, then muttered something in Spanish that included the name "Preston" and ended on a disparaging little snort. Before Jack could ask her for a translation, she said, "Harry Livermore's just some guy looking for a good cause to help ease his guilt about being filthy stinking nouveau riche. Kat's hitting him up for funding for Augusta House."

Jack cocked his head as if to say, *And that would be . . . ?*

"You don't know about Augusta House?" Pia glanced in bemusement at Chantal, then back at Jack. "What do you think Kat's been doing since she quit the school system two years ago?"

Drawing on his all too meager reserves of prudence, Jack said, "Why don't you tell me?"

"It's a little complicated," Chantal began, an echo of Kat's *It's hard to describe in a nutshell.* "But I guess you'd have to call her a full-time do-gooder." Pitching her voice low, she added, "You do know she comes from money."

"Uh . . ." Jack tracked Chantal's gaze into the living room, where Kat was deep in conversation with the Livermores.

"Big-time money, a trust fund and all that, but she'd always wanted to counsel kids, so she went to college and got a master's in child psychology."

"She wanted to work in inner-city schools," Pia said, "where she felt she could do the most good. She was great at it, too—never came off as a little rich girl slumming it. Very down-to-earth, *really* in touch with the kids. They loved her. And she loved them."

Jack stared, dumbfounded, as Kat gracefully bent her head to absorb some comment of Kirsten Livermore's, her arm on the other woman's, her smile warm and attentive.

"The family situations of some of these kids really got to her," Chantal said. "Lots of single-mother-scraping-by situations, even some homeless families. When she handed in her resignation, some of the staff thought it was because she just couldn't take it anymore. Her grandmother Augusta had just died, so Pia and I thought maybe she was in a weakened emotional state, what with the grief and all. Augusta left her this building and millions in—"

"*This* building?" Jack asked. "The building we're in?" Kat owned a five-story luxury apartment building?

Pia said, "Yep. There are seven units upstairs. She rents those out and lives on the first two floors, like Augusta did."

"So, anyway," Chantal continued, "she took the money Augusta left her and bought another building with it—this vacant old dinosaur uptown. It had been a private school for girls once—Miss Fussybutt's Academy for Young Ladies, something like that—but they shut it down years ago."

"At first we didn't know what to think," Pia said. "But then she told us she wanted to create a residence for mothers with children who needed a place to live while they got their lives together and looked for permanent housing. Augusta House has been up and running for over a year now."

"There are over sixty families there right now," Chantal said. "They get furnished apartments, crisis intervention, child care, job training, permanent housing assistance . . ."

"Chantal and I are part of the volunteer staff," Pia said. "She established a reading program for the kids, and I've recruited a couple dozen of the teenagers for a mixed chorus—they'll be here later, in fact, to sing some carols and hopefully put Mr. and Mrs. Warbucks in the check-writing mood."

Chantal said, "We've got some paid staff, too—counselors for drug abuse, mental health, AIDS, teen pregnancy, domestic violence . . ."

"Then there's CFF," Pia said. "Caring for Families. It's a coalition of volunteers that Kat's trying to get off the ground. It'll oversee programs for battered women and runaways, among other things, but to do that, she needs to buy and furnish another building. She spent buckets of her own money getting Augusta House started, so a big part of what

she does is to court deep pockets like ol' Harry and his
wife to write checks to CFF. She's one busy lady."

"So, if this is all news to you," Chantal asked Jack,
"what did you *think* she did?"

"Uh . . ."

*Hook up with sugar daddies and milk them for all
they're worth.* That was how Jack had assumed she made
her living. Now he knew that wasn't the case at all, that
she was not only wealthy in her own right, but a philan-
thropist. She didn't need to seduce prosperous men who'd
grown bored with their wives.

Maybe she just preferred them.

Kat was laughing now, head thrown back, diamonds
flashing. No wonder she reminded him so much of Grace
Kelly, another high-society blonde who, as an ingenue, had
reputedly enthralled her share of married man.

"She *is* seeing someone, you know." Chantal met Jack's
gaze with an apologetic little smile. "It's just . . . the way
you've been looking at her, ever since you got here . . . I
thought I should—"

"No, I know about that." Jack reached for his drink
again. "Preston something, right?"

"We just call him P-Four," Pia said as she drained the
rest of her eggnog, " 'cause before him, Kat dated this guy
Phil, and last year it was Pretty Paolo, and back when she
was still working, it was our old vice principal, Peter Pe-
terson."

"Pumpkin Eaterson?" Jack asked.

"You'd fit right in with the junior high crowd." Chantal
shook her head. "They seemed like great guys in the beginning, all of them—so serious about her. Pumpkin proposed to her on the third date. Turned out all they were
really serious about was her bank balance."

Pia said, "Preston's so rich himself that he couldn't care
less whether she has money or not. We think that's his
appeal, 'cause he doesn't seem to have much else going for
him. We keep hoping she'll come to her senses and jettison

the guy. It's a dead-end relationship, anyway. It can never go anywhere."

"Why?" Jack asked with studied nonchalance. "Because he's married?"

They both fell silent for a moment, then burst out laughing. "What on earth makes you think that?" Chantal asked.

They didn't know! With a careless shrug, Jack said, "I just thought maybe that was why you disapproved of him."

"Trust me," Pia said, "Kat is the last woman in the world who'd stoop to dating a married man."

Jack looked down and rubbed the back of his neck, disheartened that Kat's lie of omission encompassed even her closest friends.

"In fact," Chantal said, "I remember her telling us about her first date with P-Four. She asked him how come a catch like him was still single, and he fed her some Hallmark line of bull like, 'I've been waiting for someone like you my whole life.' "

Jack stared at her. "She said that? That he *told* her he was single?"

"Yeah, and I'm with Pia. *No way* would Kat have anything to do with a married man. She has very strong feelings about infidelity."

"I think it has to do with her parents' marriage breaking up," Pia offered. "She said the Other Woman was just as answerable as her father. The only time I've heard her curse was when she was talking about that woman."

She doesn't know! Jack realized. *Oh, my God, she doesn't know!*

He shook his head as if that would jar his brain into *getting* this. "Then . . . why is it you think the relationship is going nowhere?"

" 'Cause he's totally not her type," Pia said. "He's, like, *waaay* older than her, and this super-WASP to boot."

"So is Kat, isn't she?" Jack asked. She was Caucasian, she had an English surname, and St. Bart's was an Episcopal church, making her pretty much the quintessential white Anglo-Saxon Protestant.

"Kat's a recovering WASP," Chantal explained. "With Preston it's like a religion. The country clubs, the stuffy law practice . . . He even lives in Greenwich, Connecticut, which is, like, the old-money capital of the universe."

In fact, Preston Worth hadn't lived in Greenwich since he went away to college, and his older brother had inherited the family manse. He and Celeste lived in a penthouse co-op in the San Remo on Central Park West. Jack assumed he'd given Kat a false—and distant—address, probably his brother's, so that she wouldn't take it into her head to just drop by someday.

"My God," he whispered, gazing through the doorway at Kat, who'd donned a ridiculous fuzzy Santa hat. She noticed him looking at her, and adopted a vampish, hipshot pose so out of character with the hat—and her true personality, he now knew—that Jack couldn't help laughing. She laughed, too, her gaze linked with his across two crowded rooms, until somebody tapped her on the shoulder and she turned away.

She really doesn't know, he thought dazedly. Preston was duping her, playing her along. The reason she seemed so guileless, so sincere, was because she really was.

From his years of dealing with cuckolded wives, Jack knew that the pure of heart were sometimes the easiest to deceive, because they projected their virtue onto those around them. To a woman like that, the notion of the man she loved lying to her face was inconceivable . . . and ultimately devastating.

The weeping of the Wronged Wives, that was the worst.

But she deserves to know, Jack thought as he watched Katherine Peale laughing with her guests. She *needed* to know, even if it broke her heart, even if she ended up loathing Jack for telling her.

She *would* loathe him if he just blurted it all out: *The guy you're seeing is married, and the reason I know is I was hired by his wife to steal you away from him.* She would dump Preston, of that he had little doubt at this point. Jack would get his money.

But she would despise him for deceiving her. He imagined the look on her face, the hurt . . . fifty grand wouldn't make up for it.

How to go about it, then, without tipping his hand?

"What Kat needs," Chantal said, "is some nice, normal, regular guy who fell for her before he even knew about her family's money." She caught his eye and smiled meaningfully.

"And he should be young," Pia added. "Or at least not old enough to be her father. And cute. Oh, and tall."

"And *ripped*." Chantal eyed Jack appraisingly. "How are you in the pecs and abs department?"

Pia prodded his stomach through his shirt. "Omigod, Chantal, I think he's hiding a six-pack under there."

"You should go for it," Chantal said.

Pia nodded soberly. "You should steal her from Preston."

Jack sighed and reached for his drink.

CHAPTER FIVE

——

"You guys *rocked*," Kat praised as she high-fived the two dozen adolescent members of the Augusta House Choralists at the conclusion of their mini-concert that evening. Led by Pia, they had opened with a mellifluous "I'll Be Home for Christmas" that had brought tears to Kat's eyes—and, she noted with interest, to Kirsten Livermore's, as well. "Jingle Bell Rock" came next, and it was a rousing change of pace, but the real showstopper came at the end—a delicately harmonized Renaissance piece in Latin, which segued into an exhilarating "Feliz Navidad" that had everyone, chorus and guests alike, dancing and singing along.

Except for Jack, who sat halfway up the stairs the whole time, nursing a drink—he'd switched to club soda and lime, she noticed—and watching the revelry with mystified detachment, as if it were the arcane ritual of some long-lost tribe. In fact, it wasn't until the party started breaking up about forty-five minutes later that he came back downstairs, joining Kat, Chantal, and Pia as they emptied wrapped presents from a giant laundry basket onto the rosewood console table by the front door.

"Yo, Jack." Chantal shook her head as he approached. "Kat wasn't kidding when she called you a Grinch, was she?"

He smiled a little sheepishly. "Let's just say my festivity threshold is a little on the low side." Nodding toward the presents, he asked, "Who are those for?"

"The kids in the chorus," Kat said as she sorted them into three distinct piles. "To thank them for coming out and doing this tonight. Each kid is getting a book, a portable

CD player, and half a dozen Christmas cookies."

"Those awesome ones with the almond extract?" Pia asked.

Kat nodded. "I baked them this afternoon."

Chantal was stacking the books into an elaborate pyramid. "They're gonna sing again on Tuesday, right?"

"Absolutely," Pia said. "Eight songs. They've been practicing like demons."

"What's happening on Tuesday?" Jack asked.

"It's this holiday celebrated by Christians around the world," Pia explained as if addressing a toddler, "where people—not you, maybe, but normal people—exchange gifts and—"

"Oh, cut the poor guy some slack," Kat chuckled. "There's going to be a big party at Augusta House on Tuesday. It's to celebrate all the winter holidays, not just Christmas, and it's also to recognize our first full year of operation."

Chantal said, "Kat's cooking a turkey dinner for three hundred."

"I'm *supervising* the cooking of a turkey dinner for three hundred," Kat corrected.

"And we're gonna have games with prizes," Chantal continued, "and Kwanzaa and Hanukkah activities. Oh, and my brother Calvin's gonna play Santa and hand out presents. It'll be great."

"Assuming we can get the communal room ready in time," Pia said. "It's a disaster. It used to be a sort of combination cafeteria and auditorium, and it's never really been fixed up, 'cause our priority was turning classrooms into apartments. In fact, during the remodeling it got filled up with old desks, blackboards, gym equipment—if the workmen didn't know what to do with something, it went there. But Tuesday's just four days from now, so we've got our work cut out for us."

Kat said, "It's going to take the whole weekend to get that room ready. Tomorrow we'll concentrate on getting all the furniture and debris cleared out, then Sunday we clean and decorate. Us and the Augusta House families."

"Hey, Jack," Chantal said a little too casually as she placed the last book atop her pyramid. "You doing anything tomorrow? There won't be many guys there to help out, and there's gonna be a ton of stuff to pick up and haul away."

He grinned. "Is that all us men are good for?"

"You give me a minute, I'll come up with one or two other things," she answered with an impish grin.

"You've talked me into it," he chuckled.

It didn't take much, Kat thought, her stomach tightening with a sensation that she recognized, to her chagrin, as jealousy. Pia and Chantal had monopolized Jack almost the entire evening. On those rare occasions when the two women broke out of their cozy little huddle, it was to issue breathless reports to Kat about how sweet and funny Jack was, and how tall and buff and completely babe-alicious.

Kat wondered which one he'd gravitate to, Pia or Chantal. They were both young—well, youngish—and pretty and ultra-personable. And currently unattached.

Layered over Kat's jealousy was a fair measure of guilt. She *was* attached. She had Preston. As far as he was concerned, they were as much an item as ever. Until she worked through her reservations about the relationship and either committed to him or ended it, she shouldn't be *thinking* about Jack. Much less wondering, as she'd found herself doing this past week, what it would be like to make love to a man who looked at her the way he did.

And, oh God, last night she'd dreamed about him. She'd awakened gasping and sheened with sweat, his name a tremulous whisper in her ears. As she lay there in the dark, images from the dream began scrolling across her mental movie screen . . . their mouths meeting hungrily . . . his hands everywhere on her, shaping, stroking . . . him rearing over her, pressing into her . . .

She'd slapped a hand over her eyes, pulled a pillow over her head. Still, the images wouldn't stop coming . . .

"Since you're feeling so agreeable," Pia told Jack,

"maybe you'd like to help us hand out these gifts to the kids as they leave."

"Um . . ." Jack looked from Pia to the gift-laden table to the kids bundling into their coats and gloves. "I guess . . ."

"Great. Just put on one of these." Reaching into the laundry basket, Pia withdrew several red and white Santa hats like the one Kat had on earlier.

"Whoa." Jack took a step back, hands up. "No way. Sorry, but . . ."

"Not your scene?" Chantal cocked an eyebrow at him.

"You worried about looking silly?" Pia pulled on one of the hats and handed one each to Kat and Chantal. "Or is it just the whole Christmas thing?"

"A little bit of both, I guess."

Jack looked almost sad, or at least thoughtful, as he watched Kat and her friends hand out the gifts to the departing chorus members. It was as she was saying goodbye to the last few guests that he suggested that he linger for a while to look the apartment over with an eye toward giving her a quote on a security system; that had, of course, been why she'd invited him here in the first place.

While the caterer and his staff packed up and cleaned, Kat gave Jack the ten-cent tour, starting with the living room—the floor-to-ceiling windows being the reason she couldn't make do with bars—and ending upstairs. Kat felt a little awkward as she guided him into her bedroom, with its cabbage-rose wallpaper and Victorian furnishings. He seemed a little self-conscious himself, if curious, although he did smile when he noticed the stuffed koala bear propped up on her high, four-poster bed.

Parting the ivory damask drapes, he checked out the windows. "Again," he said, "these can be replaced and rigged up with security mechanisms without sacrificing the period look."

"Great."

Turning, he spied the framed photograph on her dresser. He crossed to it and picked it up, studying the enlarged snapshot of Preston in tennis whites, a fluorescent yellow ball in one hand and a racket in the other. It was a flattering picture; he looked tanned and vigorous and even handsomer than he was. And younger. Jack started to say something, then hesitated and looked up at her, a cryptic glint in his eye. "Who's this? Your dad?"

Her cheeks stung. "No, that's, uh . . . that's Preston. My, uh . . ." She hated calling a man of Preston's age her "boyfriend."

"Oh." He winced. "Sorry." Obviously groping for some neutral comment, he said, "Nice frame."

"It's Tiffany. Preston gave it to me with the picture." She regretted the statement as soon as it left her mouth, knowing that Jack would size Preston up as an egotist for having given her that picture.

"You'd never know he's sixty-two," Jack said as he set the photo back down.

"Sixty-two?" Kat exclaimed. "He's *fifty*-two."

"Oh. Uh . . ."

"I told you he was twenty years older than me. Do I really look like I'm in my forties?"

"No! God, you look . . ." He shook his head helplessly, his gaze lighting on her hair, her mouth, her legs. "Incredible. You're . . . wow."

The heat in her cheeks spread to consume her entire face.

"I mean, not that forty-something can't look like wow, but . . ." He rubbed his neck. "I . . . don't know what I was thinking when I said sixty-two. Slip of the tongue, I guess."

"That's all right. I guess I'm a little sensitive about his being so much older, or I wouldn't have reacted like that."

"No, it's my fault. I'm . . . real good at saying the wrong things sometimes."

"Miss Peale." Kat turned to find Marco, the caterer, in the doorway, glancing uncomfortably between her and Jack, as if loath to interrupt what looked like a lovers' tête-à-tête. "We're about done, so . . ."

"Thanks, Marco. I'll be right down."

Jack produced a tape measure and proceeded to measure the first-floor windows while Kat was settling up with

Marco. Once he and his staff were gone, Jack said, "I can do the last couple of windows and go over some security ideas right now, if you'd like. Unless you're tired."

"No, just a little stressed out. It was kind of a long night, what with all that pressure about the Livermores." Not to mention the anxiety of watching Pia and Chantal flirting nonstop with Jack. Tension always went to her stomach; she hadn't had the appetite for a single drink or hors d'oeuvre all night. "Tell you what. Why don't I open that bottle of wine you brought while you finish your measuring, and then we can sit down and go over your ideas?"

The lamps in the den had been turned off during the cleanup, producing a deliciously tranquil semidarkness relieved only by the low flames in the fireplace and the dozen or so pillar candles scattered around the room. Kat had to hold every bottle of wine on the bar up to her face to find the Fox Run pinot noir that Jack had brought, but she left the lights off because, for the first time all evening, she felt her nerves starting to unknit.

As she was twisting the corkscrew, its handle bit into the ball of her hand, and she let out a little mew of pain.

"What's the matter?" Jack asked as he came up behind her, retracting his tape measure into its case.

"Just my hand. It's still a little tender."

"From last week? The mugging?" He took the bottle and set it on the bar, then turned her hand palm up and rubbed his thumbs over it, generating a friction that sent a ticklish warmth up her arm and down into her chest. "It still hurts?"

"No, it's . . ." She cleared her throat to dispel its sudden hoarseness. "It's not pain, really, just . . . you know . . ."

Jack brought her hand close to his face to see it in the dark. He lowered his head, and then she felt his lips, hot and soft and shocking on her palm, and she closed her eyes and sighed.

Another kiss, a lingering one on her sensitive inner wrist. With her free hand she gripped the edge of the bar to keep from slumping to the ground, because her legs had gone liquid; her heart thrummed like a bird's.

Kat opened her eyes, finding his face mere inches from hers, his gaze on her mouth. She'd never felt more ready, more *desperate* to be kissed than in that hushed and breathless moment, as his head bent to hers.

Nor had she ever felt more torn. It wasn't like her, to let a man kiss her when she was involved with someone else. She wasn't that kind of woman, couldn't be that kind of woman.

"Jack." She said it softly, gently, but it was enough. He shut his eyes for a moment, as if gathering himself. When he opened them and met her gaze, there was a resignation in his expression that told her he got the message. He didn't like it, but he got it.

He released her, let out a long, unsteady breath.

"I'm sorry," she said. "I . . ."

He touched a fingertip to her mouth, lightly stroking her bottom lip before withdrawing his hand. "You're right. You're absolutely right. I should know better than to . . . muddy the waters."

"What do you mean? What waters?"

He looked away, dragged a hand through his hair. "Just an expression. Look, why don't you let me finish opening that bottle for you? Unless . . . I mean, do you want me to leave, or . . . ?"

"No, you can stay. As long as . . ."

"Yeah, I know. Don't worry. I'll keep it friendly."

He was as good as his word. They sat together on the leather sofa in the candlelit den—albeit at opposite ends— drinking wine and hashing out her security needs for the better part of an hour. Jack filled up a legal pad with notes and diagrams. She slid out of her high heels and tucked her legs under her. He doffed his suit coat and loosened his tie.

"So, how do you want to work this?" he asked after she'd green-lighted his ideas. "Should I submit a bid?"

"I'm not taking bids. The job's yours if you want it."

"Ah." He laid his pad and pencil on the coffee table and lifted his wine glass, which he'd hardly touched—whereas Kat had emptied almost half the bottle so far. She didn't usually drink this much, this fast, but that was okay. Sometimes you needed a little help unwinding.

"So, do you want it?" she asked. "The job?"

He took a pensive sip of wine, and then another, almost as if he were stalling for some reason. "I couldn't start right away."

"No problem. When do you think you can schedule it in?"

He set his glass down without looking at her. "A few weeks from now, maybe?"

"Sure, that'd be—"

"Are you in love with him?" He looked at her. God, she wished he'd stop looking at her like that.

She swallowed. "Jack."

Quietly he said, "It's just a question. I'm not gonna . . ." His gaze swept over her, then he looked away, his jaw rigid. "I'm just curious. Are you?"

"I . . . haven't known him that long."

He sat back, nodded, returned his gaze to her. "How'd you two meet?"

She hesitated.

Jack smiled. "Hey, I'm just trying to prolong the pleasure of your company by making conversation about your boyfriend. Not an entirely innocent motive, maybe, but not exactly nefarious."

She drank some more wine. "I met him at the end of October, when his firm agreed to do some pro bono legal work for Augusta House. He suggested we discuss it over lunch." She shrugged. "He was . . . different from other men I'd known. I was intrigued."

"So you've been seeing him for what, almost two months? I'm surprised he didn't ask you to go to Aspen with him. Or did he?"

She looked at him over the rim of her glass. "How'd you know he's in Aspen?"

Jack glanced away, picked up his glass, took a sip. "Chantal must have mentioned it, or Pia."

God knew what else they'd "mentioned" to him. They

both loathed Preston. "He couldn't ask me to go with him, 'cause it's this guy thing he does every year with some old pals. He was very apologetic."

He wouldn't have been if he'd known how secretly grateful Kat had been at the prospect of a respite from him. His three weeks in Aspen would give her, she'd reasoned, the breathing room she needed to think clearly and objectively about their budding relationship. More and more lately, she'd begun to wonder if Preston's refreshing lack of interest in the size of her bank account hadn't blinded her to his . . . "Faults" might be the wrong word, but he *was* different from her, and in some very significant respects. Not to mention two decades older. On the other hand, he was smart, successful, and classically handsome. She'd spent the past two months hoping for a genuine rapport to materialize between them, but it had proven slow in coming.

Three weeks. Three precious weeks in which to contemplate her future with Preston, or lack of it. That was all she'd wanted, yet no sooner had Preston flown off to Aspen than Jack O'Leary had stepped up to the plate. How could she possibly trust any conclusions she drew about Preston with a guy like Jack keeping her all weak in the knees? Her only recourse was to keep Jack at a distance unless and until she broke things off with Preston. Otherwise she'd always doubt that she'd done the right thing for the right reason.

"Do you miss him?" Jack asked.

"Of course," she answered too quickly.

"Yeah," he said soberly. "You probably spend an hour on the phone with him every night."

"He's called me a couple of times. He didn't bother giving me the number, 'cause he said he's hardly ever in his room."

"Really? You'd think he'd want you to have the number so you could at least leave a message if you wanted to. Where's he staying? You could always call information."

She shrugged. "All I know is, it's at the base of Buttermilk Mountain. Some hotel where you can ski in and ski out."

"He didn't even tell you the name of the place?"

"It just never came up."

"You know . . . maybe I shouldn't say anything, but . . ." Jack glanced uneasily at her. "Have you ever considered that he might be married?"

"What?" She sat upright, laughing incredulously. "No."

"Are you sure?"

"Of course I'm sure."

"Just 'cause he told you he was single?"

"I'd know if he was lying." She grabbed the wine bottle off the table and refilled her glass.

Jack studied the wine in his glass as he swirled it. "Married men, when they're pretending to be single, there's a certain behavioral profile. They've got to compartmentalize their life, keep the wife in one world and the girlfriend in the other, 'cause God help him if they end up meeting, or talking to each other on the phone. That's why these guys make it so hard for the girlfriend to get in touch with them."

"And you're an expert on cheating husbands because . . .?"

He looked suddenly weary. "Let's just say I know whereof I speak. Has Preston ever even had you over to his place?"

"It's a bit of a haul. He lives in Greenwich, Connecticut."

"Are you sure? Where's your Manhattan phone book?"

With a roll of the eyes, Kat pointed to the Edwardian banker's desk in the corner. Jack crossed to it and flipped through the white pages with a determined expression. *He believes this,* she realized. He'd convinced himself that Preston was married, and now he was trying to convince her.

Jack made a sound of disgust and slammed the phone book onto the desk. "Unlisted. Of course."

"Either that," she said testily, "or he really does live in Greenwich. I've got his phone number, you know. It's a two-oh-three area code. That's Connecticut."

"And you've spoken to him there?" Jack asked as he walked back across the room.

"Yes. Well . . . I've left messages on his machine. He's out a lot. There's that long commute, and he's active at his club. But he's always gotten back to me."

"Just 'cause he's got an answering machine in Greenwich doesn't mean he lives there. Maybe he knows someone—"

"And maybe you're clutching at straws." More gently she said, "Jack, I'm flattered, I really am, but you've got to let it go."

Jack sat on the corner of the coffee table, leaned forward, cupped her face in his warm hands; the air left her lungs. Earnestly, softly, he said, "He doesn't deserve you. He's just using you."

She shook her head resolutely. "I'd know it if he was."

He stood up, raked both hands through his hair. "Kat . . . no. You wouldn't. Not you. You're trusting—too trusting. You think everyone's as good as you are, but—"

"You think I'm gullible."

"No, I—"

"Maybe I used to be, but I've learned my lesson, especially when it comes to men. Why do you think I was so attracted to Preston in the first place? It's because for once there's a man in my life who's actually interested in me as a person, not in how he can profit from me."

"He's not using you for money." Jack picked up his wine glass and sat back down on the sofa. "He's using you for sex."

"Yeah, well, that just shows how little you know, because we've never even . . ." She bit her lip, wishing she hadn't blurted that out. What business was it of Jack's?

He was staring at her, his head cocked as if he weren't sure he'd heard right. He looked surprised, but pleased. She could see it in his eyes, that little glimmer of gratification. "You and Preston. You don't . . ."

Kat gulped down the rest of her wine. "We will, I'm sure. Sooner or later."

"Let me guess. Preston's lobbying for sooner. You're holding out for later."

"I've been burned too many times by letting things get too . . . intimate with a man, only to find out . . . well, we've covered that territory. The users."

"But Preston's different," Jack said. "Or so you seem to think. So how come you won't sleep with him?"

"He *is* different," she said heatedly. "And I *am* going to sleep with him. I even went back on the . . ." *Damn.* It was the wine, making her spill her guts like this. She should have known better than to drink so much on an empty stomach.

"The pill?" he said. "You went back on the pill."

"I can't believe I'm telling you all this."

"And I can't believe this guy isn't trying to coax you between the sheets every chance he gets."

"He's a gentleman."

"Even gentlemen have certain expectations once a few weeks have gone by. Surely he's made his move by now."

Kat ran her finger around the rim of her empty wine glass, generating an airy trill. "About a month ago, when we were out to dinner, he gave me these gifts. Three of them—a tiny box, a medium box, and a big box, all tied together with gold ribbon. He said to open the smallest one first. It was a pair of diamond earrings from Harry Winston. He told me he wanted me to go away with him that weekend—he's got a place in Bermuda. I said I'd go with him, but only if we had separate bedrooms, and that I couldn't accept the earrings. They were too valuable a gift."

"Not to mention that there appeared to be strings attached," Jack pointed out.

Kat didn't bother trying to deny that that had factored into the equation.

"If you gave the earrings back, then . . ." Jack reached out and brushed a fingertip over her left earlobe and the diamond stud that adorned it; she wished his touch didn't speed her heart this way. "What are these?"

"My grandmother gave me these for my fifteenth birthday. They're pear-cut. The ones Preston gave me were emerald-cut."

"Oh."

She smiled. "You don't know the difference."

He returned the smile, still stroking her ear. "No."

She lowered her head, breaking the contact. "I opened the medium-sized box next. It held that picture of him in the Tiffany frame. He took the big box away without letting me open it. He said it was something else he'd wanted me to wear in Bermuda, but that it could wait till we were a little further along in our relationship."

"Sexy lingerie," Jack said.

"That's what I was thinking."

"Let me guess. He never did take you to Bermuda."

Kat hated that he was right. "Something came up. He had to work that weekend."

"Uh-huh." Jack lifted the almost-empty wine bottle and held it over her glass, but she covered it with her hand, saying she'd had more than enough. He emptied the last couple of ounces into his own glass.

"So, you don't love him." Jack sat back, propping an ankle on his knee. "Not yet, anyway. And so far it's a platonic relationship. Yet you're bending over backward to be faithful."

She shrugged. "It's the way I am. I don't like complications, and I especially don't like to be the cause of them. And I do believe in right and wrong. Preston and I have an unspoken understanding, and that understanding is that we're exclusive and that eventually we'll take things to the next level." All of which was true enough on the surface, but nowhere near the whole story. Kat knew better than to confide her doubts about Preston to Jack, who would no doubt seize on them and make her decision even more difficult. "In the meantime, like I said, he's being a gentleman."

"*Playing* the gentleman. He's wearing you down. Sex is what he's after."

She made a little *Yeah, right* face. "He's middle-aged. Middle-aged men have other priorities."

"Not this one."

"What makes you think that?"

He turned toward her, his eyes all-seeing in the dark, his voice low and almost pained. "Because no man in his right mind could be with you, smelling the way you smell and watching you walk and listening to that laugh of yours, and not want to possess you. Entirely. Body and soul. You're the kind of woman a man wants to lose himself inside, Kat, the kind he aches to hear moaning his name in the dark. You're the one."

Kat couldn't tear her gaze from his. A log shifted in the fireplace, settling with a rustle of embers.

"You should leave," she said, so quietly even she almost didn't hear it.

"Yeah."

She fetched his overcoat, walked him to the front door, held it open.

"What time should I be there in the morning?" he asked.

She frowned in bewilderment for a moment before remembering that Chantal had drafted him to help get ready for the holiday party at Augusta House. "You really don't have to—"

"I want to."

"Nine o'clock, then?"

"I'll be there." As he stepped out into the hallway, he turned and said, "What does he call you? Kat or Katherine?"

"Katherine."

That seemed to please him, because he smiled as he turned to leave. "Good night, Kat."

There was a message on Jack's machine when he got home to Brooklyn that night.

Beep.

"Jack, it's me, Celeste. Any developments as regards the service I've retained you to perform? You'll notice I'm being discreet, in case you have company."

There came a muted snick and the crackle of a cigarette being lit, followed by a brisk exhalation.

"As you know, I expect this situation to be resolved before I return to New York on January fourth, which means you've got thirteen more days to, shall we say, close the deal. I assume you're in contact with the subject at this point—hopefully close contact. I wouldn't mind a progress report, as I'm naturally very much preoccupied with this matter. I left my credit card behind at two different stores yesterday."

Another drag on the cigarette. "Preston's getting a massage tomorrow between two and three in the afternoon your time, so he'll be out of the room for an hour—an hour and a half if he bangs the masseuse. You've got my number here. I'll be waiting for your call."

Click.

CHAPTER SIX

—

No heavy lifting. Wasn't that what Celeste had promised when she'd finagled Jack into taking this job? Then why had he spent the past five hours—with a twenty-minute break for pizza at noon—lugging literally tons of old school equipment from the Augusta House communal room out to a row of rented Dumpsters in the parking lot? In 40-degree weather.

Not that he minded the occasional blast of cold air that much. They kept the heat pretty high in the building, and it was brutal work, hauling all that crap outside. Even stripped down as he was to a T-shirt and a pair of jeans, he'd been soaked through with sweat by mid-morning.

Dragging yet another broken school desk over to a half-empty Dumpster, Jack took a deep breath, hoisted it overhead, and heaved it into the receptacle, where it landed with a clatter.

On his way back, he held the door open for Chantal's brother Calvin, a New York City firefighter who had a battered old bookcase, a big one, balanced on his meaty shoulders. There were dozens of people helping out today—the Augusta House staff and most of the moms and kids who lived here—but Calvin and Jack were among an all-too-small handful of men who'd let themselves get talked into this gig.

"Hey, man," Calvin panted on his way to the Dumpsters. "You know how chicks are always saying they're so smart and we're so dumb? You think maybe they're onto something?"

"Strong backs and weak minds," Jack said with a grin as he headed back inside. "That's us."

The cavernous, linoleum-floored communal room, book-ended by a curtained stage at one end and a kitchen at the other, buzzed with activity, as it had all day. Now that most of the debris had been cleared away and the usable furniture shoved to the perimeter of the room, it was time to break out the brooms, mops and buckets. Tomorrow they would decorate for Tuesday's party, which the children, especially the younger ones, looked forward to with an almost frantic anticipation.

Through the open doorway to the kitchen at the opposite end of the room, Jack spied Kat scrubbing down a big steel table with a sponge. She looked about seventeen in her faded Bryn Mawr sweatshirt and jeans, her hair in a slap-dash ponytail, her hands sheathed in bright yellow rubber gloves. She'd been cleaning and disinfecting that kitchen all day in preparation for Tuesday's turkey dinner, her progress hampered by a parade of staff members, volun-teers, and delivery men, each with some problem only she could resolve, some decision only she could make, some check only she could write, some paper only she could sign. It was a lot of responsibility on one person's head; Jack admired her composure, although she *was* starting to look a little frayed around the edges.

Tugging off his left-hand work glove, he checked his watch. Just barely two o'clock. He'd give it a few more minutes, just to make sure.

"Yo, Jack!" Chantal called out as she crossed the crowded room on her way to the kitchen. "Those chairs still need to go out." She pointed toward a cluster of cracked old stacking chairs.

"Yes, ma'am!" Jack saluted jauntily as Chantal rolled her eyes. "On the double, ma'am!"

He yawned twice while snugging the chairs together to lift as a unit. It had been almost dawn by the time he'd finally nodded off last night, after hours of lying there in the dark, grappling with his situation.

The message Celeste had left on his machine—*you've got thirteen more days to, shall we say, close the deal*—had served as a crude but necessary reminder of his true purpose in cultivating the acquaintance of Katherine Peale. He'd staged their initial meeting, lied to her face, charmed his way past her defenses—all for fifty thousand bucks.

That was shameful enough. What in holy hell had he been thinking last night, working up that elaborate security system for her? He *hadn't* been thinking. So effortlessly had he fallen into his cover role—so pathetically eager was he not just to be with her, but to be who she thought he was—that he'd all but forgotten who he *really* was: an opportunistic PI who'd do just about anything for a buck.

And, oh, God, he'd almost kissed her. Not because of the job—that was the thing—but because he'd forgotten about the job. He'd forgotten he was just conning her and started to think maybe he was falling in—

"Damn," he growled as he hefted the stack of chairs and headed outside. "Damn, damn, damn, damn, damn."

It was shame that had kept Jack awake last night. He wasn't used to feeling like a devious sack of crap, and he didn't like it one bit. But his long night of penitent insomnia had given him the opportunity to reflect on his situation and formulate a plan for extracting Kat from Preston's clutches that might even redeem a little of his own erstwhile integrity—or at least not add to the sick sense of shame he'd been carrying around all week.

The only smart thing he'd done last night, he reflected as he muscled the door open with his burden and stepped outside, gulping cold air, had been to rat Preston out, or try to. Kat had to find out he was married. Jack's sense of decency and righteousness—latent though it might be—demanded it, and although the news would shock her, it would be for her own good.

Thunking the stack of chairs down next to the emptiest Dumpster, Jack proceeded to hurl them in one by one.

Not that he was eager to blow his cover to accomplish that goal; the prospect of Kat's discovering his own duplicity made his stomach clutch. But at around three in the morning, Jack had thought up a way to break the news to her that would leave him entirely in the clear.

Now to execute his plan. She would end things with Preston when she found out. And she would do it without Jack's having to seduce her into it, either physically or emotionally, thereby allowing him to salvage a shred of honor in this murky mess.

What then? he wondered as he returned, empty-handed, to the communal room. The right thing would be to walk away from her then. Otherwise he'd only be prolonging the fiction that he was just some affable security consultant who'd saved her from a mugging . . . only to fall for her, hard, once he'd gotten to know her.

Well, that last part wasn't a lie, but it was the only thing she knew about him that wasn't. How could he possibly pursue a relationship with her under those circumstances?

He'd blown it. Bad.

And then there was that fifty grand, which would be legitimately his once Kat dumped Preston. The right thing would be to turn it down and thereby free his conscience from the grip of Celeste Worth's coral-tipped talons. Did he have the moral fortitude for that? Last night, he'd decided he did, and he'd set about mentally unraveling all the plans he'd made for that money. But Grady, who'd phoned him this morning for a briefing—good thing, too, or Jack would have overslept for this gig—had argued vehemently against turning it down. After all, Grady had reasoned, Jack will have saved Kat from Preston without having taken advantage of her himself, thereby, in essence, having performed a good deed. Didn't that deserve some sort of reward?

Just promise me you'll think about it, Grady had begged.

Jack, in the process of racing out of the house unshowered and unshaved, had promised.

He took off his gloves, checked his watch again: 2:09.

Show time. Detouring to where he'd dumped his parka,

he fished out his cell phone and the folded-up page he'd printed off the Internet at around 4 A.M.

When he entered the kitchen, he found Kat talking to a burly fellow in coveralls that had the name *Gus Hamm* embroidered on the chest; he was leaning on a handcart loaded with boxes labeled "Young Tom Turkeys" and shaking his head. Chantal, watching from the corner, caught Jack's eye and gazed heavenward.

"Look, lady," Gus said as he lifted a box off the cart and slammed it onto the table, "you ordered 'em, they're yours."

"But I'm telling you they weren't supposed to come today." Kat snapped her rubber gloves off. "I specifically said tomorrow. The refrigerators haven't even been turned on yet, and they're filthy. I've got no place to keep them."

"It's cold outside." Gus unloaded another box. "Keep 'em there."

"What, so every dog in the neighborhood can tear into them?"

"That ain't my problem, lady."

"No, I'm your problem." Jack shoved the cell phone and printout in his back pocket as he stepped forward, freeing his hands. "And trust me," he said, placing himself between Kat and Gus so that he had the man's full attention. "I'm a problem you don't need."

"Is that right?" Gus sneered, but the uneasy way he checked out Jack's build in the sweat-dampened T-shirt, the heft of his fists curled at his sides, gave him away. "Take it easy, Tarzan. I'm just messin' with her."

"Then you won't mind loading those turkeys back on that cart and bringing them back tomorrow, say around . . . ?" He turned to Kat.

"Uh . . . sometime in the morning?"

Jack said, "Have them here by twelve noon, Mr. Hamm. Otherwise I'll have to come looking for you, and I get cranky when I'm inconvenienced."

"Sure, no problem," Gus said with blustering nonchalance. It took him about twenty seconds to reload the turkeys and beat a hasty retreat.

Chantal let out a low, impressed whistle. "Who's the man?" She gave Jack a playful punch on the arm, then paused to test the solidity of his biceps. "Kat, honey, check this out. This is how a man's *supposed* to feel."

"I'll take your word for it," Kat said, a faint wash of pink staining her cheeks. "Gosh, Jack. I didn't realize you'd be so handy to have around. If you could only solve *all* my problems that way. It's been one thing after another today."

"Speaking of which . . . ." Chantal looked chagrined. "I'm sorry to add to your troubles, honey, but Calvin wanted me to tell you he's not gonna be able to—"

"I can't hear you!" Kat clapped her hands over her ears.

"I'm sorry, Kat." Chantal patted her friend on the shoulder. "He just found out he's got to work a full shift on Christmas."

Kat collapsed wearily onto a chair. "Great. Now, on top of everything else, we've got no Santa. The kids'll be crushed."

"I'll find someone else," Chantal promised.

"Someone else who's willing to give up his Christmas morning on such short notice?" Kat asked. "You had a hard enough time roping Calvin into it."

Chantal brightened. "Hey, maybe Jack'll do it. You wouldn't mind giving up your Christmas morning, would you, Jack? Christmas means nothing to you."

"Which is exactly why he *shouldn't* do it," Kat pointed out. "Even if we could talk him into wearing the costume."

"Which I'll be more than happy to do," Jack said cheerfully, "when hell freezes over. But I might actually know someone who *would* do it—my nephew. He loves Christmas." Jack mentally kicked himself as soon as the words were out of his mouth. Grady had snatched Kat's purse just a week ago today. She would recognize him . . . except he'd have a beard on, right? And a hat. He could pull it off, Jack decided, as long as he kept a fairly low profile.

"Is he used to dealing with children?" Kat asked.

"He's an O'Leary," Jack said with a grin. "There are nine kids in his immediate family alone. And he's crazy about them."

"Sounds like a plan," Chantal said as she headed for the door. "He'll need the costume we rented. You can take it with you when you leave today."

The kitchen seemed smaller after Chantal had left and Jack found himself alone with Kat. "Pretty big job, huh?" he asked as he withdrew the printout from his pocket and unfolded it. "Getting this party off the ground?"

"You could say that," she muttered, burying her face in her hands.

"You okay?"

"Yeah, just . . ." Kat uncovered her face. "I feel like I've done nothing but put out one fire after another all day. I'm that close to just . . ." She flexed her hands in an explosive gesture.

"Seriously? You always seem so . . . unflappable."

"Yeah, my doctor says I'm gonna get an ulcer from internalizing stress. What's that?" she asked, nodding toward the printout.

"Um . . . oh." Maybe this wasn't such a good idea after all, at least right now. "Nothing," he said, starting to refold it.

"It's something about Aspen," she said. "What is it?"

He unfolded it and handed it to her. "It's the Web site for a hotel called the Inn at Aspen. I did a little surfing last night. This is the only lodging at the base of Buttermilk Mountain where you can ski in and ski out."

Her brows drew together as she looked up at him. "I don't get it. Why did you—"

"It gives their phone number," he said, pointing. Of course, he'd had it all along, but he could hardly tell her that. "You can call Preston now."

"Why do you want me to—"

"So you can ask him point-blank if he's married."

She groaned. "Jack . . ."

He stepped closer, gentled his voice. "Tell me you haven't been wondering if I might not be right. Tell me you haven't had doubts."

"But if what you think about him is true—and I don't think it is—wouldn't he just lie to me?"

"Listen for a telltale pause, or any strain in his voice. See if he dances around the question or just comes out and denies it. Pay attention, and you'll know right away if he's lying."

She stared at the printout.

He withdrew the cell phone, held it out to her.

She took it. "If I'm satisfied with his answer, you let the matter drop. Deal?"

"Deal."

Kat punched out the number, held the phone to her ear. Jack heard it ringing on the other end, having cranked the volume all the way up so he could effectively listen in. A woman's muted voice said, "The Inn at Aspen. How may I direct your call?"

Kat said, "Preston Worth's room, please." With a glance at Jack, she added, "He probably won't even be there."

No, but Celeste would. Jack stepped back and crossed his arms, resisting the urge to snatch the phone out of her hand.

The call was answered on the first ring. "Hello?" Celeste must have been waiting by the phone.

Kat blinked. "Um . . . I think I might have the wrong room. I'm looking for Preston Worth."

"I'm his wife. If this is the masseuse, he's on his way there now."

Kat stared blankly for a moment. "I'm sorry. Did you say . . . you're his . . ."

"His wife. Celeste Worth." There came an ominous pause. "Who is this?"

Kat opened her mouth to speak, but nothing came out. The color had leached from her face.

Celeste's voice turned hard. "I know who you are, Miss

Peale. Preston really should have known better than to give you this number."

"I . . . he . . ."

"Enjoy those diamond earrings, 'cause they're the last thing you're getting from him in a tiny little velvet box. Underneath it all, you're just another high-priced whore. You weren't his first, and I'm sure you won't be his last."

Click.

"Kat?" Jack said softly, lifting the phone from her hand.

She continued to stare into middle distance. Her eyes were shiny, too shiny. The printout was balled up in her fist.

"Oh, Kat, I'm sorry. I . . ." He closed a hand over her shoulder.

She flinched at his touch, sprang off the bench. "I've got to get out of here."

He followed behind her as she grabbed her trench coat off another chair and bolted toward the back door. "I'll come with—"

"No, I'd rather you didn't," she said, her voice quavering as she pulled open the door. "I just need some fresh air. I'll be back in ten minutes."

But, of course, she wasn't.

CHAPTER SEVEN

—

It was getting dark by the time Jack got home that evening, and a steady, frigid rain had begun to fall.

Kat hadn't come back to Augusta House after leaving to get some "fresh air." Nor had she returned to her apartment; Jack had checked in three times with the doorman. Nor had she shown up in any of what Chantal had assured him were her favorite midtown haunts: a coffee shop on East Forty-seventh, a sit-down deli on Lex, and the Argosy Bookstore on East Fifty-ninth.

Assured by his contacts in the various Manhattan police precincts that there had been no violent crimes that day involving women of Kat's description, Jack had finally thrown in the towel. After swinging by her building one last time—where he left a message with the doorman for her to call him the second she got home—he'd caught the F train back to Brooklyn.

Stowing the plastic-wrapped Santa costume in his front hall closet, Jack grabbed the cordless phone off the desk in the living room, dialed Grady's number, and sprawled out on the couch.

"Are you *serious*?" Grady demanded incredulously. "You want me to play Santa to a couple of hundred kids?"

"I know it's asking a—"

"That is *so awesome*! I've always wanted to do something like that. Oh, my God. This is so cool."

"Have you been mainlining lattes again?"

"Oh! Oh! I've got this totally bitchin' idea. You know Leon, my on-again off-again squeeze from last year?"

"The female impersonator?"

"He only does the drag thing in his cabaret act. He's a Teamster during the day, for crying out loud. Anyway, I'm thinking he'd make an *excellent* Mrs. Claus."

"He probably would." Jack rubbed his forehead. "If there was a role for a Mrs. Claus. But they really just need—"

"Oh! Or *I* could be Mrs. Claus and Leon could be Santa. Why should he have all the fun?"

Jack sat up. "No, you'd better be Santa so Kat doesn't recognize you as the guy who *assaulted* her and *knocked her to the ground* last week, when all you were *supposed* to do was—"

"Look, man, you know how sorry I am about that. I screwed up, but I've said my mea culpas, and now I can maybe even make up for it a little bit by helping her out here. I'll get some wire-rimmed glasses and a wig and one of those dustcaps. Leon can make me up. I'll pluck *everything*. Trust me, she'll never know it's me."

"She'd better not."

Jack started dozing off after saying goodbye to Grady, but his empty stomach finally propelled him off the couch and into the kitchen. He couldn't recall ever having felt so utterly scorched, not just physically—he'd put in a full day of hard labor on an hour of sleep and two slices of pizza—but mentally and emotionally, as well. A bowl of Cheerios was all the dinner he felt capable of mustering up, after which he stripped down and showered off the film of sweat and grime he'd accumulated that day.

Donning a fresh T-shirt and oversized boxer shorts—his loungewear of choice—Jack flopped down on the living room couch, yawned and grabbed the remote. Five minutes of national news and he'd be nodding off, for sure. He thumbed it on, and the TV crackled to life, but he wasn't looking at it. He was looking at his desk in the corner, and the file folder that lay half on top of his computer keyboard.

Muting the TV, he went to the desk, flicked on the green-shaded banker's lamp and opened the folder. The newspaper clipping of Celeste's *Village Voice* ad lay over

Kat's face on the top photo. He brushed the clipping aside and studied her image in softly grainy black-and-white. Funny he hadn't noticed before how brightly she seemed to glow against her night-in-the-city surroundings: the radiant skin, the lustrous hair, the gleam of silk, the snap of diamonds and rhinestones. She looked ethereal, angelic . . . and a little sad, buttoning her jacket against the cold.

Jack opened the middle desk drawer, withdrew the fat kraft envelope, dumped its contents on top of the desk.

Five thousand dollars in bound twenties. He grabbed a packet and brought it to his nose; the bile rose in his throat.

Bzzt! It was the intercom on the wall by the front door; someone was downstairs. Jack crossed to it, pressed the talk button. "Yeah?"

A pause. "Jack, it's me—Kat." *Kat!* She said something else, but he was already holding down the door button so she could enter the building. She must have looked up his address; he didn't think he'd ever given it to her. He hadn't wanted her to know too much about him—just like Preston, he realized soberly.

He opened the door and stepped into the hall, swore sharply, and turned to sprint back to his desk. Jerking open the middle drawer, he scooped the money and envelope back into it, tossed the file on top, shut it and went back out to the hall.

"Up here," he called from the top of the stairs. "Third floor." When he saw her trudging upstairs, wet ponytail drooping, sodden trench coat hanging limply, he raced down to meet her. "Kat, honey, where have you been?" he asked, taking her hand to guide her back up to his place. "I looked all over for you."

"I was just . . . walking." Eyeing his attire, or lack of it, she said, "I'm sorry. I didn't mean to disturb you."

"You're not. I was just hanging."

Old Mrs. Wise was peering out through her cracked-open door with those monstrous baby-bird eyes of hers. They widened cartoonishly when she got a load of his boxers.

" 'Evening, Mrs. Wise," Jack greeted as he ushered Kat into his apartment. The old woman slammed her door shut.

Kat looked around curiously as she strolled from his foyer into his living room, dark but for the flickering bluish light of the muted television and the banker's lamp. She did a slow three-sixty, taking in the worn leather furniture, framed B-movie posters, Navajo-inspired rug. "Nice, but it could use a few t-tacky Christmas decorations."

"You're cold." Coming around to face her, he untied the sash of her damp trench coat and flicked open the buttons. "Look at you." He raised a hand to her face, brushing his fingertips lightly over her mouth. "Your lips are blue."

She rubbed her face against his hand like a kitten wanting to be petted.

"I'm sorry," he said in a raw whisper. "I'm really sorry. I never should have had you make that call."

"No, I needed to know. You have nothing to be sorry about."

If only that were true. Jack started to withdraw his hand, but Kat held on to it, pressed it to her mouth, kissed it—just a warm tickle against his knuckles, but he felt the thrill of it, the promise, right down to his toes.

Kat looked up at him, pale and beautiful in the fluttering incandescence. She skimmed her hand—so cool, so soft—over his beard-roughened cheek, curled it around the back of his head, drew him closer . . .

"Kat . . ." He shouldn't do this. This was the last thing he should do.

She touched her lips to his, just lightly.

The pleasure of it jolted him, made his heart ram in his chest, his body tighten with sudden need. He dragged her to him, clutched her hair, her coat, kissed her like a man seeking air to breathe. God, how he'd craved this, *needed* this.

She tore at his T-shirt; he whipped it off over his head. She kissed his throat, his chest, kicked off her loafers, unzipped her jeans. While shimmying out of them, she got tangled in her trench coat and lost her balance. He caught her and they fell together to the carpeted floor, she yanking at his boxers, he kneading her breasts through her sweatshirt as he kissed her ravenously, stunned by how hard he was, how ready, how desperate for this. She guided his hand between her legs, hitching in a breath at the first gentle slide of his fingertips; she was ready, too.

Naked now, he rolled on top of her, her legs cradling him snugly, her hands gripping his hips, urging him—

"Jack," she gasped as he filled her, one slick hot lunge that made them both cry out with the fierce pleasure of it. He buried his hands in her hair, kissed her in triumph and helplessness and inexpressible gratitude.

They writhed together with increasing urgency, to the escalating cadence of the blood pounding like drums in his ears. She arched her hips, dug her fingers into his shoulders, whimpered his name. He groaned with each thrust, reveling in the turbulence of their joining, the unthinking furor of it.

She cried out raggedly, her body shuddering beneath his. It was like pulling a trigger; he shouted as his own climax thundered through him, erupting over and over and over . . .

"Oh, God, Kat." He sank onto her, quaking and gasping for air. Gathering her up awkwardly, he kissed her forehead, her nose, the crests of her cheeks. "God, honey, that was . . ." He was still reeling; the words wouldn't come. Breathless, sated, astounded, he planted whisper-soft kisses all over her face. "It was . . . it was . . ."

"Yeah," she whispered shakily as her lips touched his. "Yeah."

"Her name was Jess," Jack said as he lay curled up with Kat under the down comforter on his big iron bed. "Jessica Mather. Turned out she'd been seeing her boss on the sly, and about a year ago . . ." He paused. Kat lifted her head to study his face, shadowy except for two ribbons of moonlight from the window blinds. His brow was furrowed. "What's today's date?"

"December twenty-second." Kat laid her head back down on his chest, a dense wall of muscle blanketed by hair that felt both soft and ticklish, like Shetland wool. She and Jack had spent the past two hours or so, after making love in the living room, sharing whispered confidences and reminiscences here in the sheltering dark while rain pattered against the windowpane.

"December twenty-second." A little *hmph* shook his chest. "It was a year ago today that she left."

"Right before Christmas."

"She'd bought a tree, put up decorations, the whole nine yards."

"All by herself, or . . ."

"No, I helped." He yawned; she knew he'd be asleep already if it weren't for her. "I actually got into it, if you can believe it, even though I'd basically soured on Christmas ages ago. I thought I might as well get in some practice, 'cause when we had kids . . ." He swallowed. "What a chump I was, huh?"

"Is that why you hate Christmas so much?" Kat asked softly.

His big shoulders twitched. "The holidays are famous for having bad stuff happen during them. People die, people get depressed, people decide something's missing. They blame their boyfriend, their husband, their kids, whatever, and they're outa there."

The light bulb clicked on. Kat raised her head to look at him again. "Was that when your mom left with that guy? During the holidays?"

"Well, yeah, but I never really made that connection."

"You were nine years old. You said you sobbed all night, but that you haven't shed a tear since then. Of course you made the connection."

"You sound pretty sure of yourself."

"I do have a degree in child psychology."

"Ah, those brainy beauties—they really get my engine revving."

"Do they?"

Reaching for her hand under the covers, he skimmed it

down his lower belly and wrapped it around himself. "See?"

"Mm. Very impressive demonstration," she murmured as she caressed him.

"I aim to please." He eased her on top of him and kissed her with heartbreaking tenderness.

"You do please me," she murmured against his lips. "You please me so much. I've gotten so used to mistrusting men, wondering if they're just out for a piece of me. With you, I don't have those fears. I don't feel like I've got to take things at some ridiculously slow pace just in case you turn out to be a user, like the others. You're nothing like them. You may be the only really good man I've ever been with, the only one who wasn't just exploiting me for his own purposes. I can't tell you what that means to me, Jack."

He was staring at her, his eyes—those amazing, soulful eyes—riveted on her, his expression unreadable in the dark. A couple of times she thought he might be about to say something, but he didn't.

"Too heavy for precoital banter?" she said. "Hate to tell you this, but it gets even worse. I'm gonna say the L word now, and you can't stop me. You don't have to say it back. We haven't known each other that long. But I need to say it."

"Kat." He banded his arms around her and drew her close. "Honey . . ."

"I love you," she whispered into his ear.

He held her tighter, so tight it almost hurt. "Sleep here tonight," he pleaded, his voice low and rough. "Stay with me . . . just for tonight."

"I'll stay with you tonight, and tomorrow night, and the night after that." She straddled him, taking him into her slowly, sinuously. "We'll have as many nights as you want."

They rocked together, at first with a dreamlike languor, their hands stroking, exploring, their mouths meeting and parting, meeting and parting between softly whispered endearments. Their pleasure gathered up by delirious increments, until they were thrashing together with an almost violent abandon.

"Kat . . . oh, God." He seized her hips to still her, his body taut, a growl rising in his chest as he pushed deep, deep. She came when he did, sobbing with the blissful force of it.

He pulled her back down on top of him, holding her close as the tremors eased and their breathing slowed to normal. He stroked her hair, rubbed his stubbly chin against her face.

"What am I gonna do?" he murmured drowsily, sounding almost like a little boy.

"What do you mean?"

He sighed, shook his head.

"You're tired." She kissed his eyelids. "Sleep."

His breathing slowed, deepened. A couple of minutes later she realized he had, indeed, fallen asleep, still buried inside her. She uncoupled gently, so as not to wake him, and rose off the bed. The clock read 9:16. She *would* spend the night with him, but it was early yet, and she wasn't remotely sleepy. In fact, she felt both buzzed and pleasantly intoxicated, as if she'd just chased a double cognac with a triple mocha cappuccino.

A cocktail of adrenaline and endorphins, with a dollop of chocolate syrup. New love; it was potent stuff.

Padding naked into Jack's bathroom, she took a long, deliciously scalding shower. A creamy yellow oxford button-down shirt was hanging on the back of the door. It smelled like laundry detergent and Jack. She put it on, breathing him in, feeling the lightly starched cotton floating against her bare skin; it came to mid-thigh.

She opened the door to let the steam out while she ran a comb—a black Ace, a man's comb—through her damply snarled hair.

From the direction of the living room, a phone rang. Kat paused in her combing, weighing whether to answer it. Nah. Jack would surely have either an answering machine or voice mail.

It was a machine, she discovered when she heard his recorded voice say, "This is Jack O'Leary. Leave a message at the beep."

Beep.

"Jack, it's Celeste."

Kat stared at the foggy mirror, the comb poised in mid-air, thinking, *I know that voice. I know that name.* It was the woman who'd called her a high-priced whore on the phone today. Celeste Worth. Preston's wife.

"I waited an hour and a half for your call today, Jack. I don't appreciate being made to cool my heels. I do hope you've got a good excuse and you're not just avoiding me because you haven't made any progress yet toward, uh . . . landing your prey."

Kat walked into the living room on deadened legs, following Celeste Worth's voice to the answering machine, spotlit by the green-shaded lamp on Jack's desk.

"Tomorrow is Sunday," Celeste said. "A day of rest, and a good thing, too, because you are to plant that tight little butt of yours at home and stay there until you hear from me. If I don't receive a satisfactory report from you tomorrow, the deal's off. That five grand I gave you as a down payment? I'll be expecting that back in full."

There came a pause, during which Kat heard a faint click and a blowing sound. "If you let me down, you'll just be letting yourself down, Jack. Trust me, this is the easiest fifty K you'll ever earn. And if you can manage not to get hamstrung by tiresome scruples, there are, shall we say . . . perks to be had?" Celeste pitched her voice to a lascivious timbre. "She must be a tiger in the sack, for Preston to have lost his head this way."

Click.

The endorphins had vaporized, leaving Kat in the grip of a raging adrenaline firestorm. Her head shook; her hands shook; her legs shook.

She laid the comb on the desk with absurd care, still staring at the answering machine. Something lay on the desk near it, a small square of paper—a newspaper clipping. She lifted it, but it shook too badly to decipher. Setting it down under the lamp, she bent to read it.

WANTED: SEDUCTIVE, SELF-ASSURED MALE to take my husband's girlfriend from him . . .

"No," she whispered over and over as she read the rest of it. This wasn't happening. Kat scanned the desktop, but it was nearly bare except for his computer equipment. She pulled open a deep drawer on the left-hand side of the desk, and found it stuffed with hanging files. A quick perusal revealed no "Peale" in the *P*'s and no "Worth" in the *W*'s. Shoving the chair aside, she opened the middle drawer.

A closed file folder lay on top. She placed it on the desk and flipped it open.

And sucked in a breath when she saw the photograph. It was her, shivering outside the Four Seasons that night Preston had taken her to dinner and she hadn't thought to bring a coat. Preston was in the shot, digging distractedly through his pockets for a tip for the doorman, who was stepping off the curb with his arm raised, a whistle in his mouth.

There was a whole stack of photos, she realized in stunned horror. Lifting them, she flipped through them swiftly with spastic hands, growing progressively more sick to her stomach: she and Preston through the window of that little Tuscan place on Columbus, eating tiramisu; she and Preston gallery-hopping on Madison Avenue; she and Preston leaving her apartment building; walking in Central Park; lunching at the Plaza.

"Oh, God." Looking down, Kat saw packets of money strewn in the drawer. She scooped up a fistful; they each held $1,000 in twenties. *That five grand I gave you as a down payment . . .*

"Oh, my God," she whispered. "Oh, my God. Oh, my—"

"Did the phone ring?"

Kat whirled around to find Jack walking toward her,

yawning and scratching his stomach. Wearing nothing but those boxer shorts over that well-honed bod, his hair sleep-mussed, his jaw dark with stubble, he looked like every woman's secret fantasy.

And Kat's waking nightmare.

He glanced blearily toward the answering machine, running a hand through his hair. In a sleep-deepened voice, he said, "I thought I heard the phone . . ." His gaze lit on the open folder on the desk, the stack of photos in her right hand, the money in her left.

Please don't let this be what it looks like, she silently prayed.

But the sudden dismay in his expression, the whispered epithet, proved the worst.

"It was Celeste," Kat said tremulously. "She expects a report tomorrow, or"—she gestured with the cash—"you've got to give this back."

Jack took a step toward her, his hands up, his expression stricken. "Kat . . ."

"Luckily, you've got good news to report, don't you? You've . . . how did she put it? Landed your prey. Isn't that what she paid you for?"

"Kat . . . no."

"This says differently." She flung the money and the photographs at him; they lay scattered at his feet.

"Kat, please just—"

"You were right, last night, when you said I was gullible."

"I didn't say—"

"No, that's right. 'Too trusting,' that was how you put it." Her jeans lay on the floor nearby, along with her panties, loafers, and trench coat. Remembering how she'd thrown herself at him, how she'd thrashed and moaned beneath him, filled her with red-hot mortification. Snatching up the jeans, she started pulling them on. "I was trusting, all right—the perfect patsy. I bought your scam hook, line, and sinker."

God, she'd told him she *loved* him! That memory would

make her burn with humiliation the rest of her days.

"Kat . . ." He approached her warily as she tugged her jeans over her hips and zipped them up. "I know how this seems, and I admit, in the beginning, my motives weren't exactly noble—"

"You *think*?" she spat out as she stepped into her loafers. "You answered a personals ad, for God's sake, to steal me away from—"

"No." He raised his hands again. "I didn't know anything about that ad. I was just the guy she hired to catch Preston and you . . ." He glanced down at the photographs littering the carpet.

"You took those pictures?" She felt her throat close up. "You followed me around and—"

"It was just a job. I'm a private investigator."

"A private . . . you're not a sec—" A bitter little gust of laughter shook her chest. "Of course you're not. Nothing is what it seemed, is it? Everything out of your mouth has been a lie."

"Not everything. Kat . . ." He took another step toward her, quivering from head to foot. "It's true, she hired me to . . . get you away from Preston. I did it for the money, but once I got to know you—"

"Stop lying to me!" she screamed, feeling her eyes burn with impending tears. "You know something, Jack? Preston Worth is an *Eagle Scout* compared to you. All he wanted from me was sex. With you, it was that old bottom line. Well, congratulations. You've fulfilled your end of the deal admirably. You seduced me away from Preston. A job well done."

As she circled around him to leave, he grabbed her arm. "Kat."

She hauled back and slapped him, as hard as she could, across the face. His head whipped to the side; she thought he might fall, but he held his ground. He closed his eyes, his chest pumping, his jaw clenched.

Willing herself not to cry—she'd be damned if she'd let him see her cry—Kat lifted her coat from the floor and put it on, stuffing her panties in the pocket; her right hand stung as if it had been burned. Quietly, gravely, she said, "I hope you choke on your fifty thousand dollars."

His eyes, when he opened them, were red-rimmed; a vein rose on his forehead. "Kat, don't," he implored in a voice like damp rust. "Don't leave, not yet. Please let me explain."

She shook her head solemnly. "I don't trust myself to separate the truth from your bullshit anymore. Goodbye, Jack."

"Kat, no!" He leapt after her as she strode to the door, grabbed it as she yanked it open. "We can't leave it like this."

Kat stepped out into the hallway, paused. With her back to him, she said, softly, "You didn't have to make me fall in love with you, Jack. That was cruel."

She walked away before he could summon a response.

CHAPTER EIGHT

——

Kat's bedside phone rang at 10:27 Monday morning while she lay there contemplating the ornate crown molding around the ceiling and thinking about the fact that it was the day before Christmas and she didn't care. She let the machine pick up.

"Hi, you've reached Katherine Peale's answering machine. Sorry I'm not in to take your call right now, but if you'd like to leave a message, just wait for the beep."

Beep.

"Kat, it's me again."

Jack. Kat closed her eyes.

"You're probably getting sick of me leaving these messages," he said. "I know you don't want to talk to me, you don't want my explanations or apologies. You've written me off, and I guess I can't blame you, but I need you to know that I . . ."

He sighed. "Look, it's hard to say these things to a machine, and your doorman won't let me up. I was hoping I'd see you at Augusta House yesterday. Nobody could believe you didn't want to help decorate. Chantal and Pia wanted to know what was wrong, if something had happened between you and me. I said they'd have to ask you."

They had. Other than confirming that she and Jack had parted ways, she'd basically stonewalled them.

"I don't want you to have to miss the party tomorrow just 'cause you're afraid I'll be there," he said, "so I've decided not to go. But Kat, *please* meet with me. Or at least return my calls. I'm dying here."

Why was he doing this? Why go to this trouble to prolong their acquaintance? He'd done what he'd been hired to do; he'd broken up her relationship with Preston. His "generous reward" was in the bag. Why should it matter what she thought of him?

"Kat, I do care for you," he said with such fulsome sincerity that she was almost tempted to believe him. "What happened between us, it wasn't about the money. I mean, in the beginning it was, but you've got to believe me when I say it became . . . more than that. A lot more. Celeste . . . she did call yesterday, and I told her she can keep her fifty grand. I don't want it."

He didn't want the fifty grand. Why wouldn't he want . . . ?

"Of course," Kat whispered when it dawned on her. Why should Jack settle for a mere fifty thousand dollars when Katherine Peale was presumably worth millions? She'd already proven herself to be pathetically susceptible to the Jack O'Leary brand of charisma. If he were to con her into forgiving him, he might be able to wheedle himself back into her life, her bed . . . maybe even marriage. Marriage to an heiress, pre-nup or no pre-nup, would trump fifty grand any day.

"Kat . . . honey." He sounded convincingly anguished. "Look into your heart. What happened between us Saturday night . . . you *know* it was real."

She reached for the phone, propped it against her ear.

He was saying, "How could I have just been pretending—"

"Save your breath, Jack."

"Kat? *Kat!* Honey, listen to—"

"I'm not rich, Jack."

"What? Kat—"

"I used to be, and most people assume I still am. But I burned out my trust fund and inheritance on Augusta House, which is why I'm having to go hat in hand to people like the Livermores in order to get Caring for Families off the ground."

"I don't—"

"I live on rental income from this place, which might sound like a lot on paper, but it's an expensive building to maintain. I mean, I do okay. I'm comfortable. I've got this great apartment, and some old jewelry of my grandmother's, but that's about it. So you might rethink giving back that fifty grand, 'cause if you think you're going to strike gold with me, think again. That vein played out a while ago."

"Kat—"

"Goodbye, Jack. And please stop calling."

"Kat, don't hang—"

She hung up. And waited for the phone to ring again.

It didn't. He must have stopped to consider what she'd told him, which was no more or less than the truth—or had been for the past year or two, at any rate. For the most part, Kat let people assume she was still loaded for the sake of Augusta House and CFF. *Money attracts money,* as Grandma Augusta used to say. The illusion of vast wealth made her a much more effective fund-raiser. But it also tended to make her a magnet to the wrong kind of man. Was the trade-off worth it? Usually.

It was almost noon by the time she dragged her sorry butt out of bed. Jack's yellow oxford shirt, which she'd had on for some thirty-eight hours, was creased and rumpled. And it still smelled like him. She should take it off.

She didn't. She pulled on the sweatpants she'd tossed on the floor last night and finger-scraped her lank hair back in a rubber band. Her reflection in the mirror was pretty scary. "It's the hap-hap-happiest time of the year," she informed it.

She should really shower. She should probably eat something, too. Instead, she went downstairs to the den, lay down on the couch and grabbed the remote. It was one of those shrill courtroom shows, but she watched it anyway, and then the noontime news and a battery of soaps. The boy-loses-girl storylines kept reminding her of her own romantic melodrama.

Look into your heart . . . You know it was real.

When the news came on again at five, Kat turned off the TV, went to the closet by the front door, and searched the pockets of her trench coat until she unearthed the crumpled-up printout for the Inn at Aspen's Web site. Flopping back down on the couch, she lifted the phone from the end table, dialed the hotel and asked for the Worths' room. As it was ringing, it occurred to her that Preston might answer. If so, she'd hang up and try again later.

Luckily, it was his wife who picked up. "Hello."

"Mrs. Worth? This is Katherine Peale. There's something I'd like to ask you."

CHAPTER NINE

—

" 'God rest ye, merry gentlemen,' " sang the Augusta House Choristers from the communal room stage, " 'Let nothing you dismay.' "

Yeah, right, Kat thought as she worked her way through a sinkful of dirty pots and pans in the kitchen. She'd known nothing *but* dismay in the three days since the meltdown of her relationship—if you could call it that—with Jack O'Leary. What was it he'd said about the holidays? That they were famous for having bad stuff happen during them? He'd had a point. If the torment he'd dealt her didn't qualify as "bad stuff," what did?

"You're working too hard."

Kat looked up to find Chantal scowling at her from the doorway.

"There's a dishwasher for that stuff," Chantal said. "You ought to be out there eating pie and listening to those kids with everyone else."

At that moment, "God Rest Ye, Merry Gentlemen," the Choristers' final number, concluded to exuberant applause.

"The dishwasher's full," Kat said as the roars died down. "The concert is now over. And I've got no appetite for dessert."

Chantal nodded thoughtfully. "I don't suppose you'd like some help in here."

"No, I'm good." Kat rinsed a saucepan under the tap and propped it in the draining rack, then set to work on a yam-crusted casserole dish.

"Kat . . . I was talking to Pia. We don't like the way you've been isolating yourself for the past few days. You haven't been this down since your grandmother passed away. Whatever this problem is with Jack, don't you think it would help if you just talked about—"

"No." Kat couldn't bear for her best friends to know how thoroughly and humiliatingly she'd been had by the charming Jack O'Leary. The memory of it still made her feel physically ill.

She had risen above her misery only briefly yesterday afternoon, when she'd called Celeste Worth to ask if Jack had, indeed, turned down her fifty thousand dollars the day before.

After expressing some surprise that Kat knew about her arrangement with Jack, and being assured by Kat that it was all water under the bridge, Celeste had said, "Yes, he told me yesterday that he didn't want the money—although I was more than willing to pay him. After all, he fulfilled his end of the bargain by prying your tentacles off my husband."

Kat chose to ignore Celeste's dig; why let her drag this conversation down to her level? "Did he give a reason?"

"Apparently his conscience had reared its ugly head— isn't that sweet? He said he didn't feel right, taking the money after what he'd done to you. Which begged the question of what you'd done to *him* to have gotten him besotted enough to refuse his rightful payment. What's your secret? Whips and vinyl? Or maybe that new tantric business. Do you give him ten-minute orgasms?"

"What did he say, exactly?" Kat had asked. "About me?"

"If you mean did he declare himself to be your abject love slave, not in so many words, but that was the impression I had. Until this morning, when he called back and said, oops! Changed my mind. I want the money after all."

"Oh." That would have been after his phone call with Kat. The phone call where she'd told him she wasn't, in fact, rich.

"I gathered he was no longer in your thrall," Celeste said, "thus freeing him from those pesky qualms of his. So of course I demanded to know whether you intended to continue your campaign to displace me as Preston's wife. He said no, that you and Preston were through regardless, and that he'd earned the rest of his payment, which he asked me to FedEx to him. I asked him if he had any idea what it costs to overnight something on Christmas Eve. He said either I did it or he'd tell Preston what I'd been up to, the blackmailing son of a bitch. I told him I'd send it off by noon—which I did—and that I hoped he choked on it."

Déjà vu.

So. He *had* turned down the fifty grand as a gesture to Kat of his good faith and undying devotion, only to do a complete one-eighty the second he found out she wasn't made of money. He hadn't called since yesterday morning, of course. No dummy, he knew when it was time to back away and cut his losses . . .

Kat finished up the casserole dish and moved on to the carving board as Chantal waxed effervescent about the party. "It's been awesome, Kat. You might not appreciate *how* awesome, 'cause you barely poked your nose out of this kitchen the whole time, but everyone's really gotten into the spirit, especially the kids. Santa and the missus were a big hit."

"Are they still here?" Mr. and Mrs. Claus had spent the past three hours holding court on the stage next to a Christmas tree trimmed with handmade ornaments, wooden Hanukkah dreidels, and red, green, and black Kwanzaa streamers. They'd held enthusiastic one-on-one audiences with some two hundred children, each of whom got a present, a chat with Santa, and a Polaroid by Chantal to commemorate the event. Although she'd had her work cut out for her, supervising dinner for that many people, Kat had paused in the kitchen doorway from time to time to watch the kids take their turns. Even from all the way across the room, she could see the smiles on their faces, hear their excited laughter when Santa bellowed, "Ho, ho, ho!"

She wanted to share in their joy, to laugh along with them. But after what had happened with Jack, all she felt was tired. She'd barely managed to get dressed and show up here today.

"Yeah, they're still around," Chantal said. "Their gig's over, but the kids keep coming up to them. They don't seem to mind, though. Jack was right about his nephew being into Christmas—he was born to play Mrs. Claus."

"I thought the nephew was Santa."

"No, Santa said his name was Leon."

Kat said, "I really should come out of here and introduce myself and thank them for coming."

"You're welcome." It was a man's voice, young but deep-chested.

Kat turned to find Mrs. Claus standing in the doorway bearing a mountain of gifts in her stout arms. She—he—was a jumbo-sized, mobcapped, bespectacled archetype of a well-upholstered matron—but with the kind of vampish makeup you might see on a Vegas showgirl, up to and including inch-long false eyelashes. It was stage makeup, the kind that looked clownish up close but normal from an audience's perspective; that was why Kat hadn't noticed it before, what with her long-distance view of the stage.

"You really were terrific, Grady." Kat pulled off her rubber gloves and extended a hand. "You and Leon both."

"Hey, I was thrilled to be asked," Grady said as he shook her hand. Something about him tickled Kat's memory. She was about to ask him if they'd met, when he said, "These gifts are for you."

"Me?"

"Special delivery from the North Pole." He thunked them down on the steel worktable. There were five, of varying shapes and sizes, each wrapped in red and green striped paper garnished with a gold stick-on bow. "Open this one first." He handed her a gift about the size of a coffee can.

She shook it; it rattled like dried beans. "What's the deal? Chantal, is this something you and Pia cooked up to—"

"Uh-*uh*, girlfriend. I *wish* we'd thought of it."

"Go ahead," Grady said. "Open it."

She peeled the paper away to reveal a jar of popcorn kernels. "Uh . . ."

"Okay, this one next." Grady handed her a larger, squarish gift. "I wouldn't shake this one."

It was a six-pack of Bass ale. "Santa's giving me beer?"

"It gets better." The next gift was shaped like a CD.

"What is it?" Chantal asked as Kat stripped the paper off.

"A DVD of *It's a Wonderful Life*. Chantal, are you sure you didn't have anything to do with this?"

"You think *I'm* gonna give you another copy of that movie?"

Good point. "Someone should tell Santa I don't have a DVD player," Kat said.

"Uh . . ." Grady handed her the next to last, and largest, gift. "You do now."

Kat groaned as she opened it. "I can't hook this stuff up."

A voice from the doorway said, "I'll do it for you."

It was Jack's voice. But the man standing in the doorway was . . . "Oh, my God."

It was Santa, all right, in full, red-suited regalia, the same Santa who'd been chatting up kids and laying gifts on them all morning. From a distance, Kat hadn't recognized him, but up close, even with the beard and hat and wire-rimmed glasses . . .

Holy cow, he was playing Santa? *Jack O'Leary* getting himself up in a silly red suit and booming "Ho, ho, ho"?

"Wait a minute." Kat wheeled on Chantal, who must have known it was Jack. She'd taken a couple of hundred Polaroids of him posing with children. "You told me some guy named Leon was playing Santa. You lied to me!"

"No, I told you Santa *said* his name was Leon. You never asked me if he was telling the truth." She smiled smugly.

"I am going to kill you," Kat said.

"That would be my cue." Chantal grabbed Grady's arm

and pulled him toward the door. "Your work here is done, Mrs. C."

"Wait!" Kat ordered Grady. "Where do I know you from?"

Grady winced. "I, uh, kinda snatched your purse last week. And knocked you down, but that wasn't part of the plan, and Jack danced on my head about it, which he should have, 'cause it was a totally lame move, and I'm *sooo* sorry. Really."

Kat just gaped at him.

"Okay, that would be *your* cue," Jack said as he ushered Grady and Chantal both out of the kitchen, closing the door behind them.

Kat collapsed on a chair, dazed and incredulous.

"I'm dying in this." Jack took off the hat, glasses, and beard, and wiped his sweat-sheened face with a dish towel. He unbuttoned the red jacket, exposing a damp white T-shirt beneath. She should have guessed it was him from the way his shoulders strained the seams of the costume.

"You told me you wouldn't come today," she said dully.

"Because I didn't want you to feel like you couldn't come. That's why Chantal and Pia kept my secret, so *you* wouldn't split."

"Why *did* you come?"

"Christmas is a time of heartfelt giving, right? Your words. I wanted to give you some gifts."

"Beer?" She slid a bottle out of the six-pack.

"Pale ale. You like pale ale. And your idea of heaven, if I'm remembering right, is"—he gestured toward the gifts—"a bowl of popcorn, an ice-cold beer, and a good cry at the end of *It's a Wonderful Life*." He hesitated, almost bashfully. "I'd . . . like to watch it with you sometime, if you wouldn't mind."

"Jack . . . of *course* I'd mind. How could you think I wouldn't, after everything that's gone down between us?"

"It would give us an opportunity to talk about all that. We could watch the movie and then—"

"You *hate* that movie. You told me so!"

"I said it was *not my scene,*" he corrected soberly. "There's a difference."

She refused to smile. "Jack, I know you called Celeste and had her FedEx the money to you after we spoke yesterday. And I know why."

"Uh-huh." He pointed to the fifth present, which was rectangular and about six inches long. "You haven't opened the last one yet."

"I don't want your gifts, Jack."

He pushed it toward her. "You want this one."

"Jack . . ."

"And then, if you really want me to go, I will."

Kat looked at him, looked at the gift, let out a lungful of air. "I'll hold you to that," she said as she tore the paper off.

And stared at what she'd uncovered: five bound stacks of twenties with a check on top for $45,000, all rubber-banded together. The check was from Celeste Worth, and made out to Jack. "What the . . ."

"Turn it over," Jack said. "The check."

She did. He'd endorsed it to Caring for Families.

"It's all yours," he said, "the whole fifty grand, to put toward your new programs for battered women and runaways. See?" he asked when she looked at him in shock. "I've been taking notes."

"Jack . . . my God. I . . . I don't know if I can accept this."

"You need it. You said yourself, you exhausted your own resources on Augusta House. You need cash to launch CFF."

"You wouldn't be trying to buy my affections, would you?"

"This from the woman who, not one minute ago, implied that I'd only been interested in her for her supposed millions? No, honey. I'm giving this money to CFF because it's either that or leave it with Celeste, and she doesn't deserve it. And you know what?"

He sank to his knees before her, took her hands in his.

"I'm glad you're not rich. I *exulted in my heart* when you told me you'd blown it all on Augusta House. Not only because I think it's just fantastic that you're so passionate about helping people, but because . . ." He closed his eyes; that vein stood out on his forehead again.

When he opened his eyes, they were glazed with moisture. "Because I need you to know—*really* know—that it's you I love, not what you can give me or do for me. Just you."

A squeezing pressure filled Kat's throat.

"Falling in love with you was the last thing I expected to happen," he said. "It was incredible, 'cause I was so *crazy* in love with you, but it was terrifying, too, because it seemed so hopeless. I'd started off with so many lies."

A tear trickled down his cheek. He let go of her hand to rub at it brusquely. This was the first time he'd shed tears, she realized, since he was nine. "I'm sorry, Kat, so sorry. I deceived you. There's no excuse, and I'm more ashamed than you know, but I'm also . . ." He shrugged. "I'm just so grateful we met, even if that was the way it had to happen."

She nodded, at a loss for words.

"But because of how it happened," he said, "all the stupid things I did, I could lose you now, and that . . . God, it would kill me." He clutched her hands tight. "Something else you said about Christmas is that it's a time of rebirth."

Kat smiled down at his costume, her chin wobbling. "*You* certainly look like a changed man."

"Do you think, maybe . . . we could start over from scratch?" he asked. "With no Preston and no Celeste and no fifty thousand dollars? Just us? And see what happens?"

"You know what I think?" She cupped his damp cheek as tears slid from her own eyes; he closed his eyes and leaned into her palm. "I think we already have."

Love
Bytes

—

SHERRILYN KENYON

CHAPTER ONE

——

"Could you please tell me what's wrong with me? I swear if anyone else looks at me and snickers, I might go postal."

Samantha Parker looked up from her computer monitor to see Adrian Cole standing in her cube. Or rather towering over it. At six foot five, the man reminded her of a giraffe when he moved around the office.

Not that she minded. Personally, she adored his height, just as she adored those gorgeous eyes of his. Deep and a dark chocolate-brown, they made her melt every time he looked at her.

And the sleek, loose-limbed way he walked . . .

Oooh, just thinking about it was enough to make her burn.

She'd never been particularly fond of blond men, but those dark eyes with his thick mane of tawny curls and lush golden skin just made her ache for a taste. A nervous jitter went over her like it always did when he stood this close to her, and she could smell the clean, spicy scent of him. The man was simply mouth-wateringly scrumptious, and incredibly brilliant.

"Well?" he prompted.

Sam bit her lip as she raked her gaze over his long, lean frame. "Other than the fact you look like your seeing-eye dog dressed you this morning, nothing," she teased. "What did you do to make Heather mad this time?"

He cursed under his breath. It was common knowledge that Adrian had a rare type of color blindness that rendered him completely incapable of seeing any color whatsoever. As a result, he paid his baby sister to do his laundry, and every time Heather got upset at big brother, she took it out on his wardrobe.

"What did she do to me now?" he asked warily.

"Well, you'll be happy to know your red plaid shirt is still red, but the splotchy pink Henley really has to go."

Adrian held his leg out and pulled his jeans up to show her his socks. "What about them?"

"Unlike your shirt, they actually match your Henley."

Growling low in his throat, he buttoned his plaid shirt all the way to his neck. "One day, I'm going to kill her."

Sam laughed at the threat he uttered at least twice a week. She'd met Heather a couple of times during lunch, and though Sam liked her, Heather was a bit self-absorbed.

"So, what did you do?" she asked.

"I refused to let her borrow my Vette. The last time she took it out, she hit a pole and cost me three thousand dollars in damage."

"Yikes." Sam cringed for him. Adrian loved his vintage 1969 Stingray. "Was she hurt?"

"Thankfully, no, but my car is still sulking over it."

Sam laughed again, but then, she always did that around him. Adrian had a dry, sharp wit that never missed a beat. "Well, I'm glad you stopped by. My Perforce is acting up again. I can't get it to integrate my changes." Which meant that the stupid server had her locked out and every time she tried to update a page on their Web site, it refused to let her.

She hated Perforce, and it hated her. But they were required to use it so that upper management could keep track of who made what changes to the Web site, and out of the entire network services department, Adrian was the only one who really understood the program.

"What's it doing?" he asked as he came to stand beside her.

Sam couldn't breathe as he leaned down to read her screen. His face was so close to hers that all she had to do was move a mere two inches and she would be able to place her lips against that strong, sculpted jaw.

"Scroll down."

She heard Adrian's words, but they didn't register. She was too busy watching the way his incredibly broad shoulders hunched as he leaned with one hand against her desk.

He glanced down at her.

Sam blinked and looked back at the screen. "I'm scrolling," she said as she reached for her mouse.

"There's your problem," he said as he read the gobbledygook. "You haven't enabled your baseline merges."

"And in English that would mean?"

Adrian laughed that rich, deep laugh that made her burn even more. He covered her hand with his on the mouse and showed her how to choose the right options.

He surrounded her with his masculine warmth. Sam swallowed at the disturbing sensation of his hand on hers as fire coursed through her. He had beautiful, strong hands. His long, lean fingers were tapered and perfect. Worse, every time she looked at them, she couldn't help wondering what they would feel like on her body, touching her, caressing her.

Seducing her.

His cell phone rang. Adrian straightened and pulled the phone from its cradle on his belt. He checked the caller ID, then flipped it open like Captain Kirk. "Yeah, Scott, what's wrong?"

"Radius is down," Scott, their network security specialist, said over the speaker phone, "and I can't get it up and running."

"Did you reboot?"

"Duh."

Adrian indicated her chair with his head.

Sam got up and watched as he set the phone aside, took a seat in her chair, and opened a DOS window on her computer. He tapped swiftly on her keyboard, then picked his phone back up. "It's not cycling."

"I know, and I can't fix it."

"All right," Adrian said with saintly patience. "I'll be up there in a few minutes."

He clicked off his phone, but before he could move, his phone rang at the same time his pager went off and the overhead paging system called his name. Adrian answered his cell phone again and checked his pager.

"Did you get the hacker alert?" Scott asked.

"Hang on," Adrian said, then he reached for her desk phone to answer his page.

"Hi, Randy," he said as he tucked the phone between his shoulder and cheek and started typing on her keyboard. "I'm in the process of switching the main databases over to my SQL. We should be ready to fly by five." He paused as he listened and switched her computer from the Windows over to Linux.

Sam watched in awe as he flawlessly entered line after line of stuff she couldn't even begin to follow or understand.

"No," Adrian said to Randy, "our customers won't notice at all, except the searches will take less time." He entered more lines as he listened to their senior director, Randy Jacobs, on the phone.

Another page went off for him.

Adrian nodded as he listened to Randy. "Yeah, I'll get to it. Would you mind holding for just a second?"

He picked up his cell phone. "Scott, it's not a hacker. It's an invalid SID. Someone is using a bookmark with an old Session ID attached to it."

"Are you sure?"

"Positive. I'm looking at it right now."

"Okay, thanks."

Adrian gave her a sheepish smile as he clicked off his cell phone and picked up the other line on her desk phone.

Biting her lips to keep from smiling at the chaos, Sam felt for him. At twenty-six, Adrian was known to everyone in the company as the boy genius. He had taken a billion-dollar corporation from the 1980s mainframe mentality into the twenty-first century Web-based e-commerce. He had single-handedly built the entire programming side of their million-dollar business retail site, and put together a Web design team that was second to none.

Unfortunately, though, everyone in the company turned to him every time something went wrong with the site. Which meant he was always on call and always rushing from one department to the next, putting out fires and trying his best to explain extremely complicated things to people who had absolutely no idea what he was talking about.

Adrian came into the office every morning by five-thirty, and seldom went home before eight at night.

The stress on him had to be excruciating, and yet he was the most easygoing boss she'd ever known. She couldn't count the number of times a day someone was complaining, if not shouting, about something, or begging him to help them, and yet he never let the strain of it show.

"Scott," Adrian said at his cell phone, "go get a cup of coffee. I'm headed upstairs as soon as I finish with Randy." He returned to her phone. "I'm back, Randy." He listened for a few minutes more, then nodded. "All right," he said, pulling the Palm Pilot off his belt. "I'll put it on my schedule."

Sam watched as he added yet another meeting to his already booked calendar.

"Okay," he said to Randy. "I'm on it. See you later."

Adrian left the chair, then hesitated at the opening of Sam's cube as she resumed her seat. In a rare show of uneasiness, he picked up the wooden medieval knight her brother had given her. "This is new."

She nodded. "Teddy got it Thanksgiving when he went to Germany."

"It's neat," he said, putting it back on the shelf with the rest of the knights. She had been collecting them for years. She figured they were as close as she'd ever come to having a real knight in shining armor.

He glanced around her cube at the large Santa and snowmen cutouts she had pinned up, the small Christmas tree she had next to her monitor, and the stack of holiday catalogues by her keyboard. "You really love Christmas, don't you?"

Sam glanced down at her Santa and reindeer sweater and smiled. "My favorite time of year. Don't you like it?"

He shrugged. "It's a day off, I guess."

Still Adrian hesitated, fiddling with her nameplate.

How odd. It was so unlike him to be fidgety. This was a man who made million-dollar decisions and held meetings with the stars of the *Fortune* 500 without even a minor qualm.

What on earth could he be nervous about?

"Would you mind if I asked a giant favor?"

Her heart pounded. *Oh, baby, ask me anything!*

"What'cha need?"

He dropped his gaze down to her nameplate as he slid it back and forth in its holder. "Since Heather has totally screwed up my clothes again, I was wondering if you'd mind going shopping with me after work? I'd take Randir, but even I can tell *his* clothes don't match."

"I heard that!" Randir said laughingly from the next cube.

Sam smiled. The guys in her department teased each other mercilessly, and it was what she loved most about her job. Everyone got along well and no one minded the incessant quips and taunts that were hurled about as often as Adrian got paged.

"Anyway," Adrian said, ignoring Randir's interruption. "Would you mind? I'll buy you dinner."

Yes! Her heart skipped a beat as she did her best to appear calm, while inside, what she really wanted to do was turn cartwheels. "I don't mind."

"You sure?"

"Positive."

"Great," he said with a slight smile. "Then I guess I better go to Scott before he hyperventilates."

"Okay, see you later."

Adrian took one last look at Sam as she returned her attention to her monitor. He clenched his teeth as he watched her fingers stroking the keys on her keyboard.

That woman had the lightest touch he'd ever seen, and he ached to feel those hands on his body. Ached to take them into his mouth and nibble every inch of them.

Worse, what he really wanted to do was pick her up from that chair, take her into his office, and toss everything on top of his desk onto the floor before laying her down on top of it.

Oh, yeah, he could already taste her lips as he peeled the thick sweater and jeans off her body. Feel her hot and wet for him as he coaxed and teased her body into blind ecstasy.

His groin tightened in pain at the thought.

Stop it! he snapped at himself. He was her team leader, and she was one of his best employees. Company policy stringently forbade dating between management and staff, and violation of that policy meant immediate dismissal.

Yeah, but the woman made him seriously hot.

Dangerously hot.

She always wore her long, dark hair pulled back from her face where it fell in thick waves down to her waist. He'd spent hours at night fantasizing about that hair draped on his chest, or spread out across his pillow.

And she had the palest eyes he'd ever seen. She'd told him once they were green, and it pained him that he had absolutely no idea what that color meant.

But from what he could see, green had to be beautiful.

Her eyes were a bit large for her pixie face, and they were always bright and teasing when she looked at him.

He could stare into those eyes for an eternity.

Adrian ran his gaze over her lush curves, and he hardened even more as raw, demanding desire tore through him. Sam had once complained about her weight, but he couldn't find any fault with it. After growing up with a skinny, frail mother and sister, he couldn't stand to see a woman with no meat on her bones.

Her full, voluptuous body made him absolutely crazy with unspent lust. And for the last year, he'd been forced to learn to live with a raging erection every time he got near her, or heard the sound of her smooth Southern drawl.

Sam paused and looked up at him. "Did you need something else?"

Yeah, I need you to smile at me.

Touch me.

Better still, I need you to climb me like a ladder . . .

"No," he said as another page sounded for him.

Adrian turned away from her and answered the page with his cell phone as he headed upstairs to tend Scott's antsy twitters.

Sam clenched her hands as her computer clock showed ten after five. An anxious tremor went through her as she feared Adrian might have changed his mind about going out with her.

Taking a deep breath for courage, she shut down her computer, then walked the short distance to Adrian's office.

He had his back to her as he typed like lightning on his keyboard while talking on the phone. "It's switched," he said. "Everything is clear . . . No, I ran the logs, and as of yesterday, we've cleared seven hundred thousand dollars in orders since the end of October . . . Yeah," he said with a light laugh. "Merry Christmas to you, too."

He hung up the phone, and she saw him rub his hand over his eyes as if he had a headache. His cell phone rang. Without breaking stride, he answered it.

"Hi, Tiffany," he said to their marketing director. "Yeah, I'll be here for a few more minutes. I was planning on implementing your changeover after Christmas since there's a good chance it could slow down site access." He listened as he worked and Sam shook her head.

The man was simply amazing. She didn't know how he managed to stay on top of everything, but he did.

He pushed his chair back from his computer desk and swung it around to the desk in front of her. As his gaze fell on her, he smiled that wolfish grin that made her blood race. She felt a vicious stab of desire straight through her middle.

Reaching for a stack of reports, he flipped to one of the middle pages. "Okay," he said to Tiffany. "I'll take care of it first thing in the morning."

He clicked off his phone. "Sorry about that," he said to Sam. "I didn't know you were standing there. Just give me a sec, I'll get this finished, and we can leave."

Sam let out a relieved breath. Thank goodness, he hadn't changed his mind. She moved into his office and took a seat against the window as she waited for him. "Have we really done seven hundred thousand dollars off the site since Halloween?"

He nodded. "We should easily hit a million by Christmas." He flashed her another smile. "Should make for nice bonuses."

Money, she didn't care about. So long as she made enough to cover her car and rent, she was completely happy. But she was glad for Adrian's sake. Their business-to-business e-commerce Web site was his pride and joy, and he took a lot of flak from the higher-ups when the site didn't perform the way they thought it should.

Sam looked up as Tiffany stalked into Adrian's office. "Adrian," Tiffany whined as she glanced at Sam without acknowledging her. Thin, tall, and gorgeous, Tiffany should have been a model. All the leggy blonde had to do was bat her eyelashes, and every guy in the building would drop what he was doing and rush to her side.

And every time Sam got near her, she felt like a warted troll in comparison.

"Adrian," Tiffany said again. "I got an e-mail from a customer wanting to know why he has to enter in his password every time he wants to order something. He wants us to fix it so that he can just do a one-click order option. What should I tell him?"

Adrian didn't pause in his typing as he answered. "That it's a safeguard to save his butt should one of his disgruntled employees get ticked off, and decide to order several thousand dollars' worth of merchandise and charge it to his account."

Tiffany rolled her eyes at Adrian's sarcasm. "Well, he says—"

"I don't give a damn what he says," Adrian said calmly.

Sam bit her lip as Tiffany's face flushed bright red. That was Adrian's only flaw. The man didn't pull punches, and he always spoke his mind, consequences be damned.

"Those safeguards are there for his protection," he continued, "and I'm not about to change it since he'll be the first one to whine when he gets burned."

Tiffany stomped her foot. "Would you look at me when you're talking to me?"

Sam arched her brow as Adrian turned around with a look on his face that should have sent Tiffany running. To his credit, all he said was a simple, "Yes?"

"I need a more tactful answer for him than that." She narrowed those blue eyes at him. "Look, I know you think you own this Web site, but the last time I checked, you were just another flunky here like the rest of us."

He took a deep breath as both his pager and phone went off. "I tell you what," he said in a self-controlled tone, "since I'm a flunky here like everyone else, why don't you come in at midnight tonight to post a press release because the man who signs our checks wants it to go live exactly at that time?" He picked his phone off his belt.

He checked the caller ID, flipped it open, and said, "Scott, it's not a hacker. I'm validating the PHP."

Adrian hung up the phone. "Now, Miss Klein, if you want a more tactful response, then please forward the e-mail to me and I will respond to it myself."

Tossing her hair over her shoulder, Tiffany glared at him. "I want a copy of your response."

"Yes, Mom."

Tiffany's nostrils flared. Turning on her red high heels, she stalked out of his office. But as she left, Sam heard her muttering under her breath, "What a friggin' geek."

She couldn't tell if Adrian heard it. He merely checked

his pager, then grabbed one of the reports and swung his chair back around to his computer.

"You must get tired of all this," she said quietly.

"I'm used to it," he said simply as he started typing again.

Sam shook her head. Poor Adrian. He wasn't even allowed to get sick. She remembered last summer when he had pneumonia. He'd been forced to drag himself in to work to fix some problem no one else could solve.

The man needed a break.

And how she wished she dared get up from her chair, go over to him and massage those broad, tense shoulders for him. She could just imagine the feel of his lean muscles under her hand, the sight of his handsome features relaxed.

He would be breathtaking.

Sam, you have got to quit fantasizing. Boy-genius doesn't even know you're alive.

Even though it was true, she wished things were different between them. Adrian was the first guy she'd ever met whom she really could see herself having kids with. She'd love to have a houseful of tall brainiacs who were fast on a comeback.

It was a full ten minutes before Adrian finally logged off his computer. He got up to shrug on his faded blue ski jacket.

"C'mon," he said to her. "Let's make a mad run for the door before someone catches me."

She laughed, knowing it wasn't a joke.

He locked his office, then they headed outside to the dimly lit parking lot.

"Why don't you ride with me?" he asked as she started for her silver Honda. "You're the only person in the department who hasn't ridden in the Vette."

Oh, don't tempt me, you cruel man. She hadn't ridden in his Corvette because she couldn't stand the thought of being so close to him and not being able to touch that wonderful body. "Yeah, but you'll have to bring me all the way back here."

"I don't mind."

Sam bit her lip as her pulse raced. *Don't do it! Don't torture yourself.*

But one look at his chiseled features in the streetlight and she was hooked. "Okay," she said with a nonchalance she didn't feel.

He opened the passenger side door for her, then closed it after she got in. Sam drew a ragged breath at his consideration. She'd never had a man do that for her before.

Adrian got in the other side, and she had to bite back a laugh at the sight of him cramming his long body into the car.

"Don't say anything," he said as he put the key in the ignition. "Heather already told me I look like a grasshopper in a peanut shell."

She couldn't help laughing at that. "Sorry," she said, clearing her throat as she caught his sideways glare. "I wouldn't have laughed if you hadn't said that."

Sam leaned back in the black leather seat as she inhaled the warm, spicy scent of him. Good heavens, but that masculine smell made her giddy and hot. She would love nothing more than to lean over, cup the back of his neck with her hand, and kiss the daylights out of those full, sensuous lips.

Adrian started the car and did his best to ignore just how good Sam looked sitting beside him. He ached to reach his hand over to where she had her legs slightly parted and caress her inner thigh.

Oh, yeah, he could already feel the denim and her flesh in his palm. And then, he imagined where he'd like to take his hand next.

Up her thigh to cup her between her legs.

Grinding his teeth, he could see them locked in a kiss, feel her hands sliding over him as he undressed her.

It had been a long time since he'd made out in a car, but for the first time since high school, he found the idea appealing.

A surge of lust ripped through him as he shifted uncomfortably in his seat.

She'd taken that stupid clip out of her hair and brushed her bangs with her hand so that now her hair fell around her face, framing it to perfection. And it was torturing him.

Pulling out of the lot, he headed toward Hickory Hollow Mall. He hadn't even gone a mile when he noticed Sam tensing in her seat. "What's wrong?" he asked.

She flinched as he changed lanes. "You know, Adrian, this isn't a video game, and cars don't evaporate if you hit them. Jeez, you drive like you have a death wish."

He laughed and backed off his speed. "Come on, half the fun of this car is pushing its limits."

She crossed herself. "I hope you have a good life insurance policy."

He did, but there wasn't anyone to reap the benefits of it. And it was one of his biggest regrets. He'd never been the kind of guy to date much. Taking care of his mother, sister, and work left him very little time to socialize.

Not that it mattered. As soon as he opened his mouth and said something, most women got a blank, dazed look on their faces and stared at him like he was speaking a foreign language.

But not Sam. She understood even his most obscure references.

"Adrian!" she snapped as a semi cut them off. "That's a truck!"

He hit the brakes. "Don't worry, I don't dare die before I put the Christmas press release up. And even if I did, I'm sure Randy would be at the funeral home with a laptop asking me to take care of some last-minute thing."

"You're not funny," she said, even though she was smiling. "Do you really have to go in later and do that?"

"Unfortunately, yes." Adrian pulled onto Bell Road. "Want to eat first?"

"Sure."

"What are you in the mood for?"

"Anything."

"How about Olive Garden?" he asked, knowing it was one of her favorites.

"Sounds great."

Adrian pulled into the lot, then went to open the door for her. But by the time he got to her side, she was already getting out. She looked up and smiled. "And they say chivalry is dead."

"You have a hard time letting anyone do anything for you, don't you?" he asked.

"What can I say? My brothers broke me in well."

Adrian shook his head. "I can't believe your mother didn't nag them into doing more for you."

"She might have had she ever been home, but since she had to work all the time after my dad left, it was pretty much just us."

Adrian tucked his hands into his back pockets to keep himself from subconsciously reaching out to touch her.

God, how he wanted her. She barely reached his shoulders and every time he stood this close to her, he had the worst desire to pick her up in his arms and bury his face in her neck where he could inhale the sweet scent of her skin.

Clenching his teeth, he tried to banish the thought of laying her down on his bed, and spending the rest of the night exploring her body. Slowly. Meticulously.

He opened the door to the restaurant and let her enter first. As she passed him, his gaze trailed down the back of her body and focused on her round hips. His groin instantly hardened. Thank God, he wore baggy jeans.

The hostess led them to a booth in the back. Adrian hesitated as Sam sat down. His first impulse was to sit beside her, but he knew it wouldn't be appropriate. The only time he got to do that was when all of them went out to lunch, then he always made a point of being the one to sit closest to her.

His gut tightening as another wave of desire hit him, he forced himself into the opposite booth.

"It's weird to be here without the guys," she said as she glanced over the menu.

Adrian stared at her as she read the menu. He didn't know why she bothered since she always ordered the Manicotti Formaggio, and he loved the way she said it. It rolled off her tongue like smooth whisky.

Sam tightened her hands on the menu as she felt Adrian's gaze on her. Unnerved by its intensity, she tried to cross her legs, but ended up kicking him under the table. "I'm sorry," she gasped as he grimaced.

"It's okay," he said, reaching beneath the table to rub his leg. "I tend to take up a lot of space."

"Don't knock it, I'd kill to be tall."

"I don't know why. I think you're a perfect size."

She glanced up at his unexpected compliment. He cleared his throat and dropped his gaze to his menu.

After they ordered, they sat in awkward silence.

Sam sipped her drink as she tried to think of something to say to him. Normally, they never had a bit of trouble finding things to talk about and laugh over. But tonight, she was just a little too aware of him. A little too nervous about being alone with him, knowing there was no one here to see her if she were to reach over and touch his hand.

No one to see if she . . .

"Did you decide to call that guy about the programming position?" she asked, remembering the résumé he'd given her to review that morning.

"I did, even though my first impulse was to toss it."

"Why?"

"Dear *Ms.* Cole," he said, curling his lip. "I hate it when someone gets my gender wrong. It's the reason I called you so fast when you submitted your résumé. You're the only one who hasn't made that mistake. I knew you had to be brilliant."

She smiled. "Yeah, well, I have to say I was stumped, which is why I wrote 'Dear Adrian.' I figured you had to be a guy, since there are so few women programmers, but just in case you weren't I didn't want to tick you off."

"Thanks, Mom," he muttered bitterly. "It wasn't bad enough she passed along the oh-so-wonderful color-blind genes, but she had to curse me with a godawful name to boot."

"If you hate it so much, why don't you use your middle name?"

"Because it's Lesley."

Sam felt her jaw go slack. "Your mother named you Adrian Lesley Cole?"

He nodded. "She *really* wanted a daughter. When the nurse told her she had a son, she told the nurse to check again. 'That just can't be right,' " he said in a falsetto, mocking a thick Southern accent.

Was he serious?

"You know," she said. "I really like the name Adrian. I think it suits you."

He snorted. "Gee, thanks for the affront to my manhood."

"No," she said with a laugh. There was absolutely *nothing* feminine about him, or his features. "You just have a classical, romantic look to you, like the hero from some period movie."

He looked a bit sheepish at her compliment. Sam dropped her gaze down to his hands again and watched the way he trailed the empty straw wrapper through his long fingers.

Oh, she loved those hands of his.

How she wished for the courage to reach over and cover them with hers. But she was terrified of what he might do. Terrified of him rejecting her, because in her heart, she knew she'd already fallen for him.

She needed to be able to see him every day. Needed to feel his presence even if it was at a distance.

No, she would never chance running him off. He was her boss, and she would have to satisfy herself with just being his friend.

*   *   *

As soon as they finished dinner, Adrian drove them up the street to the mall. Sam led him through the men's section of Dillard's, looking for things she thought would be hot on him.

She paused as she found a stack of button-fly jeans. "You know, these would look great on you."

Adrian didn't miss the gleam in her eyes. He hated button-fly, but if Sam liked them . . .

"I need a thirty-two waist and a thirty-six inseam."

"Oh, my God, you're tall."

He laughed. "I know and it's a bitch to find them. But if you can locate a pair in this mess, I'll try them on."

She did. Adrian tucked them under his arm as he followed her around and did his best not to be too obvious in his ogling of her.

"You're not going to put me in anything weird, are you?" he asked suspiciously as she stopped to look at a rack of V-neck sweaters. "I might not be able to see colors, but I know guys don't wear pink, or pastels. And please, nothing in bright yellow because I can't stand light-post jokes."

"I wouldn't do that to you. I'm thinking blacks and dark blues. Maybe red. You look really good in red."

He smiled. "Really? How good?"

"*Very* good." She plucked at his shirtsleeve. "But I don't like your plaid shirts. They make you look like a lumberjack."

She'd noticed him! Adrian wanted to shout in happiness. He couldn't believe she'd actually been looking at him.

"So, what do"—he had to bite back the word *you*—"women want on a guy?"

"Not those baggy jeans," she said, looking at his rear and making him even hotter. Harder.

His breathing tense, it was all he could do not to pull her to him and find out exactly what those lips of hers tasted like.

"I don't know who came up with the idea," she continued, "but ew. Women like to see a man's . . ."

He arched a brow.

"Never mind. I'm having a weird case of déjà vu."

"Why?"

"I used to buy clothes for my brothers and we'd always get into similar discussions." She ran her gaze over him. "No offense, but you could really use a makeover."

Adrian hesitated. Maybe if he let her, she might be a little more receptive to his . . .

You're her boss.

Yeah, but he liked her more than he had ever liked any other woman. She made him laugh; made him happy every time she looked up at him.

Better still, she made him burn.

"You feel up to it?" he asked before he could stop himself.

"You'd let me?" she asked in disbelief.

"Sure, just so long as you don't paint my fingernails pale pink."

She frowned at that. "What?"

"Heather did that to me in high school as a joke. One night while I was sleeping, she sneaked into my room and painted my fingernails. I didn't notice until I got to school the next day and people started laughing."

"Why is your sister so mean to you?"

He shrugged. "She doesn't mean any real harm. She's just impulsive, and never seems to think before she acts."

Shaking her head, Sam searched through a rack of black button-down shirts as she thought about what he said. "She really painted your fingernails?"

"Yup."

"My brothers would have killed me."

"Yeah, well, she's my kid sister. My mom always said my one job was to protect her, not pulverize her."

Affected by his protectiveness, she reached out without thinking and touched his arm.

Her heart stopped.

Holy cow!

Up until now, she'd thought he was on the skinny side

like his sister, but there was nothing thin about that arm. His biceps were harder than a brick even while relaxed.

"Okay," she said, trying to distract herself from that delectable muscle. "Makeover with no nail polish."

Sam picked out several shirts and more jeans, then sent Adrian to try them on. She was busy looking through another rack when she felt someone behind her.

Turning around, she froze. Adrian was standing at the mirror outside the dressing room with his sweater lifted while he tugged at the back of his jeans. "I don't know about this," he said.

She only vaguely registered his words. Because she was captivated by him. The faded denim cupped a rear so tight and well formed that it made her ache to touch it.

He was wearing a thin, black V-neck sweater that clung to his broad shoulders, biceps, and pecs. And worse, the hem of the sweater was lifted up to where she could see his hard, flat stomach and dark brown hairs curling becomingly around his navel.

Oh . . . My . . . God! The man had the body of a well-toned gymnast. Why he had kept that yummy body hidden was beyond her.

"Buddy, you got abs!" she said before she could stop herself.

Adrian met her gaze in the mirror. "What?"

She closed the distance between them and lifted the shirt hem a tad higher as she stared in awe at that body. "You got abs! A whole six-pack of them." She looked up at him. "You didn't get those on the computer."

"Well, no. I do other things on occasion."

No kidding!

And right then, there was a whole series of other things she wanted to do to him. Starting with those hard abs and working her way up and down that luscious, tanned body. "If I were you, I'd burn all those baggy jeans and oversized shirts as soon as I got home."

"You like these jeans?"

Biting her lip, she nodded.

Suddenly, Adrian liked them, too. But what he liked most was the hunger he saw in her eyes, the feel of her hand against his stomach. It sent chills all over him.

It was all he could do not to kiss her.

Worse, an image of her lying naked beneath him tore through him. He shuttered his eyes as his breathing faltered. He wanted her so badly, he could already taste the moistness of her lips. Feel the softness of those full breasts in his hands.

It was a such a raw, aching need that it sliced through him.

Sam looked up and caught the heated look in his eyes. He had his lips slightly parted. And she became all too aware of the fact she was still holding his shirt in her hand, and was so close to his hard belly that she could feel his body heat.

Her breasts tightened as a wave of lust singed her.

Please kiss me!

But he didn't. He swallowed and took a step back.

Sam sighed. What was she thinking? Smart, gorgeous guys like Adrian didn't date short, fat co-workers. They were friends, plain and simple. There could never be anything between them.

By the time they finished, Adrian was almost a thousand dollars poorer, but he had an entire new wardrobe. And if it would keep Sam staring at him like she was doing, he decided it was worth every penny.

He changed into a new T-shirt, sweater, and jeans before they left.

Their next stop was MasterCuts. "What's wrong with my hair?" he asked as he sat down in the chair.

"Nothing, Shaggy-Doo," Sam said playfully as she brushed her hand through his hair. His entire body erupted into fire as he savored her light touch against his scalp. "I love the tawny color and curls. With the right cut, you would stop traffic."

Sam watched from the side of his chair as the beautician

trimmed his silken curls into a shorter cut that looked incredibly sexy and stylish.

Oh, yeah, now he was cooking. She stared in awe as the woman moussed his hair.

"Now that is a great look," Sam told Adrian. "You get rid of that goatee and watch out."

"Now you hate my goatee?" he asked, aghast.

"For the record," Sam said as she met his gaze in the mirror, "all women hate goatees."

The beautician concurred. "She's right. They're nasty."

Adrian stroked his goatee with his thumb. "Really? You don't think it's manly?"

"Do you think a billy goat is manly?"

"Oh, thanks, *Heather*."

Sam's eyes twinkled.

Adrian paid for the cut and for the bottle of mousse Sam insisted he'd better use, but personally, he'd rather stick a pair of tweezers in an electrical outlet.

All too soon, the night was over and he had to drive her back to her car.

"Thanks," he said as she got into her Honda. "I really appreciate your taking pity on my clothes tonight."

"It was my pleasure."

God, he wanted to kiss her. He stared at her lips, trying to imagine what they would taste like. He'd give anything to have a single night with her. To sink himself deep between her soft thighs as she held him close and moaned in his ear.

Then again, one night with her would never be enough.

"You be careful," he said, his voice hoarse. "How far is Spring Hill from here?"

"A good fifty minutes."

"Jeez, I shouldn't have kept you out so long. Do me a favor and call my cell phone and let me know when you get home, okay?"

"Okay."

Adrian forced himself to close her car door. He stepped away from her car as she started it. The light from the control panel lit her face as she buckled herself in.

In that moment, he ached for something he knew he could never have.

Her.

She looked up and waved. He returned the gesture, then watched as she drove off.

His heart heavy, and feeling twice as lonely as he had before, he got into his car.

Adrian froze as he reached for the ignition. He could still smell her floral scent in the air. Taking a deep breath, he relished it and dreamed of being able to bury his face in her neck where he could just breathe her in all night.

And in that moment, he made a decision.

Right or wrong, company policy be damned, he was going to find some way to make her his.

CHAPTER TWO

—

"Hey, Sam, could you come here for a minute?"

Sam cringed as Tiffany waylaid her outside of the break room at ten A.M. "What do you need?"

Tiffany huffed in agitation. "Adrian isn't here yet—"

"That's because he was here from eleven-thirty last night until three o'clock this morning. I imagine he's sleeping in."

"Whatever. I have to respond to the Waverley Valley customer, and he has yet to send me his e-mail."

Sam pursed her lips to keep from laughing. Oh, he'd written the e-mail all right. He'd answered the customer's complaints, point by point, with the most hilarious sarcasm she'd ever read. The last line of it had said, "All hail the goddess Discordia the day we let Lord Bone-Head's twenty-two teenage employees have unrestricted ordering capacity on our system."

Adrian was a riot.

And at the bottom of the e-mail, he'd pasted in the much more professional response that he had sent to their customer.

"I know he wrote it," Sam said seriously. "I'm sure he'll forward a copy as soon as he gets in."

"Well, he better, or I'm telling Randy about it." Tiffany glanced down the hallway, did a double-take, then gaped.

Sam turned her head to see what was going on.

She froze at the sight.

Oh, my.

Like all the other women in the hallway, Sam was transfixed by Adrian and that sexy, loose-limbed swagger of his as he came toward her. Dressed all in black, except for the hint of his white T-shirt peeking out of the V of his tailored black button-down shirt, he was dazzling.

The black leather jacket she had talked him into looked even better on him than she had imagined it would.

His goatee was gone and the new haircut gave a deeply poetic look to his chiseled features. He wore a pair of Way-farer sunglasses, and when he smiled, she saw deep dimples that had been masked all this time by his thick whiskers.

The man was *seriously* hot.

Regina, the receptionist, was headed to her desk when she passed him. Turning her head to watch him, she stared so intently at his rear that she walked straight into the wall.

Oblivious to the gaping women around him, Adrian made straight for Sam.

"Good morning," he said, flashing those dimples as he took his sunglasses off.

"Morning," Sam said, amazed at how normal her voice sounded given the amount of havoc his new look had on her senses. Now that he was this close, she could smell the leather and his Old Spice aftershave. Yum! Her entire body burned.

"Oh, Adrian!" Tiffany gushed as she twirled a strand of blond hair around her index finger. "We were just talking about you."

Adrian arched a brow at her. "What did I do now?"

"Oh, it was nothing bad. I was just asking about that silly old e-mail, but I know you're busy. So, you take your time and when you're ready, I'll take care of it for you."

My, how her tune has changed, Sam thought irritably. *Why is it, you find a good man, clean him up, and then the vultures start swooping in?*

Life was not fair.

"I sent the e-mail last night," Adrian said.

"How strange," Tiffany said with an obviously practiced frown. "I didn't see it in my in box."

"Did you forget to change it over from your personal e-mail account to the company servers again?"

"Oh," Tiffany said, stroking him lightly on the arm as she giggled and preened. "How silly of me. You know, I just can't keep all this computer stuff straight in my head. I'd really appreciate it if you'd show me to how to fix that."

"I'll send Scott down."

His phone rang. Adrian answered it while Tiffany ran a hungry look over his body.

Sam wanted to choke her. "Don't you have something you need to do?" she asked Tiffany.

Tiffany glared at her until Adrian hung up, then she smiled sweetly at him. "You know, if you've got a minute, right now—"

"Actually, I don't. I need to talk to Sam. Excuse us?"

"Oh, absolutely. I'm sure you *guys*—no offense, Sam—" she said, sweeping a hard look to Sam before giving Adrian a worshipful smile, "have computer problems to talk about. I'll see you"—she punctuated the word by touching Adrian on the chest—"later."

Sam had to force herself not to clobber Tiffany.

As soon as they were alone, Adrian bent down to whisper in her ear. "I did put the right colors together, didn't I?" he asked.

"Oh, yeah," Sam breathed as two women who were staring at Adrian collided behind him.

He let out a relieved sigh. "I was having a bad Heather flashback as I came in the door and three women looked at me and started giggling."

Sam could well imagine that. She felt giddy herself.

Adrian stroked his chin with his hand. "And I'm not sure about the face. I've had a beard or mustache since I turned seventeen. I feel really naked."

At that moment, she wished he *were* naked. Naked and in her arms doing the Wild Thing with her. "You shouldn't."

"You're sure I don't look like a girly-mon? Because I really don't want the guys up in design to start following me around."

"Oh, no," she said with a laugh. "There's nothing girly about the way you look."

"All right, but if the guys start harassing me, I might have to fire you."

She laughed at the empty threat.

His phone rang again and Regina paged him.

"It starts already," Sam said.

"Already? Hell, it started two hours ago, which is why I came on in," he mumbled as he flipped open his phone, and headed toward his office.

Sam bit her knuckles as she watched him walk away. She ran a lecherous gaze down his lean back and well-shaped rear. An image of those flat abs tormented her, and it was all she could do not to follow him into his office, lock the door, and keep him there until they were both sweaty and spent.

"Yo, A-dri-an!" Scott called as he passed by Sam's cube.

Sam cringed, knowing how much Adrian hated for someone to do that to him.

"What?" he snapped as he stuck his head over Randir's cube.

"Oh," Scott said. "You're not in your office. I was wondering what we're doing for lunch today?"

"We haven't discussed it."

"Well, it's eleven-thirty and I'm starving. Let's discuss it."

Adrian peeped over the cube wall to look at her. "Sam, you coming?"

"Depends on where you go."

"Well," Scott said to Adrian, "I was wondering if your sister's working at Chik-Fil-A today. I'm kind of broke, so if she'd spot us again, I'd really appreciate it."

"You mooch," Randir said. "I say we take him out back, and shoot him."

Adrian laughed as he picked up his phone and dialed it. "Hey, Mark? This is Adrian. Is Heather working today?"

"Hey, Sis," Adrian said after a brief pause. "Scott's

broke and wanted to know if you'd feed him again? Okay, we'll see you shortly." Hanging up, he looked at Sam. "Chik-Fil-A?"

"Sure, I'll go."

"I'll drive," Jack said from the cube opposite her. "I have the minivan today. But I warn you, it's full of toys."

The six of them gathered their things and headed for the door. Adrian fell in beside her, then reached an arm toward her.

Sam froze in nervous anticipation as it appeared he was about to put his arm around her, then he bent it up quickly and raked his hand through his hair.

Disappointed, she had all she could do not to pout.

Adrian cursed at himself as he realized what he'd almost done. And at work no less! Jeez! What was wrong with him?

But then, he knew. Sam had been sneaking looks at him all morning.

And he'd loved every minute of it.

Jack unlocked his van. Sam took the seat behind the driver's and Adrian quickly sat beside her. When she looked up and smiled, he felt like someone had sucker-punched him right in the gut.

"I really like that jacket," she said to him.

"Oh, Adrian," Scott teased from the front passenger seat as Jack started the van, then backed up. "You're just so cute today," he lisped. "Can I have a ride in your special Love Bytes machine after work?"

"Would you guys leave him alone?" Sam said.

"It's all right," Adrian said as he picked up a Game Boy from the seat and turned it on. "I'll just fire his ass after lunch."

Adrian played Centipede while Sam and the guys exchanged insults. He listened to them, all the while glancing sideways at Sam. Man, how he loved the way her eyes sparkled when she laughed.

*   *   *

As soon as they reached the mall, they piled out and headed to the food court. They had just entered the area when Sam caught sight of Heather standing beside a table with a guy dressed in a leather motorcycle jacket. He had three days' worth of black stubble on his face, and a death grip on Heather's arm.

Sam held her breath.

Rage descended on Adrian's face as he rushed toward them.

"Josh," Heather said in a pain-filled voice, trying to pry the man's hand off her upper arm. "You're hurting me."

"I'm going to do more than that if—"

"Let her go," Adrian growled as he grabbed Josh's hand and removed it from Heather's arm. He shoved the man back.

Josh raked a sneer over Adrian's body, but there was fear in his eyes as he took in the size of Adrian. "Look, pal, this is between me and my woman."

"No," Adrian said. "It's between you and my baby sister. And if you touch her again, it's going to be between you and me."

A wave of apprehension crossed Josh's face as he looked from Adrian to Heather. "I thought you said Adrian was a geek."

"He is," Heather said. "But he's a really *big* geek."

Josh angled a finger at Heather. "You remember what I said."

"Let me tell *you* something," Adrian said with a killing glare. "If I find you near my sister again, I'm going to play Picasso with your body parts."

Heather postured. "And he can do it too, he has a black belt."

Josh snarled at the two of them, then stalked off.

"Jeez, Heather," Adrian said as he turned to face her. "Can't you ever find a decent guy?"

"He's not always like that," Heather said dismissively. "He can be really sweet, sometimes."

Adrian's face turned hard, cold. "I better not find you near him again, and I mean it."

"Back off, Adrian. It's none of your business. You know, I'm not eleven years old anymore, and I don't need you coming to my rescue all the time."

"Fine," he snapped. "Then stop calling me every time you get into a jam."

"Fine," Heather snarled back at him. "Mom's right, you are just like your father. Worthless and mean."

Sam held her breath as a dark, angry pain descended over Adrian's face.

It was then Adrian must have remembered they were there, listening, because he looked to his left, saw them and locked his jaw.

Without a word, he walked off.

The guys stayed in the food court to comfort Heather while Sam ran after Adrian. He was halfway down the mall before she finally caught up to him.

"Hey?" she said as she pulled him to a stop with a gentle hand on his arm. "You okay?"

Adrian stared at her as he felt her soothing touch all the way through his body. "Why does she have to act that way?" he asked rhetorically. "I'll never understand you women, and why you're only attracted to pricks who run all over you, then turn on you if you dare open your mouth to defend yourself."

"Not all women are attracted to men like that."

"Yeah, right. Prove it."

Before he knew what she was doing, she stood up on her tiptoes, reached her arm around his neck, and brought his head down for a scorching kiss.

Adrian's head swam at the softness of her lips, of the feel of her tongue against his. He cupped her face with his hands and closed his eyes to better savor the moment.

She had her hand buried in his hair, sending chills the entire length of his body. He felt himself harden even more as a wave of her sweet feminine scent permeated his senses.

In that moment, he couldn't think of anything except

taking her home, stripping her jeans and sweater from her body, and keeping her that way until breakfast.

Sam didn't know where she'd found the courage to finally kiss him, but she was glad she had. She'd been dreaming of it all day long. And now that she'd actually done it, it was all she could do not to moan from the incredible taste of his lips. The warm, masculine smell of him.

Until it dawned on her what she was doing. She was kissing her boss less than five miles from work, in the middle of a mall crowded with Christmas shoppers where four of their co-workers could see them any second.

Pulling back, she let go of him. "I'm sorry," she whispered. "I shouldn't have done that."

But Adrian didn't let her get away. He caught her in his arms and pressed her against the store window behind her. Then, he kissed her so fiercely that she thought she might faint from it.

It was raw, demanding, and it made her so hot that she couldn't breathe. Couldn't think as she felt his heart pounding rapidly in time with hers.

Good Lord, the man knew how to give a kiss. Every part of her throbbed and ached for him. And when he ran his hands down her back to press her closer to his hips, she felt his hard erection against her stomach.

He wanted *her*.

In that instant, she felt she could fly.

"Neither should I," he whispered against her lips. "But the bad thing is, I want to do it again."

So did she.

He took a step back and put his hands in his jacket pockets.

"What are we going to do about this?" she asked tentatively.

"I don't know." He looked around them. "You probably should get back to the guys before someone sees us."

She took a step toward the food court, then noticed he hadn't budged. "Are you coming?"

He shook his head. "I'm not hungry. I'll go play at Radio Shack while you guys eat. Just pick me up on the way out."

"I'll stay with you."

He smiled. "I appreciate the thought, but Ms. Hypoglycemic can't go without lunch."

It was so like him to think of her, and that was one of the things she loved best about him. "All right."

He caught her hand before she left him, then kissed the back of her knuckles. "Thanks for coming after me."

"You're very welcome."

He let go and she felt a strange vacant hole in her stomach. Glancing back at him and the striking image he made smiling at her, she headed to the food court.

Sam waved at the guys as she went over to Chik-Fil-A and ordered a value meal.

"Is Adrian okay?" Heather asked.

"No. You embarrassed him."

"Well, you know, it's not my fault. He always has to act like he's Mr. Macho out to defend my honor all the time. It gets really old."

"He loves you, Heather. What's he supposed to do? Sit around and let you get hurt? Jeez, I'd kill for one of my brothers to do the things for me he does for you. I mean damn, girl, you let him go to work, knowing he's the boss, in ruined clothes while he *pays* you to embarrass him. I just don't understand you."

Heather looked away guiltily. "I do love him, you know. I just wish he'd quit trying to parent me all the time."

"Well, from what I've heard, he was pretty much the only parent you had growing up."

"I know," Heather said. "I remember when he was twelve and I was six, Mom couldn't afford a Christmas tree. I was crying on Christmas Eve because I didn't think Santa would come without one, so Adrian rode his bicycle down to the supermarket and talked the tree dealer into letting him work for one."

Heather sighed. "He's always doing really sweet things like that for me. I guess I really do take him for granted."

"Personally, I think a whole lot of people do."

Heather handed Sam her food.

"Wait," Heather whispered as Sam started to leave. She quickly bagged a sandwich, fries, and brownie. "Would you take this to him and tell him I'm really sorry?"

"Sure."

Sam made her way over to the guys who were eating. They were back to their usual bantering, but as she ate, she couldn't get the taste of Adrian's kiss out of her mind. That kiss had really done something to her.

Worse, she kept imagining him as a kid working on a cold Nashville parking lot so his baby sister would have a Christmas tree. It was such an Adrian thing to do.

And she wondered if anyone had ever done such a thing for him. But in her heart, she knew they hadn't.

Adrian took care of the world while no one took care of him.

Sam cracked open Adrian's office door. "Hey, I just wanted to let you know that I was leaving."

He turned around in his chair to face her. "Is it five already?"

"Five-thirty, actually."

"Oh." He rose from his chair and shrugged on his leather jacket. "I'll walk you out."

"Okay," she said, her heart pounding as every hormone in her body instantly fired.

There was an awkward silence between them as they walked down the hallway toward the side door where she parked.

"I, um . . . I had something I wanted to ask you," he said as he opened the door for her.

"Sure," she said in dread as she led the way across the lot to her car. "If you're worried about what happened this afternoon, don't be. I'm not going to tell anyone."

"Oh, I don't care about that. I mean, I care about that, but . . . shit," he breathed. "I never was any good at this.

So, I'll just do what I do best, and blurt it out. Would you like to go to the Christmas party with me?"

Sam smiled as her heart raced even faster. "Yes, I would. But only if you bring the mistletoe."

His gaze dropped to her lips and she wondered if he was imaging the feel of their kiss like she was.

"Great," he said. "Pick you up at three?"

"Sounds good. I'll give you the directions to my house tomorrow."

"Okay." He bent his head down like he was going to kiss her again, then he quickly shot back upright. "We're still at work."

Adrian watched as she got in her car, and a chill went up his spine that had nothing to do with the cold winter wind and everything to do with her.

She was something else. And he liked it.

She rolled her car window down.

Adrian leaned down to where he could speak to her without someone overhearing them. "You know, I really want to kiss you right now."

"Me, too."

Ask her back to your place. It was on the tip of his tongue, but he didn't dare.

"You better get back in," she said. "It's cold out here."

No, it wasn't. Not when he was standing so close to her. "Yeah," he breathed, "You're probably freezing."

She reached out and touched his hand. "I'll see you tomorrow."

Adrian gave a light squeeze to her hand even though what he wanted to do was hold it tight.

Letting go, he walked away from her, and with every step he took, he cursed himself for the stupidity. Why hadn't he asked her back to his apartment?

But then, he knew. If he had her alone in his place, his hands would be all over her. It was too soon, and the last thing he wanted was to drive her away from him.

He'd never wanted anything in his life the way he wanted Samantha Parker.

Closing his eyes, he did his best to banish the image in his mind of her naked in his arms. The imagined feel of her breath falling across his neck as he lost himself inside her body.

"I want you, Sam," he breathed as he watched her pull out of the lot. "And one way or another, I'm going to have you."

CHAPTER THREE

—

"Sam?"

Sam looked up to see Adrian's head poking out of his office door. "Yeah?"

"In my office. Now."

She swallowed at his low, even tone. It sounded strangely like the one he used to crawl all over Scott when Scott did something stupid.

Worse, he'd been avoiding her all day. He hadn't even gone to lunch with them.

Had she done something wrong?

Nervous, she got up and took the five steps that separated her cube from his office.

As soon as she was inside, he closed the door.

Sam's heart pounded. This wasn't good. Adrian never closed his door unless it was time for a major performance talk.

Eyes dark and features grim, he turned toward her.

Sam expected him to tell her to sit, so when he cupped her face in his hands, and pressed her back against his wall, she was stunned.

His breathing ragged, he lowered his head down and captured her lips with his.

And it wasn't just any kiss. It was scorching and demanding. Every hormone in her body jumped to attention. Closing her eyes, she relished the warm scent of him. The masterful feel of his tongue dancing with hers as his hands roamed over her shoulders and back, down to her hips. She wrapped her arms around his shoulders and moaned softly as her desire for him tripled.

He separated her legs with his thigh and cupped her buttocks as he set her down on that taut muscle. Sam groaned at the feeling of him between her legs. Her feet barely touched the floor as he surrounded her with warmth.

Her head light, she throbbed and ached for more of him.

Adrian knew he shouldn't be doing this, but he hadn't been able to stand it any longer. All day long, he'd been unable to think about anything other than the fact that she was only five feet away.

She was so intelligent, so much fun.

He wanted to devour her.

Adrian pulled back from the kiss to where he could nibble her lips as he buried his hand in her thick, dark hair. He laved a trail from her lips to her neck where he inhaled her.

He skimmed his hand up from her waist to the side of her breast. At the sound of her murmured pleasure, he felt his control slipping.

He ached for her. Burned for her in a way he'd never burned before and all he could think of was being inside her.

"I want you, Sam," he whispered.

Sam gave him a chiding stare. "I thought I was in trouble."

Adrian shook his head as he lost himself in those light eyes of hers. "I think I'm the one in trouble. Serious trouble."

He dipped his head to kiss her again.

His cell phone went off.

Growling, he answered it. "Scott, I'm in the middle of a damn important meeting. Send an e-mail."

Someone knocked on the door.

"Just a minute," Adrian snapped, then he brushed her cheek with his fingers, even though what he really wanted to do was lay her down on his desk and alleviate the vicious, throbbing ache in his groin.

Not to mention the one in his heart.

His breathing ragged, he let go of her. "I better let you get back to work."

She nodded, then kissed him hard on his lips.

The knock sounded again.

She smiled. "Duty calls."

Sam spent the rest of the day dreaming about that kiss. And as she watched people traipse in and out of Adrian's office, she felt like cursing. Couldn't they just leave him in peace?

"Hey!" Randir said as he came around her cube. "It's snowing really bad outside."

Sam looked up with a start. "What?"

"Oh, yeah, the roads are freezing." Randir stuck his head in Adrian's door. "I'm going home."

Adrian came out of his office. "Tell everyone to head out."

Since she lived fifty minutes away, Sam dialed her oldest brother's cell phone.

"Don't you dare head home," Teddy said sternly. "The roads are awful. I had to leave my Blazer at the bottom of the hill and walk home. Is there some place in La Vergne you can bunk for the night?"

"I guess. Thanks." She hung up.

"Why are you still here?" Adrian asked.

"My brother said the roads are frozen solid. Looks like I'll be spending the night on the cot in the first-aid room."

Adrian frowned. "You can't do that."

Like she had any choice, she thought wistfully. "Sure I can. I have the vending machines and the security guard for company. I'll be fine."

"Why don't you come home with me?" he asked stoically.

Sam hesitated as her heart pounded. If she did that, she had a really good idea what would happen.

But then, how bad would it be to make love to him all night?

She bit her lip in indecision. "I don't know."

At the hurt look on his face, she quickly added, "I bet

you get stuck here with me. I'm sure the Corvette isn't any better in this weather than my Honda."

"I'm not in the Vette. I drove my Bronco in."

She arched a brow. "I didn't know you had another car."

"Yeah. I love the Vette, but she's temperamental and she hates snow." He took her jacket off the peg inside her cube and held it open for her. "C'mon. I promise I'll behave."

Her stomach knotted in excitement and fear, she shrugged her coat on. "Okay."

Adrian led her out of the building, across the virtually empty parking lot to an older-model black Bronco and opened the door for her.

After he got in and started the car, Sam sat beside Adrian with her heart in her throat. She was so nervous, she was actually trembling. It'd been a long time since she'd been with a guy. A long time since she'd gone to a guy's place.

And she'd never loved a man as much as she did Adrian.

Should I make a move on him? Or should I wait for him to do something?

What if he thinks I'm fat? He was so well toned and she was . . . well, fleshy. What if it turned him off?

Good grief, her doubts and fears plagued her silly.

Adrian tried to think of something to say as he drove the ten-minute commute to his apartment.

But he couldn't.

His hands were actually sweating inside his gloves. He hadn't taken a girl home with him since college.

Should I make a move on her? Or should I wait for her to do something?

Is it too soon?

He didn't want to scare her off. He really liked her. And the last thing he wanted was for her to bolt for the door.

But he couldn't stand the thought of not having her.

By the time he pulled up next to his Corvette, his stomach was absolutely knotted.

"Do you have a roommate?" she asked as he walked her to his door.

"With the hours I keep? No one would put up with me." He unlocked the door and let her in.

Sam entered the living room, then froze. She'd never seen anything like it in her life.

"Good Lord, it looks like a Circuit City showroom," she said as her gaze darted over the big-screen TV, three leather recliners, DVD player, double-decker VCR, two computers, and a stereo bigger than her car.

His walls were stark white and completely bare. But at least the whole apartment was amazingly clean and well kept.

"Jeez. Adrian, you live like a bear in an electronic cave."

He laughed as he locked the door, then set his keys, security badge, and wallet in a bowl on the breakfast counter.

He shrugged his coat off and hung it up in a closet to her left. Sam took hers off and handed it to him.

"Should I ask about the three recliners?"

He shrugged. "Sometimes the guys come over to watch a game."

"So, why don't you have a couch?"

He looked offended by the very idea. "I'm not sitting my ass down next to another guy. Jeez, Sam, I thought you were raised with five brothers."

"Oh, yeah, how could I forget?" she said as she rolled her eyes at him. "The male and his territory."

He laughed as he gave her a brief tour of his place.

"Do you really need a PlayStation 2, Dreamcast, and Nintendo 64?" she asked. But what really amused her was the small TV next to the big one. She arched a questioning brow.

"Sometimes I play games while I'm watching the big TV," he said as if there were nothing unusual about it.

Sam smiled, until she glanced down at one of the chairs. Then she sobered. "You know, Adrian, you're quite a guy."

He gave her a puzzled frown.

"There's not many men who let their underwear watch TV while they're at work," she said, glancing to the pair in the seat of the chair closest to the window.

"Oh, jeez," he moaned as he grabbed them and rushed to the laundry room in the kitchen.

"I'm sorry," she said as she followed after him. "I didn't mean to embarrass you. I think it's funny. Besides, I used to have to do my brothers' laundry, and all I have to say is—"

He turned around at the same time she took a step forward. They collided.

Adrian's breath left his chest as soon as her breasts touched his arm. She looked up at him with her lips parted and before he could stop himself, he took advantage of it.

Sam wrapped her arms around his shoulders as she kissed him with all the passion and love flowing through her. And in that moment, she knew what was about to happen between them.

This was the moment she'd spent the last year dreaming of.

Scared and excited, she couldn't wait.

Adrian deepened his kiss as his hands roamed freely over her back, pressing her closer to him. Growling low in his throat, he pulled back from her lips and buried his mouth against her neck.

Sam hissed in pleasure as his hot tongue, lips, and teeth nibbled and suckled her. Chills swept through her entire body as her breasts tingled in response to his expert, masculine touch. Heat pooled itself into an aching throb between her legs.

The scent of leather and Old Spice tormented her unmercifully. Gracious, how she wanted this man.

No one had ever made her feel the way he did. Desirable. Beautiful.

And best of all, needed.

Tonight, she would show her love to him. Tonight, she would hold nothing back and she would hope for a time when perhaps he might love her in return.

Adrian's vision dulled as he inhaled the warm, sweet scent of her skin. And he wanted more of her.

He wanted all of her.

That need foremost on his mind, he ran his hand over her breast, and squeezed it gently. He moaned at the softness, and at the feel of her hardened nipple through her Santa sweater.

To his amazement, Sam answered the caress with one of her own as she reached down between their bodies and cupped him in her hand, through his jeans. Adrian growled as she stroked him, teased him, making his entire body quiver and burn for her.

She was bold with her caresses, and more than generous with her lips.

His body on fire, Adrian returned to her mouth as she unbuttoned his jeans, then slid her hand beneath the elastic band of his briefs to take him into her hand.

He sucked his breath in sharply between his teeth as he hardened to the point of pain.

"You are a big man," she whispered against his lips as she gently stroked his shaft.

"You're the only one who does that to me," he whispered. He ran his hands under her sweater, over her smooth, soft skin, to the back of her bra where he released the catch.

His breath caught as her breasts spilled out of the satin bra and into his hands. He reveled in the feel of those taut nipples in his palms and he couldn't wait to taste them. To run his tongue over the tiny ridges as he breathed her scent in.

Her soft flesh filled his hands past capacity and he loved it.

Then, she untucked his shirt and ran her hands over his chest and back, clutching at him in a way that made him dizzy.

The damned phone rang.

"Do you need to answer it?" she said breathlessly.

"To hell with it."

"What if it's work?"

"To hell with it."

She laughed.

He heard his answering machine pick up.

"Adrian?"

He flinched as he heard his mother's nasal, Southern drawl.

"Adrian, this is Mom. Are you there? If you are, pick up, honey. I need to talk to you."

His hormones instantly iced by the sound of his mother's voice, he pulled back. "I better answer it or she'll call every ten minutes from now on and start beeping me."

Devastated by the interruption, Sam licked her lips and tried to pull herself together as Adrian left her and picked up the cordless phone from the counter. He tucked his shirt back in and buttoned his pants.

"Hi, Mom," he said coolly as he left the kitchen, then went to his bedroom, and closed the door while Sam straightened her own clothes.

"Adrian, where have you been? I've been calling for an hour."

Sam went over to his answering machine to turn it off so that she wouldn't overhear their conversation, but it had so many unmarked buttons, she didn't know which one to press.

"I was at work."

"I wish you'd give me your work number. I need to be able to get a hold of you when something comes up."

"What do you need now, Mom?"

"I need you to come over and salt my driveway, so that I won't get stuck here tomorrow."

"Jesus, Mom, it's a forty-minute drive and the roads are iced over."

"I know, that's why I need you to come over, right now."

Sam frowned at his mother's insistence.

"Mom, I can't. I'm busy."

His mother gave a dramatic sigh. "Busy doing what? Playing with your stupid computers again? All I ask is a little, tiny favor and this is the thanks I get. Do you know,

I was in labor for thirty-six hours with you? I almost died giving birth."

"Yes, Mom, I know."

"Don't you take that tone with me, young man. I gave my life to you kids, and the least you can do is take care of me in my old age."

"You're only forty-seven."

"Don't you dare get smart with me. It's not like you have anything better to do. God forbid you should actually date and marry someone, and give me a grandchild."

"Would you please lay off me, Mom? I'm not in the mood."

"Fine," she said in a sarcastic tone that made Sam want to choke her. "You just stay there, and let me fend for myself. You're just like your worthless father."

"Would you leave Dad out of this?"

"You're just like him, you know. Selfish and worthless. It's a good thing you don't have a girlfriend. You'd probably just knock her up, and leave her, too."

Sam's heart lurched. Poor Adrian. It was a good thing he didn't have another phone or she'd pick it up and give his mother a piece of her mind.

"Just my luck," his mother continued. "To get stuck with an ungrateful son. I knew you should have been a girl. That's fine, though. I'll just call Heather and get her to do it."

"Jeez, Mom, Heather can hardly drive when the weather's clear and she lives farther away than I do."

"What do you care? At least I can depend on her."

"All right," Adrian snapped. "I'm coming, okay? Don't get her killed because you need your driveway salted."

"Oh, good."

Sam gaped at the sudden change in the woman's voice. Now that she was getting her way, she actually sounded nice.

"Love you, sweetie."

"Me, too." By his tone, Sam knew he had his teeth gritted.

The answering machine clicked off. Sam shook her head. She'd never heard anything like that in her life.

Adrian came out of the bedroom with his jaw ticking. "I have to go out for a little bit."

"Adrian, you can't do that. What if you have a wreck and get killed?"

"Trust me, I'm not that lucky."

"You're not funny."

He shrugged his heavy ski jacket on. Sam zipped it while he fixed the collar. "You be careful," she said, standing up on her tiptoes to kiss him.

Adrian nibbled her lips as warmth spread through him. Only Sam had ever said that to him. "I will. Lock the door behind me."

As soon as he was gone, Sam sighed. Adrian reminded her of a tolerant lion with cubs hanging off him while they nipped his skin. How could he stand it?

Shaking her head, Sam went to get herself a Coke. She opened the fridge and stared in disbelief. It was bare except for an almost-empty gallon of soured milk and a six-pack of beer.

Frowning, she opened his kitchen cabinets, taking inventory. One plate, two mismatched bowls, a cookie sheet, one medium-sized pot, three glasses, two coffee cups, coffee, and two half-empty boxes of cereal. That was it.

Unbelievable. She'd had no idea he lived like this. And now that she thought about it, she realized he didn't even have a Christmas tree in his apartment.

The phone rang again.

Sam ignored it until the answering machine picked up.

"Adrian?" Heather said. "Hey, I need you to call me back as soon as you hear this, okay? Um, I need you, big brother. And please don't yell at me. I had to write a check out for tuition today or else they'd cancel my classes. And I don't have the money to cover it. I'm also two weeks overdue on my rent again. I really need twelve hundred dollars by tomorrow. I swear, I won't ever again ask you for money. I know I said that last time, but I mean it this time. Anyway, please call me tonight. Love you."

Sam ached for him. When he had told her he watched out for his sister and mother, she'd had no idea just what a challenge the two of them were.

"That's *it*," she muttered as she grabbed her coat out of the closet. "It's time someone did something for you."

It was almost three hours later when Adrian finally got home. His head throbbed from his mother's incessant criticism. And the woman wondered why no man would ever stay with her for more than a few months.

If he had any sense, he'd take off, too. But he refused to do that to Heather. His sister could barely look after herself, let alone watch after their mother.

Pushing the thoughts out of his mind, he opened the door. He frowned as he caught a whiff of something really good.

Must be his neighbor's dinner again, he thought as he closed and locked the door. He hung up his coat.

"Sam?" he called, not seeing her in the living room.

"I'm right here," she said from the kitchen.

Adrian turned, then froze as his breath left his body. Sam was standing at the sink wearing nothing but one of his flannel shirts. It was huge on her, reaching all the way to her knees.

The sight floored him.

"I hope you don't mind," she said as she pulled at the collar. "I fell on my way back and got mud all over my clothes."

"Fell?" It was then he realized the warm, delicious aroma was coming from his stove. Damn, the thing actually worked!

He frowned. "What did you do?"

She moved toward him with a coffee cup in her hands. "Here," she said, handing him hot chocolate. "I'm sure you're frozen."

He had been until he saw her half-dressed. Now, he felt as if he were on fire. "Where did this come from?"

She smiled. "I walked down to the market on the corner."

He was stunned. He'd never in his life come home to such a warm welcome.

And in that moment, he knew he loved her.

Setting the cup down on his breakfast counter, he pulled her into his arms and held her close.

Sam trembled at the contact. He ran his hands down her back, then to her bare hips.

"Oh, God," he breathed. "You're naked under there."

Sam laughed. "I know."

Adrian's thoughts scattered as he touched her bare buttocks. Her skin was so incredibly soft while he was harder than he'd ever been before.

Bending down, he scooped her up in his arms and carried her to the bedroom.

Sam wrapped her arms around his neck, amazed he was able to carry her so easily. And when he laid her on the bed, she smiled, knowing this was what she'd wanted since the first time she'd seen him greeting her in the lobby for her interview last year.

She got up on her knees and pulled his shirt over his head. Her gaze feasted on the sight of all that strong, tawny skin as she ran her hands over his delectable flesh.

Good gracious, the man had a gorgeous body, and she couldn't wait to taste every inch of it.

The way he watched her with his eyes dark and hungry, his breathing ragged, made her burn even more for him. How could a man like this want *her*?

Sam hesitated as she placed her hands on the top button of his jeans. "I want you to know that I'm not easy," she whispered.

"It never crossed my mind," he said as he cupped her face in his hands. He moved to kiss her, but she pulled back.

She met his confused gaze. "I've only been with one other guy. My college boyfriend."

"Okay," he said, dipping his head toward hers.

She laughed as she dodged his lips again. "Would you listen for a second?"

He arched a brow at her.

"I wanted to let you know that I'm not on the pill or anything."

Adrian went rigid. Cursing, he took a step back from the bed. "Well, since we're confessing things, I have to tell you, I haven't been with a woman since college, either. And I threw out my condoms last year after it occurred to me that they were older than I was." Adrian retrieved his shirt from the floor.

Damn it, he was so hard it hurt. And all he could think of was taking her, consequences be damned.

But he couldn't do that. He wasn't about to take a chance on getting her pregnant. In spite of what his mother thought, he wasn't his father.

It figures. Whatever made you think you could have a woman like her, anyway?

Sam frowned as he stalked out of the room. She started to call him back, then reconsidered. He needed to eat first.

She went after him. "You hungry?"

Adrian nodded, but by his face she could tell food was the last thing he wanted.

Sam served him a bowl of chili.

Adrian stood at the counter while he ate it.

Bemused, Sam watched as he refused to look at her. And the only words he uttered were a very brief compliment on how good her chili tasted and a simple thank-you.

As soon as he was finished, Adrian placed the bowl in the sink, then went to sit in his recliner.

Picking up his remote for the stereo, he clicked on his CD player. He had to do something to distract himself from those luscious legs peeking out from under her shirt. He rotated the discs to Matchbox 20.

Suddenly, he felt Sam beside his chair. He glanced at her, then did a double-take as he saw her shirt unbuttoned all the way to her navel. Even worse, the swell of one breast was so obvious that it sent a wave of heat straight through his groin.

"Don't tease me, Sam," he said hoarsely.

With a tight-lipped smile, she lifted up the hem of the shirt to gift him with a glimpse of the dark curls at the juncture of her thighs before she climbed into his lap.

"Sam," he groaned as she reached to unbutton his pants. His entire body burned and, worse, her feminine, floral scent was making him insane. If she didn't get up, he was going to have her regardless of his common sense. "Please don't."

She took his hands in hers and led them to her breasts.

Adrian leaned his head back and moaned at the softness of her bare breasts in his hands.

Sam kissed him then, and he felt something strange in her mouth.

Adrian pulled back to see her with a wrapped condom between her teeth.

The smile on her face was devilish as she removed the package. "I bought them at the store, just in case."

Growling low in his throat, he kissed her fiercely.

Sam gasped as he rose to his feet with her still in his lap. She wrapped her arms and legs around him as he carried her back to his bed with his hands firmly gripping her bare bottom.

He set her on the bed, then pulled his shirt over his head again as she finished unfastening his jeans. She removed his clothes from him.

Sam gaped at the sight of his lean muscles as she saw him naked for the first time. Every single inch of his lean, hard body was toned and perfect. Never had she seen anything like it.

Her face burned as she saw the size of his erection.

She ran her hands over the veins on his forearms, over the strength of a body she'd never dared hope to touch. His skin was so soft, his muscles so hard. It reminded her of velvet stretched over steel.

She'd never imagined her programming genius would

have the body of a Greek god. But he truly did.

Adrian hesitated as he stared at her in his bed, wearing his shirt. She was beautiful there. So soft, warm, and giving.

His desire surged through him like lava as he joined her in the bed and laid her back against the mattress. He rained kisses over her face and neck as he did his best to control himself.

His body demanded he get down to business with her, but his heart wanted to savor her for as long as he could. Even if it killed him.

Adrian groaned as she rolled him over onto his back and straddled his waist. He liked her feistiness. But most of all, he liked her on top of him.

She leaned over his chest and ran her tongue along the edge of his jaw, sending a thousand needlelike chills over his body as she rubbed herself against his stomach.

It shook him all the way to his soul.

"I'm so glad you got rid of that goatee," she whispered in his ear a second before she ran her tongue around the curve of his jaw.

Adrian held her against him. "If I'd known you would do this, I'd have shaved it off the first week you came to work."

She laughed.

He buried his lips in the curve of her shoulder, inhaling the sweet scent of her skin. His head swam from the moistness of her on his stomach.

Needing her in a way that terrified him, he unbuttoned her shirt and pulled it from her shoulders. "You are so beautiful," he breathed as he saw her naked.

Her curves were every bit as full and lush as he had imagined. And her breasts . . .

He could stare at those luscious breasts all night long.

His breathing ragged, he reached up and cupped them in his hands. She trembled in response, delighting him even more.

He dropped his gaze down to the moist curls that were

driving him crazy, the moist curls that covered the part of her he couldn't wait to have.

Sitting up, he kissed her furiously as he skimmed his hand from her breast, down her smooth, soft stomach to the tangled curls and into the sleek, wet cleft.

Sam hissed at the pleasure of his long, lean fingers stroking her intimately. She'd never felt anything better, until he slid them inside her. In and out, and around, those fingers tormented her with a fiery pleasure she feared might actually consume her.

Shamelessly, she rubbed herself against him, wanting him in a way that went beyond the physical.

Her body on fire, she pushed him back against the bed, then moved to kiss a trail down his chest.

Adrian hissed as Sam brushed her lips against his taut nipple and when she drew it into her mouth he thought he would die from the pleasure of her tongue on his skin.

He buried his hands in her hair, cupping her face gently as he let the love he felt for her wash over him. She was so giving, so kind. Never in his life had anyone taken care of him. Never had anyone cared.

But Sam did, and it rocked him all the way to his heart.

"Touch me, Sam," he breathed, wanting to feel her hand against him again.

She moved herself lower, trailing her tongue and lips down his abdomen, to his navel, his hip, where she tormented him mercilessly with little nibbles that rocked his entire body.

Delirious from her touch, he closed his eyes in painful anticipation as she finally brushed her hand through the curls at the center of his body. She cupped him in her hand.

Adrian arched his back, growling at the softness of her fingers stroking his shaft.

"Yes," he moaned, writhing from the unbelievable sensations that ripped through him.

And before he knew what she was doing, she moved her head lower and licked a slow, torturous path from the base of his shaft, all the way to the tip.

Adrian hissed at the unexpected, blind ecstasy that tore through him.

Sam smiled as she felt him shivering around her. Her only thought to give him more pleasure, she took him into her mouth.

She knew she was making him crazy, and she loved every minute of it. Adrian deserved to be loved by someone who wouldn't take him for granted, and she wanted to show him just how much he meant to her. Just how much she needed him.

Adrian clenched his fists in the sheets at the incredible sensation of her tongue and lips covering him. No one had ever done that to him before, and he couldn't believe just how good it felt.

His body trembling, he couldn't stand not tasting her in return.

He had to have her. Now!

Sam lifted her head as Adrian sat up. His eyes dark and shuttered, he moved until his body was lying in the opposite direction of hers. He ran his mouth and tongue over her stomach as he skimmed a hand down her hips, blazing a scorching trail of heat.

His touch literally burned her from the inside out as he trailed it up her inner thigh, urging her to open her legs for him.

He nudged her legs farther apart, then buried his lips at the center of her body.

"Adrian!" she breathed as he tormented her.

Sam moaned at the sensation of his mouth on her as he nibbled and licked. His tongue and fingers swirled around her, intensifying her pleasure.

Trembling, she returned to torment him the same way.

She writhed as he continued and as she tasted him.

There was such fire and magic in his touch. It scorched her in a way that was indescribable. No wonder she loved this man.

She gave herself to him without reservations or fear. There was something so special in this equal sharing, equal giving. It touched her profoundly and she knew in her heart that she would never be the same.

Sam's head was light as he gave careful consideration to her, and when he slid two fingers inside her body and stroked her, she moaned in ecstasy.

Biting her lip, she closed her eyes as his fingers delved deep and hard inside her, swirling around with the promise of what was to come while he laved her even faster.

Sam's entire body shivered and jerked involuntarily in response to his touch.

Her head spun from the intense sensations. The pleasure was so incredible, so extreme, as it built inside her until she could stand no more.

Suddenly, her entire body exploded as white-hot ecstasy tore through her in ever-increasing waves. Sam cried out as her release came.

Panting, she couldn't move.

"That's it," he said, his skin covered in sweat. "I have to be inside you."

Sam pulled back from him and reached for the condom a few inches from her.

Adrian tensed as she gently slid the cool condom over his hot, swollen shaft. Then she cupped him in her hand. Her touch singed him as his body quivered in response.

How could such tiny hands wreak so much havoc on him?

Needing to feel her more than he needed to breathe, Adrian pressed her back against the mattress, then separated her thighs with his knees.

You are about to violate your Web designer.

He didn't know where that thought came from, but it ripped through his mind as he pressed the tip of his shaft against her core.

What was he doing?

"Adrian?" she asked as she looked up at him with a frown. "Is something wrong?"

"Are you sure you want this?" he asked as he looked down at her. "If anyone finds out, we could get fired."

"Then I'll find another job," she said, lifting her hips toward his.

Joy ripped through him. Taking her hand into his, he stared into her eyes, then drove himself deep inside her body.

They moaned together.

Sam couldn't believe the fullness of him as he rocked his hips against hers. He went so deep inside her, she could swear he touched her womb as fierce, hot stabs of pleasure tormented her.

She wrapped her legs around his lean waist and savored the feel of his muscles flexing in and around her. She ran her hands down his back, over the chills that covered his body as she met him stroke for stroke.

He was spectacular.

"You feel so good," he breathed in her ear as he rocked his hips, hard and fierce, against hers. "I could stay inside you forever."

She was sure she didn't feel half as good to him as he felt to her. He lowered his upper body to where she could nuzzle his neck as he thrust into her.

Sam wrapped her legs tight about his hips, then she rolled over with him.

Adrian looked up, startled, as he found himself beneath her. She took his hands in hers and placed them on her hips. Then, holding them in hers, she lifted herself up to the tip of his shaft, before she lowered herself onto him.

He growled at the feel of her body on his as she rode him fast and furiously. He'd never felt anything like it.

"You're making my toes curl," she breathed.

"I plan to make more than that curl before the night is over," he said as she released his hands and leaned forward.

Adrian ran his hands over her breasts, cupping them gently as she continued to stroke him with her body.

Why had he waited a year before kissing her?

It terrified him when he thought of how close he'd come to never acting on his desire. What if he had let her get away without ever having tasted her lips? Her body?

And in that instant, a wave of possessiveness washed over him. He would never let her go.

She belonged to him.

Sam watched Adrian watch her. His dark eyes were shuttered, but the look of pleasure on his face tore through her.

She ran her hand over his stubbled cheeks, grateful that she had finally kissed him. This moment far exceeded any fantasy she'd ever had about him.

Her body aching with bliss, she could feel her pleasure mounting again with every forceful stroke she delivered to him. She moved her hips faster as Adrian lifted his hips to drive himself even deeper.

"Oh, my goodness," she breathed as her body became even hotter as massive, wrenching stabs of pleasure tore through her.

Adrian rolled over with her then, and placed her beneath him. His eyes wild, he quickened his pace.

Sam moaned at the feel of him sliding in and out, fast, deep, hard.

And then suddenly, an indefinable ecstasy exploded through her body in resounding ripples. Sam gasped at the same time Adrian threw his head back and roared as he delivered two more long, deep thrusts to her. His entire body convulsed around her as he released himself.

He collapsed on top of her and buried his face in her neck.

Sam held him there, cradled in her arms and legs as she just listened to him breathe. She felt his heart pounding against her chest and sweat covered them both.

This was a perfect, peaceful moment that she wished she could hold on to forever.

"That was the most incredible experience I've ever had," he whispered in her ear as he cradled her gently in his strong arms.

"No kidding," she said as she ran her hands over his hard biceps, then kissed him tenderly on his chest. "You know, I've never done that before."

"Done what?"

"Orgasmed."

Adrian smiled. He was glad he'd been the man who had shown her the full depth of her sexuality. Cupping her head in his hand, he pulled her lips to his for a scorching kiss.

The phone rang.

"I swear, I hate those things," he snarled.

"Oh," Sam said as she let go of him. "I forgot to tell you Heather called."

Carefully, he withdrew from her. "Then I'm sure that's her," he said, reaching for the cordless phone on his nightstand.

"Hi, Heather," he said in a tone that was half a growl.

Sam could hear just a hint of Heather's chattering on the other end.

"Damn, Heather. What do you do with your money? I pay you two hundred and fifty dollars a week to do my laundry and buy groceries for me, and half the time you don't even do it."

She heard Heather chattering again as Adrian ran his hand through his hair and clenched it tight.

Adrian got out of bed and reached for his pants as he listened to her. Biting her lip, Sam admired the perfect shape of his buttocks and rear as he stooped over.

"Give me a break," he said as he fastened his jeans. "I worked three jobs in college and no one ever . . ."

He went rigid. "I'm sorry," he said. "Just stop crying, okay? Heather, please stop crying."

Sam sat up as he walked out of the room.

Frowning, she pulled her shirt on and followed after him.

He wiggled his mouse at his computer. "I'm doing it right now," he said in a gentle voice. He cursed again. "You only have two dollars in your account, did you know that? What are you living on?"

His jaw ticked, but his voice was patient. "All right, I'm transferring two grand over to you, but this is it, Heather. I work too damned hard just to give it away to you because you decide you need a Christmas vacation in Daytona for a week."

He clicked the phone off and tossed it on his desk.

Sam moved to stand behind him. She ran her hand over his back. "You are a wonderful man."

"I'm an idiot," he said under his breath. "I don't know why I put up with them."

"You love them."

"I wonder sometimes. God, I'm just so tired of everyone needing me all the time."

Sam went cold at his words. His dependability was what she loved about him most, and in truth that was what she wanted. Someone she could depend on who wouldn't disappoint her. She was tired of unkept promises.

Sam, you fool. No one is ever going to put you first. When are you going to realize that?

Her father had done what Adrian's had, he'd abandoned them. And her worst fear was to fall in love with some thoughtless, woman-chasing jerk who dumped her for a trophy girlfriend the minute she passed the age of thirty.

She didn't want a little boy, she wanted a man.

And she had hoped Adrian would be that man.

"Is something wrong?" he asked.

She shook her head, then brushed her hand over his whiskered cheek.

Please don't disappoint me, too. The words were on the tip of her tongue. But she didn't dare utter them aloud. Didn't dare give him any more ways to hurt her. He already held a place in her heart where only he could destroy it.

"Why don't we go back to bed?" she whispered.

He looked up at her with those dimples flashing. Then, he scooped her up in his arms and ran with her back to the bedroom.

CHAPTER FOUR

—

"Hi, Adrian," Sam said as soon as he answered his cell phone.

"Hey, sweet, what's wrong? You sound upset."

God, how she loved the sound of his deep, caring voice. It comforted her on a level that defied explanation.

"My brother forgot to pick up my mom's Christmas tree and she's having a hissy fit. I'm over here at the lot and there's no way I can make it back home and get ready in time. Is it okay if we just hook up at the hotel?"

"Sure. Is there anything I can do for you?"

She felt tears well at his offer. This last week had been the best of her life. After they had returned to work, they had kept quiet about their relationship, but it hadn't been easy. More nights than not, she'd left work first, then gone over to his apartment to fix dinner and wait for him.

He'd even given her a key.

"Thanks," she said, "but I've got it. I'll see you at the hotel."

"I'll be waiting for you in the lobby."

Worried, Adrian paced the hotel lobby. The temperature outside was steadily falling, and the news had been calling for a bad snowstorm later that evening. He'd tried to call Sam a dozen times to warn her not to come out this far, but she'd turned her cell phone off.

The door opened.

Adrian looked up and felt his jaw drop as Sam swept in.

She was wearing a Renaissance-style dress with a high

waist, long flowing sleeves, and ballerina slippers. Her hair was down around her face and she had a light ribbon braided across the top of her hair with flowers. She looked just like Guinevere.

And he loved it.

No, he corrected himself, he loved her.

Sam paused as she caught sight of Adrian staring at her. He looked gorgeous in his black jeans and sweater. He'd even gone to the trouble of fixing his hair and she knew how much he hated doing that.

Better still, his entire face lit up as his gaze met hers.

"My lady, you are beautiful," he said as she drew near him. He took her hand in his and kissed the back of her knuckles.

The warmth of his hand startled her. He took her coat from her hands and offered her his arm.

Feeling like a heroine in a romance novel, Sam took his arm and allowed him to lead her into the party.

"Wow, Sam," Randir said as he saw them. "You clean up good."

She laughed. "Thanks, I think."

While Adrian went to get her something to drink, she took a seat at the large, round table with the guys from her department.

"Oh, Adrian," Scott teased as soon as he returned. "You're just so thoughtful. Want to go get me a Coke?"

"No," Adrian said as he sat down beside her.

Sam did her best to appear nonchalant and distanced from Adrian, but it wasn't easy when all she wanted to do was lean back into his arms and have him hold her like he did in the early morning hours.

How she loved curling up with him in his favorite recliner, watching TV or listening to music while they fed each other popcorn. Naked.

She'd never been overly comfortable with her body, but Adrian seemed to love it and she loved him for it.

He gave her a meaningful look, then slid his gaze toward the lobby. "I need to go make a call."

Sam waited until he was out of sight before she excused herself to go to the bathroom.

She met Adrian in the lobby where he pulled her into a hidden, dark corner. "Why are we here?" he asked as he pressed her back against the wall.

She trembled at the strength of his chest against her breasts as he cupped her face in his hands and stared down at her with heat in his eyes. "Because it's a free meal?" she asked impishly.

"I'd rather be at home, making love to you."

"Mmm, me, too."

He kissed her then.

"Hey, Adrian!"

They both went tense at hearing Randy's voice.

Adrian stepped out of the corner while Sam pressed herself against the wall, hopefully out of Randy's sight.

"Hi, Randy. How's it going?"

"Great. I meant to tell you that Greg Wilson is going to applaud your team tonight after dinner. We hit the million-dollar mark for the Christmas season this morning. Congratulations. Greg says he's going to double your bonus and give you a raise."

"Thanks."

"So, what are you doing out here?" Randy asked. "C'mon, let's go say hi to Greg. I know he wants to shake your hand."

Sam listened with pride. Greg Wilson was on the pompous side, but he owned one of the largest privately held corporations in the country. For him to want to spend six seconds in your company was a big compliment.

As soon as the coast was clear, she went to the ladies' room.

She had barely closed the door on her stall when she heard Tiffany and a gaggle of her girlfriends sweep into the bathroom.

"Did you see Adrian?" Tiffany said to them.

"Are you kidding?" Barbara Mason said breathlessly. "How could anyone miss such a baby doll?"

"I heard that." Sam didn't recognize that voice.

"Yeah, well," Tiffany said in a loud whisper, "I'm going to nail that boy tonight."

Her friends laughed as Sam saw red. Tiffany better lay off Adrian, if she wanted to keep that perfect nose of hers.

"Right," Barbara said in disbelief.

"I am," Tiffany bragged. "I rented a room upstairs and as soon as I see him, I'm going to get him up there and have my wicked way with him."

They left the bathroom.

Sam clenched her fists. How dare she.

Her eyes narrowed, she left the bathroom and went after Adrian to warn him.

There was no need.

Tiffany had him cornered outside the ballroom. Worse, they were locked in a fiery kiss with Tiffany's hands on his waist and neck.

Sam froze at the sight as pain tore through her.

Her first impulse was to tear them apart and slug Tiffany. And if she wasn't so stunned, she might have actually done it.

But she couldn't move.

Not while her heart was slowly splintering into a million pieces.

And what hurt her most was the fact that Adrian would kiss Tiffany out in front of everyone while he wouldn't even so much as touch her hand when anyone was around.

Her tears swelled, but she blinked them back. She wouldn't give either one of them the satisfaction of seeing just how much damage they had done to her.

God, she was such a stupid fool. How could she have thought Adrian was any different than her own father?

Tiffany pulled away, and handed him a card key. "It's room 316," she said seductively. "I'll see you in twenty minutes."

Sam went numb as even more pain washed over her. How could he?

He's a man! Look at Tiffany.

How on earth could you ever compete with that?

Heartsick and aching, Sam rushed back to her table. She gathered her purse and coat.

"You okay?" Randir asked.

"No," she said, swallowing her tears. "I need to go home. I'll see you guys Monday."

Adrian waited and waited for Sam. Where was she? Had she gone back in when he wasn't looking?

He went to check, and as soon as he saw her coat was missing, a feeling of dread washed over him. "Where's Sam?"

Randir shrugged. "She went home."

"What?"

"She said she didn't feel well."

Adrian pulled his phone out of its cradle and dialed her cell phone.

No answer.

Cursing, he ran after her.

A heavy snowfall had started as he reached his Bronco, got in, and went to find her.

Sam wept the whole way to Spring Hill. She didn't really notice the icy roads until she had to turn onto Nashville Highway to reach her house. Her car started skidding.

Terrified, she held her breath until she landed safely in a ditch.

Her heart pounding, she was glad she hadn't been physically hurt. She picked up her cell phone to call her brothers, then saw the battery was dead.

"Damn it!" she snarled as she slammed her fist against the steering wheel. "What next?"

Angry and hurt, she wiped her eyes, then shoved open her door and started the five-mile walk to her rented house.

Adrian's heart raced as he realized how hazardous the roads were becoming. Sam's little Honda was about as safe in weather like this as his Corvette.

Why had she left? It didn't make any sense to him.

He turned onto Nashville Highway and saw her car in the ditch. Terrified at the sight, Adrian pulled to the side of the road and got out. Running up to her car, he saw it was empty.

She was out walking in 26 degrees?

He shook his head as he remembered her thin shoes and dress. She would freeze to death! Damn her independence. Couldn't she ever let anyone do anything for her?

He ran back to his Bronco. Getting in, he tried to start it.

"No!" he snarled as the starter clicked without firing the engine. He tried again, but still the car refused to start.

Pulling out his cell phone, he called the only other person he knew who lived in Spring Hill.

"Hey, Trey," he said as his friend picked up. "I need a huge favor from you."

Sam was absolutely freezing. Her shoes were soaking wet and she had all but lost the feeling in her feet.

Worse, she still had a mile to go to get home. And over and over again, all she could see was Adrian kissing Tiffany.

"Why, Adrian?" she breathed, clutching her coat tighter around her. "Why wasn't I good enough?"

Suddenly, she heard a strange clip-clopping sound coming from behind her.

What on earth?

It sounded vaguely like hooves. Turning around, she saw . . .

No, it couldn't be.

Sam blinked, not trusting her eyes.

The image only got clearer as the snowfall became heavier.

It was a knight. A knight in black leather.

Frowning, she watched as Adrian rode up to her on the back of a white stallion. Her mouth wide open, she looked at him as he reined to a stop by her side.

"Methinks milady damsel doth be in distress."

She shook her head at his fake medieval English way of speaking. Those deep, dark, chocolate-brown eyes stared at her with a heat that instantly warmed her freezing bones.

"Adrian?" she gasped.

"Sir Adrian," he corrected with a smile. He reached his hand down to her.

Without thinking, she took it and allowed him to pull her up to sit before him on the medieval-style saddle. He wrapped her up in two blankets as he adjusted her in front of him.

"What are you doing here?" she asked in disbelief. "I thought you were with Tiffany." As she said the name, her rage ignited.

"Tiffany?" he asked with a frown. "Why would you . . ."

She saw the color darken his cheeks.

"Yes," she snarled at him. "I saw you two. And you took her room key."

"Didn't you see me give it back?"

Sam hesitated. "You gave it back?"

"Yes. A few minutes after she left."

"You kept it a few minutes?" she snarled. "You skunk. How could you do—"

He stopped her words with a heated kiss.

"Don't yell at me, Sam," he said as he pulled back. "It wasn't my fault. I was waiting for you when she grabbed me from behind. At first, I thought it was you. Then she swept around me and put a lip-lock on me so fast I didn't know what to do. In case you haven't noticed, women don't usually do things like that to me. She caught me off guard."

"You looked like you were enjoying it to me."

"I was too stunned to move. And when she handed me the key, it took a full minute before it dawned on me what it was."

"A full minute?"

"I know you don't believe me, but if I wanted Tiffany, then why am I out here on a horse, freezing?"

"I don't know. Why are you here on a horse, freezing?"

"Because I love you, and I wanted to come to your rescue."

Sam choked on a sob. "Really?"

He tilted her chin up to look at him. "Don't ever doubt me, Sam. You're the only woman I've *ever* wanted to take care of."

Coming from him, that meant something.

She smiled as he kicked the horse forward toward the setting sun.

And in that moment, Sam knew she had the best Christmas present ever. She had her knight in shining leather.

EPILOGUE

—

CHRISTMAS DAY

Adrian let out a tired sigh as he pulled up to his apartment, just after noon. He'd spent most of the morning at work, alone, doing his best not to call and disturb Sam. She was spending the day with her family, while his had fled. Heather had gone to Daytona, and his mother was on a cruise in Alaska with her latest boyfriend.

But then, there was nothing unusual about that. He hadn't had a family Christmas since he was fifteen.

For the last eleven years, Christmas had meant nothing more than a heated TV dinner eaten in front of bad television shows.

"I hate Christmas," he muttered as he got out of his car, and went to his apartment.

He opened his door. Then, he froze dead in his tracks.

Someone had put a small Christmas tree in his living room and decorated it.

Frowning, Adrian closed the door and took his coat off, then went to the tree where a medieval-looking note card was tied with a ribbon to a branch.

He flipped it open.

Milord, Knight in Shining Armor, methinks thou hast a present in thy chamber.

He smiled at Sam's writing. She must have stopped by while he'd been at work. How he wished she'd called him. He'd love to see her today.

Oh, well, she'd be at work tomorrow.

Holding the card to his heart, he went to see what she'd left for him. He opened the door to his bedroom and went stock-still as his jaw fell open.

Sam was lying on his bed dressed in a teddy that made his mouth water, and she had a bow tied around her neck.

"Where have you been?" she asked with a seductive smile as she closed the book she'd been reading and put it on his nightstand.

Adrian couldn't speak, since his tongue was hanging on the floor.

Her smile widened as she left the bed and moved to stand in front of him. "Carpet got your tongue?" she asked.

He smiled.

Cupping her face in his hands, he stared in awe. "I thought you were going over to your mom's."

"I am for dinner. But I wanted to surprise you."

Adrian pulled her to him and kissed her until he couldn't stand it anymore. He wanted her in a way he had never wanted anything else.

And that flimsy outfit that barely covered her and left nothing to his imagination, was making him way too hard for comfort.

Growling, he pulled his clothes off in record time, then tossed her over his shoulder and deposited her gently on the bed.

Sam laughed.

Adrian ran his hand down the curve of her thigh, amazed at how much he loved her.

Sam kissed Adrian's bare shoulder as he reached into his nightstand for a condom.

He turned to her then, but instead of handing the condom to her as he normally did, he kissed her.

She felt something strange in his mouth.

Pulling back, she frowned as he pulled a ring out from between his teeth and handed it to her.

"I was going to give this to you tomorrow at dinner," he said, looking a bit sheepish. "But since you're here . . ."

Completely stunned, Sam couldn't breathe as she stared at the ring. It was a one-carat, heart-shaped diamond engagement ring in a medieval-style setting that made her heart pound.

Tears welled in her eyes as she blinked in disbelief. "Are you sure about this?"

He ran his hand down her arm. "You're the only thing in my life I've ever been sure about," he whispered before he took the ring back.

He left the bed and went down on one knee beside it, then took her hand into his.

Tears fell down her cheeks at the sight of Adrian naked on the floor.

"Samantha Jane Parker, will you marry me?"

She launched herself at him and knocked him flat against the floor. "Of course I will."

He laughed as she straddled his bare stomach.

Adrian placed the ring on her left hand, then he kissed it. "I love you, Sam."

"I love you, Adrian," she whispered, knowing in her heart that she had finally found her one, true knight in shining armor. And she was never, ever going to let him go.

Naughty Under
the Mistletoe

—

CARLY PHILLIPS

To Mom and Dad
who made me believe I could do anything.
To Phil
who loves and supports me through everything. And
to Jackie and Jennifer
who make it all worthwhile.

CHAPTER ONE

—

Antonia Larson fastened the white fur anklet adorned by three silver bells and a green velvet bow, closing the accessory around her leg with a single snap. From the radio on the edge of her desk, a traditional Christmas carol ended and the Bruce Springsteen version of "Santa Claus Is Coming to Town" now reverberated through her small office. Pulling her hat over her head and securing it with bobby pins, she hummed her own off-key rendition of her favorite Christmas tune. She twirled once, pleased with the jingling accompaniment to the gruff voice of The Boss.

If Santa was coming to town, he wasn't going to find Toni being a good girl. Not this year. Not this night. Tonight she was a woman on a mission. A mission to seduce the man she'd been attracted to for too long. She planned to act on what was a physical attraction and indulge in a safe interlude she could easily walk away from when their time together was through. Something Stephan, the firm's confirmed self-proclaimed bachelor, would appreciate and understand.

Because they'd been working closely as colleagues, acting on her desire had been impossible until now—but today had been her last day of work before the long holiday vacation. When she returned after the New Year, she'd be in the new suburban offices of Corbin and Sons. Work and office protocol no longer stood between them. Nothing did except her courage and the nice-girl role she'd played all her life. A role she could afford to let go of, at least this once.

After yet another night of tossing and turning for hours

in her lonely double bed, she'd pulled out the December issue of the women's magazine she'd subscribed to on a whim. What other reason could there be since she had no time in her busy lawyer's life to read tips on how to attract men and what turned them on?

But as she'd read the steamy article on naughty versus nice, Toni realized she'd spent the better part of her life as a nice girl, following the rules to get ahead and working overtime to make a good impression. Her two thousand–plus billables over the last few years had put her in a prime position for a promotion. The ailing Mr. Corbin had been thrilled when he'd named her the senior associate to work with the as-of-yet unnamed partner who'd run the new office. She'd never have come this far without performing to perfection. Being naughty had had no place on the ladder to success. Neither had coming on to a man she worked alongside.

But having earned her position, she felt free to act on other, impulsive desires. Then with the onset of the new year, Toni would put Stephan behind her and step back into the stable, secure, independent life she'd created for herself.

If the article were to be trusted, the clichéd adage was true and nice girls finished last. So Toni would just have to be bad. She smoothed her skirt and straightened her hat, giving one last jingle of her bells for good luck. In matters of the hormones and the heart Toni intended to come in first.

No matter how naughty she had to be to accomplish her goal, Toni intended to get her man.

They called this a party? Maxwell Corbin glanced at the dark suits milling about the large conference room. Muffled laughs, discreet corner discussions, and a handshake every now and then to clinch a deal. Not an ounce of fun in sight, he thought and immediately remembered why he'd traded in his SoHo apartment and his family's downtown New York City law firm for a place in the suburbs and his PI office on the Hudson River. An office he'd return to. No matter how happy it would make his father if Max decided to return to the fold, he had to live his own life, his own way. Three years at the family firm had taught him practicing law wasn't it.

As he made for the eggnog across the room, his sneakered foot crushed a stray pretzel, marring the otherwise pristine carpet. Beside him, someone made a toast to an upcoming merger, increased income, and the guaranteed all-nighters to come. Max shook his head in disgust. The only thing worth staying up all night for was sex—something he hadn't had in too damn long, mostly because no woman had interested him enough. But lately he'd begun to wonder what being discriminating and picky had gotten him besides a cold bed at night.

He lifted the ladle to pour himself a drink when the faint ringing of bells caught his attention. He turned toward the sound and the expensively decorated Christmas tree, a pine, lavishly trimmed with white and gold, with dozens of boxes beneath the branches to increase holiday spirit. He stepped to the left so he could see around the tree and caught sight of a dainty elf kneeling over a bulging bag of toys. As she reached inside the large bag, the hem on her miniskirt hiked up higher, revealing black lace beneath white fur trim.

Max swallowed hard. So much for disinterest, he thought wryly. A longer glance as she dug through her huge bag and he discovered the lace ended at mid-thigh. He wondered what she wore beneath that green suit, if the hands-on exploration would be as satisfying as his imagination.

He tried to swallow but his mouth had gone dry. If he had to spend time in the hallowed halls of Corbin and Sons—make that Corbin and Compliant Son, he thought, thinking of his twin—then maybe the pixie in the corner would make his time here worthwhile. He dodged his way around the business suits and headed for the tinsel-laden elf.

On his way, he realized that not only was she the sole focus of his attention, but he was the center of hers. She'd straightened from her chore and looked at him dead-on, heat and something more in her smoky gaze. Drink forgotten, he walked the rest of the way to where she stood. Despite the drone of preoccupied, chattering attorneys, Max felt as if he were approaching her in silken silence.

As he closed in, he raised his gaze from the white fur anklet to her belted, trim waist to her green-eyed stare. Sea-green scrutiny made more vibrant by the interested flush in her cheeks. After promising his father he'd show up at this gig, he'd mentally called the day a bust, but when she pulled him behind the tree, rose onto her booted tiptoes, and touched her mouth to his, he reassessed his opinion.

He'd been kissed before—but he'd never *been* kissed. Not with such intensity and single-minded purpose. She tasted sweet and smelled sensual and fragrant, making both his mind and his body come alive. Her hands gripped his shoulders in a death-lock as her champagne-flavored tongue darted past his willing lips.

She had a potent effect, yet despite it all her touch was endearingly hesitant, turning him on while arousing a fierce protectiveness within him at the same time. He gripped her waist to anchor himself, something she obviously took as a sign of acceptance because a soft but satisfied sigh escaped and he caught the erotic sound with his mouth, deep in his throat. Though he hadn't a clue what he'd done to become the lucky recipient of her attention, he wasn't about to question good fortune. He'd rather make more of his own.

He began an arousing exploration, mating his tongue with hers in a prelude she couldn't misinterpret or mistake. And obviously she didn't. Her head tipped backward and she welcomed the onslaught of his roving tongue and hands. His fingers locked onto her petite waist and he pulled her forward, her breasts flush with his chest, her hips brushing his.

Such close contact with his elf had him aching for more and he sucked in a startled breath, inhaling deeply. The scent of pine assaulted his senses and reminded him of their surroundings and the possibility that despite the barrier of the Christmas tree, they might have an audience of attorneys taking copious notes. With regret he raised his head and took a safe step back from temptation. Emerald eyes glazed with desire stared back, an engaging smile on her well-kissed lips.

"Mistletoe," she said in a husky voice, pointing upward.

He glanced at the bare ceiling. So she had passion as well as a desperate need for an excuse. A grin tipped the edges of his mouth as he wondered what other surprises this mystery lady had in store. "Whatever you say."

She touched her lips with shaking fingertips. "I say you're not *him*. You're nothing like Stephan."

Kind of her to point out something he'd been told hundreds of times before. But she'd spoken low, more to herself than to him, and not with the well-aimed need to hurt, the way the information had been used against him in the past.

Her gaze darted from his worn basketball sneakers, up the length of his dark denim jeans, and focused on his face. "In the dim lighting and from a distance you kind of looked like him." He saw as well as heard her searching for answers. "The same dark hair and piercing blue eyes, though yours are somewhat warmer." A glimmer of passion infused her voice. "Similar dimple but yours is deeper." She reached out with the same hesitant determination he'd sensed behind the kiss.

Her touch burned him straight to his soul.

"And when he works weekends, he . . . dresses . . . like . . . you." She jerked her hand away from the same fire consuming him.

Max was surprised to learn Stephan ever veered away from conservative suits and ties. Maybe he and his twin had come from the same egg after all. Maybe they had more in common than either of them let on. And maybe they *could* be friends as well as brothers. The thought arose, not for the first time in ages, but it was the first time he considered acting on the impulse.

He had his elf to thank for revealing the surprising similarities and possibilities. *His* elf. Funny how proprietary he'd become in such a short span of time. But it wouldn't be funny if she had any kind of relationship with his twin, and based on that hell of a kiss, the odds tipped against Max.

"Since it's not the weekend, I should have known," she murmured. Scrutiny complete, she settled her stare on his New York Rangers jersey, an obvious attempt to avoid his gaze. Then she folded her arms across her lush chest, chewing on her bottom lip as the enormity of her mistake obviously set in.

He remembered the feel of those curves pressed intimately against him, recalled the sweetness of her mouth, and he struggled not to groan aloud. "Something against the Rangers?" he asked, seeking the more mundane.

She shook her head, her button nose crinkling in answer. "I don't have time for basketball."

"Hockey."

"Whatever. But baseball's another story. How 'bout those Mets?" A twinkle sparkled in her glorious eyes.

Apparently she'd been giving him a hard time and was probably as big a sports fanatic as he, something he'd never expected to find in a woman.

"Hard to believe a Corbin would wear a jersey to an office party, though." Her brows rose in surprise.

On any other woman, the gesture would remind him of his judgmental federal court judge mother. But on *her,* the otherwise critical display indicated curiosity and interest, not disdain. "You've got that right. But I'm not a typical Corbin." He felt the welcome tug of a smile.

She inclined her head, her silky black hair brushing her shoulders much the way he'd like it caressing his skin. "Tell me something I don't know."

Once again, her trembling fingers touched her mouth, this time tracing the outline of her reddened lips before she caught herself and stepped around the tree, reaching for the first gift-wrapped package she could find. He allowed her escape for the moment, watching the sexy sway of her hips in retreat. And in that instant, her words immediately after that mind-blowing kiss came back to him. *You're not him. You're nothing like Stephan.*

She'd kissed him and known instantly. And she wasn't all that upset and she definitely wasn't unaffected. The thought pleased him. Though Max could never compete with his twin as a Corbin son, he'd obviously made headway with . . . his brother's woman? His gut clenched at the thought.

"Hello, Max." Stephan walked up beside him.

"Hey, little brother." Catching the scowl on his twin's face, Max grinned, feeling on safe, sibling-sparring ground. " 'Little brother' is a figure of speech. You know that. But you also know I got sprung first."

"Three minutes isn't enough to hold it over me our entire lives," Stephan said with characteristic grumbling. "But I'm glad you made it." He surprised Max by slapping him on the back. Obviously his brother wasn't threatened by his father's summons of his wayward, prodigal son. Another reason for Max to suddenly hold out hope he'd leave this party with more than he'd walked in with.

At the very least, a renewed connection to his twin and at best a new woman in his life? Possible, Max thought, unless—he glanced at his brother. "Who's the elf?"

Stephan folded his arms across his chest and glanced around the tree to where the woman who'd kissed Max senseless now tried to feign interest in her bag of toys and not the Corbin brothers. Max stifled a smile.

"Who, Toni?" Stephan asked.

"Toni." Max tested the name on his tongue, liking the sound as well as the incongruity of a man's name on such a feminine creature.

"She's an associate—something you'd know if you didn't make yourself so scarce."

His brother was right. Other than the obligatory holidays at home, Max avoided family situations—especially family business functions like this one—if only because they were always fraught with tension between himself and his parents.

"Any interest?" Max asked, ignoring his brother's jibe but still needing to lay other cards on the table.

Stephan shook his head. "Maybe when she first started working here, but that was a while ago. And once we became colleagues and friends . . ." He waved his hand in dismissal. "No interest."

It was obvious to Max that she didn't feel the same—at least she hadn't before kissing the wrong twin, but no point in informing his brother now. "You sure?"

"No interest. Not that way." Stephan glanced at him, surprised but obviously certain. "Field's clear."

And so were his brother's words. Nothing stood between Max and his elf.

He turned, determined to stake his claim, but she was talking with a female colleague, and then without warning the conference room was overrun with scampering, chattering children. "What's this?" Max asked over the din.

Stephan laughed. "*This* is Toni's contribution to the annual firm Christmas party. We always made a cash donation to a charity, but she insisted we do something more personal, too. Now we buy gifts for the kids at one of the local women's shelters and Santa hands them out—with her help."

"Santa?"

"Dad. But not this year. He'll be here but the doctor's banned him from anything too stressful like picking up the kids and putting them on his lap. At least until next year."

A twisting pain lanced through Max. "You sure?"

"That he'll be around till next year?" Stephan asked, finishing Max's unspoken question in a way only a twin could. "I'm sure. Spend some more time with him and you will be, too."

Max had seen the older man in the hospital and again when he'd been released, but they'd never been alone long enough to get into serious conversation. Yet apparently the stroke had prompted a renewal in the older man's determination to get Max back into the family firm, because he'd been summoned here by his father, who claimed he had an offer Max couldn't refuse.

"He's determined enough for four men," Stephan said.

"Swell." Determined to stick around and determined to get his way with his one ornery son. Well, one out of two wouldn't be bad. Max glanced at his twin, knowing he had to be honest about not wanting to take over in the office, or in his brother's hard-worked-for domain. "Hey bro, you should know I have no intention of coming back—"

Stephan cut him off with a slug to the shoulder. "*I* know. The only one you have to convince is Dad."

Max nodded. His brother was obviously secure in his place and position within the firm and the family. One potential problem taken care of.

He looked over. His elf—Toni—was kneeling down with kids beside her, tickling one, laughing with another. Not only did she have an altruistic streak but from the looks of things she was a natural-born nurturer, too. Add that to her sexy-as-hell appearance and her knock-out kiss and Max knew he'd found a gem. Getting to know her would be a real pleasure.

"Who's replacing Dad as Santa this year?" Max asked.

"Even cash couldn't sway any of these uptight jokers to do the job and I wasn't sure I'd make it on time, so Toni's handing out the gifts herself," Stephan said.

"Really."

His brother chuckled aloud. "You sound awfully pleased. Aren't you too old to be telling Santa what you want for Christmas?"

Max grinned. "Hell, no. Especially not if it'll let me get close to his sexy emissary." And as soon as the children were finished, he planned to tell Santa's helper exactly what he wanted for Christmas.

CHAPTER TWO

—

Toni was one part mortified and two parts completely turned on. She was in a sweat that owed nothing to the crowded, overheated room and everything to the man watching her out of the corner of his eye. With hindsight and the rush of adrenaline to act on impulse gone, she saw the differences in the brothers more clearly. This man had slightly longer though equally black hair, and razor stubble gave him a more rugged, less clean-cut appearance. He exuded a raw masculinity that appealed to her on a deeper, more carnal level. One she hadn't known existed inside her until that kiss.

That kiss. Toni hugged her arms around her chest, as if she could hold tight to the feelings he inspired. As always, she forced herself to take an honest look at herself, her actions, and the situation. She couldn't deny the truth. At a crossroads, about to embark on a new professional life, she couldn't afford more than a one-night stand, no matter how out of character it was. She'd thought Stephan Corbin was the perfect man on whom to test her feminine wiles, but she'd been wrong. Whatever attraction she'd felt for Stephan paled in comparison to what she'd experienced under the nonexistent mistletoe with his twin. And darned if she didn't want an instant replay.

But with the onslaught of children from the shelter, she had no choice but to wait. In the meantime, she continued the cat-and-mouse game of eye contact he'd begun earlier. Her heart beat frantically in her chest and anticipation flowed through her veins.

"Only two more kids, Toni," Annie, her secretary, whispered in her ear.

"I don't know whether to say thank goodness because I'm beat or thank goodness because even one child here is one too many." She ought to know, having spent more than one night in a shelter as a child.

"How about thank goodness so you can go play get-to-know-you with the Corbin twin?"

Toni felt the heat rise to her cheeks. Had Annie seen that consuming kiss behind the tree?

"He hasn't taken his eyes off you since you sat down in this chair."

Toni shifted in her seat to accommodate the next little girl. "Did you know Stephan had a brother?" she asked Annie.

"No, but I wish I had, at least before you nailed him for yourself. I've got to run. I have a date. Have fun tonight," she whispered on a laugh and walked away before Toni could respond.

The last two children and their requests for Santa went quickly. Toni kept her mental list of extra things to send over to the shelter from Santa and soon the kids, their chaperones, and the gifts were bundled up and on their way. She started to rise, knowing she still had an office to pack before the night was through.

"Not so fast."

She recognized the seductive voice that rumbled from behind.

She curled her hands around the arm of the office chair she'd appropriated, steadying herself with a firm grip. "Something I can do for you?"

"Since you have a special relationship with the big man in the red suit I was hoping you could relay a wish." His strong fingertips brushed her hair back from her face and around her ear, strumming across her skin with perfect precision.

Her stomach fluttered with longing and she forced an easy laugh. "Aren't you too old to believe in Santa?"

"Aren't you too young not to?"

"I'm dressed like one of his elves. Doesn't that tell you something about who and what I believe in?" And right now she believed in this man—and anything he said or did.

She tipped her head to the side and found herself sharing breathing space, close enough to kiss him if she desired. And she did, badly. She'd never experienced anything as strong as her immediate attraction to this stranger.

"It tells me some. But I know too little about you and I intend to change that." He walked around and eased himself onto the arm of her chair, not on her lap but close enough to increase her growing awareness.

His hip brushed her arm and her body heat shot up another ten degrees. She glanced around at the thinning group of people. Though she and her companion didn't seem to be garnering added attention, Toni was still aware of this being a place of business.

Even if she had temporarily forgotten once she'd gotten him behind the tree, they were in full view of the masses now. "I'm not Santa Claus so there's no lap-sitting involved," she warned him.

He bent closer. "I'll accept those barriers . . . for now."

She inhaled a shaky breath. His masculine scent, a heady mix of warm spice and pure man tempted her to throw caution aside. Before she could lose common sense she grasped onto the one thread of the conversation she could remember. "So what can I tell Santa you desire . . . I mean want. What can I tell Santa you want?"

She'd caught her phrasing, an obvious extension of her thoughts and needs, and attempted a too-late retraction. But the word "desire," once spoken, hovered in the air, teasing, arousing, and building upon the electricity arcing between them.

"I know what you meant." He laughed and the deep sound both eased and aroused her in ways she didn't understand. "I also know what you want and it's the same thing I do."

A tremor shook her hard. "And what would that be?"

"To finish what we started under the so-called mistletoe."

A rousing round of applause erupted around them, interrupting their banter and his huskily spoken words. Despite the beat of desire thrumming inside her, she forced herself to look for the cause of the stir. She glanced up and saw Mr. Corbin, the firm's senior partner—Stephan and his twin's father—standing in the doorway. *His twin.* But beyond the obvious resemblance Toni drew a sudden blank.

Oh, Lord. For as quickly as they'd connected, she didn't even know his name.

He brushed his knuckles across her cheek in a gesture more tender and caring than overtly sexual. She could have melted at his feet. And then there was the heat rushing through her body. She felt on edge, the desire inside her out of control.

He rose to his feet. "I've got to go greet the old man but no way are we finished."

She bit the inside of her cheek. When she'd decided to go after Stephan, the firm's bachelor, she'd known nothing long-term could come of it. She'd just wanted to enter the new year feeling good and knowing she could get the man she thought she desired, if just for a brief time. But she'd kissed the wrong brother—or the right brother depending on her perspective—and knowing nothing about him, all bets were off.

So she could continue her bold act and see where things led or she could run, something she'd seen her mother do too many times. Toni Larson didn't run.

"Oh, we're finished all right." She licked at her dry lips. "At least until you tell me your name."

"It's Max." Amusement mingled with desire in his blue-eyed gaze.

She grinned. " 'Bye, Max."

He shook his head. "Only until later, Toni." His words held certainty, his voice the promise of sharing more than just an introduction. With a last glance, he reluctantly turned and walked away.

She watched as he approached the older man and witnessed what was so obviously a reunion between a father and a son he loved deeply. A lump rose to her throat. Looking at Max, Toni saw concern and love cross his handsome features, no hint of the playful man in sight. Apparently this reunion was emotional for both men.

But as Max broke from his father's arms, he said something light enough to make Stephan laugh. Then he turned and, from across the room, his compelling gaze met hers and he treated her to a sexy wink. One that assured her he hadn't forgotten her or his promise of seeing her later.

Her stomach curled in anticipation and searing heat assaulted her senses. She shook her head, amazed. Not only had she been naughty, she'd most certainly gotten her man. Just not the man she'd expected. Fate and irony were at work tonight. She touched her fingers to her lips and imagined the feel of his mouth working magic over hers, his warm breath and his masculine scent wrapping her in seductive heat.

She let out a breathless sigh, knowing the night she'd desired was about to get much, much hotter.

Max hadn't wanted to leave Toni's side, not for an instant, which he supposed told him something about the strength of his attraction to a woman he barely knew. An attraction he wanted to explore further.

After spending time and discussing everything *but* business with Max, the older man had grown tired and said he'd see Max at home tomorrow. He just hoped the truce they'd begun to forge today lasted once Max told his father that no offer, no matter how supposedly enticing, could coax him back into the family firm. The most the older Corbin could expect from Max was a loving son who'd always be there for him. Max hoped it would be enough.

But before he had to deal with tomorrow, he had tonight ahead of him and he looked forward to every last minute. He walked down the darkened hallway, lit only by lights from some occupied offices, and stopped by the door his brother had told him belonged to Toni.

Light shone from beneath the partially closed door and the low strains of music sounded from inside. Anticipation and arousal beat heavy inside him as he let himself in. Toni was emptying her office, packing boxes and singing while she worked.

The woman couldn't carry a tune to save her life. Max folded his arms across his chest and grinned. "You can serenade me anytime."

She yelped and jumped. "You shouldn't sneak up on me like that."

He stepped forward, moving closer. With each step he took toward her, she inched back until she hit the wall, looking up at him with wide eyes. "What are you doing?"

"What you asked. Making my presence known."

"As if I could miss it," she said wryly.

"But you're afraid of me."

She shook her head in denial but he backed off anyway. He wanted this woman in many and varied ways but frightened wasn't one of them.

"You don't scare me . . . Max." His name fluttered off her lips. Then as if to prove her point, she held her hand out for him to shake. "And it's nice to officially meet you."

"Likewise." He eased his hand inside hers. Warm and soft, her skin caressed his coarser flesh.

"You just surprised me," she said in a husky voice.

"A good surprise, I hope."

"Definitely that. So why are you here?"

"I was hoping to talk you into going for dinner."

She bit down on her lower lip. "What if I have plans?"

He propped a shoulder against the wall beside her. "Break them," he said with more confidence than he felt. His biggest fear was that she'd blow him off before they had a chance to explore what was between them.

"Convince me." Her teasing smile invited him to do just that.

He curled his fingers around her hand and pulled her

toward him, wrapping one arm around her waist and holding her other hand out in front of them. "Let's dance."

Her eyes opened wide. "You're kidding?"

"Do you see me laughing?" He pulled her flush against him and swept her around the small office in time to the beat of the music. He had no idea what had come over him except he had no intention of losing her now.

She anchored her hand around his back for support, molded her body to his and let go. He felt it in the sway of her hips and saw it in the sassy tilt of her head. She was enjoying herself and he was glad.

His body couldn't ignore her lush curves and his groin hardened, unsatisfied with a single dance. But Max wasn't in this for a one-night stand. He was a man who'd spent his life trusting his own instincts and he wasn't about to question his gut now. He wanted much more than sex with this woman and for Max that was a first.

She tilted her head back. "You've got good moves."

"I give my partner all the credit."

Her smile was nothing short of incredible. "Is that what I am?"

"You tell me." He turned her once and stilled. They were so close, their warm breath mingled. So aware of one another he thought, as he stared into her expectant eyes.

Toni's legs shook beneath her and she tightened her grip on the only available means of support—Max's waist and hand. Then she waited as he lowered his mouth to hers, slowly, surely, his blue-eyed stare never wavering until his lips touched hers.

Their first kiss had been spontaneous, unplanned, and yes, she admitted to herself, a bit desperate. But this was so much more. He took his time, his tongue delving and discovering the deep recesses of her mouth, learning *her,* not once rushing the moment.

Her stomach curled in response to the drugging kiss, much the way her fingers curled into his skin.

His lips slid gently over hers, making the most of the moisture they generated together. Strong yet gentle, he took control, mastering the moves that made her sigh into him and spin dizzily out of control. Toni needed to participate on equal footing and she traced the outline of his strong lips with her tongue and reveled in his uninhibited verbal response. He was a man who not only expressed his physical desire but was bold enough not to hide his emotional reaction. The masculine groan found an answering pull deep inside Toni, in a place she'd kept hidden, uncharted until now.

Without warning, he pulled back, leaning his forehead against hers, his breathing rough in her ear. But the intimacy of continued body contact felt both good and right. Teetering on an emotional precipice, Toni shook deep inside.

"Have I convinced you yet?" he asked.

"Convinced me of what?" She was out of breath, stunned by the intensity of the short but extremely emotional encounter. She couldn't call it just a kiss, not when he'd engaged her heart and soul in every move he'd made. Did he really expect her to think clearly now?

"I am so glad to see I can make you forget everything but me." He laughed, a husky, tender sound that sent ribbons of warmth curling through her. "I asked you to break dinner plans to go out with me. You said I should convince you, remember?"

He reached out and traced the outline of her moist lips with his fingertip, reminding her of the kiss and all that had passed between them. "So did I convince you?"

Her tongue darted out, coming into contact with his salty skin.

He sucked in a startled breath and he met her gaze. "I'm going to take that as yes," he warned.

He could take her anywhere, anytime, but she wasn't about to tell him that. Instead she cleared her throat and straightened her shoulders. "Dinner sounds great. But I can guarantee you that without a reservation there's not a place around that doesn't have at least an hour or more wait."

Dinner, reservations, Toni hoped everyday conversation

would center her somehow, but after this interlude, she doubted her feet would touch the floor again tonight.

"Then it's a good thing I have an in at someplace special. You ready?"

"Dressed like this?" She glanced down at her green tights and fur-lined skirt and wished she hadn't come to work dressed as an elf but had changed at the office instead.

He took in her outfit, one she hadn't thought of as sexy until she saw herself in his glazed eyes. "The place I have in mind doesn't have a dress code."

"How about a people code?" She pulled at her hat until the pins gave way and she tossed it aside.

He slid his fingers over a long strand of her hair. "Everyone's allowed, bar none, including elves." His eyes twinkled with mischief. "Just leave the reindeer outside."

"Cute."

"No, I'm serious. The place is called Bar None and you're more than welcome. My old college roommate owns the joint. So will you come with me?"

In his eyes, she saw the same hope and anticipation alive inside her and grabbed for her courage. "Okay, Max. Lead the way."

Max had a hard time concentrating on driving with Toni beside him. She shifted in her seat and he felt the heat of her stare.

"While you were twirling me around my office . . ." she began.

"And kissing you senseless . . ." He couldn't help but remind her of what he'd never forget.

Toni shot Max a wry glare. "You didn't mention this place was in the boonies."

"That's because you didn't ask."

She held her hands out in front of the heater, but he doubted she needed the warmth. He pulled his truck past the train station, lit by traditional colored Christmas lights that gave the place a festive look, much like the rest of the smaller town. Another half-mile down, Max turned into a private street and pulled the car into a gravel parking lot. The Bar None, an old-fashioned pub and restaurant, was in the same upstate town where he lived and worked, a good forty-minute car ride from New York City.

"Forget me asking. I think you were more afraid I'd say no."

He grinned. "That, too." After their second kiss, the one where they'd connected on too many levels to count, Max hadn't been about to lose her by mentioning a little detail like distance. "I gave you the chance to turn around, didn't I?"

She laughed. "While you were doing fifty-five, yeah, you did."

He'd then proceeded to find out as much about his elf as possible, discovering she was at a turning point in her life. Feeling overburdened and overworked, she had the new year pegged as a fresh start. She hadn't elaborated and he'd given her the freedom to reveal as much or as little as she desired.

Though he didn't want to spook her by getting too serious too fast, Max knew he had every intention of being part of her new beginning. He shifted to park.

"So your friend owns this place?" she asked, glancing around her.

He nodded.

"Gorgeous decorations."

Max took in the icicle lights dripping from the shingles and overhang along with the colored lights circling the surrounding shrubbery, seeing the setting he viewed daily from her new, awed perspective. "They are incredible." And so was she.

"How do you plan on explaining me? My outfit, I mean." She laughed, a lilting but embarrassed sound that reminded him of her jingling bells. Those she'd removed somewhere during their ride up the West Side Highway and they lay in the center console.

"I'll just tell him you're Santa's helper." He turned in his seat and reached for her hand.

She tipped her head to one side, a wry smile curving her lips. "And you think he'll buy that?"

He shook his head. "Doesn't matter to me what Jake believes. But it matters to me what you believe." He'd only known her a few hours but the connection he felt with her was real.

Her lashes fluttered upward as she met his gaze. Deep and compelling, her eyes settled on him. Did she know? Understand? Feel the same overwhelming attraction and need as he felt pulsing through his body at this very moment?

Max wondered. He'd never fallen hard and fast for a woman he barely knew, but he had now. Feeling vulnerable wasn't something he was used to and he suddenly needed proof she felt the same. "Tell me something. Since you brought it up, what was behind the elf outfit?" He'd heard his brother's version. He wanted to hear hers.

She glanced away. "I was just spreading some holiday cheer."

"Maybe that's part of the reason, but I doubt it covers everything. And before we go into that crowded bar, I want to know more about you." Something that would show him she trusted him. Something to prove to him that this . . . thing . . . between them wasn't all one-sided.

She bit down on her lower lip. "What did Stephan tell you about me? And don't tell me you didn't ask."

He laughed, admiring both her intuition and nerve. "That you organized the children's visit to Santa and the gifts. That's all."

She inclined her head. "And you want to know why."

He shook his head. "I want to know *you*."

Looking into his eyes, Toni believed him. Though nothing had been said aloud, somewhere between kissing him and . . . well . . . kissing him, a sense of caring had developed, too. They didn't know nearly enough about one another but he was giving her the opportunity to change that.

She'd never admitted her past to a man before, never felt close enough—yet she felt that closeness now. The vulnerability she normally associated with opening up to a man was nowhere to be found. Considering she wasn't planning anything more than the here and now, the notion rattled her. Badly.

His hand brushed her cheek and remained there. "You can trust me, sweetheart."

As she turned her head so his palm cupped her face, a renewed sense of rightness swept through her. "I spent my childhood in and out of a women's shelter," she admitted. "Whenever my mother got up the courage to leave, we'd find one my father didn't know about. Then when things got rough, she'd go back to him and it would start all over again."

He let out a low growl. "That shouldn't happen to any child."

"Exactly." She shrugged self-consciously. "Which explains the Christmas party and my elf outfit."

"Which explains my attraction to you," he murmured.

"You have a thing for little women dressed in green?"

"You make yourself sound like a Martian." He burst out laughing but sobered fast. Nothing about what she'd revealed was funny. "Actually, I have a thing for a certain raven-haired beauty with a big heart."

She shook her head, flushed. "Don't give me that much credit. Really. It's all very self-serving. When I got out of high school, I swore I'd finish my education somehow. No matter how many student loans I had to take, I promised myself I'd find a way to be self-supporting so I'd never run out of options like my mother had."

"And you've accomplished that."

"With a little unexpected help," she said, gratitude evident in her tone. "I found out when my mother passed away she'd taken out an insurance policy. Enough money to cover my education—after the fact. So my loans are paid off, but I spent years working like a demon for that sense of security."

"But you've got that now."

"Most definitely." She turned away, reaching for the

door handle. "I'm starving," she said, changing the subject.

Obviously she didn't want to take things too quickly, but Max made a mental note to find out more. "Toni, wait."

She glanced over her shoulder.

"One more question."

"Yes?"

"You thought you were kissing my brother."

Even in the darkened car he could see the heat of a blush rise to her cheeks. "Mistaken impulse," she said.

"Any feelings behind it?"

"Just one."

He waited a beat before she finally finished.

"Regret."

Max felt as if he'd been kicked in the gut. Until she turned completely and scooted over in the seat, so close he could smell her perfume. "I regret that you obviously think there was something going on between me and Stephan. Or that I have feelings for your brother other than friendship."

"Don't you? You initiated that kiss. I have a hard time believing it was born of feelings of friendship." Despite the fact that she'd let him into her heart and the painful parts of her past, she'd yet to openly admit her interest in him.

"This is so humiliating and I'm going to sound so desperate." She laughed and shook her head. "I thought I was interested in your brother and I acted on the opportunity." She shrugged. "Turns out I was wrong." Those velvet green eyes met his. "I thought I wanted Stephan—until the second I kissed you."

Max had his answer and let out a ragged breath of air. She wanted him, too. So, he thought, let the night begin.

CHAPTER THREE

—

"Hey, Detective, how's it going?"

"Just fine, Milt."

Detective? Max had grabbed Toni's hand and she followed him through the crowd at the bar to the back of the paneled pub, decorated with silver and green tinsel along the top of dark wood. There was no way he could hear her above the din so she waited until they'd reached their destination before yanking on his hand and capturing his attention. "You're a detective?"

"Private investigator. Why?"

"No special reason. I just had no idea what you did for a living."

"And now you do." He turned toward the bar. "Hey, Jake, give me a round of . . ."

Max turned toward Toni and she shrugged. "Whatever you're having is fine."

"Two Coronas."

The man he'd called Jake, a light-haired man about the same age and height as Max, nodded in return. "Hey, Brownie," Jake called to someone across the room. "Get your ass up and give the detective his table."

Max laughed. "I have a standing seat in the corner." He gestured toward a high table with two barstools where an older man was clearing out.

"He doesn't have to give up his seat for us," Toni said.

"He damn well does. If we don't boot him out of here, he drinks too much. He's too lazy to stand on his feet all night. This way he'll go home and sleep it off." Max caressed her face with his knuckles. "Trust me. I've been through this routine before."

"You've booted him out for his own good? Or booted him out to make room for you and another woman?" She bit the inside of her cheek, hating herself for asking but needing the answer just the same.

"There are no *other* women."

Toni liked the answer, but couldn't help wondering if he was telling her what he thought she wanted to hear. Seconds later, he dispelled her concerns by cupping her cheeks in his palms and lowering his lips for a seductive, heated kiss. One that left her gasping for air, unable to think, and the subject of intense speculation, she realized, as he lifted his head.

The stares of onlookers turned into a slow round of applause and more than one whistle of approval. "Way to go, Detective."

Embarrassed, she lowered herself onto the nearest barstool with shaking knees, just as Jake arrived with their drinks.

"You sure do know how to make an entrance, Corbin. Now are you going to introduce me to your lady?"

"*His* lady?"

Jake laughed. "I've owned this place nearly ten years and he's never brought a woman here before. If you can think of another label, just let me know."

Max joined his friend's amused chuckling. "See? Proof to back up my claim. Jake Bishop meet Toni . . ."

"Larson," she said, extending her hand before his friend realized how little they knew about each other.

"Nice to meet you, Toni." Jake swung a towel over his arm. "Can I get you two something to eat? My burgers are the best." Without waiting for an answer, he disappeared into the kitchen.

"Modest guy."

Max dragged the empty stool close to hers and swung himself into it. "He can afford to be full of himself. Look at this place. It's a gold mine. Of course it is the only bar for miles."

She nodded. "And one where you've got your own table and everyone seems to know you. Do you call this place home?" Toni liked the rustic, comfortable decor. The place emitted warmth and a down-home atmosphere that welcomed its customers and she could see Max spending his free time here.

"As a matter of fact I do." He gestured upward. "I rent the place upstairs."

"Really." She leaned forward and rested her chin on her hands. "And here your friend said you don't make it a habit of luring unsuspecting women to your lair."

He shook his head, his gaze never leaving hers. "I haven't lured you anywhere you didn't want to go. And if you want me to drive you back to the city after dinner, I will."

Her heart beat out a rapid crescendo in her chest. She didn't want to go anywhere without him. They'd just met tonight but she'd never felt so much so fast. "And if I don't?" she asked softly.

Max leaned closer. "If you don't want to go back, then you stay with me."

His warm breath tickled her cheek and she realized she could easily fall hard for this man. All six feet of him put her at a petite disadvantage, yet for a woman who prided herself on her independence, she had to admit she liked his overpowering air and the heady way he made her feel.

Enough to consider spending the night?

"Burgers, folks." Jake arrived, interrupting the electric current of awareness running between them. After serving them their meals, Jake grabbed a chair and dragged it over.

Max eyed his friend warily. Jake never knew when to butt out. Max ought to resent Jake's intrusion, but hell, the man was a bartender. Being nosy was his business, and besides, Max needed a break or else he'd grab Toni's hand and drag her upstairs to his bed—the one thing he wanted and the last thing he ought to do. He needed to build on the tentative start they'd made, not rush into a one-night stand. Which wasn't to say he wouldn't follow her lead, Max thought.

"So where'd you two meet, a costume party?" Jake asked, then gestured to the food in front of them. "Go 'head and eat."

Max rolled his eyes. "We met in the city."

"I work with his brother," Toni explained.

"She's a lawyer?"

"Not a typical one," Max said, knowing Jake was already questioning why he'd fall for one of what Max had always labeled a stuffy breed.

"This true?" Jake asked.

"I guess." Toni shrugged. "At least no more than he's a typical Corbin."

"You two seem to have a handle on each other."

Not nearly well enough, Max thought. Not yet.

Jake leaned forward in his seat, ready for more conversation. "Sounds like a match made in heaven to me."

"You realize the place is emptying out while you're hanging out here?" Max asked.

"Are you looking to get rid of me?"

"Could I if I tried?"

Toni laughed. "You two sound like brothers."

Max shrugged. "Live with a guy for four years and you get the urge to kill him every once in a while."

"The man speaks the truth." Jake leaned back and took in the emptying bar. "Less money, more family time. I don't know whether I love or hate the holidays."

"He closes early during the week before Christmas," Max explained.

"That's nice."

Max wondered if he mistook the wistful look in Toni's eyes when Jake mentioned family time and holidays in the same breath. Recalling her childhood, he doubted he was off base and he wanted the opportunity to replace older, sadder memories with newer, happier ones.

"Well, you two be good." Jake turned to Toni and

winked. "I'm going to start wrapping things up for the night."

For the next hour, while Jake cleared out the remaining customers and then locked the door behind Max and Toni, promising to return early for a real cleanup, Max ate and watched Toni do the same. He wasn't a man prone to talking about himself but she had him explaining the types of cases he handled and describing the thrill of working in the field as opposed to behind a desk or in a courtroom. To his surprise, she didn't turn her nose up or question his choices. If anything, she not only approved but seemed to envy his ability to walk away from the pressure and grind to do what he enjoyed.

Max studied her. Now that she'd paid off her student loans, she could afford to start making choices out of enjoyment and not necessity. He wondered if she even realized she had that option, but before he could delve deeper into her life, the conversation detoured yet again.

But no matter what they discussed Max found himself drawn to her. Not just because they shared a passion for take-out Mexican food and Rollerblading in fresh air, but because she was unique: She was a woman who made him want to open up, a woman who interested him so much he wanted to know more about her life, and a woman who accepted the choices he made. A woman he desired not just in his bed, though that was a given, but in his life, to see where things led.

And if her footwork was any indication, she wanted the same thing. She'd obviously let her elf boots fall to the floor and she'd brushed her foot against his leg once too many times for comfort or accident. The light flush in her cheeks and her inability to look him head-on told him she didn't find her overt moves easy. But he was grateful for her interest and he intended to keep things light and fun—to give her space to decide how far she wanted to take things, knowing he wouldn't accept just tonight. It would be *her* decision to stay or go, no matter how much his body throbbed with growing need.

Conversation became more difficult as she intentionally massaged his calf with the arch of her foot, inching upward beneath the table.

He leaned closer. "You're a naughty girl, Toni." He captured her foot between his legs, stilling her arousing movements.

It was either stop her or let her continue her upward climb, in which case their evening would end before it ever began. And with the bar empty and Jake gone, Max would much rather start their time together fresh and new.

"Being naughty's the whole point, Max."

"You sound like a woman with a plan." He paused, thinking of their unusual meeting. "And it started with that kiss."

"You're astute. No wonder they call you detective." Her lips lifted in a smile. "I already told you I acted on opportunity."

"In a way that was out of character." Max was as certain Toni wanted him as he was that she had a bad case of nerves.

"And you know this how?" She drummed her fingertips on the table, trying hard to maintain her nonchalant façade.

Max grinned. "Gut instinct."

Toni inclined her head. Not only did he understand her well but he seemed to see inside her, too. Her aggressive act was just that, but in no way did that minimize how badly she wanted this night.

He stopped her nervous tapping and threaded his fingers through hers. "Relax, sweetheart."

The softly spoken endearment wrapped around her heart and her adrenaline picked up speed. "You really think that's possible?"

He shrugged. "I know so. We're going to get to know each other better. We'll have fun. And nothing will happen that you don't want to happen. So relax and come with me."

She'd follow him anywhere, Toni thought. And despite the fact that she'd never done anything that resembled a one-night stand before, she wanted *everything* to happen. She just needed to gather her nerve. Her hand entwined with his, she let him lead her around the bar and into a back room she hadn't seen earlier because of the crowds.

In the corner, beside the rack holding the pool cues, a Christmas tree took up a lot of space in the small room. The tree beckoned to her, with its worn ornaments, aged by time and handling, hanging from its branches. Though it wasn't professionally decorated with pricey ornaments like the one in the office, this Christmas display showed thoughtfulness, warmth, and caring.

She reached out and lightly fingered a cut-out teddy bear hanging from a crudely bent pipe cleaner. "This is so sweet."

Max came up behind her. His body heat and masculine scent put her nerve endings on high alert.

"Jake's daughter made it her first year in kindergarten," he said.

"And this one?" With a trembling hand, she pointed to a clay angel, made with obvious talent and love.

"A customer." Max's warm breath fanned her ear. "Jake could tell you who gave him each one."

Toni nodded, impressed. "And what was your contribution?"

"What makes you so sure I made one?"

"Intuition." The man would put his mark on everything in his life, she thought. Including herself.

"Smart woman. I supply the tree each year."

Toni turned to find him very close and what little composure remained nearly shattered beneath his steamy gaze.

"Ever play pool?" he asked, changing the subject.

Toni's shoulders lowered and she smiled, feeling on safer ground. "Too many times to count."

"Then we don't need lessons." He grabbed her hand and strode the few steps to the pool table. Wrapping his hands around her waist, he lifted her onto the lacquered edge.

She licked her lips, wondering why she'd deluded herself into an illusion of safety. Around Max, she was constantly off balance, desire never far away. "No lessons," she agreed, wondering what would come next.

"Then how about we play each other? For intriguing stakes." His deep eyes bored into hers.

"What do you have in mind?"

"It's called getting to know you. For every ball I miss, I admit something about myself. Something deep and personal or . . . something I desire." His voice deepened to a husky drawl.

She tried to swallow but her mouth had grown dry. "And if you get the ball into the pocket?"

She watched the pulse beat in his neck, and acting on impulse, she pressed a light kiss against his skin. He let out a low growl. "If I make my shot, you remove an article of clothing. Same rules apply for you. What do you say?"

Arousal beat a heavy rhythm in her veins. Naughty or nice, Toni thought. Did she have the nerve to participate in his game? To take their night to its ultimate conclusion?

Under ordinary circumstances, probably not. But nothing about Max or her growing feelings for him was typical— or easy. However, her pool game had never been a problem—not since she'd waitressed in college and learned from the best. "I say why not?"

He handed her a cue, then proceeded to set up the table. "Do you want to break or should I?"

"I'll do it." Toni figured it was a win-win situation. Either she revealed something about herself or he revealed a bare body part—either way *she* wouldn't be the one overexposed.

Max stepped back, leaning on his cue as Toni lined up her shot. The one thing he'd forgotten when suggesting this game was her skimpy outfit—and if the thought of their rules had him hot and bothered, the reality of watching her bent over the table inspired erotic images to rival his steamiest daydream.

"You do realize the lighter the stick the farther the follow-through," she said.

"It's also been said a heavier stick gives you more

power," Max replied but he wasn't concentrating.

The white fur trim of her skirt had lifted a notch, revealing thigh-high stockings and an enticing glimpse of the pale skin peeking above the elastic lace trim. The sudden rise in heat owed nothing to room temperature and everything to his sexy elf. His fingers itched to cup her soft flesh and his body begged to be cradled in her feminine heat.

The sudden crack of the stick hitting the cue ball broke his train of thought and echoed in the otherwise silent room. Still in a sweat, Max forced himself to focus on the game in time to see a flash of color and a ball ease into the corner pocket. "I'm impressed."

She straightened and grinned, looking pleased with herself. "One lesson I learned early in life was to never agree to a game I couldn't win."

"I'll keep that in mind." He reached for the bottom of his shirt and yanked it over his head, grateful for her decent shot and the opportunity to cool off.

Her lashes fluttered quickly and her eyes opened wide as she stared at his bare chest.

"What's wrong? Did you forget the rules?" he asked.

She shook her head. "Of course not." Appearing more flustered than before, she settled in for the next round of play. But this time her hands shook and Max knew for sure his lack of clothing had rattled her. At least now they were on equal footing, he thought, taking in the seductive wiggle of her behind as she lined up her shot.

Sure enough, the next ball went shimmying toward the back wall, missing the pocket. "Sorry, sweetheart. Confession time."

She turned toward him, eyes big and imploring, a pout on her lips.

He shook his head. "No poor-me look is going to sway me, now spill." He paused, thinking of her alternatives. "Or you could always opt to speed the game along and remove an item of clothing."

"My sweet sixteen was my worst birthday," she said quickly, obviously making her choice.

He suppressed a laugh. "What happened?" He stepped closer, wishing she'd taken him up on his alternative offer.

"My dog ran away."

"I'm not buying that." He folded his arms across his chest, gratified when her eyes followed the movement. "But I am listening."

Her arm brushed his and she didn't break contact as she said, "My father died suddenly, the day before I turned sixteen."

Max breathed in deeply. A punch in the gut would have been more gentle, but it was his own fault. He'd suggested they reveal something deep and personal, and she had. She trusted him, showing it far more than if she'd removed her clothes.

"What happened?" he asked softly. Though she couldn't have any fond memories of the man, losing a parent couldn't be easy. "Heart attack?"

She nodded. "And instead of grief, I felt nothing but relief." The strain in her face and the guilt in her eyes were obvious. "And here I thought my shooting first would leave *you* more exposed." She shook her head and treated him to a brief smile. "Your turn." She gestured to the cue.

Max swallowed hard. Had he really thought this would be light and easy?

"Okay." Still shaken, he bent over the table and took in his options before lining up his shot, missing the pocket by too much.

He felt her light touch as she tapped him on the shoulder. He turned to find her in his personal space, within kissing distance. He reached for her shoulders and held on.

"You didn't have to do that," she whispered, calling him on his deliberately missed shot. An easier play had sat by the corner pocket but he'd chosen to forfeit instead.

"No, I didn't. But I wanted to." He'd had two choices. Open a vein and exchange information or watch her peel off the clingy green suit.

No matter how much he'd rather see her undress, he owed her and had to reveal a personal secret. She'd opened up to him tonight. Twice. If his goal was getting closer, he had to return the favor. Besides, he wanted to let her in. For the first time, he wanted to connect with a woman in more places than in bed. He'd proven himself adept at making selfish choices in life, Max thought, but not when it came to Toni. She was too special.

Gratitude flickered in her eyes and she waited in silence for him to pay up. He wasn't comfortable and hated like hell for having put himself in this position, but he supposed that spoke of Toni's effect on him. "My father resents me for leaving the business and I've never measured up to Stephan as Dad's favorite son." He tensed, having admitted his deepest vulnerability and laid it out there for her to see.

Her gaze softened. "Your father's a fool, and if you repeat a word of that to my boss, you'll pay in spades," she said, then wrapped her arms around his neck and pulled him closer.

Her lips lingered over his and as his chest rasped against her fur-lined V-neck, he needed more than a simple kiss. He fumbled for her zipper, the one that would allow him to peel off the outfit and bare her for him to see. But she pulled back before he could get a decent grasp and he groaned.

"Your last miss didn't count," she said in a husky voice. "Now play pool."

He wagged a finger in the air. "Like I said, naughty girl."

"What fun is it if you don't have to work for it?"

"Trust me, sweetheart, it'd be plenty fun. But if you insist, I'll take another turn." Having laid his soul bare, he knew it was time to turn up the heat. "But before I make this next shot . . ."

"You're too confident about your gaming abilities," she said, interrupting him.

"Aren't you the one who said never play a game you can't win? But if at any point you change your mind . . ."

She shook her head. "I wouldn't have let you drive all the way out here if I wasn't sure."

He let out a slow breath of air that did little to help his

rapidly beating heart. "Just remember, it's your choice."

She looked at him in a way no one—no woman—had ever looked at him before, with just the right mixture of trust, reverence, and desire to make a man fall to his knees.

"You're a nice guy, Max."

He'd never been called nice before and he knew his actions tonight were as unique as she was. "You're pretty damn special yourself." He leaned over the table and easily made his next shot, then walked a few steps to line up the next. "But something tells me you won't be thinking such great thoughts about me after this," he said, sinking another ball as he spoke, then his third before shifting her way.

He focused on her and his breath caught in his throat. She'd left her shoes under the table in the other room and Max hadn't realized how little remained—the shirt, skirt, and belt, all three items she'd discarded while he was upping the ante and making his shots.

She faced him now, his most erotic dream come to life. Her clothes lay in a pile beside her. Her black hair, tousled and full, caressed her shoulders. The body he'd glimpsed through the barrier of clothing and imagined in his mind had nothing on reality. A black lace bra cut in a deep V contrasted with and revealed creamy white mounds of flesh, while a whisper-light-looking bikini barely covered her feminine secrets.

She met his gaze and shrugged, a deep blush staining her cheeks and an embarrassed fidget to her stance. "I forgot to mention that when I lose—no matter how unlikely— I always pay up."

He edged his finger beneath one delicate bra strap, savoring the feel of her soft flesh beneath his roughened fingertips. "If you consider this a loss, then we have nothing further to—"

"Shh." She placed one finger over his lips. "That was a figure of speech."

His tongue darted out and he tasted her, a combination of salty skin and female softness. She sucked in a startled breath but she didn't remove her hand. Instead she traced the outline of his mouth with her fingertip, leaving him incredibly aroused by her touch.

"The game's over, Max, and I'd call it even."

He grinned. "Win–win."

"Mmm-hmm."

Taking that as his cue, Max did what he'd been dying to do since he'd laid eyes on her standing beside the Christmas tree—he spanned her bare waist with his hands, curling his fingers around her back and kneading his palms into her skin.

She let out a low, throaty moan. Need, want, and desire collided as her back arched and her breasts reached toward him, almost as if in supplication. Max didn't want to deny her.

And he could no longer deny himself.

CHAPTER FOUR

One night. Toni told herself she'd earned one night with this very special man. Then she could hang on to the memories and get on with her busy life. She refused to let herself dwell on what kind of emptiness that life would hold now that she'd known Max.

He'd settled her on the table and the lacquer felt cool against her hot, fevered skin, making her more aware of her surroundings and what was to come. She spread her thighs and he stepped inside, then bent his head and captured her nipple in his mouth, suckling her through the filmy black lace. His teeth grazed her flesh, then his tongue soothed and white-hot darts of need pulsed inside her. Her reaction was immediate, the pull starting at point of contact and causing intense contractions deep in her belly and down lower.

"You like that?"

Her answer came out a low, husky growl.

"Is that a yes?" He cradled her tender flesh in one hand and treated her other breast to the same lavish attention as the first.

She squirmed against the hard surface and slick moisture trickled between her legs as warmth and desire exploded inside her. "That's a yes."

He lifted his head and met her gaze. "You like to play."

"When it goes both ways." She raised her hands, placing both palms not just on his bare chest, but against his nipples.

Slowly, she raked her nails downward, watching, gratified, as his eyes glazed with heated emotion.

He groaned aloud. "You have no idea what you do to me."

"Oh, I think I can guess." Because she knew what *he* did to her. Every nerve ending came to life, raw and exposed, sizzling with live currents of desire.

"No need to guess when I can show you," he said, bringing his mouth down hard on hers. Frenzied, his kiss expressed an immediate need to be as close as possible.

His tongue swept inside the deep recesses of her mouth, mimicking the ultimate act. It wasn't a joining of bodies in the biblical sense, but another, just as intimate means of climbing toward satisfaction. His strong hands slid from her waist to her thighs and he grazed the tops of her stockings with his thumbs while his fingertips teased the outer edges of her panties. With his whisper-soft and erotically arousing movements, he let her know what he had in store.

And Toni wanted more. She arched her back and her hips jerked forward, reflexively, searching for his harder, deeper touch. He didn't deny her. He broke the kiss and concentrated on her need, cupping her feminine mound in his palm. The heat and weight of his hand against her barely covered flesh stirred long-dormant sensations and when he pushed aside the thin lace and dipped his fingers inside her moist, waiting heat, she thought she'd died and gone to heaven.

She was hot and aroused, on the brink of falling over a precipice, a tumble she had no desire to take alone. She leaned back to catch her breath, intending to make her desire known and she caught a glimpse of their position. She was barely dressed, her legs spread wide, with Max's lean body settled between them. She was open and vulnerable, physically as well as emotionally. The intimacy they were sharing struck her as strongly as her rampaging emotions. And when he leaned over, covering her body with his so he could rest his cheek against hers, he found a way closer to her heart.

She shut her eyes against the wave of emotion she wasn't ready to deal with and instead wrapped her legs around his waist in a provocative suggestion. "Make love to me, Max."

His deep blue eyes met hers. "Be sure, Toni." His breathing was as ragged as her emotions. "Because if we go any further there's no way I can stop."

She'd come into this night with seduction in mind and though everything had changed, including the man, there was no way she could walk away from him now. Still, he had to understand her behavior wasn't normally so wanton. She didn't know why it mattered so much, but it did.

She caressed his face with one hand. "I wouldn't have asked you if I wasn't sure, but . . ."

He grabbed for her hand. "But what?"

"No matter how bold I've been tonight, I want you to know I don't usually sleep with a man I just met."

"I know."

"You do?"

He nodded. "Because I feel like I've known you all my life."

She felt the same but couldn't bring herself to admit the truth out loud. She licked her already moist lips. "There's something else you need to know." She couldn't think beyond now. Not that he'd asked but the emotional pull between them was too strong to ignore.

He shook his head. "Enough talking, don't you think?" To make his point, he slipped one finger back into her panties, parting her sensitive folds and moving his fingertip deeply inside her.

She closed her eyes and exhaled a soft moan as he encountered the desire he'd created inside her.

"So wet, so ready for me."

The man did have a point. "Talking can wait." She forced her heavy eyelids open. "So what did you have in mind?"

"I'm going to do what you asked, sweetheart. I'm going to make love to you. But I want you to do something for me first." He reached into his front pocket and pulled out the anklet she'd had on earlier in the evening.

She eyed the object with surprise.

"I took it from the car." He answered her unspoken question and shook the accessory in the air. The light chime of bells echoed in the silent bar. "Wear these for me."

Her heart beat out a rapid pulse and excitement tingled inside her. "Mind if I ask why?" she asked, curiously aroused by the suggestion.

"I want to hear bells when I come inside you," he said and his blue eyes flared with heat. "And every time you hear the ringing of chimes, I want you to think of me."

She never broke eye contact as she raised her leg and perched it on the edge of the table. With a nod of approval, he turned to his task, taking his time, rolling the stocking down her leg, inch by tantalizing inch. When he finished one, she propped her other leg so he could peel off another of her few remaining layers.

Then he snapped the anklet closed. "Perfect," he said, taking in her wanton pose.

With her legs spread wide, Toni ought to be embarrassed, but all she felt was a keen sense of carnal anticipation. "Well, you've got me where you want me."

She shifted her leg, shaking her foot so he could hear the light tinkling of bells. To her surprise, the sound turned from light and playful to highly erotic, charging the already electric atmosphere even further. "So what do you plan to do with me?"

With her help, he eased the last remaining undergarment off her legs, letting her panties fall to the floor. "I already told you. I'm going to make love to you." Then he knelt down, dipped his head, and proceeded to do just that, in a way she hadn't expected or anticipated. In a way much more intimate than she'd imagined.

His hot breath covered her feminine mound and his tongue delved deep into her core. Resting back on her elbows, she gave herself up to sensation, to the masterful strokes and fiery darting motions that had her hips gyrating and her body arching, beseeching him for more. He complied, bringing her higher, nearly to the brink of orgasm.

"Max!" She writhed beneath him, unable to express her desire further, not with her body tense and her climax so close. But she knew she didn't want her first time to be alone. Wonderful yet unfulfilling at the same time. He seemed to understand because his nuzzling caresses slowed and the waves subsided, leaving her empty.

Next thing she knew, she was being lifted and carried in his arms. "We're going where?" she wondered aloud, her body protesting the very cessation of pleasure she'd asked for.

"Upstairs." Max made his way to the back door and up a dimly lit staircase. "Somehow, thoughts of our first time on a pool table don't work for me."

Not that he'd had the presence of mind to realize that before she'd called out his name, he thought. Prior to that moment, he'd have taken her on the hard surface without thought or reason, he'd been so far gone. Lost in her dewy essence.

"See? I told you you were a nice guy." Her arms snaked around his neck, her bare body crushed against his chest. "Now hurry."

He managed a laugh, barely able to make his way up the stairs, open his door, and hit the bedroom before lowering her to the bed and sealing his mouth to hers. But kissing wasn't enough for either of them and her hands fumbled with the snap on his jeans. Frustrated with the barrier between them, he rose to shuck his pants and briefs, and to dig protection from the back of his nightstand drawer, not an easy task in the dim room, lit only by the glow of light from the street lamp outside.

As he knelt over her, a wash of emotion swept through him, strong and tender, something he knew damn well he'd never felt before. He cupped her thighs, widening her legs, then slid his fingers over her damp flesh. He met her velvet gaze, watched as her eyes glazed at the same moment her hips rose in response to the slick strokes of his hand.

A soft purr escaped her throat, a sound of frustrated need.

"Just making sure you're ready for me, sweetheart."

"I am." She took him by surprise, managing to flip him to his side, switching their positions, her ending up on top. "I realize you're trying to be a gentleman our first time." Toni swung her leg over his until she straddled his thighs. "But there's no reason to wait."

"I like the way you think." And he more than liked her.

After making use of the condom he'd found earlier, he grasped her hips, fully participating as she lowered herself onto his hard erection. He gritted his teeth as heaven surrounded him and he entered her tight, moist heat.

She let out a shuddering sigh. "It's . . ." She bit down on her lower lip. "It's never been like this before." Awe and something more infused her voice, letting him know she felt not just the physical, but the emotional connection, as well.

Needing to touch her in other ways, he lifted his upper body to meet her lips in a too brief kiss before leaning back against the pillows. She shifted slightly and his body shook with the restraint of holding back, of letting her mentally adjust to a connection he'd already recognized and accepted.

He reached up to unhook the clasp of her bra and she let the flimsy garment fall to the side, revealing twin mounds of rounded flesh. Her black hair fell over her shoulders, in stark contrast to her pale skin. He'd never seen a more incredible sight. His body swelled and hardened further while her muscles contracted to accommodate him, arousing him even more.

Max had said he felt as if he'd known her forever, and cocooned inside her, he knew he was right. His heart pounded as hard and fast as the adrenaline flowing through him. And then she began to move, beginning a rhythm he picked up immediately. Each circular motion built upon the already growing waves rocking his body. Every clench of her thighs ground their bodies more intimately and drove him that much deeper inside her. Fire licked at his skin and waves of desire pushed him higher, and from the soft cries escaping her lips, he knew she felt it, too.

Carnal sensation mixed with a basic awareness. He'd had sex before, but Toni was right. They were making love.

He glided inside, her tight, slick passage accepting him, taking him with her just as her frenzied movements carried her up and over the edge.

"Max." She cried out his name, her body pulsing around his, beckoning him to follow. And as his climax hit, engulfing him in sensation, Max heard the ringing of bells.

Toni curled her legs beneath her and poked around in the candy dish he'd brought from his small kitchen. She clenched her thighs together and the waves of awareness hit her once more. How could she still be so sensitive and aroused?

She glanced over at Max through hooded eyes. He watched her intently, not saying a word. What was there to say? What they'd just shared defied description. Though she knew she'd clammed up on him afterward, her thoughts were in turmoil. She'd planned a seduction she could walk away from, not a relationship that would be hard to let go of. But no matter how she tried to tell herself she barely knew him, he'd not only touched her body, he'd touched her heart.

"Do you always work up such an appetite?" He rested his arm across the pillows, skimming his fingertips along her shoulders.

"I already told you I don't do this often, so how do you expect me to answer that?" She knew she'd snapped and held up her hands in apology. "I don't know what's wrong with me."

"I do."

He gently took the bowl out of her hands and placed it on the nightstand. "It was intense and it scared you."

She narrowed her gaze, not sure if she liked how well he read her. "If that's the case then how come you're so calm and composed?"

He took her hand, his thumb tracing slow circles into her palm and her stomach curled with warmth. "I'm a jaded guy who's been around?" he said lightly.

Toni sensed more beneath his words but she couldn't tell if she was projecting her hopes and dreams into his unspoken words.

"And if I'm not thrown, I think the more important question is how come you *are*?" he asked.

She bit down on her lower lip. She couldn't very well tell him she'd slept with him wanting only one night. For one thing it was callous, and regardless of what he wanted from her, she had no desire to hurt him. And for another, what she'd wanted going into this night was no longer what she desired now.

Now she wanted a chance to see where things with Max could lead, but the thought frightened her beyond reason. After all, what did she know of long-term, stable relationships? Of depending on another person when she only knew how to depend on herself? Most of all, she feared losing her independence to a man and what it could cost her.

But she wanted to learn about sharing and caring, and she wanted to see that being in a relationship didn't mean losing the autonomy she cherished. She wanted to learn all those things.

With Max.

"Let's say you're right." She forced herself to meet his compassionate and oh-so-sexy gaze. "And let's say what's between us is passionate and . . ."

"Intense." He treated her to his most charming grin.

Then again, any grin she'd seen from him was appealing and her heart twisted with emotion. "Okay, intense. It's been one night. What exactly are you proposing we do about it?" she asked and her heart clenched with possibilities.

In response, he pulled her into his arms and toppled her to the mattress, sandwiching her body between his and the bed. "I suggest we go with the flow and see where things lead."

And if his hard erection against her stomach was any indication, she knew exactly where they were headed. At least for now. "You do know how to tempt me." And going with the flow wasn't a high-pressure situation.

In fact, it was one she couldn't wait to handle. She reached down and grasped his hard erection in her hands. He exhaled and a masculine groan reverberated from his body through hers.

He somehow managed a harsh laugh. "Tempting you is a pleasure." He brushed a sweet kiss across her lips. "Then I have one day at a time to show you we can be as good out of bed as in."

His hips jerked forward, brushing against her thigh. Heat rocked her and arousal began a steady pulsing rhythm.

Toni closed her eyes. Easier to concentrate on the physical than on the emotional, she thought, letting sensation take over. He had only to let his desire be known and her body came alive.

"Look at me."

She opened her eyes but she wasn't able to meet his gaze.

"I'm not going to let you hide from me." He cupped her cheek in his hand but didn't turn her head for her.

The tender gesture brought an unnerving lump to her throat. Not only did he understand her so well but he cared, too. What they'd found in one night was rare and special and she sensed he felt it, too.

She fought the inclination to flee and met his patient gaze. "I don't want to hide from you." Her words came out a whisper and she realized she meant it. Reservations be damned.

"Then don't." Max pulled the covers back, revealing their bare bodies to the cooler air, then reached over and turned on a bedside lamp. He wanted her trust, wanted no secrets, no clothing, not even darkness between them. Physical intimacy was the only way he knew how to start.

The rest would have to come. They'd already made love once, and when they did again, there'd be no hiding.

For either of them.

He caressed her body with his gaze, following the slender lines and full curves, appreciation and more settling inside him. Then he watched as she did the same. She took in his body, her eyes widening as they traveled from his face, down to the erection he couldn't hide.

"What do you want from me?" she asked softly, but he had a hunch she already knew because as she spoke, she slid backward, settling into the pillows behind her.

Her black hair fanned across the ivory sheets. *His* sheets. A primitive urge to possess her, to make her his again—this time forever—took hold. "I want everything, sweetheart. But I'll take as much as you're willing to give."

He inched forward, making his way toward her. Her eyes lit with excitement and desire, diluted by an apprehension only his time and trust could overcome.

She surprised him by extending her arms. "I want to make love to you, Max. Lights on, nothing hidden."

Her vulnerability hit him hard where it counted most—his heart.

Toni awoke feeling decadent and relaxed after falling asleep without trouble for the first time in ages. Of course her late-night activity could have had something to do with that. So could her . . . lover.

Lover. She tested the word on her tongue, realizing it was too generic, too detached and indifferent, to describe their encounter. Whatever sexual relationships she'd had in the past, no one had made it past the walls she'd built up since she'd been a child. How could any man have gotten inside her when she'd feared emotional closeness would result in unhealthy dependence? But Max had not only found her heart, she'd willingly let him in.

"Max?" She sat up in bed, realizing she was alone.

Noise from the shower in the bathroom alerted her to his location. She was in Max's bedroom while he showered for the day. Soon he'd come out—would he wrap a towel around his neck? His waist? Neither? Curling her legs beneath her, she forced deep breaths into her lungs. Whatever sharing a morning together entailed, it couldn't be any more intimate than the night they'd just spent.

And it wasn't reason for panic, she told herself, until the waves of anxiety began to ease. The man wasn't asking her for anything more than she was willing to give, and a nurturing, caring relationship would be a wonderful start to both the holiday season and a brand-new year.

The ringing of the telephone startled her and the answering machine picked up soon after. "Hi, Max." Toni recognized Stephan's voice. "Dad tells me you'll be running the new office. Since Santa's helper will be your assistant, it won't be too much of a strain," he said, a wry sound to his voice. "You owe me one. Later, big brother."

No sooner had Stephan's voice clicked off than Toni tossed the covers off, adrenaline flowing fast in her veins. Or maybe she was feeling a full-blown anxiety attack coming on. Was this fate's version of a joke? Or was she being punished for her descent into the world of the less repressed?

Where were her clothes? She glanced around the room, desperate to find something to put on. She'd finally found a man she could relate to, a man she desired, a man she trusted enough to let down her guard with.

And he'd be her new boss. A man she'd slept with the first night they'd met. A man who was now in control of her job—the symbol of the very independence she cherished. One-night stand or full-blown affair, it didn't matter. Because office romances never worked out, and when they fell apart, who was the one gone? Not the boss, but the co-worker. Office-wrecker.

She'd be out on her ear, no job, no references, no money—her blessed independence shot to hell, all because she'd fallen for the wrong man. "Where are my clothes?" she wailed aloud.

Downstairs. Scattered around the poolroom. She rolled her eyes, realizing her life had taken on surreal proportions. Her gaze fell to a pile of clothes on the chair which obviously substituted for a laundry hamper or a closet. She grabbed a sweatshirt and then turned to the desk and pilfered a sheet of paper.

"Dear Max," she wrote, feeling as if it were like "Dear John" and hating herself for it. She finished her letter, hoping what she said would be enough to save, if not her job, then at least a letter of recommendation for a position at a new firm. Starting over, Toni thought. Like her mother had each time she'd tried to make a stand and failed.

Her stomach clenching, she bolted for the door without looking back.

CHAPTER FIVE

Max looped a towel around his neck and headed out of the bathroom. He had to be at his parents' house early but damned if he'd miss one minute of time he could spend with Toni—who, he realized, was nowhere to be found.

Max glanced around but all he saw was a rumpled bed. "Son of a bitch." He muttered more under his breath.

He didn't need to look around his small apartment. Every instinct he had and prided himself on told him she was gone. What he didn't know was why.

He ran a frustrated hand through his hair. Yes he did. He knew exactly why she'd bolted. Fear, pure and simple. Because Max Corbin, ace detective, had made a major miscalculation when dealing with a vulnerable, skittish woman. Despite her calculated seduction, he didn't kid himself that Toni was anything less than vulnerable. That innocence was what held him in thrall. Her beauty would never fade but her looks weren't what had caused him to fall so damn hard. It was the whole package.

And Max had blown it. He'd tread lightly when he should have hit harder. He'd kept his feelings to himself, afraid of frightening her after one night. Maybe if he'd let her know he was certain they had long-term written all over them, she'd still be in his bed and not on her way back to New York City.

"Damn." Curses and regrets were the only things he could manage about now. He walked to the bed they'd shared and lowered himself onto the mattress. The sheets had cooled but his body hadn't. Not even a cold shower could dull the aching need she inspired.

He glanced at the clock but a folded note blocked his view of the numbers and his stomach plummeted as he read her hastily scrawled words. "Dear Max, Please remember I don't normally sleep with men I don't know. And don't hold last night against me. Toni."

Confusion mingled with a deep pain in his gut as he realized what she must have felt on waking up alone. Another reason to kick himself in the ass, Max thought. He should have let his family wait, and would have if not for his father's frail health.

Another choice curse rose to his throat but he stifled it, knowing it would do no good. He just needed to find Toni. He crumpled the note and tossed it to the nightstand, noticing his blinking answering machine for the first time. He wondered who'd called so early and hit play.

Listening to his brother's message provided not only insight into Toni's run but another reason to kick himself hard. Only Max would understand the sarcasm in the message and the fact that his brother was giving him a heads-up before his meeting with the old man. Only Max and Stephan realized he had no intention of returning to Corbin and Sons. But Toni, to whom he'd admitted his biggest failing and disappointment, might well believe he'd want to make his sick father happy.

She obviously thought she'd slept with her boss. For a woman who needed security as much as other people needed air to breathe, that had to have been one hell of a slap in the face.

Max pulled on his jeans and made his way down to the empty bar. The pool table was just as they'd left it last night, but Toni had retrieved her clothing. Not a trace of her remained except in Max's heart.

Max entered his brother's luxury condo, an apartment opposite in furnishing and feel from Max's own casual over-the-bar rental.

"So what brings you to my neck of the woods?" Stephan asked, gesturing to a chair in the kitchen.

Max shook his head. He didn't have time to sit. Still, his brother had asked a fair question since Max couldn't remember the last time he'd shown up here unannounced. But today was different, just as his relationship with his twin had undergone a subtle shift since last night. Many things had changed since last night, he thought wryly.

Including his priorities. Max had driven into the city, postponing his meeting with his father in favor of finding Toni. Unfortunately, he had no idea where to begin, so he'd landed on his brother's doorstep first. Swallowing both his pride and his rule against talking about the women he slept with, Max unloaded on his brother. It was the first time in too damn long he'd had a heart-to-heart with his twin. Realizing how much he missed it and seeing the same in Stephan's face, Max knew the distance had closed.

Distance Max had placed there for no good reason. Just as Toni's insecurities drove her to succeed and to bolt this morning, Max now knew his own insecurities had driven him from his family. He planned to rectify both his and Toni's misperceptions—immediately.

Max finished relating last night's history to his brother.

Stephan nodded, while shaking his head at the same time. "I'm glad to see you screw up every once in a while. Makes the rest of us feel like you're human, too."

"Come again?" Max raised an eyebrow. "I screw up more than once in a while. Isn't that what Dad always says?"

"Dad says it to instill guilt and you buy into it every time. But you always hold your ground and live your life. To me that's not screwing up, that's playing it smart. A part of me has always envied that."

Shock rendered Max mute. For twins, he and his brother had been operating on opposite wavelengths for too long. "You don't want to be a lawyer?" Max asked.

"I never gave it a thought. It was expected and I followed through. Now it's all I know and I can't imagine doing anything else. But sometimes I wonder 'what if.'" He shrugged. "Then I take a look at how following a different road has kept you far from the family and I figure I'll accept my life as it is. But in case you're wondering, distancing yourself is the only screwup I think you've made." His brother let out a wry laugh. "Until now."

"Now meaning Toni." Just saying her name caused the twisting in Max's gut to return. He had the rest of his life to process his brother's admission and make things right. He had too little time to catch Toni and explain before she withdrew for good. "I need her address."

"There's no point." Stephan pushed off the wall and headed for the mugs in the cabinet. "Coffee?"

"No, thanks, and why the hell not?"

"She's not at home. I stopped by the office to pick up a file and she was there sorting through boxes." Stephan laughed. "Damn but you need to calm down."

"After I talk to her."

His brother eyed him in surprise. "This is a hell of a lot more than a one-night stand, isn't it?"

Max clenched and unclenched his fists. "It'd better be or I'm looking at a lousy Christmas and a miserable New Year."

"Well, I'll be damned. I wonder what I missed in her."

"Too late for you to find out now," Max said in warning, turned and started for the door before spinning back to face his brother. "Hey, Stephan, I owe you one for the heads-up on what the old man wanted."

His twin shrugged. "I figured since you showed up last night, it was the least I could do."

Max laughed. Showing up had brought Toni into his life. "Then it looks like I owe you double. See ya later." Max opened the door and stepped into the hall.

"Don't think for one minute that I won't cash in," Stephan called as Max slammed the door shut behind him.

Toni needed to keep busy or else she'd think and she could not afford to think. Not about last night and how much she'd enjoyed herself, not about Max and how much she'd grown to like and care for him, and certainly not about the fact that she'd slept with her new boss. What irony. After years of avoiding the situation with Stephan, she'd stepped right into it with his twin.

She let out a slow breath of air. Okay, apparently she couldn't avoid thinking but maybe she could drown out the sound of her own thoughts. She flipped on the radio in her near empty office. As expected, Christmas music filled the air. She tried humming and when that didn't work she sealed the last box, while singing out loud, but no way could she escape the fact that she'd fallen in love with Max Corbin.

Fallen in love. She shook her head, unable to believe the truth. She was a woman who hadn't grown up watching a loving relationship and who'd never once deluded herself that happily ever after was in her future. Yet in one meeting, over the course of one night—one glorious night— she'd fallen in love. And all the security she'd worked for, all the independence she'd strived for, now hung in the balance.

Her heart beat out a rapid cadence, panic and other undefinable emotions parading inside her while the music mocked her thoughts. No merry Christmas, no happy new year for her this year. She closed her eyes, singing the final verse along with the song. "We wish you a merry Christmas, we wish you a merry Christmas, we wish you a merry Christmas . . . and you're out on your ear." Toni added her own ending to the well-known tune.

"Is that really what you think of me?"

Startled, Toni whirled around to find herself face-to-face with Max. Leaning against her doorframe, he was the epitome of her fantasy come to life. And to think, she hadn't known she had any. "Hello, Max."

He inclined his head. "Toni."

She attempted to swallow but her mouth was too dry. "What are you doing here?"

"I wanted to get a few things straight." He walked into her office, making the small area even smaller by virtue of his overwhelming presence.

She grasped the cardboard edges of the box. "I can tender my resignation if it would make things easier." She spoke without meeting his gaze.

She heard him exhale hard. "Again, is that what you think of me? Do you really believe I'd have taken you home and made love to you, knowing I was your boss, and then demanded your job the next day?"

Toni wondered if she imagined the hurt in his voice. She shook her head. "Truthfully, I haven't thought things through."

"No, you're just feeling, aren't you?" His voice softened. "Acting on instinct and fear."

"What do you expect, Max? I woke up to find out I had slept with my soon-to-be-boss. Whose job is on the line now? Yours or mine?"

"No one's, I hope." He eased himself onto the edge of her desk, too close for her peace of mind.

So close she could inhale his masculine scent and arousal hit her all over again, but he wasn't asking permission and she wasn't in a position to argue. "So you're suggesting we put last night behind us and work together?" She tried to laugh but the sound was harsh and she didn't mean it anyway.

If he could work side by side with her, after what they'd shared, she'd misjudged him. Yet even before she met his serious and compelling gaze, she knew better. How could she not? She'd accepted him into her body, felt him hard and hot inside her, giving as much as he got in return.

Then there were the emotional revelations, Toni thought. Men didn't open up and share unless they cared. But she was still at a loss.

"I'm not suggesting we work together, either. I told you last night I do my own thing. And yes, my father's disappointed, and no, he's not finished trying to convince me to return. But he's been unsuccessful in the past and he'll continue to be unsuccessful in the future. Law isn't what I want. I am *not* going to be your boss."

She glanced down and saw her hands were shaking. "But Stephan said . . ."

"Stephan was giving me advance warning about what to expect at my meeting with Dad. You heard what Dad wants, not what will be." He touched her cheek, his hand strong and gentle. "But that's not the real issue, is it?"

She forced herself to meet his gaze. "If you know so much, then tell me what is."

"I'm not your boss. I'm just a man who's desperately in love with you. So the issue is, are you going to run from your feelings because of your past? Or are you going to stay and face them . . . and give us a chance?"

In that instant, Toni's past and present flashed in front of her eyes, a kaleidoscope of memories, some good, some bad, some satisfying, but way too many lonely ones. Lonely by choice not necessity, she thought. Last night she'd chosen Max and last night she hadn't felt alone or isolated.

She was a woman who'd always prided herself on her ability to stand on her own two feet, yet she wanted nothing more than to throw herself into his arms.

"So what are you waiting for?" he asked.

She blinked, refocusing on her surroundings. On Max. "Did I speak out loud?"

He watched her intently. "No, I'm just a mind reader."

Her mind was jumbled, her heart racing, and his earlier words came back to her. "What did you say?"

"I'm just a mind reader."

"Before that."

"I'm not your boss," he said.

"In between those two things."

"I'm a man desperately in love with you?" He grinned.

His devastating smile nearly knocked her off her feet and a sparkle twinkled in his blue eyes. A weight she hadn't been aware of carrying her whole life eased and lifted inside her.

She could run and hide or give the future a chance. No contest, Toni thought, a smile pulling at her lips.

"I asked what you're waiting for?" His voice was gruff

with emotion, his once-certain smile faltered as his inse-
curity became obvious.

More than anything else, his ability to own up to his
feelings and emotions touched her heart. She could free
hers and learn from him. Be independent and still be in
love.

If she dared.

His gaze locked with hers. He lifted his hand, revealing
a green sprig of mistletoe and holding it up high. "I thought
we could try it again." He extended his free hand, holding
it out to her. "Get it right this time."

Toni rushed into his arms and Max lowered his head for
a kiss that felt too long in coming. He'd never admit it out
loud but she'd had him sweating there for a minute. But
now she was his.

Her lips were soft and willing, welcoming him. His
hands slipped around her waist, beneath the band of her
sweatshirt until he encountered soft skin. She let out a faint
sigh and leaned back against the desk, letting his body mesh
with hers. Her thighs spread and his groin settled hard
against her stomach.

But warning bells went off in his head. "Not again,
sweetheart. Not until we've got a few things settled."

"Mmm." She purred in his ear and her hand slipped to
the bulge in his jeans.

Max nearly caved right then, but knowing his future was
on the line, he forced himself to pull back. He'd messed
up once and she'd run at the first opportunity. He wasn't
about to screw up again. "I love you" was saying a hell of
a lot for a man who'd always lived alone—but it wasn't a
declaration of future intent. And a woman like Toni both
deserved and needed one.

And for the first time, Max realized, so did he. "Toni."

She met his gaze.

"I don't usually sleep with women I just met."

She grinned. "That's good because I feel as if I've
known you all my life."

"Then prove it. I'm a slob. I don't put my clean clothes

away, I wear them straight from a pile on the chair. I squeeze the toothpaste from the middle, I drink milk out of the carton, and those are the positives." He paused, deadly serious. "But I still think we have a chance."

Her eyes were misty and damp but her smile never dimmed. "I've been known to hang stockings from doorknobs and eat Chinese food out of the carton. For breakfast." She smoothed one hand down his thigh, the other hand never leaving its strategic position on his groin.

His body protested his prolonged wait in making her his but his mind and heart knew he was doing it right this time. "I go to sleep too late and wake up too early. But I promise to give you the best that I've got to make us work. You can trust me and you never have to fear me—" Max never got to finish.

She covered his mouth with hers in the sweetest, hottest, most honest kiss he'd ever known. He paused only to slam her door closed and undress her, dropping his jeans as quickly as possible. He entered her quickly, this time on the desk she'd be leaving behind. When the aftershocks subsided, his body was still deep inside hers.

"This was naughty," she murmured.

"I thought that was your plan."

She laughed. "Only with you, Max. You bring out my decadent side."

"My pleasure, sweetheart. It's something I plan on doing again." His groin began to harden once more, and Max proceeded to seal their bodies, just as they'd sealed their future. Being naughty under the mistletoe.

A Christmas
Charade

—

KATHRYN SMITH

For Laura.

CHAPTER ONE

*My first is a most singular word. Alone it defines the
whole of myself.
Without it, there is no "us" or "we."
And though it is nothing without you,
Its very existence depends on "me."*

Garrett Maxwell, Viscount Praed, was not a man who
dwelled on the negative.

"We're going to die in here," he announced with a re-
signed sigh, staring through the barred window at the night
beyond. Even if he had been more familiar with the French
landscape he wouldn't have been able to ascertain their surroundings, although from the smell, he'd guess they were
somewhere near a harbor.

"I'm sorry, sir." The announcement preceded a series of
bone-jarring coughs.

Garrett's gaze followed a shaft of silvered moonlight
across the small cell. Sitting on the cot against the wall was
Willis, one of his officers, his sickly features ghastly in the
blue-white light.

"For the last time, Willis, it's not your fault we were
captured. It was just bad luck." He kept his voice steady,
hiding his frustration. If anyone were to blame, it was him.
He should have been more careful. It should be him slowly
dying, not this young pup who'd followed him out of blind
devotion.

Willis closed his eyes. Garrett had seen many men die,

but never as slowly as Willis was doing. "Do you think anyone will ever come for us?"

Turning back to the window, Garrett stared up at the stars. "Yes." He knew they would send someone for him. He was valuable. Willis wasn't. He wouldn't tell the boy that.

There was no reply and Garrett knew his friend had slipped into an unnatural and fevered sleep.

How long had they been in the prison? A month? Perhaps longer. They'd been on a simple "reconnaissance" mission, as Wellington called it. Posing as a French peasant, Garrett had gone to meet Willis at their meeting place to hand over what information he'd managed to uncover. That's when they'd been caught. Garrett had been smashed in the head by their captors and had remained in a stupor for several days after. He had no idea how long he'd been unconscious, neither did Willis. Thankfully the headaches that had plagued him had ceased.

The only thing that had kept them both from being killed on the spot was that the French found proof of his identity. A peer of the English realm was a good bargaining chip, but only if they kept him alive. Instinctively, his fingers went to his head, to the thick scab underneath his hair. Blood, grease, and dirt made his scalp itch. At least he hoped it was just blood and dirt.

"You Maxwell?"

Garrett turned toward the door. He hadn't even heard it open. Someone dressed like a guard stood barely visible in the shadows, but unless he'd lost his hearing along with his other senses, this was no ordinary guard. It was a woman.

"Who the hell are you?" He wasn't about to introduce himself just because she had a nice voice.

She stepped just inside the door, as though she were afraid to get too close to him. "I'm from the Home Office," she whispered. "Are you Maxwell?"

The agreement he'd made with the Home Office was that as few people as possible know his true identity. He didn't want special treatment because of his title, and it made it difficult for any double agents to use him to their advantage. The only way his captors had determined his identity was through the personal correspondence in the lining of his jacket. He knew he should have burnt those letters from his sister.

"I'm Maxwell," he replied. "Do you have a message for me?"

She sighed, as though she thought the whole situation a waste of her time, but Garrett wasn't about to trust her until he knew she was the real thing. For all he knew, she could be a delectable-smelling diversion cooked up by the French to ferret information out of him.

"I'm supposed to mention the draperies, not that there are any here to comment upon."

Close enough. "Drape" was the code word he and the Office had agreed upon. It was a simple anagram for his title, but could be worked into most conversations if one had a little imagination. Obviously, his rescuer had little of that.

Or maybe not. As she stepped farther into the cell, Garrett got a look at her face. She was wearing a faux beard and moustache. The disguise did nothing to hide her sex, at least he didn't think so, as his gaze raked over the barely concealed curves of her body. Apparently it had been good enough to get her inside the prison. Obviously the guards hadn't gone without a woman as long as Garrett had. Just the smell of her—clean and fresh—was enough to heat his blood, bad disguise or not.

"We don't have much time," she whispered. "Follow me."

He pointed at Willis, still shivering on his cot. "He's coming with me."

She shot him an annoyed glance. It made her moustache twitch. "My orders are for you and you alone."

Folding his arms across his chest, Garrett stared at her.

The woman's jaw tightened. "Fine, but you'll have to carry him."

As if Garrett had any other choice.

"Maxwell?" came Willis's groggy voice as Garrett shook him awake. "What's going on?"

Garrett smiled, not sure if his friend could even see his expression through his fever. "We're going home, Willis. Can you stand?"

"I'd dance a jig if I thought it would get us home." Leaning heavily on Garrett's arm, the soldier struggled to his feet.

They barely made it to the door before Willis's limbs gave out and he sagged to the floor, almost taking Garrett with him.

"I'm so sorry, sir. Leave me. Save yourself."

Garrett crouched before him. "Willis, you gallant idiot, you know that's not an option." He grabbed Willis's arm in his left hand and scooped his right shoulder under the other man's belly. Grunting, he lifted and rose to his feet with a strength he didn't know he had.

Adjusting Willis's weight on his shoulder, he turned to the woman. "Let's go."

Slowly, they crept out into the dark corridor. Each step seemed louder and heavier than the last to Garrett as he struggled to remain upright on his trembling legs. His shoulder and back were beginning to ache mercilessly under Willis's weight, and his lungs ached from the effort to keep his labored breathing quiet. If the guards caught them now, they'd surely kill them. His knees were shaking so badly Garrett wouldn't even be able to run.

"We're almost there," the woman whispered as if reading his thoughts. "This tunnel leads out onto the docks. I have a boat waiting there to take us to England."

England! The very sound of the word gave him the strength to go on.

They broke out into the darkness. The chill night air struck Garrett full in the face and he sucked it greedily into his lungs. The smell of sea and fish were sweet when compared to the fetid air of the prison.

"This way," the woman hissed, quickening her pace. "Hurry!"

Somehow Garrett found the strength to run. Willis jostled heavily against his shoulder and moaned.

"Apologies, old man," Garrett huffed. "We're almost to the boat."

And then they were running up a gangplank, Garrett's lungs bursting and his muscles shaking. Suddenly, they were surrounded, and for one split second he thought it was a trap and he hadn't the strength to fight.

Two men tried to take Willis from him and Garrett raised his fist, even as his knees began to buckle beneath him.

The woman laid a hand on his arm. "It's all right, Mr. Maxwell, these men work for me. They're going to take your friend inside and care for him. Trust me, he'll be in good hands."

The odd thing was that Garrett did trust her. After all, she had saved them, hadn't she? Warily, he allowed her men to take Willis, who had passed out again. He watched them take his friend away before turning to the woman who had saved them.

"What happens now?"

She smiled at his bluntness—a bizarre sight given her false facial hair. He couldn't really see her lips, but her amber-colored eyes crinkled and her moustache pulled up at the corners. "We set sail for England. There's a hot bath and an excellent meal waiting for you below. You might want to take advantage of both."

Garrett followed her as she picked her way down a set of steps into the ship. The ship left the docks shortly after he lowered himself into the hot bath. Sighing in pleasure, he scrubbed himself pink and washed his hair, taking care with his wound. A razor, soap, and mirror had been set on the side for him to shave with and he scraped off the heavy growth of beard with long, satisfied strokes. He wanted nothing more than to soak in the water until it cooled, but it was so dirty from his body he couldn't bring himself to sit in it any longer.

He toweled off quickly, the chill in the air dancing along

his bare skin. A stack of clothes had been placed nearby and he grabbed a pair of trousers and shoved his leg in. Whoever had sent her had underestimated his size. He wasn't huge by any stretch, but he was tall and used to physical activity. The man who owned these clothes was much smaller.

The trousers were a bit snug through the thighs and the crotch, but at least they went on. The shirt was another matter altogether—it wouldn't even go down over his shoulders. Sighing, he tossed it aside and picked up his discarded one. The smell hit him like a hammer and he tossed it into the bath.

He hoped his hostess wasn't too modest, because he was about to walk out into the dining area in nothing but a pair of trousers!

Oh, Garrett had long ago given up any false perception of his looks. His was a fierce countenance, one that had made the girls giggle nervously in his youth and made ladies' eyes widen in trepidation as he became older. He attributed the brunt of the problem to his low, straight brows that made him look as if he were always scowling, and to a mouth that was a tad too wide and too thin to give the illusion of good humor. However, his intimidating appearance had served him well during his career as a soldier and spy.

Stepping out into the corridor in his bare feet, Garrett moved toward the warmth and light of the outer cabin. The smell of food, hot and savory, tantalized his nostrils, drawing a low growl of anticipation from his stomach. His mouth watered.

A female he assumed to be their savior stood at the table, her back to him. She too had recently bathed because a cascade of damp, ebony hair fell over her shoulders almost to her waist. Gone was the grimy uniform, replaced by a gown of soft plum.

"Smells good," he spoke, announcing his presence.

She turned, and if her golden eyes widened at his appearance, Garrett didn't notice. He was too busy staring at her.

She was the most beautiful woman he had ever seen. Her skin glowed in the lamplight, all ivory and pink and gold. Her eyes shone like newly minted coins fringed by thick black lashes. Her lips parted at the sight of him. Was that a good thing or a bad? One could never tell with women. bj10Her gaze dropped to his chest and then to his pelvis. Judging from the flush creeping up her chest and neck, he'd wager it was a good thing.

It was also a little uncomfortable. It had been months since he'd enjoyed the physical company of a woman, and his savior's knowing stare was a painful, *stirring* reminder. "I apologize for my state of dress, but the clothes you provided were too small."

That brought her gaze up to his face. "I'm sorry. The Home Office didn't provide any of your clothing. I brought you some of my late husband's."

A widow, then. That would explain her blush. It would also explain why she looked in the first place. Had her husband been smaller than him in other areas, as well? He pushed the crude thought aside with a rush of shame. He shouldn't think such things. The woman had lost her husband—recently for all he knew—and she had saved his life. She deserved more respect than that.

"Why don't you come eat?" she suggested, gesturing to the table. "You must be famished."

He was hungry—hungrier than he had originally thought. But as he watched the gentle swish of her skirts about her hips as she walked toward the table, Garrett wasn't entirely certain food was what he hungered for.

"You have me at a disadvantage," he remarked as he held her chair for her. "You know my name but I don't know yours."

"Vail," she replied, staring at her plate. "Mrs. Vail."

"Thank you for coming to my rescue, Mrs. Vail." Moving around to the other side, Garrett seated himself across from her.

She draped a napkin over her lap. "You're welcome, but I was just doing my duty."

Her duty? What a strange way of putting it, especially since her tone was so distasteful.

They made small talk as they ate. Well, actually Mrs. Vail talked. Garrett savored every bit of the delicious meal in virtual silence. He was content to listen to the low, throaty pitch of her voice as he filled his belly with as much food as he dared. It wouldn't be much, but he was determined to memorize every savory bite.

Mrs. Vail told him how her husband, Thomas, had been a spy and that she had sometimes worked with him—that was how she knew the layout of the prison he and Willis had been held in. She told him how Thomas had died when the boat he was on was sunk by the French, and that he had died the way he would have wanted, serving his country.

"He sounds like an incredible man," Garrett commented, uncorking another bottle of wine. In fact Thomas Vail sounded like a bloody saint.

She stared at his hands as he filled their glasses. "He loved his work."

Garrett sipped his wine. "And you didn't." The alcohol loosened his tongue, and coupled with his diet over the last few months, succeeded in making him more light-headed than he normally would be after one bottle.

Her face was pale as she jerked her gaze up to his. "What gives you that idea?"

He shrugged. "The way you said it, as though he loved being a spy more than anything else in the world."

He didn't have to define "anything else."

"No woman likes to feel she comes second, Mr. Maxwell, not even to a man's country."

He shook his head and rose out of his chair. "I can't imagine anyone thinking you second to anything." He picked up the bottle and his glass, ignoring the fact that she was staring at him in shock.

He'd said too much—much more than was proper—but it was true. He couldn't imagine any man making this woman feel as though she weren't loved. She was brave, intelligent, and beautiful. What kind of man could ignore that? He certainly couldn't. He'd been in her company not even an hour and already he wanted her. Wanted her more than he'd ever wanted a woman before. Perhaps it was the wine, or the fact that he'd never thought he'd make it out of that damn French prison. Maybe it was just her.

"Come sit over here," he said, walking across the cabin to where two chairs sat. It was warmer there, near the large overhead lamp that lit most of the room.

She rose from the table to join him. As she moved across the gently swaying floor with the kind of grace only someone used to sea travel possessed, Garrett realized that it wasn't the wine, and it wasn't the prison.

It was the raw vulnerability in her golden eyes, the emptiness he knew his own gaze reflected. It was the way she made him feel as though she understood him. She'd seen too much death and destruction, as well.

It was all of that and more that made him want to feel her lips—her body—beneath his. He hadn't felt such a startling, uncontrollable need since he was an eager boy. It was she who brought out these feelings.

And he wasn't certain if he could control them or not.

Sweet heavens, what a man!

Elizabeth could do little more than stare as Mr. Maxwell sauntered across the dining area clad in nothing but trousers that left little to the imagination. Despite weeks in a French prison, he was far from thin, as most men would have been. The entire cabin seemed to shrink around him as his presence filled every corner.

It had been too long. Too long since she'd seen a man wearing so little clothes and looking so good as he did it. Her husband, Thomas, God rest his soul, had been in fine physical form, but had been much slighter, and not as tall as Mr. Maxwell. And not as strong, either. She'd almost gasped aloud when he slung Willis over his shoulder as though the man were no more than a sack of potatoes.

He'd shaved during his bath, revealing the arresting fea-

tures the beard had hidden. The lines of his face were fierce
and strong, but there was a vulnerability around his eyes.
The sweetness of a kitten inside the body of a lion.

Staring at his body was one thing, but romanticizing
about his character was just plain foolish. She knew better
than to think such girlish thoughts.

A widow who'd spent the last two years mourning a
man who'd loved his work more than he loved her. A
widow who'd been in close quarters with a stranger before
but never been attracted to him. Until now.

He watched her as she moved toward where he stood.
She shook off the feeling that this—*rugged*—stranger
could see far, far too deep inside her. It was silly to think
that he might actually understand her, not when no one else,
not even her husband, had ever seemed capable of it.

She seated herself in one of the heavy, comfortable
chairs. Instead of taking the other, he dropped to the floor
near her feet, curling his knees up to his chest and crossing
his bare ankles. Her eyes took in the curve of his spine, the
lines of his ribs showing through the skin of his sides. Even
before his capture she doubted there had been an extra
ounce of fat on that frame. He was all sinew and muscle.

"You really should have put some shoes on, Mr. Maxwell," she admonished, trying to take her mind off his body.
Instead her gaze went to his feet.

His big, slender feet.

"I've been wearing those shoes for at least a month
straight, Mrs. Vail," he replied in the same tone. "It feels
good to have them off."

She laughed at that and sipped her wine. She was beginning to feel very relaxed and mellow. Whether it was
him, or the wine, or a combination of the two, she didn't
know.

Tucking her feet beneath her, she snuggled into the chair
and gazed down at him. "So, I've told you all about me,
now tell me all about you."

He looked up, his hazel eyes dark and warm in the fire-
light. "What would you like to know?"

"Where you're from, why you left, and how you came to end up in a French prison. And perhaps why you risked so much to rescue a man who might not live to see his family again." Yes, she was very curious as to why he'd risked the success of his mission, on getting the information he had back to England, for one man. Thomas wouldn't have. And she'd been told by the Home Office herself not to allow her "sensibilities" to interfere with getting the job done.

He smiled. "You don't want to know much, do you?"

Elizabeth blushed and shook her head.

He took a drink of wine. "I'm from the south of Devonshire, a little village not far from Exeter. It's the most beautiful spot in all of England. Don't look at me like that, I'm serious. From my family's house all you can see is beach and sea and green rolling hills."

"It does sound beautiful," she agreed. "I've never been to Devonshire."

"Oh, you should go." He took another drink. "You'll never want to leave."

She drank from her glass as well, admiring the way the lamplight picked up the red in his hair. In this light it was the color of rich tobacco, darker where it was still damp. It curled around the edges, the tips just brushing his shoulders. "Why did you leave?"

His expression shuttered. "I left because I wanted to prove myself."

Another drink. Her glass was almost empty. "To whom?"

He met her gaze and winked. "To myself."

And that was the end of that subject.

Elizabeth reached down to grab the wine bottle. Her hair fell like a heavy curtain between them, and the next thing she knew, his fingers were in it, pushing it back over her shoulder like a mother might. Except that his touch was anything but maternal. He stroked her hair as though he'd never felt a woman's hair before. And the heated expression in his eyes as he did it made Elizabeth's heart pound.

"I'm sorry," he said, releasing her hair. "I forgot myself."

Seizing the bottle, she sat up before she forgot herself and kissed him. "So, is there a Mrs. Maxwell waiting for you at home?" she asked, draining the last of the wine from the bottle into her glass. She wanted him to be married so she could put a stop to these shameless thoughts.

"No," he replied with a shake of his head. "There was a girl, but I doubt she waited for me."

"Why not?"

His gaze was clear and open beneath those slashing brows. "I imagine she thinks I'm dead."

Elizabeth remembered what that was like. Going weeks, months at a time with no word, only to think the worst and then get a letter from some godforsaken part of the world proving her wrong. It wasn't an existence she would wish on any woman. It was part of the reason she'd eventually started to work with Thomas. Being with him had been easier than not knowing. Most husbands wouldn't have wanted their wives to endanger themselves in such a way, but Thomas had mistaken her fear of losing him for loyalty to the crown—a misconception she'd never had the courage to correct him on.

"If she loves you, I'm sure she's waited." She made the mistake of patting his shoulder when she said it. His flesh was smooth and warm beneath her fingers. She snatched them away before she could embarrass herself by actually caressing him. What the devil was wrong with her?

He captured her fingers in his, holding them until the heat from his hand chased the chill from her bones.

"Some women won't wait, Mrs. Vail. Not even for love." His gaze bored into hers. "But you're not like that, are you? You've been waiting a long time."

Elizabeth's heart stopped. How could he tell? How could he know these things?

"I—" She didn't know what to say.

He took pity on her discomfort. "Why do you do these things? Why do you risk your life for people you don't know? Are you still in mourning for your husband?"

Mourning? For Thomas? No, that wasn't it. She mourned many things about her marriage, but sadly her husband's death was no longer one of them. That pain had passed a long time ago. She'd never told anyone why she continued Thomas's work. She doubted anyone would truly understand. She let them all believe it was out of love. Out of devotion.

"I made a promise," she whispered. "I promised my husband that if anything happened to him I would do what I could to prevent England from falling into French hands."

He smiled. For a moment she almost thought he envied her. Why? "You loved him enough to risk your life."

Elizabeth took a drink of wine to wash the bitter taste out of her mouth. "That was part of it."

His head tilted to one side. It gave him a boyish look. "What was the other part?"

She met his gaze, surprised by her need to confess her sins to him. "Have you ever been cuckolded, Mr. Maxwell?"

He looked surprised by her question. "Not that I know of."

She shrugged. "I suppose I had a need to get as close as I could, to learn as much as I could, about the 'other woman.' Yes, I loved my husband, and I know he loved me, but England always came first, and I had to know why she meant so much that he'd die for her."

Mr. Maxwell frowned. "I'm sure he would say he died protecting you."

Elizabeth's smile twisted. It was humiliating to admit the truth, but at the same time, it felt as though a great weight were being cast off her shoulders. "It wasn't me he went to war for, Mr. Maxwell. It wasn't my virtue he sought to protect, trust me."

"I'm so happy that the fate of England means as much to you as it does to me, Lizzie. Our country has stood proud and regal for centuries. She must not fall to France. You must promise to protect her at any cost . . ."

Thomas's words rang in her head. It wasn't the first time he'd spoken of England as a lover or a child, to be protected "at any cost." At the time, she'd believed it was the price to be paid for marrying a soldier, but Mr. Maxwell was a soldier . . .

"Would you have been proud to die for your country, Mr. Maxwell?"

He shrugged those magnificent shoulders and drank his wine. "Dying in a prison cell wouldn't be much of a hero's death. I suppose dying in battle would be a better choice, if one had to choose. To be honest, Mrs. Vail, I'd rather die an old man snug in my bed than die for England." He drained his glass. "On the other hand, I'd give my life in a minute if it meant my loved ones would be safe."

Boneless with too much wine, Elizabeth slouched in her chair and regarded him with open admiration. "I should like very much to be one of your loved ones, Mr. Maxwell." The instant the words left her mouth, she realized how they sounded, and so did he.

He stared at her, the ferocity of his expression making her tremble. "At the risk of being bold, Mrs. Vail, I dare you to find any man who wouldn't gladly die for the privilege of loving a woman like you."

Did he mean love in the emotional or in the physical sense? Elizabeth didn't really care. His words thrilled her right to the very core of her. She shivered as parts of her body she'd long forgotten tightened and tingled under the weight of his gaze.

Dear heavens, what was happening? She'd never reacted to a man this way before, and she'd easily met hundreds during the last few years, while working with Thomas and after his death. She'd seen so many of them, brave men like Thomas, fighting for their country; or cowards, desperately trying to find a way to save themselves no matter what the cost. And she'd seen so much death, almost touched it a few times herself. She'd thought she'd hidden that vulnerable part of herself, thought she was as cold and hard as the war itself, but this man saw through her façade as if it were made of gauze.

In her soul, it was as though she'd known him her entire life.

God, she just didn't want to feel alone anymore. Even if it was just for this crossing, just until they reached wretched England, she wanted to feel as though she were all that mattered, that she was the most wanted, cherished thing in a man's—this man's—life.

He saw it. He saw the desperation in her eyes. She knew because for one split second, she saw it reflected in his own. They were both mature, experienced adults, there was no reason for them to fight their attraction. They both knew that this moment was a chance to unleash all the fear and cold the war had heaped upon them, to share it with someone who understood what they'd gone through—what they would continue to go through until families were safe and promises fulfilled.

He could fill her emptiness, fill her body with his own, and make the numbness go away, if just for one fleeting moment.

Silence stretched between them as he rose to his knees before her. Her legs flanked his ribs as he pulled her closer. He was solid and warm between her thighs as his body pushed her skirts up as high as they would go. He didn't even seem to notice the difference between her stockings and flesh, or the pretty flowered garters she always wore for luck when on a mission.

His hands gripped the arms of her chair, tension making the muscles and sinews from his wrists to his shoulders stand out against the reddish hair and golden skin that covered them.

Mouth dry, Elizabeth raised her gaze, past the bold line of his jaw, past the jut of his cheekbone, to the molten, earthy green of his eyes.

"In fact," he murmured, pulling her closer as he eased further between her thighs. "I think I just might die if I *don't* love you."

Elizabeth's moan of surrender was lost as his mouth seized hers. How could she possibly resist? She didn't want to resist. She wanted him to make her whole again.

Her lips parted at the first gentle probing of his tongue. He tasted of wine and man and something Elizabeth had feared she'd never taste again—warmth, compassion, and desire. She opened her mouth to him as she pressed her body to his, eager to give as much as she wanted to take.

His back was smooth and firm beneath her palms as he deftly unhooked the back of her dress. Had Thomas ever felt like this? Had Thomas ever made her want him this badly? Did it matter? Poor Thomas didn't exist anymore. She was no longer Lizzie the wife, or Mrs. Vail, the spy. She was Elizabeth, the woman.

A woman who wanted—no, *needed*—this man so badly she wanted to weep.

She lifted her hips when he tugged, allowing him to lift her skirts and pull her gown over her head. Her shift followed, and soon, she was sitting on the chair, the cool, worn wood smooth against her bare flesh, in nothing but her garters and stockings.

Mr. Maxwell—God, she didn't even know his name— looked at her. Really looked at her. Never in her life had she felt so open—both physically and emotionally—to a man's gaze. His eyes were everywhere, lingering on the roundness of her thighs, her belly, her breasts.

"You're perfect," he told her, sliding his hands up her ribs to cup a breast in each palm. His thumbs brushed her nipples, sending a hot jab of sensation spiking between her thighs. She stared as he teased the pink flesh into dark, hardened pebbles that ached for his mouth. She wanted him to make her cry out. She wanted him all over her until nothing else existed, until the world didn't matter anymore.

He took a nipple into his mouth, laving it with his tongue, nipping it with his teeth until Elizabeth's head spun. She held his head in her hands for fear that he might stop. His hands had gone to the falls on his trousers, and her knees clenched against his arms as the itch built deep inside her, making her squirm in the chair. She felt him push at his trousers, peeling the snug fabric down his thighs to his knees.

She reached down and brushed the head of his sex with her fingers. He was hard and hot against her palm. A bead of moisture greeted her curious caress. He was ready for her, and wanted her as much as she wanted him.

"You're so lovely," she whispered brazenly against his ear. "I want you inside me, filling me."

He groaned against her breast, his hand slipping between her thighs, to the heated, damp flesh that craved him.

Elizabeth gasped, her face still pressed against the smoothness of his cheek, as he slipped a finger inside her. His flesh was cool against her heat. The intrusion was sweet, but only increased the frustrated ache inside her. Even as her hips moved with every languid stroke she wanted more. Even as his thumb parted her slick folds to rub the swollen hardness within, she gasped for breath and pushed against him. It wasn't enough.

"I can't . . ." It came out as a sob. "I want . . . please."

He withdrew his hand. Whimpering, she clenched her muscles, trying to keep him inside her. She failed.

His mouth left her breast, and he stood, leaving her restless and bewildered.

She stared at him as he kicked off his trousers. He was naked and beautiful, hard and desirable. God, please don't let him be leaving her. She couldn't bear it if he left her now!

He held her gaze as he offered her his hand. "Come here."

Even if she wanted to refuse him, the hypnotic timbre of his voice would have made it impossible. Rising as quickly as her trembling legs would allow, she placed her hand in his and allowed him to lead her to the table.

He swept their supper dishes to the far end of the cloth and lifted her up onto the other side. Their faces were level.

He didn't speak. He just caressed her, his fingertip tracing the embroidered flowers on her garters.

"Delicate," he murmured, that same finger trailing along the inside of her thigh. He raised his gaze. "Just like you."

It was on the tip of her tongue to tell him she was anything but delicate, but as his finger slipped inside her again, she realized just how close to shattering she truly was.

Leaning back on her hands, Elizabeth tried to focus solely on his face, but she couldn't help but glance down at the hand on her breast, and at the one between her legs. Heat flooded her cheeks at the sight of the glistening wetness on his fingers, but despite her embarrassment, she spread her legs further when he nudged them with his wrist.

God, it felt so good, so urgent. Moving her hips, she closed her eyes and thrust against his hand, sweat beading her brow as she fought to ease the growing ache deep inside her.

He released her breast, removed his fingers from inside her. Frustration reared its head, making her want to scream.

Then she felt it. Felt the table shift as his hand gripped its side, felt the blunt head of him push against the entrance to her body. She arched toward him. He pulled back.

"Please." She didn't care if she had to beg. She'd beg if that was what he wanted. Just as long as he gave her what she wanted, she didn't care what she had to do.

"Please what?"

Her eyes flew open. He was right there, looming over her, his face just inches from her own. His gaze was hot and heavy-lidded. There was no denying he was as far gone as she was.

Angling her hips closer to the edge of the table, Elizabeth wrapped her arms around his neck at the same time as she wrapped her legs around his waist. She didn't look at him as she pulled him to her. "Please come inside me."

He closed his eyes, his mouth parting in a silent moan. Elizabeth thrilled at his reaction. It was so intoxicating to know she affected him as deeply as he affected her. Roughly, he pulled her against him, as though his fine hold on his control had snapped. Her heart pounded in anticipation rather than fear. She didn't want loving and gentle.

She wanted hard and pounding. The only thing she wanted to feel was his body inside her, and afterward, she would revel in the exquisite tenderness his lovemaking left upon her flesh.

She was sitting upright, perched on the very edge of the table, her breasts against his chest and his hard sex pushing insistently against her. Reaching down, she guided him to her, pushing against the small of his back with her calves.

He slipped inside her, filling her, stretching her so deliciously that she couldn't help but cry out.

He stilled. "Are you all right?"

Unexpected tears burned the backs of Elizabeth's eyes. He shouldn't care if he hurt her. She was nothing to him, nothing but warm, wet comfort. That was all he was to her—a little sanity in an insane world. They were using each other. Just because they were sharing their bodies didn't mean there was any deeper bond between them.

If she kept thinking it, perhaps she'd eventually believe it.

"Don't speak," she whispered, her voice low and thick as she began moving her pelvis against his. "Just take the emptiness away. Please."

Clinging to each other as though they were drowning, their bodies moved together, slowly at first, then faster, more desperately, until the tablecloth bunched beneath her hips and the rough edge of the table dug into her upper thighs. Sweat beaded above her lip as every muscle—muscles that she hadn't used in two years—in her body flexed in time with the movements of his body. With each thrust of his hips Elizabeth felt as though he filled her a little more, until the emptiness inside her was gone and all that was left was pure, sweet pleasure aching to be released.

The arms around her tightened, lifting her into every plunge his body made into hers. Faster he moved, their moans merging into one solid gasp of pleasure as her flesh clung to his, shuddering as the ache grew. Mouth open, brow furrowed in an attempt to keep from crying out, Elizabeth clung to him, numb to everything except the sweet, fast friction where they were joined together.

And then the ache exploded into breath-stealing, heart-stopping rapture as spasm after spasm of release shook her. Grabbing her by the hair, he forced her mouth to his, swallowing her cry as he fed her his own. Slowly, he released her as they both began to breathe again.

Opening her eyes, Elizabeth glanced up to find him staring at her. He smiled. Tentatively, she smiled back.

"Is there a bed on this boat?" he asked, gingerly withdrawing from inside her.

Elizabeth nodded, already mourning the loss of him. "In the cabin where you bathed."

"Good." With one fluid movement, he swept her up into his arms and carried her across the floor, leaving their discarded clothing where they'd tossed them. "Can we get there without being seen?"

"Of course. What few crew I have are either on deck or with your friend. What are you doing?" Elizabeth demanded, even as she marveled at his strength and reveled at his confidence.

"I'm taking you to bed, Mrs. Vail," he replied in a light, yet determined tone. "We've still got some time before we reach England and I intend to spend it making love to you in a proper manner."

In a proper manner? Elizabeth raised a dubious brow. "You mean you can do better?"

He grinned as he carried her down the corridor, kicking open the door of the room where he had bathed earlier. "Much."

They laughed together as the door swung shut behind them. Elizabeth allowed him to take her to bed. She gave him her body as many times as he wanted it, did things with him that she had never done with any other man and might not live to do again. She took everything he offered her and gave him everything she had.

Even her heart.

"I want to see you again," he told her later as they prepared to dock.

Elizabeth's heart froze. Whether in joy or dismay, she didn't know. "I have to leave again soon."

He cupped her face in his hands, smiling even though she frowned in return. "I want to see you again. Meet me tomorrow."

It wasn't wise. In her line of work she couldn't afford . . . "Where?"

"The Pultney Hotel," he told her. "We'll take it from there."

Elizabeth nodded. "All right. I'll meet you there." And as he kissed her good-bye, she dared to let herself dream that they actually had somewhere to take it to.

CHAPTER TWO

—

My second is universal. Placed by God in all our hearts.
For its favor, wars have been fought and empires shaken.
But no army on earth is powerful enough to claim it
For though it can be given it can never be taken.

LONDON, DECEMBER 1815

"Garrett? What is it?"

Lifting his head to meet his fiancée's concerned gaze, Garrett forced a smile. They were in the dining room of the Pultney Hotel, having a quiet dinner away from family and servants. It was supposed to be a pleasant evening, but it had been her decision to come here, and Garrett found the surroundings anything but pleasant.

"It's nothing, Caroline. I was just thinking." Thinking, yes. Thinking about the woman who agreed to meet him there eight months earlier and never showed up. He'd thought of her often since that night—sometimes with anger, but more often than not, with regret. And when he'd faced Napoleon's army at Waterloo, it had been the thought of her that kept him alive.

Caroline smiled that serene smile of hers. "It's nothing serious, I hope?"

"No," Garrett lied, raising his glass to his lips. "Not at all." *I'm just obsessed with a woman who saved my life and then saved my soul and left me. Forgive me, my dear, but I didn't go to Waterloo to protect you. I went looking for her.*

It was true. He couldn't even bring himself to feel guilty

for it. When she didn't show up for their arranged meeting, Garrett had torn London—and the Home Office—apart looking for his mysterious "Mrs. Vail," only to discover she'd left again for the Continent.

The Season had just started and he knew he couldn't leave again without seeing his sister, and as fate would have it, he saw Caroline, too. Everyone expected them to marry now that he was back, but he couldn't bring himself to actually propose—not when *she* was out there. So he went to war and came back with nothing more than a hole in his shoulder, and an even larger one in his heart. He didn't even know if she was still alive. The Home Office wouldn't tell him anything.

He returned a hero and, with the war against Napoleon over, settled back into his role as viscount. With his return to his former life came his former responsibilities. He needed to marry, they said. He needed an heir, they said. Caroline's been waiting, they said. So he proposed, and the girl who'd always been more a friend than a lover said yes.

And now he sat across the table from her, watching unease flicker in her gaze and he felt awful for it. Awful because he wanted her eyes to be the color of sherry, not the summer sky and because he wanted her hair to be black instead of blond.

"I've decided to go to Devon for Christmas," he announced as the waiter refilled his glass. "Regina's been after me to make a visit. I thought this would be the perfect time."

Caroline smiled. She always smiled at whatever he said. He couldn't remember ever seeing her frown. He'd never seen her eyes darken in passion. And she'd certainly never whispered hot little sex words in his ear as he took her on an old, rickety table.

"I think that's a lovely idea. The children always love to see their war-hero uncle."

Garrett smiled at the mention of his niece and nephew. It had been too long since he'd spent any real time with them and Christmas had always been one of his favorite times of year.

"I think you're right to spend Christmas with Regina. It's better than spending it here alone in London."

"I wouldn't be alone," he reminded her. "Your family is here."

Something flashed in her gaze. Was it panic? Nonsense. What would she have to panic over? But she did look uneasy . . .

"Spending Christmas with my family is not the same as being with your own," she replied, smile firmly back in place. "Besides, we've decided to go to Cornwall this year. When do you leave?"

"The day after tomorrow."

Was it his imagination or did her perpetual smile brighten just a bit? Did she want to be rid of him? No, that couldn't be. She'd accepted his proposal. Surely she would have refused him if she hadn't been expecting to marry him just as everyone else had been expecting him to ask her.

"Give Regina my love, will you?" Caroline sipped her wine. "I miss her now that they rarely come to town."

His younger sister Regina and Caroline had been at school together. That was how Garrett had met her in the first place. The last few months, Garrett had taken to wondering how different his life would have been had Regina never invited her friend to Devonshire for a visit.

He would probably just be engaged to someone else, he thought as he told Caroline he would be happy to deliver her message to his sister. And it probably still wouldn't be the woman he wanted.

After taking Caroline back to her family's house in Mayfair, Garrett had his driver take him to the docks. It wasn't the safest of places for a man of his rank, dressed in his black evening finery, but Garrett didn't doubt his ability to defend himself. Nor did he doubt the blade concealed within his walking stick.

It was cold this close to the water, and Garrett welcomed

the icy air on his face, even as his nose started to numb. The blue-white light of the moon gleamed on the patches of ice that peppered the walkway, and made it easy for him to scan the names written on the sides of the ships tied up nearby. He made this journey twice a week, one visit during the day, the other at night. And every time, he walked this same route, looking for a sign. Every time, he was disappointed.

He would soon have to stop this nonsense. Very soon he would be a married man, and even if he didn't love his wife like Regina's husband loved her, he would still respect and honor her as she deserved. And that meant giving up this ridiculous obsession with a woman he knew only by her surname. He should have given up a long time ago, but he couldn't stop. He couldn't spend the rest of his life not knowing . . .

Dear God.

Hoisting his stick, he ran on shaky legs toward the small ship shifting on the waves in front of him. He forgot to watch where he was going and lost his footing on a patch of ice, falling to one knee.

He scarcely felt it. As soon as both feet were under him again, he continued toward the boat; slower this time because his knee refused to work as fast as he wanted. The most he could manage was a fast hobble. Still, it brought him close enough so that he could see that his eyes hadn't been playing tricks on him. They hadn't been.

There, sitting pert and pretty on the surface of the Thames was *The Vail of Tears*. It was the boat that had brought him back from France all those months ago. It was the boat he'd been searching for ever since. It was *hers*.

Heart pounding, Garrett limped up the ramp as quickly as his knee would allow. "Hello," he called. "Hello?" Leaning heavily on his stick, he started for the stairs that led below.

A burly man with a lantern met him at the top. " 'Ere now! Wot's all the racket about?" Then, as his gaze took in Garrett's appearance, his expression relaxed somewhat. "What can I do for ye?"

"I'm looking for the owner of this ship," Garrett informed him, resisting the urge to push his way past the man to the cabin below.

The man puffed up like a peacock surrounded by a flock of hens. "Yer lookin' at him."

Dismay hit Garrett like a boot in the stomach. "How long have you owned this vessel?"

The man scratched his chin as he thought. Garrett's hand tightened on the handle of his walking stick. He'd run the great oaf through if he didn't answer him soon!

"About four or five months now. It were summer when I bought her." He grinned. "Ain't she a beaut?"

"She certainly is," Garrett agreed from between clenched teeth. "Do you know where I might find the previous owner?"

The man shook his head. "I bought 'er from a gent who said his mistress wouldn't be needing her anymore." His eyes narrowed. "It was all done legal like, guvnor. I got the papers to prove it."

Shaking his head with the heaviness of defeat, Garrett managed to smile weakly at the man. "I'm not questioning the legality of your ownership, my good man. Did the gentleman happen to say why his mistress wouldn't be needing *The Vail of Tears* anymore?"

"No, sir. 'E didn't say much about her at all."

So she could very well be dead after all. The very best scenario was that she had given up the spy trade after Waterloo, but even that did little to satisfy him. She may be alive, but the Home Office certainly wouldn't give him any information about her, and she could be in a different country for all he knew.

"I'm sorry to have disturbed you," he said, his voice rough and empty. "Thank you for your time."

He limped back to the docks, suddenly very aware of the throbbing pain in his knee. Fortunately, his driver had seen his mad dash to the *Vail* and was waiting a short distance away for his return.

"Where to, my lord?" the man asked just as Garrett was about to climb inside the carriage.

"Home," Garrett replied, his body now as tired as his soul. "I'll be leaving for Devon in the morning, however. Have the horses ready to leave by eight."

He had to get the hell out of London.

"Eliza! I'm so glad that you could join us!"

Elizabeth stepped into her friend Regina's jasmine-scented embrace with a contented smile. "Thank you for inviting me."

"Oh, I couldn't bear to see you spend Christmas alone!" her friend cried, releasing her. "It just isn't right. A person should be with the people who love them."

And sadly, Elizabeth realized just how few of those people existed in her life. Her own parents were long gone and Thomas's family, while kind, just served to remind her of how much of a failure she'd been as a wife.

And then there was *him*. She couldn't help but wonder what he was doing for Christmas. He probably would spend it in London, surrounded by all his rich, titled friends. Perhaps he'd married. There were bound to be plenty of women who'd love to be his viscountess. Hadn't she even foolishly entertained the notion?

Yes, for all of five seconds.

She'd gone to meet him that night at the Pultney Hotel. She'd even worn her best dress—it was a season or two out of style as women in her profession didn't often have time to visit the dressmaker unless it was part of the job, but certainly it would be good enough for her Mr. Maxwell, spy and soldier.

But her Mr. Maxwell wasn't a mere mister at all. As Elizabeth had stepped out of the hired cab, she'd spotted him also climbing out of a carriage—a splendid equipage with matched grays at the front and a fancy crest upon the door. And how incredible he'd looked in his evening clothes! Right then, she knew he was out of her league. She watched him enter the hotel and then asked his driver who his master was.

"The Viscount Praed, ma'am," he'd replied.

A viscount! Elizabeth stood in front of the hotel in her outdated gown and wondered what to do. It didn't take her long to decide. As much as she was attracted to him, as deep an impact as he'd had on her life, viscounts did not marry widows who were spies—not that she had even entertained the idea of marrying him, but now that she knew his true identity, it changed everything.

The only thing men of his station could want a woman of hers for was a mistress. She was worldly enough to accept that. She just hadn't expected it from him. And even if it wasn't what he wanted from her—even if he did want something more, Elizabeth wasn't foolish enough to think it could actually work, not after being foolish enough to hope that what had happened between them had been more than just sex.

She hadn't been able to keep herself from feeling something for him any more than she'd been able to make marriage to Thomas work, and he was only a spy, a soldier. She certainly couldn't be a wife to a viscount—a man who would want a lady for his wife. A man who would want an heir. In the five years before Thomas's death, Elizabeth had spent the better part of those years learning how to be a spy, learning how to be anything but a lady. And she'd never once had the joy of even suspecting herself of being pregnant. She'd never been the wife Thomas deserved.

She would never be what Mr. Max—*Viscount Praed*—deserved either. He would not be content with someone like her, someone who didn't want excitement and intrigue in her life—someone who'd rather live out the rest of her life in peace and quiet. He thought she was mysterious, alluring, and wanted her because of it. One look at her gown, one look inside her heart, and he'd know she wasn't what he wanted.

And at the exact moment when that realization sank in,

Elizabeth turned on her heel and walked away from the Pultney Hotel. The next day she went to the Home Office and instructed them to give no personal information to any-one—*anyone*—who came looking for her. And then she left England as quickly as she could. She went back to war, to do the one thing she knew she could do well.

But she thought of him. She thought of him for months after that. She still did, when she was feeling particularly weak.

It had been one of those weak moments, after returning from the Continent and Waterloo, that had driven Elizabeth to Devonshire, to the coast near Exeter, and to the tiny little village she now called home. She didn't think it was the same village Viscount Praed called home—she'd never heard anyone mention him. She couldn't bear the idea of accidentally meeting him again—but it was close enough that she could almost feel him near her, and share the beauty of his home.

She let a cottage near the beach and sold the house she and Thomas had shared in London. She made a new life for herself on the comfortable nest egg she'd stored away from her spy work and the sale of the house. She'd even made a few friends. The dearest of which was Regina Ab-bott.

"Would you care for some tea, Eliza?" her friend asked as they seated themselves in the comfortable warmth of the ladies' parlor.

Regina's husband was an MP and the younger son of an earl, and they lived in the manner befitting their station. Oddly enough, Elizabeth never once felt inferior to her friend. Regina always made her feel at ease.

One of the reasons Elizabeth felt so comfortable with "Reggie," as her husband called her, was because Regina never referred to anyone by their title. Anyone close enough to be her friend was called by the first name. Social rank didn't matter in her home, and oftentimes Elizabeth would sit through an entire dinner party not knowing if the person talking to her was socially above her or not. It was eccentric behavior, and no doubt London society would frown upon it, but no one ever seemed to complain—at least not that Elizabeth knew of.

In fact, Regina reminded her of someone, but Elizabeth couldn't quite put her finger on it. She didn't know anyone else who shared her friend's exotic coloring of rich auburn hair and bright green eyes, but still the feeling was there, like an itch in the back of Elizabeth's mind. Sometimes she almost thought Regina reminded her of *him*. Depending on her mood, however, just about anything could have the same effect.

"Have you heard from your brother?" she asked, as Regina handed her a cup. "Will he be joining us for Christmas?"

"Oh, yes!" Regina's eyes sparkled at the mention of her beloved sibling. Elizabeth didn't know much about her friend's brother other than that his name was Garrett, that he was the ideal brother, and that he'd been injured during Waterloo. But Regina's face lit up so brightly whenever she talked of her brother that Elizabeth looked forward to one day meeting this paragon of brotherly virtue.

"I expect him to arrive sometime today, as well. I can't wait for you to meet him. Cake?"

Never one to turn down sweets, Elizabeth set her cup and saucer on the table and accepted a thick slab of frosted goodness. Regina didn't believe in being skimpy with her cake, and Elizabeth didn't believe in pretending she couldn't eat it all.

The first bite elicited a moan of pure pleasure. "Oh dear, this is good."

"It's Garrett's favorite," Regina replied, helping herself to a large slice. She giggled. "I hope there's some left when he arrives."

Licking a dab of frosting from her lip, Elizabeth grinned. "I'm sure we can save him a little piece. You're looking forward to seeing him, aren't you?"

Regina stared at her as though she thought the answer obvious. "Of course I am. I haven't seen him since the summer. Of course, there was the Season and then he and Caroline announced their betrothal."

"Oh, so the paragon has found his match, has he? The way you go on about him, I'm surprised such a woman even exists."

Regina waved her fork in the air. "The only woman who comes even close to being perfect enough for my brother, my dear, is you," she replied with a teasing grin. "But Caroline is a precious girl and she'll do."

Elizabeth laughed. It was a running joke between them that Regina was constantly trying to find her a new husband. In fact, Regina had declared that the only man she knew who could possibly match Elizabeth's incredibly high standards was her brother, the noble and honorable Garrett.

"I'm so glad that my fiancée meets with your approval, Egg Head."

Elizabeth's heart froze at the sound of that low, rough voice. Icy-hot pinpricks danced along her skin and behind her eyes. No. It couldn't be.

"Garrett!" Regina cried, her plate clattering to the table as she leapt to her feet. She raced toward her brother, her arms outstretched.

Elizabeth sat hunched in her chair, barely hearing the joyous voices behind her. Slowly, her hands trembling, she placed her plate and fork on the table. *Please, God, let me be wrong. Please.*

"Eliza," came Regina's bubbly voice. "Come meet my wonderful brother, Garrett."

Her knees shook so badly, she had to cling to the arm of the chair for support. There was no escape, so she might as well face them. Besides, there was always the chance that she was wrong, that it wasn't him.

"Ah, the much talked-about Eliza," she heard Garrett say, his voice light and teasing. Lord, but it sounded like *him.* "I've been eager to make your acquaintance."

Standing, she released the chair and turned. Oh, God.

"I believe, my lord, that we've already met."

*   *   *

Garrett couldn't speak, couldn't breathe. He could only stare. That hair, those eyes, that mouth. It was her. He'd found her. Eight months too late, but he'd found her, and in the most ironic of places. Here she was, in the one place he hadn't looked—the one place that always called him.

Why was she there? It wasn't to see him—he could tell that from the horrified expression on her face. She wasn't happy to see him, not one bit.

"You two know each other?" Regina's face was bright with surprise. "How very extraordinary! However did you meet?"

Garrett's gaze fastened on the woman standing stiffly before him. Anger flared within him. After all he'd gone through trying to find her and here she was hiding in Devonshire—in his own sister's house! And now he was engaged to someone else and she was lost to him forever.

"Mrs. Vail was the woman I told you about, Reggie." Those golden eyes widened, no doubt wondering just how much he'd told his sister about her. He stared at her, a bitter smile curving his lips. "You know, the woman who saved me."

Regina's head whipped around to face her friend. "You're a *spy*?" She made it sound so wonderfully naughty. "Oh, Eliza, why didn't you tell me you knew Garrett?"

"I didn't know I did," Eliza—the name didn't suit her—replied, breaking their stare to address his sister. "I knew him only as Mr. Maxwell."

"We didn't even know each other's first names," Garrett added in her defense, wondering why he should even care if she was the least bit distressed.

Obviously it was the wrong thing for him to say, for she fixed him with a gaze that was filled with anger and mistrust. "Or titles, for that matter."

Garrett's eyes widened. She was angry because he had a title? His heart seized in his chest. Or was she angry because she hadn't known? Would she have shown up for their meeting that night if she'd known who he truly was?

He didn't want to believe her capable of such behavior,

but the fact remained that she was angry at him, and for the life of him, he had no idea why. After all, he'd been the one who'd waited at the hotel for three hours for her to show up. He'd been the one who looked like an idiot, sitting at that table by himself with an unopened bottle of champagne and a dozen roses.

"No," he said, surprised at how cold his own voice sounded. "We really don't know each other at all."

Her chin rose a notch. "And how's your friend? Mr. Willis, did he recover?"

Garrett held her gaze and replied in the same frostily polite tone, "He's quite well, thank you."

From the corner of his eye he watched his sister as her gaze moved back and forth between the two of them. Reggie wasn't stupid; she knew there was something going on.

"Yes, well . . ." Regina cleared her throat. "I think I'll just go check on dinner and leave the two of you to get to know each other a little better."

From what little Garrett could see she practically ran from the room. Neither he nor Eliza turned to watch her go. Neither of them said a word until the door clicked shut again.

Garrett made the first move, literally and figuratively. "I never would have pegged you for an Eliza," he remarked, stepping toward her.

"It's Elizabeth, actually," she replied. She didn't retreat, but he noted with some satisfaction that she gripped the back of the chair so hard her knuckles were white.

He took another step. "Why didn't you come that night?"

Elizabeth—now that regal name suited her—stiffened. "Why didn't you tell me you were a viscount?"

"Would it have made a difference?" He wasn't sure he wanted to know the answer.

Her eyes flashed with anger. "You know it would have!"

His stomach clenched. "When? On the boat, or after?"

She flushed. Two deep crimson spots of color stained

her otherwise pale cheeks. "Both. Neither. I wouldn't . . . wouldn't have . . . if I'd known."

Garrett stood directly in front of her now. Close enough that he could smell her perfume—she smelled of flowers, like the tiny ones embroidered on her garters that night.

"Wouldn't have what?" he taunted, staring at her cleavage when she wouldn't meet his gaze. He could still feel her breasts in his hands. "Wouldn't have begged me to come inside you?"

Her flush deepened. "No," she whispered.

He took another step closer. Her breasts pressed against his chest. She didn't try to move away, but her breathing had quickened—as had his own. He placed his hand beside hers on the back of the chair, just enough so that their fingers touched.

"I still would have wanted to be there, Elizabeth." His lips brushed her ear as he spoke. She shuddered.

God, but he wanted to be inside her now! The last eight months didn't matter. Lord help him, but his engagement didn't matter. He didn't care why his title meant so much to her, he just wanted to bend her over the back of the chair and show her what she'd missed by not meeting him that night.

No, that wasn't true. He didn't know what she'd missed that night, other than the chance at something that he thought could have been pretty special. She'd touched something within him that night. He'd thought she'd felt the same way, and it hurt to think the only thing she'd felt inside her was him.

That didn't stop him from wanting her, but he suspected what he was feeling right now was a mixture of attraction and the need to vent all his anger and frustration. All these months, he'd feared she was dead and now she was alive, and it seemed the only reason she had for not showing up that night was that she hadn't wanted to.

He'd never felt any rejection so acutely in his life.

She raised her gaze. Her eyes glittered like a thousand

tiny daggers. "You can say that even though I didn't come that night?"

His smile was mocking. "But you did come that night."

It took a minute for the meaning of his words to sink in, but he knew the minute they did. Her cheeks bloomed with color and her mouth, that incredibly sensuous mouth, parted in exclamation.

"In fact," he continued, enjoying disconcerting her, "I seem to remember you coming several times."

God, but she was magnificent when she was angry! Her entire face was a study in bright and dark.

"What do you want?" she snarled. "A medal? Anybody with the right equipment and a little stamina could have achieved the same result, my *lord*."

He couldn't help it, he laughed. It felt good to get a response—any kind of response out of her. At least he knew that he wasn't the only one who remembered what had happened on the boat. He hadn't been the only one affected. He had touched her. Only someone who'd made herself vulnerable to a person—him—could be this angry.

So why hadn't she met him?

"Is that why you didn't meet me? Because you'd gotten what you wanted and had no further use for me?" He let his gaze roam over the pale expanse of bosom revealed by her gown. "You could have used me some more if you'd wanted."

Hurt flickered across her features, stabbing him in the heart with remorse. He didn't want to hurt her. He thought he did, but now that he had . . .

"I didn't want to use you," she replied, her voice dangerously soft. "I wasn't the one who lied."

Lied? What the devil was she talking about? His title? "The Home Office was under strict orders not to reveal my identity."

She glared at him. "And what about you? Were you under strict orders, too?"

Garrett sighed. He was getting tired of this. Why wouldn't she just come out and admit what bothered her so much about his title? He would almost rather hear her admit to being a fortune hunter than continue on in these verbal circles.

"I didn't think it mattered," he admitted. And it shouldn't have. That night on the boat they'd simply been a man and a woman, not spies, not a viscount and a widow, just two people sharing themselves, body and soul. At least that's what he had believed it to have been.

There was that hurt look again. "You should have told me." Oh God, was she going to cry? Her voice had that low timbre to it that women always had before they burst into heart-wrenching sobs.

"Tell me why," he pleaded, feeling dangerously emotional himself. "Tell me why it matters so much."

Then the hurt was gone, replaced with what experience told him was her spy face. Perfectly neutral, perfectly blank.

"It doesn't matter anymore." She took a step back. He hadn't realized just how close they'd been standing until she was gone, when all the parts of him she'd been pressed up against—his stomach, his chest—felt the chill of her absence. "Congratulations on your betrothal."

Was that what had been bothering her? "I wasn't engaged when I met you."

Her expression was cool. She looked nothing like the hot-blooded woman he remembered. "Would it have made a difference?"

"Of course it would have!"

She didn't look convinced. "I'm sure she's perfect for you, my lord. I wish you both happiness."

Desperate, Garrett grabbed her. Pulling her hard against him, he brought his mouth down on hers. She stiffened but didn't respond.

A silent scream of frustration welled up inside him. He couldn't have been wrong, he couldn't have been. She'd been as shaken by their lovemaking as he had been. It hadn't been a dream and these past months hadn't distorted his memory.

He slipped his tongue between her lips, tasting her. She tasted of buttercream frosting—his favorite. Groaning, he deepened the kiss, softened the pressure of his lips against hers, poured all the heartache and loss of the past few months into her, and prayed for a response.

Slowly, her arms wound around his neck. Her fingers tangled in his hair as her tongue met his, tentatively at first, then with more deliberation, as though she were searching for something, something within him.

His fingers splayed along her back, feeling the warm softness of her through the fabric of her gown. He'd never thought he'd hold her again, and now that he was it felt so completely, utterly right.

And it was so hopelessly wrong. He had a fiancée, and no matter how Elizabeth affected him, he'd made a vow of honor and he couldn't just walk away. Even if Elizabeth wanted him, even if she could forgive him for whatever wrongs she accused him of, he could no more turn his back on Caroline than he could pretend Elizabeth didn't exist.

He released her. It was one of the hardest things he'd ever done. She stared at him as though she'd found the answer to whatever she'd been searching for in his kiss.

"That can never happen again," she told him, her voice trembling. "Whatever happened in the past is the past. We can have no future, so please . . . don't touch me again."

She left the room with her spine and shoulders as straight as any soldier's. Garrett watched her go with a mixture of hope and sorrow.

He couldn't forget the past, no matter what she said, and he had no idea what the future held in store for either of them. But he did know about the present, and if she wanted to carry out this charade that they meant nothing to each other, then so be it.

But things weren't over between them. Of that, Garrett was certain.

Closing the door of her room behind her, Elizabeth fought the urge to cry. Of all the people who could be Regina's brother, why, why did it have to be him?

And why did he have to be bigger and more virile than she remembered? And why did she find it next to impossible to stay angry with him?

Probably because she had nothing to be angry about. Not really. No, he hadn't told her who he was, but he was right, at the time it hadn't been important. And it wasn't the kind of thing one dropped into casual conversation. No doubt he would have told her had she met him that night at the hotel, but by then it would have been too late.

And now it definitely was. There could be no future for them. Even if he weren't above her, even if she dared believe she could be what he wanted, he was engaged to another, and she could never be a man's mistress. That night on the boat had been different—they'd used their bodies to comfort each other, to fill the emptiness inside them both. She wouldn't cheapen it by selling herself. It was worth more than that.

But that didn't stop her heart from racing at the sight of him. And it didn't stop her body from responding to his kiss.

How was she going to survive the next few days under the same roof as him? There was no point in wishing he'd leave. This was his sister's home. He had more right to be there than she did. She should be the one to leave, but she didn't want to. She didn't want to spend Christmas alone in her little cottage. She wanted to spend it with people she cared about, like she had growing up.

But how could Regina not have mentioned he was her brother? Oh sure, she knew Regina was the daughter of a viscount, but not caring about titles, she'd never mentioned it. And Elizabeth had been intimidated enough by her friend's social status that she hadn't bothered to ask. Oh, if she'd only asked!

She drew a deep breath. She could do this. She had to. It was only for a few days and then he would be gone.

Crossing the plush blue and cream carpet, Elizabeth moved toward the window. The heavy blue velvet drapes were tied back with cream and gold cord, giving her a wide, clear view of the grounds below. She could hear David and Elsa, Regina's two children, laughing below.

Through the chilled glass, she could see the two children romping in the few inches of snow that covered the grass. It wasn't enough to make a fort or to lie down and make angels in, but it was sticky enough for making snowballs, and that's what the two youngsters were doing.

Smiling, Elizabeth pressed closer to the window. Little Elsa's face was pink with cold and bright with joy as she drew back her arm and let her snowball fly. She laughed, loud and hard, when it struck its target. Her brother followed suit.

Suddenly, two snowballs flew back in retaliation. One hit Elsa square in the bottom as she bent to pack more snow. The other struck David in the shoulder. Who were they playing with?

The answer should have been obvious, she realized as soon as she saw their opponent. Her smile faded. Of course it would be *him*. Neither Regina nor her husband, Henry, were the snowball-throwing sort.

Her heart twisted painfully as she watched him laugh as a sloppily packed snowball struck him in the face. He looked different when he laughed. Silly, and young, not at all the fierce warrior who'd made love to her on her boat.

Regina said he'd been injured during the war. She noticed he limped a bit as he chased after the children. Had it been a leg wound? He could have been killed and she never would have known what happened to him.

No, she would have known if he'd died. Somehow she knew she would have felt it, somewhere in her soul.

Shaking snow from his hair, he looked up at her window. Their gazes locked. His smile faded a bit, but not completely. He stared up at her as if waiting for her to either approve or find him lacking. Against her better judgment, she returned the smile.

"Eliza!" Elsa yelled at the top of her lungs. "Come help me!"

Elizabeth shook her head at the girl. No, she couldn't.

The expression on Garrett's face changed slightly. He was still smiling, but it was almost as if he were daring her to come out and face him. What did he think? That she was frightened of him?

She was. Terrified, actually, but not in any way that made sense. And she certainly wasn't going to let one little toe-curling kiss keep her from enjoying time with the children.

Besides, it would please her to no end to wipe that smug, arrogant expression off his face with a hard, icy snowball.

Just as the thought occurred to her something struck the window directly in front of her face. Snow. And she didn't even have to ask which one of them had thrown it.

So he wanted to play that way, did he? Well, she certainly wasn't going to disappoint him. If it came down to childish behavior or having him kiss her, she'd take the childish behavior.

Lord Praed needed a little cooling off.

CHAPTER THREE

—

My third is another word as familiar as your own name
And although it is beautiful alone
I much prefer it stay by me.

Three days.

For three days he'd been trapped under the same roof as her. And for those seventy-plus hours, he'd done his best to respect her wishes and stay away from her as much as he could. It was difficult considering that they were expected to join in family entertainment and meals. All he had to do was look at her and the rest of the world faded away.

From his seat near the fire, he watched as she played the piano for David and Elsa, coaxing them into singing along with her. It didn't take much effort. The youngsters adored her. Garrett couldn't say he blamed them. He adored her, too.

Oh, he was still angry with her for not showing up eight months ago, and he was still determined to find out why. He just couldn't bring himself to fully believe it was because she thought him penniless. A woman who becomes a spy because of a promise was not the kind of woman angling after a rich husband.

It really didn't matter now. Knowing wouldn't change anything. He'd still be honor-bound to marry someone else. He had no idea how Caroline felt about him. He'd never asked and she never volunteered, but he knew that she had never kissed him like Elizabeth did, and that her body wouldn't respond to him like Elizabeth's did. Nor would he ever give himself to his wife like he'd given himself to the woman singing with his niece and nephew.

He'd allowed himself to foolishly believe that spending time with her would diminish the hold she had over him, that the more he got to know her, the more she would slip from the pedestal he'd once placed her on. He couldn't have been more wrong. Everything she did only made the ache in his heart worse.

His fingers went to the tender spot on his temple where she'd hit him with a snowball. Maybe not *everything* made the ache worse.

"Uncle Garrett, come sing with us!"

Fixing his nephew with an amused look, Garrett shook his head. "I don't think Elizabeth is quite ready to suffer through my singing, thank you, David."

"Let's play charades, then," Elsa suggested, eyes like big, brown saucers. "We can act them out. You go first, Uncle Garrett."

Garrett smiled. "Elizabeth is the guest. She should go first."

For the first time that evening, her gaze met his, and the impact of it sent a jolt right to his toes.

She smiled. It was a strained smile. "But I'm certain you're so much better at charades than I am, my lord."

That was it! Garrett didn't care that his sister and her children were present, he was going to find out just what it was that had her so angry at him. He'd had enough of her barbs.

"Well, it's my house and I decide who goes first," Regina piped up before he could say a word. "And I agree with Garrett. Elizabeth shall go first, if for no other reason than as punishment for 'my lording' in my presence. You may call him Garrett or Cubby or even You There, Eliza, but do not inflate his ego by calling him 'lord.' "

Garrett groaned at her mention of his childhood nickname and hoped Elizabeth didn't pick up on it.

No such luck. "Cubby?" She arched a brow in his direction before turning to Regina. "Why Cubby?"

Smiling slyly, his sister rose from her chair and came toward him with that squishy baby-talk face that he absolutely abhorred. She wouldn't . . .

She would. Regina clutched his chin in her hand and stuck that deformed face right in his. "Because he always wooked just wike a wittle bear."

"At least I wasn't born with a head shaped like a goose egg," he murmured as she laughed and released his chin.

"Oh, come now," she admonished, turning her teasing gaze to an equally amused Elizabeth. "Eliza isn't some young miss to be put off by embarrassing stories of your youth. Why, she's practically family, and as an engaged man, you have no need to impress her."

The reminder of his engagement made Garrett more uncomfortable than his sister's teasing. Elizabeth didn't like it, either, he noticed. Her smile was stiff and forced on her pale face.

"No," she agreed, her voice husky. "I'm in no need of impressing."

Regina noticed, too. She had to. In fact, Garrett wouldn't have been surprised to learn she'd made the remark on purpose just to gauge his and Elizabeth's reactions to it. But to what purpose? Reggie didn't have a malicious bone in her body, so she certainly hadn't done it to hurt either one of them.

His sister also didn't seem convinced by her friend's compliance. "Then impress us, dear Eliza, with your wit." She cast a glance at her husband, who was fixing himself a drink at the bar. "Get over here, Henry, so we can have an equal number of players."

With the efficiency of any general, Regina divided them into two teams. She said it was because a little competition made everyone try harder, but Garrett had to wonder if she didn't have an ulterior motive when she put him on the same team as Elizabeth.

For the benefit of the children, they acted the charades out rather than making riddles or word puzzles out of them. It wasn't commonly how charades were played, but nothing was common in his sister's house. And so Regina would actually be able to guess, they could only use characters or titles from books or poetry. His sister was notoriously bad at charades.

As dictated, Elizabeth went first. She held up two fingers.

"Two words!" Elsa cried, grinning at Garrett. They were on the same team.

Garrett tried to keep his attention on what Elizabeth was doing rather than the woman herself, but it was difficult. Stooping a bit, she waved her arms out around her, as if trying to draw the entire room to her bosom. It was her bosom that had Garrett captivated. So full and round, he remembered the pink hardness of her nipples, how she moaned when he took each peak into his mouth . . .

"Room!" Elsa cried.

Shaking her head, Elizabeth gestured to each of them and then spread her arms again.

"Family!" shouted David.

"Many!"

Elizabeth nodded at Elsa, signaling that she was close.

Garrett's gaze went back to that spectacular chest. "Lots," he suggested with a smirk.

She clapped her hands, jumping up and down excitedly. She didn't even seem to notice where he was looking.

Frantically, she gestured toward Regina, not even bothering to face the other team. Her efforts were solely for Garrett and Elsa. Had a bit of a competitive streak, did she?

"Mother!" David shouted from the other team.

"Beautiful woman," Henry suggested calmly, sipping his port. Regina smiled at him.

"Lady!" Elsa cried.

Elizabeth shook her head.

"Egg Head!" Garrett cried, laughing when Elizabeth's mouth tightened grimly and she pointed a stiff finger at his sister.

Regina laughed too. In fact, the only person not laughing was Elizabeth. Stomping her foot, she thrust both hands toward the other woman as though it should be obvious.

"Oh!" Regina gasped, eyes bright. "Wife! Lot's Wife!"

Shoulders slumping, Elizabeth nodded. "That's it."

Henry hugged his wife while David triumphantly crowed his sister's defeat. Grinning, Garrett clapped for his sister. She was practically giddy at having guessed the right answer.

"How could you not get Lot's Wife?" Elizabeth demanded as she flounced onto the sofa beside him.

Stunned, Garrett glanced to his right. Elsa was arguing with her brother. He looked back at the flushed woman on his left. "Are you talking to me?"

"Yes, I'm talking to you!" Her eyes glittered like gold coins. "How could you not get something so inanely simple?"

He didn't know whether to laugh or be offended. "Because," he explained in a low tone, "I always let my sister get the first one right. Always have, always will." He glanced down. "And not even watching your glorious bosom jiggle when you stomp your foot could persuade me to change." He grinned.

She stared at him, mouth open, eyes wide. She made a noise that sounded very much like a cough, and for a moment, Garrett suspected she was choking on rage.

But then a twinkle lit in her eyes as they crinkled at the corners, and the cough turned into a chuckle and the chuckle turned into full-throated laughter.

They laughed together for what seemed like an eternity, but then their gazes locked and smiles faded as they both realized how comfortable they'd gotten. The softness of her expression reminded Garrett of that night on the ship, which reminded him of how her body had felt wrapped around his. She remembered, as well. He could tell by the nervous way she licked her lips as she looked away.

"My turn!" Regina announced, leaping up from her seat. "I want to play next."

Turning his gaze to his sister, Garrett tried to concentrate on her actions, but his mind refused to cooperate. All he could think about was the woman beside him, and how godawful much he wished he'd never met her.

Because she was there for the taking, and he wanted her, but she wasn't his to have.

"Still angry with me?"

Elizabeth jumped at the sound of his voice. She thought the entire house had gone to bed. She'd gone to the library looking for something—anything—to take her mind off the man who'd plagued her thoughts for the past three days. But not even Shakespeare could sway her from her thoughts.

"Angry?" she echoed, her heart hammering in her throat as she turned and met his frank gaze. He stood just within the glow of the candles, half haloed, half shadowed, in nothing more than a wrinkled shirt and trousers. Just the sight of him made her mouth go dry.

"Now, Cubby, why would I be angry with you? You only humiliated me by using me in your *Taming of the Shrew* charade."

His laughter was soft and teasing, shivering down her spine like a trickle of warm water. "You have to admit it was effective. Even Elsa-Wheezie-Bird figured it out." He stepped closer, so that the branch of candles on the desk caught the hollows of his face. "But that wasn't what I meant."

Elizabeth turned her back on him, slipping the book she'd been skimming back into its place on the shelf. She knew exactly what he meant. "Do all the people in your family have nicknames?" she asked, her voice tremulous. She was such a coward where he was concerned.

"Yes," he replied. She heard him take a step closer. He wasn't even within arm's reach, and yet she was certain she could feel the heat of him against her back. "It's inevitable. If we care about you, you get a nickname."

She glanced over her shoulder, her gaze resting on his chest. She was too afraid to look at his face. "Like Cubby if you're always scowling?"

She'd meant it to be a dig, but he just laughed. "Exactly. Or Elsa-Wheezie-Bird if you're a little girl who can't whistle to save her life." He was directly behind her now, his breath warm on her neck. "You've been christened with one, as well."

Elizabeth shivered. "Really?" She stepped to the side, putting distance between them again. "What is it?"

He folded his arms across his chest and grinned. "Right now it's 'Elizabeth Rex, Spy Queen of the World, Slayer of Dragons and Rescuer of Uncles.' "

"What?" She turned fully to face him. "You're making that up."

Garrett shook his head, smiling that stupid, silly, unbelievably wonderful smile of his. "No, my niece and nephew did. The 'Rex' was Elsa's idea. She didn't want to use 'Regina.' "

Against her will, a smile lifted the corner of Elizabeth's mouth. "Why? Because it's her mother's name?"

"No, because she's at that age where she believes your sex infinitely more superior to my own, and much more deserving of the title."

Elizabeth laughed at that. "Smart girl."

"She is. I suspect the moniker will eventually be shortened to just 'Eliza Rex,' but you never know with this lot." He moved toward her again. "Now, are you going to answer my question?"

"Question?"

He wasn't fooled. "What did I do, Elizabeth? Why didn't you meet me that night?"

Her chin rose a notch. "What difference does it make now, Garrett?" It felt odd to call him by his Christian name. He'd been "Mr. Maxwell" for too long. *Her* Mr. Maxwell.

"Because," he said, stepping directly in front of her, "I waited for you for hours. It was humiliating to sit there, knowing everyone could see I'd been duped."

Shame chilled Elizabeth's blood. But wouldn't he have been more humiliated had she actually met him? A man of his station would have been embarrassed to be seen with her.

"You broke my heart," he told her, his fingers coming up to brush her cheek. "And I would love to be able to forgive you for it. Why didn't you come?"

She could lie. She could make up some foolish story that would make him sorry he asked, but vulnerability shone in his eyes beneath those slashing brows. She owed him the truth.

Locking her gaze with his, she swallowed. He was so close, she could feel the heat and strength of him. He was bigger than she remembered, obviously having regained the weight he'd lost in prison. If she pressed against him, would he be as hard as he had been that night, or would he feel softer, more forgiving?

"I did go to the hotel that night," she confessed, her voice little more than a croaked whisper. At his shocked expression, she continued. "I saw you arrive in your fancy carriage, dressed like the lord you are. I couldn't... couldn't face you."

His brow furrowed, making his features even more fierce in the dim light. "Couldn't face me? Why the hell not?"

Elizabeth took a step back. This wasn't the Garrett who'd held her and made love to her. This was the man who'd kept himself alive on the battlefield while those around him perished.

Her back came up against the wall. There was nowhere left to run. Funny how a woman so renowned within the intelligence world for bravery could spend so much time running from one man.

"Answer me," he demanded, the softness of his voice a sharp contrast to the tautness of his face and body. "Why couldn't you face me?"

"Because you weren't what you were supposed to be!" she replied, pressing her shoulder blades into the plaster as he closed the distance between them.

His chest brushed her breasts. Her nerves jumped and tightened in response. He was too close. She couldn't think with him this close, not when she could feel his anger and see the hurt in his eyes.

"What was I supposed to be?" He placed a hand on either side of her head, fencing her in.

"A soldier," she whispered, licking her lips as he leaned closer. His breath was warm against her temple. "A normal man. My equal."

"I am." His lips brushed her cheek. "I am your equal, and you are mine."

Liar! Slamming the palms of her hands into his chest, Elizabeth pushed. Hard. He stumbled back a few inches— not nearly as far as she would like.

"You are not my equal," she informed him through clenched teeth. "And I am most assuredly *not* yours."

His eyes narrowed. "What are you talking about? Of course you are!"

God love him for being so obtuse. Sighing, Elizabeth pinched the bridge of her nose between her thumb and forefinger. "Garrett . . ." Dropping her hand, she raised her weary gaze to his. "You were born to be a viscount. I'm a clergyman's daughter who had the good fortune to marry a soldier who did well for himself. We never would have met if not for my vocation. I am beneath you and we both know it."

She waited for him to make an innuendo out of her words, but it never came. He just stared at her as though she'd kicked him.

"Beneath me?" He stepped toward her. "How can you even think such foolishness? Elizabeth, you rescued me from prison. You saved Willis's life. How can you believe yourself to be anything but my equal? If anything, I'm beneath you."

He had been beneath her once. Closing her eyes, Elizabeth turned her head away. She couldn't stand this. She didn't want to hear she'd been wrong, because that would mean he cared, and if he cared, that would mean she'd done a great disservice to them both eight months ago.

Strong, warm fingers cupped her face, forcing it up. She

opened her eyes. It hurt to look at him, but she did it anyway.

A lock of hair fell over his forehead, softening his features. "Did I do something that night to make you feel as
though you weren't good enough?"

How could he ask such a question? She shook her head,
feeling the smoothness of his palms against her cheeks.
"No. You made me feel as I'd never felt before." Her heart
clenched at the truth in her words.

Smiling faintly, he brushed the pads of his thumbs under
her eyes. "Then why did you throw it away?"

Elizabeth swallowed. "Because I knew someone of your
stature could never marry someone like me, and no matter
how you made me feel, I could never be your mistress."

His smile faded. "Mistress?" He dropped his hands.
"You thought I'd ask you to be my mistress?"

"Wouldn't you?" she challenged, angry that he'd made
her admit the truth. "You already had someone waiting for
you and you couldn't marry both of us."

His jaw tightened, the muscle ticking beneath the skin.
"I didn't propose to Caroline until I'd lost almost all hope
of ever finding you. And even then, I still searched the
docks for your boat, harassed the Home Office for information about you." He drew a breath. He was shaking—it
was in his voice. "The only thing I asked of you was that
you meet me for dinner. All I wanted was the chance to
get to know you, to see if what I *thought* we shared was
real or all in my mind."

"Garrett . . ." What could she say?

He ran a hand through his hair. "I don't know if I would
have proposed marriage to you or not, but it wouldn't have
mattered if you were the queen of Egypt or a bloody chimney sweep! I just wanted to discover if Mrs. Vail the
woman and Mr. Maxwell the man could have had a future."

Tears stung the back of Elizabeth's eyes and clutched at
her throat. He shouldn't be telling her these things. It only
made her wish things could have been different. She didn't

want to know, because she knew the truth. She knew the answers to his questions.

"They couldn't have," she whispered as her vision blurred. "I couldn't make my husband love me. How could I ever keep you?" She dragged the back of her hand across her eyes. She would not cry!

Shock washed over his features, followed by yet more anger.

"Your husband," he hissed, hauling her to him, "was an ass."

His mouth came down hard on hers and Elizabeth welcomed it. His anger was something she could deal with. The implication that she had been wrong was not.

Slipping her arms up the solid wall of his chest, she pressed herself against the length of him. How did he manage to awaken such emotion in her? How could he make her want him with a desperation so intense she thought she might die without him? She could no more resist him than she could the need to breathe.

His tongue was hot and wet against hers as her palms pressed against his chest. Beneath the thin lawn of his shirt, his flesh was warm to the touch. His heart hammered against her palm in time with her own frantic pulse. She wanted to feel his skin, taste him on her tongue . . .

His hands slid down her back, pressing her even closer. His groin was hard against her belly, and she could feel him growing harder and thicker still.

She gripped the open edges of his shirt as his fingers cupped her buttocks, lifting and tilting her so that her pelvis was closer to his. His hips moved against her, igniting the spark of ache that flared between her legs. Arousal, sharp and swift, knifed through her, and with one impatient tug, Elizabeth tore his shirt open, baring his chest and stomach to her searching hands.

His nipples were hard against her palms, and her own tightened in response to his soft moan. She slid her hands all over him, across his ribs, the plains and contours of his stomach, up through the crisp mat of hair to his shoulders.

She wanted him naked. Wanted to feel all his glorious body beneath her hands.

Her breath quickened as he increased the rhythm of his hips. She could orgasm just by having him rub against her. Pushing against him, she slid the tattered remains of his shirt down toward his shoulders, reveling in the silky hardness of his flesh.

Then she felt it. Beneath her right palm, just beneath the knobby bones of his left shoulder, his skin was different. It was smoother, thicker—puffy. It was a scar. A scar that hadn't been there eight months ago.

Her head suddenly very clear, Elizabeth pushed him away, despite the silent protest her body made at the loss. He stared at her, his dazed expression slowly giving way to something far more guarded and wary.

She dropped her gaze to his shoulder. And gasped at what she saw.

It was all that was left of a bullet wound—two of them. She'd seen enough of those to have no doubt. It was still pink and ugly, despite looking as though it had been well cared for.

The tears were back as she reached up and tugged on his arm, turning him just enough so that she could look at his back. The exit wound was bigger and not as neat. This was the wound he'd received at Waterloo.

He'd almost died. Tears, hot and fat, slid down her cheeks even as she fought to keep them at bay. A few inches lower and they would have gotten him through the heart. As her fingertips gingerly ran along the satiny expanse of flesh, she remembered what he'd said to her that night on the boat—about dying in battle. He said he'd die protecting his loved ones, but not for England.

"You got this fighting for the woman you love." Her voice was flat in her own ears. God, how she hated this woman—this Caroline. Did she know what this man had gone through for her? Did she appreciate it? Elizabeth hadn't seen the actual battle, but she'd seen the product of it.

Garrett caught her fingers in his own. His gaze was dark and intense as it met hers.

"I got it fighting for you," he murmured huskily.

For her. The implication of his words was more than Elizabeth wanted to face. She didn't want to be responsible for this. Better it be a tribute to his family than to something fleeting, something that could never last. The woman he thought he loved was an illusion. She wasn't real. At that moment, Elizabeth would have given almost anything to be what he wanted.

Choking on the sobs that threatened to consume her, Elizabeth pulled free of his grasp. "Your efforts would have been better spent on Caroline, my lord. Or perhaps even England. I'm sure either one of them would be more appreciative of the gesture."

And then, before she could make an even bigger fool of herself by bursting into tears, Elizabeth ran from the room.

This was just ridiculous.

It was Christmas Eve and the last of Regina's guests had just arrived for her annual party. The ballroom had been opened up especially, and decorated with boughs of holly and mistletoe. Jewels flashed and glittered as dancers whirled by and the air rang with music and laughter. Even Elizabeth seemed to be having a good time.

Until she looked at him.

Whenever their gazes met she looked away so fast Garrett was amazed her neck didn't snap in two.

He didn't understand. How could such a woman possibly think she wasn't good enough for him? Aside from his title, which wasn't very grand, and his wealth, which was by no means staggering, there was nothing terribly special about him. He was just a man.

A man who was engaged to another woman. Honor held him to the betrothal, but there was part of him who'd toss honor to the wind if he thought Elizabeth would have him. Would she have him?

He watched above the rim of his glass as she danced

with Reverend Jones. The good reverend's expression was
far from holy as he stared down into Elizabeth's smiling
face—and the impressive amount of cleavage displayed by
her stunning amber silk gown.

She looked like a goddess. The color of the gown
matched her eyes, brightening them. The square neck
plunged low across her breasts as was the fashion, and
flaunted the porcelain smoothness of her skin. Her hair was
drawn up onto her crown in a thick coil, with one long
chunk left free to snake over her shoulder like a lush black
snake. Her only jewelry was a pair of dangling diamond
earbobs.

She was magnificent, and everyone there knew it. Men
made idiots of themselves just to get near her, which was
why Garrett kept to the shadows, sulking.

It hadn't bothered him when she danced with Lord Pos-
seton—Harry, as Regina called him. And it hadn't bothered
him when she danced with the Marquis of Cheltenham—
Charles. If she didn't think herself good enough for a mere
viscount, an earl and a marquis were certainly no threat.

No, it was the young, handsome clergyman who had
Garrett grinding his teeth and drinking far more Scotch than
his normal habit. He could tell just from the relaxed line
of her back and shoulders that Elizabeth felt at ease with
this man. He was her equal in her eyes.

Garrett snorted and then drained his glass. As if a soft-
spoken, easy-going man like Jones could ever match a
woman of Elizabeth's passionate nature. It was ludicrous
to even think about. Still, that didn't stop him from wanting
to stomp out onto the dance floor and peel the clergyman's
hand off the small of Elizabeth's back and slap him with
it.

She belonged with him, not with some lily-handed book-
worm who would compare her to an angel and compose
psalms in her honor. And she certainly didn't need to be
with another man who would make her feel second to his
occupation.

He'd meant it when he called her husband an ass. Why

couldn't Elizabeth see the fault was with Thomas, not with her? Had she been that in love with him that she refused to see his faults? It would explain why she had promised to carry on with his work. But she'd referred to that promise as her "duty." Surely that wasn't the term a grieving widow would use?

And he doubted a grieving widow would have allowed a stranger to take her on a table. In fact, he didn't doubt for a second that he was the first—if not the only—man Elizabeth had been with since her husband's death. Perhaps it was just wishful thinking, but there was a bond between them, forged that night on her boat, and it was stronger than either of them wanted to admit.

She laughed at something Jones said. Garrett's heart leapt in his chest.

Oh hell, he loved her. There was no point in even trying to deny it any longer. At first he'd thought it was obsession, plain and simple, but as he watched her sparkling eyes gaze up at the good reverend, the painful revelation hit him like a fist in the chest.

He couldn't stand that she could smile like that at another man. He couldn't stand another man touching her. In fact, he wouldn't stand for it any longer.

Setting his glass on the tray of a passing footman, Garrett threaded his way through the swirling dancers with steely determination. Guests scurried to clear a path for him, nervous of his fierce expression. He didn't care that they watched with interest as he approached Elizabeth and Jones. All that mattered was the flicker of excitement he saw in Elizabeth's eyes before they clouded over with trepidation.

The music faded to a halt as he stopped in front of them. Flashing his brightest and most charming smile, Garrett turned to Jones. "I believe the next dance is mine. You don't mind, do you, Arthur?"

The smaller man smiled in return, completely oblivious to the tension between Garrett and Elizabeth—or that people were staring. Lord, Jones didn't have a sexually aware bone in his body. He was definitely the wrong man for Elizabeth.

Of course, they were all wrong. He'd already established that fact.

"Not at all, Garrett," the reverend replied, adhering to Regina's rule about no titles being used under her roof. He bowed toward Elizabeth. "I hope to enjoy your company again this evening, Elizabeth."

A snarl bubbled in Garrett's throat, but he forced it down. Gesturing to the orchestra for another waltz, he turned to Elizabeth. "Shall we?"

Warily, she stepped into his arms. He was made to hold her like this, close enough that he could smell the spicy warmth of her perfume. Close enough that he could watch the pulse jump at the base of her throat.

"You're holding me closer than is proper," she informed him in an icy tone as he drew her through the first turn.

"I'm not proper." He turned her again. She followed him effortlessly, every step perfectly attuned to his. It only strengthened his conviction that they were perfect for each other.

"So I noticed." Her gaze locked with his, full of censure. "It was rude of you to chase Arthur off like that."

His sister's rule or not, the sound of another man's name on her lips infuriated him. "Arthur's easy to chase off."

"He's a very nice man."

"He's boring." He twirled her faster this time, catching her off guard. She gasped, but could not be swayed.

"He's dependable."

"He's unemotional."

Her eyes hardened. "He's *available*."

Garrett stiffened, almost stepping on her foot as he faltered. So that's why the good reverend was getting all her attention, was it? To punish him for *not* being available?

"He also loves God more than he could ever love any woman."

All the blood save for two angry red splotches drained from her face. "Maybe he just hasn't met the right woman."

Lord, but she was like a dog with a bone! "For men like that, like Arthur and Thomas, there is no such thing as the right woman."

Her eyes were bright with unshed tears. Her lips, red from mulled wine, tightened. "And for some men there seems to be more than one."

The blow hit its mark. Drawing a deep breath, Garrett stared into her eyes, letting her see the depth of emotion there. "No," he replied honestly. "There's only ever been one. I'm looking at her."

Her lower lip trembled. "I'm certain your fiancée would be pleased to hear that."

Sighing at her sarcasm, Garrett steered her away toward the edge of the dance floor.

"What would you have me do, Elizabeth? Would you have me dishonor myself and break the engagement?" He couldn't believe he was even suggesting it. It was one of the lowest things a gentleman could do. Caroline would be able to take legal action against him for breaking their betrothal. It would be an awful scandal.

"Because I'll do it, if that's what it takes to prove how much you mean to me." He wanted to tell her just how much he loved her, but he couldn't, not here where everyone could see her reaction.

Elizabeth blinked, her tears evaporating as a shocked expression froze her face. "If you broke your promise because of me you wouldn't be the man I think you are."

Frustration clawed its way up from Garrett's gut, sinking its talons into every fiber of his being. "Then what?" he demanded. "What do you want from me?"

She opened her mouth, and for a moment he thought she might actually—miraculously—have the answer, that she might admit her feelings for him, that she would desist in the foolish notion that she wasn't good enough and that they would live happily ever after.

"Nothing," she replied. "There's nothing you can do, Garrett."

He opened his mouth, but nothing came out. He couldn't

believe this was it, that it was over, not after he'd tried so hard to find her. He'd waited all his life for a woman like her. There had to be a way. There had to!

The music was fading. In a moment he would have to let her go. He couldn't. If he did, he knew he'd never have the chance to hold her again.

"Look, everyone!" cried a voice Garrett instantly recognized as Elsa's as the music stopped. "Uncle Garrett and Eliza are underneath the mistletoe!"

Garrett froze. Elizabeth stiffened in his arms. Together, they lifted their heads, gazing up at the ball of leafy green above them with a mixture of excitement and dread.

"A kiss!" someone cried.

"We demand a kiss," yelled another.

Laughter and voices rose up around them, roaring in Garrett's ears as he lowered his gaze to Elizabeth's. Their last kiss and it wouldn't even be in private. It would be chaste and proper, for all the village to witness. God, he didn't want to say goodbye this way.

Swallowing against the dry, hard lump in his throat, Garrett pulled her closer, dropping her hand so that both of his could circle her waist. Could anyone watching see the horrified expression on her face? Could they see the sorrow and grief that seemed to surround them both like a heavy shroud?

He lowered his head.

"Garrett!"

He could have cried. He laughed instead. Straightening, his arms still wrapped around the woman he loved, he turned toward the door where his betrothed stood, a blue and blond blur as his eyes filled with tears of laughter and despair.

"Caroline."

CHAPTER FOUR

—

My whole is the three united
And it's very simple to do
And these little words will tell the world
just how I feel for you.

Garrett didn't waste any time. As soon as the study door clicked shut behind him he turned to his betrothed. "What are you doing here?"

Caroline arched a pale brow. "Merry Christmas to you, too, Garrett."

Now it was Garrett's turn to be surprised. He'd never heard Caroline speak with such sarcasm.

"Merry Christmas, Caroline. Now—" Crossing the blue and cream carpet to the desk in the far corner, he perched one hip on the polished rosewood top and folded his arms across his chest. "What brings you to Devon on Christmas Eve?"

She wrung her hands. "I had to see you."

Just what Garrett didn't want to hear. If Caroline wanted to make some kind of declaration to him, she'd picked a rotten time to do it. Or maybe it was the perfect time, depending on whether or not she wanted to watch him torture himself with guilt.

"What did you want to see me about?" How cool he sounded, how detached!

Caroline dropped her gaze. "Who was that woman you were in the ballroom with?"

Garrett sighed in frustration. He didn't want to play this game. He wanted all the cards on the table—now.

"Her name is Elizabeth Vail, and she's a friend of Regina's. She's also the woman who rescued me from the French prison I was in."

Caroline's head snapped up. "She's the reason you waited so long to propose."

So surprised was he by her insight, that Garrett couldn't keep his shock from showing on his face. "Caroline, you know very well that I didn't propose because I was going to Waterloo—"

"To look for her." Gone was the nervous rabbit. This Caroline was confident, almost cocky as she sauntered toward him. "You didn't propose before you went because you were hoping to find her again. It wasn't until you came home and my family made their wishes known that you finally asked me."

Frowning, Garrett swallowed. She made his actions seem so devious and underhanded, which of course they were. He wasn't going to lie to her—not when so much was at stake. He couldn't marry her and give her the love and respect she deserved, not when his heart belonged to someone else.

"Yes," he admitted. "She's why I put off proposing."

She stared at him, realization brightening her delicate features. "You're in love with her."

He was such a cad. "Yes."

If he expected tears, he was disappointed. In fact, Caroline looked almost . . . *pleased* by his announcement. Not the reaction one would expect from a cuckolded fiancée.

Hand on her head, Caroline chuckled. "I can't believe I was so worried about coming here. Had I known she would be here, I would have done this much, much sooner."

"Done what?" Garrett's tone was wary, uncertain whether her laughter was from relief or some kind of mental imbalance.

She met his cautious gaze with a smile. "Released you from our engagement, Garrett. In fact, had I known that you loved someone else, I never would have said yes in the first place."

"You wouldn't?" He knew he wasn't much of a catch, but the fact that she would have dismissed him so easily came as a bit of a surprise, considering the nature of their relationship before he went off to war.

Laughing again, she shook her head. "No. You see, Garrett, I've met someone else as well."

"You have?" It was his turn to chuckle in disbelief. "Why didn't you tell me?"

"Because I thought you wanted the marriage as much as my family did." She grinned. "I came here to break the engagement. In fact, Jonathan is meeting me here in the morning and we're joining my family in Cornwall."

"Your parents don't know, then?"

"They think I just wanted to spend Christmas with you." Her smile faded a bit, but there was a twinkle in her eyes that Garrett hadn't seen for a long time. This Jonathan made her happy. Good. "Does she know you love her?"

He shrugged. "I don't see how she couldn't."

Caroline didn't bother to try to hide her surprise. "I don't suppose you've tried telling her?"

His smile was rueful. "It didn't work. I don't know what else to do."

She placed her hand on his forearm and squeezed. "Tell her you're a free man. Tell her how you feel. Beg if you have to." She grinned. "That's what Jonathan did with me. He told me how much he loved me and begged me to stop being so stupid until I finally gave in."

Unfolding his arms, Garrett took her hand in both of his. Her joy was infectious. "I'll give it a try. Thank you. Be happy, Caro."

She kissed his cheek, her expression one of warmth and genuine affection. They would always be friends, the two of them.

"Merry Christmas, Garrett." Straightening, she tugged her hand free of his. "I'm going to go tell Regina. You go find Elizabeth."

Standing, Garrett nodded. He was going to do just that. They left the study together, re-entering the ballroom as friends and more at ease with one another than they had been in months. Garrett had to shake his head. Imagine, neither of them had wanted to go through with the marriage, but they had both been willing to sacrifice their own happiness out of a sense of duty.

It would have been laughable if it wasn't so bloody pathetic.

But now he was free, and there was no reason for Elizabeth not to listen to him, no reason they couldn't be together if he could only convince her to take a chance. And this time, he'd use every weapon in his possession to coax her into surrender, even if it meant carrying her off to his bed like some kind of randy caveman.

He searched the ballroom for her, even asked people if they'd seen her. No one had, and his own search only led to one disheartening discovery. Elizabeth wasn't in the ballroom.

And neither was that "nice man," the Reverend Arthur Jones.

Christmas morning came early for Elizabeth. She'd stayed up until almost dawn, sitting in Regina's kitchen pouring her heart out to Reverend Jones over several cups of rum-laden eggnog.

The poor man had listened patiently as she went on and on about Thomas, their marriage, and her feelings for Garrett. And when she was done, he'd patted her on the shoulder, told her she had to be honest with herself before she could be honest with anyone else, and then helped her up to her room as most of the staff were either still in bed or at home with their families.

She undressed herself and fell into bed in her shift, wondering what the devil he'd meant by such a cryptic remark. Then she fell into a deep and dreamless sleep, only to be jostled awake a scant few hours later by a very excited little girl who wanted her breakfast and her presents, and wasn't allowed to have them until everyone was up.

Her head hurt and her mouth felt as dry as dirt, but

Elizabeth rose, washed, and dressed with Elsa's help. Then, the two of them went hand in hand down the stairs to the dining room where the rest of the family was waiting.

The rest of the family, including Garrett's lovely fiancée.

"Good morning, everyone," she greeted the family, amazed by the strength of her voice. She might feel like hiding under the table, but at least she didn't sound like it.

She met Garrett's gaze as she seated herself in the only vacant chair—the one across from him. He regarded her strangely, as if he were disappointed with her. What was the matter with the man? He was the one getting married, not her. All she'd done was reminded him of that fact. If he didn't like it, that was just too bloody bad.

"It's so nice to finally meet you, Elizabeth." Caroline spoke from her seat next to Henry. Lud, but the girl even sounded pretty! She spoke just like a lady. Uncharitably, Elizabeth wondered if she made love like a lady, too. Although, she couldn't imagine anyone just lying there while Garrett was inside her . . .

And the mental image of Caroline and Garrett in bed together was not something Elizabeth wanted to think about.

She shook her head. "Thank you, Caroline. I'm happy to meet you, as well. Garrett's told me so much about you."

Garrett made a small, choking sound as he sipped his coffee.

Caroline cast a sly glance in his direction. "Has he? How nice."

Elizabeth frowned. Caroline didn't sound like a woman in love. How could she marry someone she didn't love? For that matter, how could she *not* love a man like Garrett? Why, he was brave and strong and honorable and devoted . . .

Oh, God. *She* sounded like the woman in love. Horrified by the direction of her thoughts, she glanced at Garrett. He looked awful, as though he hadn't slept well the night before, either. Had he been thinking of her, wondering, as she had done, of what might have been if she'd only met him that night at the hotel?

What did it matter? Even if she had met him, it was very unlikely they could have made things work. She didn't belong in his world. She didn't know how she could possibly hold his interest. He wanted her to be strong and mysterious and she was neither.

And quite frankly, she was terrified. Arthur had told her to be honest with herself, and there it was. She was scared of Garrett. She was scared to give her heart to another man—a man so totally capable of breaking it. Her heart, her love, hadn't been enough for Thomas. How could it possibly be enough for Garrett?

But hadn't he already proven he wasn't like Thomas? He'd rescued Willis from prison. He'd gone to Waterloo to fight for the woman he loved, which wasn't England, but . . .

Her gaze shot back to Caroline. It wasn't his betrothed, either. It was *her,* or so he said. Had he actually gone into battle to fight for her, and her safety? Why should it be so hard for her to believe? After all, she'd gone back hoping that her work would somehow make life safer for him, as well. In fact, when she'd heard the news that Napoleon had been defeated—hopefully for good this time—it hadn't been her promise to Thomas that she'd thought of. It was Garrett, and whether or not he was still alive.

Oh, her head hurt. She didn't want to think about Garrett and how much he loved her. It didn't matter—not when he was marrying someone else.

The dim thumping of the door knocker against the front door sounded through the room. Spooning a liberal amount of ham and coddled eggs onto her plate, Elizabeth looked up, surprised to see Caroline rise to her feet.

"That will be for me," she announced with an angelic smile. Bending down, she gave Garrett a lingering kiss on the cheek. Elizabeth swallowed hard against her eggs. She was quickly losing her appetite—the one thing that always made her feel better after too much to drink.

"You're leaving?" she asked, cringing at the hopeful note in her own voice.

Caroline smiled like a mother might at a recalcitrant child. "Yes, I'm afraid so. It was lovely meeting you, Elizabeth. I hope to see you again soon." She cast another glance at Garrett.

Elizabeth desperately wanted to hate this woman, but something about her made it impossible—perhaps the fact that Elizabeth felt so guilty for wanting Caroline's fiancé?

Taking another bite of ham, Elizabeth watched as the other woman said her goodbyes to the rest of the table and left the room. Everyone watched her go. Everyone, Elizabeth noticed, but Garrett. He was watching her. In fact, he looked decidedly glad to see Caroline leave. And as much as Elizabeth secretly thrilled at his reaction, she also thought it was rather badly done on his part. He should have at least shown the girl to the door.

After a quick breakfast—Elizabeth was the last one eating—the family practically ran to the drawing room to open their presents.

She'd never seen such an excited bunch. In her family, opening presents was a subdued thing. One always knew that Aunt Martha would give slippers she knitted herself. Aunt Dorothy was always good for a new pair of fancy stockings, and Uncle William, the bachelor, would give peppermints. Nothing new, nothing terribly exciting. Apparently, things were different in the Abbott household.

She watched with an awed smile as the children vibrated with excitement. This was what Christmas should be: happy time spent with loved ones. She glanced at Garrett. He didn't look happy. How joyful would Christmas morning be in his and Caroline's house? Would he think of her? Maybe once he and Caroline had children . . . she didn't want to think about that girl having his children.

The next hour passed in a blur as presents were opened and exclaimed over. Elizabeth almost cried over the gifts the children gave her. David had given her a book of sketches that he'd done himself. He'd drawn everyone in the family, including his uncle. The boy was incredibly gifted, for he'd captured Garrett's combination of ferocity and vulnerability.

Elsa gave her some music for the piano, each note copied with shaky, painstaking precision.

When it was over, she turned to Garrett, who looked absolutely foolish in the cap Regina had knit for him. It was too big and flopped down over his ears and forehead. Most men of his station wouldn't be caught hanged in such a thing, but there he was, grinning like an idiot over his sister's lack of talent.

"I'm sorry," she told him in a low voice. "I didn't know you were going to be here. I don't have a gift for you."

His smile was strained at best. "Seeing you again was gift enough."

Oh, that hurt, because he sounded so sincere.

A short while later, Elizabeth took her bounty and headed upstairs to her room to add the gifts to her trunk. She was going back to her cottage tomorrow. She'd miss the warmth and gaiety of this house, and the people in it. No doubt her visits to Abbott House would be a bit more frequent than normal as she tried to escape the loneliness of her cottage and her regrets.

But she would make it a point to first ask if Garrett and his wife would be there before she came.

A knock sounded on her door just as she closed her trunk.

"Come in."

It was Garrett. He'd removed his cap, and his thick, tobacco-brown hair was tousled from it. In his hand, he carried a small package.

"What are you doing here?" she demanded as he shut the door behind him. Her throat felt like hot sand. She was alone with Garrett. In a bedroom with Garrett. And it didn't matter that he belonged to another, she still wanted to throw herself into his arms and beg him to make love to her again.

"I wanted to say goodbye." He held out the package. "And to give you this."

"Goodbye?" He was leaving? No! He couldn't leave, not just yet. She wasn't ready to let him go. She thought she had been, but now that it was here she didn't want it to end.

Her movements jerky, she took the package he offered. The paper was plain but the ribbon matched the plum of the dress she'd worn that night on *The Vail of Tears*. It wasn't a coincidence, either, if she knew Garrett.

"I have business to attend to in London that won't permit me to stay away any longer." His gaze met hers, deep and bare of any pretense. How could he let her see inside his soul like that? One would think that after years of being a spy he'd refuse to give anyone that kind of power. "I couldn't leave without seeing you first."

There was no use denying it any longer. She'd loved him from the moment he'd informed her that he wasn't going to leave his friend to die in a French prison. And even though he'd been weak from hunger and exhaustion, he'd slung Willis over his shoulder and carried him to the boat with nothing but sheer determination driving him on. Yes, he was a man who put his loved ones above all else.

But what about her? Would he rank her above all else? Or would he one day discover that the woman who had rescued him was a fraud? That her knees shook and her stomach rolled at the least little prospect of danger? What would he think of her then when she'd rather stay at home by the fire than attend a fancy ball?

What was she thinking? He would never find those things out because he was marrying someone else.

She stared at the package. "The children will miss you." *I'll miss you.*

"Did you . . . are you . . . ." She looked up at his distress. Scowling, he raked a hand through his hair, mussing it further. "Oh, damn. Did you make love to Arthur Jones last night?"

If he'd slapped her she wouldn't have been more surprised—or angry. "What if I did?" she demanded, planting her free hand on her hip. "Are you trying to tell me you didn't make off to the nearest table with Caroline?"

The expression on his face said it all. He knew she hadn't been intimate with Arthur and the smile on Garrett's face was so smug she wanted to wipe it off with the package he'd given her.

"Caroline broke our engagement last night."

Now it was her turn to be shocked. "What?" Caroline had left him? But she was so friendly this morning. He was unattached? Dear God, he was unattached!

He stalked toward her, like a big cat after a little mouse. "Turns out she fell in love with someone else while I was chasing after a certain female spy. Convenient, don't you think?"

Elizabeth's heart was pounding so hard she couldn't even speak. He wasn't engaged. They could be together. After months of wondering, days of longing, they could finally be together as she'd dreamed . . .

No. Nothing had changed. She was still a nobody and he was still a viscount. He was still a man of complex emotions and passions and she was a simple widow who wasn't the woman he thought she was—he didn't know the real her. And once he did get to know her, his interest would wane as Thomas's had, and he'd find something or someone else to give his love to . . .

"Come to London with me, Elizabeth," he murmured against her ear. "Let me show you how it could be between us."

She closed her eyes against the shiver that raced through her. She wanted to go with him, wanted him to show her everything he promised. But it was just an illusion. It wouldn't take long for him to realize that she was lacking. It wouldn't take him long to find something or someone to replace her as the most important thing in his life. And it wouldn't matter what she did, she'd never, never win him back. She'd never been able to win Thomas back—not even by fulfilling that stupid, stupid promise to protect England at any cost. It hadn't changed a thing—except it had brought Garrett into her life.

"I can't," she whispered.

His lips were soft against her temple. "Yes you can. Give me a chance, Elizabeth. Give *us* a chance."

"No!"

Panicked, she pushed against his shoulders, shoving him away. It was tempting, so very tempting to believe him. But if she took that chance and it didn't work, then she would know that it wasn't just that Thomas had loved England more, it would confirm all her fears—that it was her fault. That there was something wrong with her, and she didn't know if she could face being that much of a failure.

He stared at her. No doubt he thought her some kind of lunatic. She certainly felt like one.

"Why not?" he demanded.

"Because," she countered lamely, not sure how to put it into words and make him understand. "Because I'm not that woman who rescued you that night. I'm a coward—I'm frightened of spiders, for God's sake!"

He stepped toward her, a sympathetic smile on his face. "You don't have to be spy queen of the world for me, Elizabeth."

She held up her hand, preventing him from coming any closer. "I'm not exciting and I'm not of your class, and eventually you'll get tired of my wanting to stay home rather than dance until dawn." Her eyes filled with tears. "You'll get tired of my looks and my body and my boring conversation, and then one day you'll find yourself something—or someone else—to love and I'll be alone again."

Biting the inside of her mouth to keep the tears at bay, Elizabeth pressed the package against her heart, wrapping her arms around herself in an attempt to keep from trembling. "I know men like you, Garrett, brave, adventurous men. You crave excitement in your life, danger. I'm tired of all that. I never liked it to begin with. How can I give you what you need?"

And then he was on her, seizing her by the arms and shaking her. "*You're* what I need! I don't want adventure and danger! If I'd wanted those things, I would have stayed in the army and hied myself off to some far corner of the world. I want *you*. You're all the excitement I want or need in my life."

Elizabeth swallowed a sob. "You say that now, but what if you do miss the intrigue? You'll want to go off and fight again."

He smiled and the love in his eyes wrapped around her heart so tightly it hurt. "Unless you or my family is in danger, I don't ever want to fight again. I went to war in the first place so they'd be able to live in peace. I went to Waterloo in an insane attempt to find you. I don't care if I never see a battle again. I hate the bloodshed."

She looked up. "You do?"

He nodded.

She hit him in the shoulder, fear and overwhelming love driving her to the brink of hysteria. "You fool! You shouldn't have gone! You could have been killed!"

Garrett laughed. "But I wasn't, and neither were you. We've been given a second chance, Elizabeth. Don't you think we should take it?"

"I . . ." She didn't know. She just didn't know if she could do it. "I need some time."

He saw the hesitation in her eyes and his expression clouded. She knew this would happen. She knew he would change his mind when he discovered that she wasn't the woman he wanted her to be.

"Then by all means," he muttered, his voice tight as he backed away. "Take your time. I'll give you three days to come to me. Three days to come to your senses and get over whatever is keeping you from allowing yourself to be happy."

Her chin came up. An ultimatum? She hated those. "Or what?" she challenged.

His smile was crooked, humorless. "Or then I come after you. I'm not letting you get away this time, Elizabeth."

And with that threat hanging over them, he turned and left the room.

*   *   *

It was evening before Elizabeth could bring herself to open the package Garrett had given her. He'd left shortly after their "discussion" and the entire house felt his loss. Footsteps seemed to echo where they hadn't before. Conversation seemed less animated, lacking in wit and laughter.

Sitting in a chair by the window, she watched as the night wind tossed around the light top layer of snow on the ground. It sparkled like fairy dust in the moonlight.

Where was Garrett now? Still on the road, or had he stopped for the night and was busy charming a pretty barmaid? No, that was hardly his style. No doubt he was in a room somewhere wondering whether or not she had opened his present yet.

With that image in mind, Elizabeth slipped a folded piece of parchment from beneath the plum ribbon and opened it.

"To Eliza Rex, Queen of My World, Object of My Desire, Rescuer of My Heart."

Nice touch. She hadn't even opened the package yet and already he had her near tears. God, he made her want to believe, to trust, so badly.

She read on. It was a charade. Smiling, she carefully picked through the verses. He must have realized how much she loved them from how competitive she was that night they all played. Or maybe he thought she would be better at the written ones since she was so awful at acting them out.

An uneasy prickling sensation washed over her as she re-read the first three verses. Did it mean what she thought it did? Her gaze went to the last line: *"And these little words will tell the world just how I feel for you."*

Oh God, it did. *I love you.* That was the answer. He loved her.

Thomas had once said he loved her, too—but it hadn't lasted. It hadn't been enough.

Thrusting thoughts of the past aside, Elizabeth tore the ribbon from the paper and opened it. A mixture of tears and laughter burst forth as she saw what lay wrapped within the folds of the delicate paper.

It was a pair of garters embroidered with tiny gold crowns. She didn't know how or when he'd purchased them—sometime after the children had given her their royal nickname, no doubt.

How had he known that such a gift would be perfect? She'd never told anyone about her lucky garters—not even Thomas—but she remembered Garrett that night on the boat, tracing the delicate embroidery with the tip of his finger.

How could she let a man who knew her that well slip through her fingers?

He loved her. She loved him. What if it didn't last?

What if it did?

Clutching the garters in her hand, she stared at her own reflection in the window. She was Eliza Rex, Spy Queen of the World, Slayer of Dragons and Rescuer of Uncles. Surely a woman worthy of a title like that could risk her heart for the possibility of a lifetime of happiness? Couldn't she?

Yes, yes she could.

Bolting from the chair, she ran down the stairs to the parlor where Regina sat sewing.

"Regina, I need to leave for London first thing tomorrow morning."

Regina's gaze was disinterested at best. "Do you? Well, then, I'll have one of the carriages ready for you. When do you need to be there?"

"In two days."

Regina didn't blink. "You should be able to make it. It's not a journey I would like to make. I take it that it's a matter of some importance?"

Elizabeth nodded, too embarrassed to tell her friend that she was chasing after her brother.

"Very well. You'd better get some rest."

Her friend's behavior was a little odd, even for Regina,

but Elizabeth was too scared and nervous to care. Shaking, she started to leave the room.

"Oh, Eliza," Regina called.

Elizabeth turned. Grinning, Regina held up a length of gold embroidery thread. "I trust you liked your gift?"

She wasn't coming.

Seated once again at a somewhat secluded table at the Pultney Hotel, Garrett realized that he was about to be made a fool of once again.

Maybe he should have given her more time. Maybe three days hadn't been enough time for her to make up her mind and come to London. Maybe he should have given her a week, but he'd stupidly thought she'd come to her senses quickly.

Or maybe she just didn't love him as he loved her. Maybe she didn't think it was worth the risk. Maybe she'd decided to play it safe with Reverend Jones rather than take a chance on loving him.

She really wasn't his Elizabeth Rex if that was the case.

"Excuse me, Lord Praed, but I have a message for you."

Garrett took the small, heavy note from the waiter with a slight smile. Was it from Elizabeth, telling him she wasn't coming?

He opened it. Inside was a room key. The paper simply had the letter *E* written on it.

Garrett's heart thumped wildly against his ribs. She was here! Elizabeth was here!

Not caring who or what had finally changed her mind, Garrett jumped up from the table and ran from the dining room. Let them stare, let the gossips speculate as to what could have a peer of the realm actually running in a public place. He didn't care. Nothing else mattered now that Elizabeth was here.

Up the stairs he went—two at a time until he reached her door. He paused just long enough to compose himself before knocking.

The door opened, and there she stood. The woman he

loved, in that same plum gown she'd worn their first night together. No wonder she hadn't wanted to meet him downstairs; the gown was hardly evening dress. No doubt she'd worn it on purpose.

He didn't speak, didn't allow her to speak. Kicking the door shut behind him, he pulled her into his arms and kissed her with all the joy he felt inside.

"What made you change your mind?" he demanded, breathless and hard for her.

Her hands came up to cup his face. "Don't talk, Garrett. We've talked so much at Regina's. I don't want to talk anymore." And when she pressed her lips to his again, Garrett didn't care why she'd changed her mind. All that mattered was that she had.

They shuffled across the floor to the bed, bodies and mouths pressed together so tightly not even light could pass through them.

Her hands pushed his coat to the floor. His fingers fumbled with the buttons along the back of her gown. One by one, garments fell to the floor. Naked and vulnerable, Garrett stared at the pale beauty of her body. Soft and round, she was perfection in every sense of the word, from the top of her head to the ribbons on her garters.

He smiled. She was wearing the garters he'd had Regina embroider for her.

"You wore them."

Smiling as she sat on the bed, Elizabeth held out her arms to him. "They're for luck."

"You don't need luck," he told her, pushing her onto her back and lowering himself on top of her. "Not with me."

"Show me."

Velvety softness closed around his hips as he slipped between her thighs. The flesh there was warm and humid, and oh so inviting as he probed it with the head of his shaft. He wanted to take his time with her, but that was impossible. They'd both been waiting eight months for this moment. They could take their time later.

"You're ready for me," he murmured against her lips as he slid a finger into that tight, hot passage.

She smiled as she tightened her inner muscles around him. "I've been ready for you for a long time." Reaching down between their bodies, she wrapped her fingers around him, stroking the hard length of him with firm, determined strokes. Garrett shivered. God, she was going to make him come just like that.

He withdrew his finger, allowing her to guide him to the entrance of her body. With one quick thrust, he was buried to the hilt inside her and both of them gasped at the sensation.

"Are you all right?" he asked, his voice hoarse with passion and emotion as he stared down at her flushed, beautiful face.

"I'm fine." Her hips moved against his. "Stop talking."

Wrapping an arm beneath her, Garrett rolled onto his back, taking her with him so that she was now the one on top. He wanted to watch her ride him until she exploded with pleasure.

She did just that. Slowly sliding her body up and down on his, Elizabeth drove him to the brink of ecstasy time and time again, until sweat beaded on his brow and his entire body was tight with tension.

She was close as well, he could see it in the rosy hue of her skin, in her heavy-lidded gaze as she took him as deep inside her as he could go. Stretching herself along the length of his body like a cat, she quickened her movements, grinding her pelvis down hard on his, her hard nipples brushing his chest as she locked her arms on either side of his head.

Sweet, aching pressure built between his legs. Arching his hips, he lifted his lower body to hers, matching her thrust for thrust, lifting them both off the mattress.

Elizabeth's moans quickened with her movements. Her forehead puckered as Garrett gripped her hips, holding her in place as he pumped himself into her. Her thighs stiffened and her back arched as she tossed her head back and cried out loud as her climax shook her.

Her orgasm sent Garrett over the edge. One fierce thrust sent him spiraling into the abyss after her, ripple after ripple of intense pleasure shuddering through his body.

It was some time later before either of them could find the strength to speak. Pinned beneath the soft weight of her body, Garrett drew what blanket he could over them as their flesh began to cool. Her head nestled between his jaw and shoulder, and he stroked the glossy surface of her hair.

Now was the time for talk. "Why did you come here tonight?"

Elizabeth lifted her head, her face just inches from his. She smiled. "I thought I'd save you the trouble of hunting me down."

Chuckling, Garrett shifted so that they lay on their sides facing each other. He slipped his leg between hers, stroking her hip as he did so. He didn't think he could ever tire of touching her. "Seriously. What changed your mind?"

With a sigh, she placed the palm of her hand against his chest, her fingers toying with the hair there.

"I was so scared that I wasn't . . . *couldn't* be the woman you thought I was, but when I read the charade, and saw the garters . . ." Garrett moved his hand down to her knee and slipped his finger inside the band of fabric there. "I realized you knew me better than anyone else ever has. I knew I'd be foolish to let that go."

He smiled. "Very foolish. I love you, you know."

She nodded, and he thought he could see the shimmer of tears in her eyes. "I know."

His own throat was tight as he spoke. "I'm not handsome and I'm not perfect, but I can promise you that you will always—always be the most important part of my life. You are my life."

A tear slipped from the corner of her eye. "I love you, Garrett."

He rolled on top of her, his body already hard for her

again. Kissing away her tears, he positioned himself between her thighs.

"You're going to have to marry me after this," he told her as he entered her.

Her mouth brushed his ear, her breath soft and warm as she whispered, "Merry Christmas, Cubby."

Laughing, Garrett turned his head to kiss her. "Merry Christmas, my love."

ROMANCING THE ROGUE

BARBARA DAWSON SMITH

When Michael Kenyon, the Marquess of Stokeford, finds his grandmother having her palm read by a gypsy beauty, he's convinced that Vivien Thorne is a fortune hunter. The Marquess is determined to expose her as a fraud—and Vivien is equally determined to claim her rightful heritage. Yet neither the spirited gypsy nor the notorious rogue foresee the white-hot desire that turns their battle into a daring game where to surrender is unthinkable . . . impossible . . . and altogether irresistible.

"Barbara Dawson Smith is wonderful!"
—*Affaire de Coeur*

"Barbara Dawson Smith makes magic."
—*Romantic Times*

**AVAILABLE WHEREVER BOOKS ARE SOLD
FROM ST. MARTIN'S PAPERBCKS**

Wish Upon a Cowboy

KATHLEEN KANE

Jonas Mackenzie isn't sure what to make of the beautiful stranger who showed up at his Wyoming ranch with marriage on her mind. While he's trying hard to ignore the sparks flying between them, Hannah Lowell is a woman on a mission with a stubborn streak as wide as his own.

Hannah hadn't been thrilled at the idea of marrying a man she didn't know . . . until she had a good look at the lean and rugged cowboy who was her destiny. But how is she going to convince a man who doesn't believe in magic, that he's got the power to save a town from a terrible fate? And that it all boils down to his belief in his legacy, his heart, and in the most powerful magic of all . . . their love.

"True to her talent, Kane keeps the conflicts lively to the end and fills the plot with many surprises."
—*Publishers Weekly*

AVAILABLE WHEREVER BOOKS ARE SOLD
FROM ST. MARTIN'S PAPERBACKS